MARGARET WAY,

a definite Leo, was born and raised in the subtropical river city of Brisbane, capital of Queensland, the Sunshine State. A conservatorium-trained pianist, teacher, accompanist and vocal coach, she found that her musical career came to an unexpected end when she took up writing—initially as a fun thing to do. She currently lives in a harborside apartment at beautiful Raby Bay, a thirty-minute drive from the state capital. She loves dining al fresco on her plant-filled balcony overlooking a translucent green marina filled with all manner of pleasure craft—from motor cruisers costing millions of dollars and big, graceful yachts with carved masts standing tall against the cloudless blue sky, to little bay runabouts. No one and nothing is in a mad rush, and she finds the laid-back village atmosphere very conducive to her writing. With more than one hundred books to her credit, she still believes her best is yet to come.

CARA COLTER

lives on an acreage in British Columbia with her partner, Rob, and ten horses. She has three grown children and a grandson. She is a recent recipient of an *RT Book Reviews* Career Achievement Award in the Love and Laughter category. Cara loves to hear from readers; you can contact her or learn more about her through her website, www.cara-colter.com.

Margaret Way
Mail-Order Marriage

Cara Colter
Husband by Inheritance

TORONTO NEW YORK LONDON
AMSTERDAM PARIS SYDNEY HAMBURG
STOCKHOLM ATHENS TOKYO MILAN MADRID
PRAGUE WARSAW BUDAPEST AUCKLAND

Recycling programs
for this product may
not exist in your area.

ISBN-13: 978-0-373-68821-0

MAIL-ORDER MARRIAGE & HUSBAND BY INHERITANCE

Copyright © 2011 by Harlequin Books S.A.

The publisher acknowledges the copyright holders of the individual works as follows:

MAIL-ORDER MARRIAGE
Copyright © 1999 by Margaret Way Pty., Ltd.

HUSBAND BY INHERITANCE
Copyright © 2001 by Cara Colter

CONTENTS

MAIL-ORDER MARRIAGE

Margaret Way

CHAPTER ONE

WHEN he reached the top of Warinna Ridge he reined his bay mare a few short of the cliff face. This was a favourite aboriginal resting place when on walkabout and a magnetic spot for him, too; the best vantage point on the whole of Jabiru. From the high elevation he could look down on the herd scattered over the shimmering, wonderful, emerald-green valley. From umber to emerald. All it took was a drop of rain. Only this time they got a mighty deluge courtesy of Cyclone Amy. Danger was a woman, didn't they say? Now the danger had passed.

The rich-coated Brahmans with their distinctive floppy ears, dewlaps and humps didn't have to walk anywhere to graze. The country all around them was in splendid condition now that the floodwaters had withdrawn. Paruna Creek and the Oolong Swamp, home to countless waterbirds, pelicans, swans, ducks, brolgas, magpie geese, the jabirus, the large tropical storks that gave the station its name, were running a bumper and the cattle grazed face-high in rippling pastures. Blue and green couch, para grass, spear grass, you name it. The richest green feed any herd could need to thrive and fatten.

Deep pools of water like miniature lagoons glittered in the metallic noonday sun, a heat haze rising off the surface creating an illusion of hot mineral springs. The pools were everywhere, natural cooling-off spots for the herd, numbers of them wallowing in the silver lakes.

Cherish the earth, he thought, some of the restlessness in his mind quietening as he looked out over a vista that ravished the eye. It was still very hot and humid but a light aromatic breeze scented so sweetly of sandalwood cooled his dark-tanned skin. Though he had a million and one other things to do, it was hard to tear himself away. He looked for a long time, drawing strength from the land. Jabiru filled him with such a sense of pride, of achievement. Not bad for a kid born on the wrong side of the blanket. Nevertheless he felt the taste of bitterness on his tongue. Maybe he would never get rid of it.

The distant hills, spurs of the Great Dividing Range that separated the hinterland from the lush coastal strip, glowed a deep pottery purple, the colour the Aboriginal artist Namitjira had used so wonderfully. An extraordinary brilliance lay over the land. It gave him infinite pleasure. A compensation for the loneliness and isolation. Sometimes at night on long rides under the stars he felt at absolute peace. That wasn't easy for a man like him. Not that Jabiru was a glamour property. It was a lean commercial operation geared for results.

Jabiru cattle were becoming sought after now. But, God, it had taken years and years of backbreaking toil. Now, when he was starting to realise the rewards, he had no one to share it with. Not a soul. There had only ever been him and his mother. Going from town to town.

Never staying long enough anywhere to be accepted, until they had come up to tropical North Queensland, over a thousand miles from where they had started, where no one went hungry or cold. Abundant tropical fruit dropped off the trees, superb beef was cheap, the rivers and the glorious blue sea teemed with fish, and the weather ranged from halcyon to plain torrid.

He'd been around twelve at the time. A difficult age for a boy. At least it had been for him, his mum's protector. His mother, always so very pretty but so soft and vulnerable, had found permanent work helping out in a pub. Marcy Graham, the publican's wife, had taken the two of them under her wing. A good sort was Marcy. The sort that prompted the accolade "heart of gold." They had even lived at the pub for a time until Marcy found them a bungalow they could afford on the outskirts of town. It had been lonely but beautiful on the edge of the mysterious, green rainforest. He even got used to the snakes, mostly harmless. His mum never did.

It had taken a long time to make friends at the local school. Something about him made the other kids keep their distance. He had a wicked temper for one thing, mainly because he wouldn't take the least little gibe about his mother or him. And there had been plenty in those early days. He was tall for his age and strong. It had only taken a couple of fights for the bully boys to get the message.

It wasn't until he was around fourteen and the efforts of the school principal had paid off he found himself with the reputation for being "clever." He didn't know how it happened. He had missed out on so much schooling moving around, yet when he decided to throw himself into it—after all it was he who had to look after his mum—he took off like a rocket. He had graduated from high school with the highest score of any student, giving him the pick of the universities when places were hotly contested. Hell, he could even have become a doctor, a scientist, or a lawyer, only there was no money for all that stuff.

"It's a shame!" Bill Carroll, his old headmaster, told his mother, bewildered to be so confronted. "Matthew could have a great future. He could be anything he sets his mind to."

Only he was a cattleman. And hell, he enjoyed it. He thrived on it. Even when he was living a life of near slavery he'd been happy. He hadn't been able to realise any dream of university but he'd brought the brain and the spirit of an achiever to bear on all his endeavours.

It was Marcy who found him a job as a jackeroo on Luna Downs. Filthy rich absentee owner, swine of a manager. Absolute swine: he had made all the young guys' lives hell, but he got square for all of them before he left.

Once he was old enough—he was plenty strong enough—he bought a very rough slice of scrub with what he thought of then as a hefty loan from the local bank. Somehow despite his youth he had convinced the bank manager he could turn the wilderness into a viable cattle empire. Finally he had sold it three years ago for a handsome profit, launching a full-scale assault on Jabiru.

Jabiru was owned by the Gordon family. In their heyday the Gordons had held significant pastoral hold-

ings, but times had changed. Jabiru had been allowed
to run down. Everyone in the business knew it would
take a lot of hard work to get it up and running again.
Then, everyone knew he wasn't afraid of hard work. It
worked for him, too, old man Gordon had taken quite
a shine to him.

Of course Gordon knew the story. Everyone did.
There were no secrets in the Outback. He was the skeleton in the closet. Jock Macalister's son. Illegitimate son.
Difficult to hide it when even he knew he was the image
of him as a young man. Sir John Macalister, nowadays
referred to as the grand old man of the cattle industry.
Macalister had three beautiful daughters but he had
never conceived a son in wedlock. Wasn't that sad? He
didn't even have a grandson to inherit. The daughters
had married, had children. All girls. Perhaps it was the
Big Fella up there getting square with Jock's dishonour-
able past.

His mother had always sworn Macalister had never
forced himself upon her. He could have, as he flew
around his cattle empire enjoying the traditional *droit
de seigneur.* His mother, then working as a sort of nanny
on one of Macalister's properties, swore she had wanted
him as much as he had wanted her. Only when their
relationship was suspected, she found herself shown the
road by "The Missus," her immediate employer, who
gave her enough money to move far away. Macalister
was the Boss; a man with a reputation that needed up-
holding if necessary by his staff. He was already married to the Mondale heiress at the time. With two small
children to think about. Matthew's mother had been
young, pretty. In the final analysis—*forgettable.*

He would have been, too, except for his red setter hair, the jet-black brows and his unusually blue eyes. Struth! He even had the same chiselled cleft in his chin. It hadn't taken that North Queensland town a week to uncover their secret.

He was Jock Macalister's kid. Only the rich and powerful Macalisters would never accept that. He had never set eyes on his so-called "father" in his life, though he had seen him plenty of times in the newspapers or on television. He wouldn't actually like to confront the old man. Only Sir John's age would prevent him from being beaten up.

Matthew's own burden in life was grief. Too deep for words. His mother had been killed two years before. She and a few friends had been enjoying a night out on the town, a night which ended in tragedy. His mother and her current boyfriend, not a bad guy, had inexplicably taken a wrong turn. They knew the area well, but ended up in a swollen canal. The dangers of drinking. The car with them in it had been fished out the next day. The same day he had been flown in by the police helicopter to identify the bodies. My God!

"You need to understand your mother, Red," Marcy had tried to console him. "She always felt so alone."

Alone? Who, then, was he? A nobody? He had worked like a slave getting a better home for his mother. It had been far too rough to take her out into the bush. Not that she would have gone. His mother loved people. But he had always provided her with money. Always made the journey into town looking like a wild man with his too-long hair and beard, to see how she was faring. She couldn't have been too lonely. There was always a man. A couple of them he had personally thrown out.

His mother had come from England to Australia with her parents as a little girl. All had gone well for some years until her parents split up. She had stayed with her mother who eventually remarried.

"I never got on with my stepfather," was all his mother ever said, but anyone could read between the lines. His mother, pretty as a picture, was simply a born victim. It made him feel quite violent towards his natural father whose life must hide a multitude of sins.

He went by his mother's surname, of course, Carlyle, and his first name came from the grandfather in England she remembered with such affection. Matthew. But no one had ever called him anything but Red. No one outside his mother who always called him Matty even when he topped six-two and his body had developed hard muscle power. Well perhaps there were one or two others. His old headmaster and a Miss Westwood who had taught him to love books. Books were a great relaxation for a man who led a very solitary life. Not that he was a monk. He found time for women. There always seemed to be plenty but he picked ones who knew the score. No laying traps for any vulnerable little girls. And he took good care he never made one of them pregnant. That would have been carrying on the sins of his father.

Matthew lifted his battered akubra and raked a hand through his thick too-long hair—heck, it touched the collar of his denim shirt, then set it back low down over his eyes. The sun was throwing back searing silver reflections off the serpentine line of the creek and multiple pools. He had five men working for him now, two part Aboriginals. Wonderful bushmen, stockmen and trackers. He wouldn't swap them for the top jackeroos off any of the stations. And they were real characters, always ready for a laugh despite the endless backbreaking work. He had no troubles with the other men, either, all tough self-reliant, occasionally given to terrible binges in town when he had to take the four-wheel drive on the long journey and haul them back home.

What he needed now was a woman. The right woman. But how the hell was she to be found? He didn't have the time to start up any courting. His life was packed from predawn to dusk and then he was too damned tired to throw himself into the Jeep and drive a couple of hundred kilometres into town. And back. He was thirty-four now. He was well on the way to seeing results, so he kept thinking about starting a little dynasty of his own. From scratch. He had no past anyone wanted to acknowledge. His much-loved and despaired-over mother was dead. He wanted family, he wanted kids of his own. He wanted to make something of his life. Only there would never be a woman he'd force or a child he'd abandon.

Late that afternoon, icy-cold beer in hand, he sat on the veranda of the modest homestead he had built himself, breathing in the pure aromatic air and contemplating his future. Single-storey, the bungalow had its feet planted in the rich tropical earth, a wide veranda that ran the length of the house and a roof that came down like a great shady hat. To him who had never had a real home it seemed like a miracle. It was then as he rocked back and forth, a solution of sorts came to him.

Why not advertise for a wife? Frontier men had had

to advertise in the old days. In a way Jabiru was still frontier country. If he kept to what he really *wanted* in a wife he might weed out the empty-headed adventuress or the woman who just wanted to find herself a home.

The idea kept his mind occupied while he prepared himself a solitary but far from don't-give-a-damn dinner. Beef, of course. He ate lots of it and even if the health freaks had cut it out of their diet, the last time he'd seen Doc Sweeney in town he'd been labelled a superbly fit individual. So, grilled eye fillet served up with all the freshly picked salad greens he could lay his hands on.

Aboriginal Charlie, who must have been a Chinese market gardener in another life, had quite a garden going. Different kinds of lettuce, lots of herbs, cucumbers, peppers, tomatoes, shallots—you name it. Waxy little potatoes that came up so clean from the red volcanic soil they only needed a brush off to shine. There were already thirty or more avocado trees on the property that fruited heavily to add the finishing touch.

He didn't allow himself to fall into the habit of eating junk food or those frozen meals plenty of guys on their own settled for. He sat down to a civilised table, a couple of checked tablecloths he got Marcy to buy for him, decent plates.

"Damn it, I'm a civilised man," he told himself. His mother, very dainty herself, had instilled manners in him. He would offend no woman with rough talk or crude ways. Breeding had triumphed, he thought ironically. One day when he could, he would find his mother's family in England. Look them up.

Right now, an enormous gulf separated him from his roots. His maternal grandparents were dead. He knew that much. Strange, his mother had never attempted to go home. Was it pride, or a kind of shame? When he thought about her, which was every day, his heart, or what passed for it, broke. He shook his head. I've got to get a life. And a life means a woman. *A wife.*

CHAPTER TWO

IT SHOULD have been perfect holidaying up here in the blue and gold tropics, but something was missing. It's a long time since I felt good, Cassie realised. Not that it seemed to matter to anyone. Not to her estranged socialite mother who spent her whole life partying and really had never wanted her. She'd had a nanny almost from the moment she was born. A nanny she had come to love until, when she was seven, Rose left.

She had a clear mental picture of herself running into her mother's bedroom after school, her eyes filled with a tearful dread. "Where is she? What happened to her?"

"Don't be tiresome, Cassandra." Her mother, seated at the dressing table, had waved her away. "The usual reason. You're too old for a nanny."

"But why couldn't we say goodbye?" All these years later she could still feel the terrible pull in her throat.

"Why? Because I can well do without your hysterics," her mother had said firmly, turning back to the mirror that showed her elegant reflection in triplicate. "You're growing up now, Cassandra, and you have to move on to a new stage. You're going to boarding school. St.

Catherine's, the very best. I expect you to get used to the idea. Daddy and I will be doing a lot of travelling this year. All connected to the business."

Which simply wasn't true. Daddy was a very rich businessman who felt vaguely ill-at-ease with a small girl. Tall, strikingly handsome, seldom at home. But whenever he saw Cassie he patted her kindly on the head then vanished again.

It was a big thing for her, going to boarding school. She learned quickly and, in the end she actually enjoyed it. She made good friends and became very popular both with her peers and the staff. She was head girl in her last year. The top student. That had her parents drooling. With her little successes they moved closer, expressing their pleasure in her achievements. Even better, she had grown from a rather frail, pale child into a highly gratifying reflection of her father's side of the family. Aunt Marian especially, a perennial beauty. There was a general feeling she had turned out rather well.

"It does a child no good at all to smother them with affection," her mother once told her friend Julie's mother, in Cassie's hearing. "Look at Cassie. While Stuart and I were off adventuring, she grew up, became self-reliant."

Julie's mother had smiled back, but the smile never did reach her eyes. Cassie always got the feeling though her mother was always invited everywhere and appeared to have scores of friends, it was just *noise*. No one genuinely *cared* about her. How could they when she had nothing to give?

As soon as she possibly could, Cassie tracked down her darling Rose living quietly in a dreary flat. They had fallen into each other's arms reliving the old grief of separation. She had set Rose up nicely. They couldn't stop her. She was eighteen and had come into a good deal of money, a legacy from her maternal grandmother who had always spoken up for her and was outraged when she was shunted off to boarding school. Grandma had died too early. There had been long-running differences between her grandmother and mother. Mostly about her.

"She might look like me, but honestly I don't know where your mother came from," Grandma often remarked. "Some other planet. Very cold."

Grandma had left Cassie well off. Something that shocked her mother out of her mind. It was a dreadful sin she had been excluded from the will except for a very valuable jade collection she had long coveted.

At university Cassie had a mild eating disorder. Not anorexia or anything like it, but still a bit of a problem. God knows what that was all about, but anyway she got over it. Maybe she'd been trying to take control of her own life. Her own body. Though she did extremely well with her studies, so far as her parents were concerned that was filling in time. Her job was to get married and marry well. Her mother introduced her around relentlessly and found her just the right man. God, he was awful. It was around that time she found the guts to challenge her mother. On *everything*. Instead of shutting up and going away, she found a highly articulate tongue. Heck, hadn't she been a valued member of the University Debating Group?

"What are you trying to do to me, Cassandra?" her

mother had cried, off balance with the shock. "You're tearing me to strips."

She had no choice but to leave home. It was never hers anyway. Her mother and herself were very different people. Her father was a benevolent fringe figure. She realised now, in her various relationships since, she had always been looking for a father figure. The men she had gone out with were mostly older, wiser, established in their professions, but alas, no spark, no flame to feed on.

I wish I could share with someone, Cassie thought. I wish I could run into strong comforting arms. I wish I could look at a man with love and respect. Wishful thinking more like it! A consequence of her pretty dreadful childhood. She prayed if she ever became a mother she would know how to show love.

The sun was getting too hot, Cassie noticed now.

She moved languidly off the recliner and stood up. Another dip in the aquamarine pool then she and Julie could start thinking about lunch. Maybe that wonderful little Italian place built on a ridge overlooking the sea. The seafood up here was out of this world, fresh from the Reef waters and straight onto the table. Second thought, pasta. She loved pasta. Who didn't? Hadn't the ancient Etruscans made pasta? The Chinese? Didn't they make *everything?* Marco Polo was supposed to have enjoyed delicious pasta in China. Pasta and noodles were essentially the same thing. Many a time she'd tossed either pasta or noodles with a simple tomato, basil and extra-virgin olive oil sauce.

She was the cook here. Julie, her friend from their very first day at St. Catherine's was almost totally undomesticated. Sometimes it came with the territory. Cassie herself had barely been inside a kitchen until she had moved out of her parents' house. Her parents had a housekeeper, an excellent cook who presided over her domain jealously. Her father had a full-time chauffeur, as well.

Julie's father, head of the stockbroking firm for which they both worked, was a lovely man. Her mother, who did a great deal of charity work along with the partying, was lovely, too. Lucky Julie! It was their tropical hideaway—really a fabulous retreat—she and Julie were staying at. They were supposed to have come up much earlier, but Cyclone Amy had put a halt to that. They had had to wait a full month before things settled down and the weather returned to glorious. Now they would dress in something easy and go into town.

"Why not try the pub?" Julie suggested when they were out on the sea road. "They have a nice little setup out the back. The food's supposed to be very good. Heck—" she swung her head to admire the splendid produce in one of the many roadside stalls fronting the local farms "—can you believe the tropical fruit? The size and the variety. I don't recognise half of it."

Cassie sat stiffly upright, her face paling. "Goodness, Julie. Watch out!" A station wagon was rapidly approaching them and Julie, in a hired BMW—she didn't know how to drive anything else—was holding the middle of the road like some hooligan playing chicken.

"Sorry." Julie corrected her positioning with a loud gulp that turned into contrite giggles.

"In the interests of survival, I think I'll drive," Cassie said firmly. Julie had developed the very risky habit of turning her head to look at things when she should have been focused on the road. It was more pronounced up here where the scenery was astonishingly beautiful and the sea road was bordered on one side by an almost continuous rampart of blossoming white bougainvillea like great foaming breakers, on the other, the crystal blue seascape. "People like you need a chauffeur."

"Yeah. Like your dad. Spoken to him lately?" Julie asked wryly, knowing full well the answer.

"I plug away but I think he's aware I've gone missing."

Julie shook her head. "You've had a terrible time, Cass."

"Only with my parents," Cassie quipped, but didn't smile. "Pull over, lady." She did her imitation of a traffic cop. "Like *now*." Life mightn't be all that brilliant but she didn't fancy going off one of the steep slopes.

They were both standing at the side of the road getting ready to change positions when a dusty four-wheel drive with a formidable bull bar pulled up alongside them.

"Everything okay?" The driver, a man, lowered his head to look out at them.

Cassie, overcome by an intensity of awareness, stood rooted, but Julie let out a quite audible, "Wow!"

"Excuse me?" One distinctively black eyebrow shot up, mockery laced with a certain amount of mischief.

Cassie predictably was the first to gather her wits. "We're fine, thank you," her breath expelled on a rush of air as she tried to overcome her confusion. "Just changing drivers."

"Well, take care, then." Brilliant blue eyes sought

and challenged her gaze. "Next time I wouldn't pull up quite so close to the edge. We've had a lot of rain. There could be slippage."

"Many thanks." Cassie gave a quick jerk of her head, wondering why she was behaving like she was.

"No problem." He lifted a hand to her, the intensity of his own gaze undimmed.

The engine of the four-wheel drive started up with a roar, another brief salute and he was off.

They were silent for quite a few moments, then Julie burst out in amazed ecstasy. "Did you see that, Cass? That had to be the best-looking guy I've ever seen in my life. Colouring to die for! Dark red hair, copper skin, jet-black eyebrows, the hottest blue eyes on the planet. Where has he been all my life?"

"Out bush." Cassie was surprised her voice sounded normal. "At a guess, I'd say he's a cattleman on one of his periodic forays into town. The long hair and the physique, the gear."

"Boy!" Julie gave a feline growl. "Talk about ten years searching for my hero. I've found him." She gave Cassie a little punch on the arm. "Sure he wasn't an apparition?"

"I'm hoping not," Cassie laughed, suddenly sounding exuberant.

"So let's get our skates on," Julie urged, running to the passenger side of the car. "It'll take us another twenty minutes to get into town."

They recognised the battered four-wheel drive parked outside the pub. "What did I tell you? The best people eat here!" Julie crowed in delight.

"No." Cassie was surprised by her own reluctance.

Normally she might have seen it as a bit of fun. But that guy, stunning as he was, wasn't a man to be trifled with.

Julie stared at her friend in amazement. "If you say you weren't impressed, you're lying in your teeth."

"He's very handsome, I agree."

Julie shook her blond head. "Handsome doesn't say it. I thought I was going to swoon."

"All right, he's terrific," Cassie conceded, yanking the thin strap of her camisole top back onto her shoulder. "But kind of dangerous, didn't you think?"

"As in what?" Julie reluctantly considered it. Cassie was extremely smart. Even her dad said so and he was sparing with the praise. "I thought he was very gallant, stopping like that."

"Well, we're not exactly bad-looking are we," Cassie retorted. "I know he wasn't giving us any come-on, rather the reverse, but he looked pretty complicated, complex, not your ordinary kind of guy. I'd say he's done a lot of living and done it hard."

"Heck, you noticed a lot." Julie, as usual, was impressed. "All I latched onto was the beauty of those *eyes!*"

"I know." Cassie smiled. "I saw the lightning strike. Don't follow it up, Julie. I'm only speaking in your best interests. Guys like that need a sign around their neck—Beware."

"Cassie, don't worry. Trust me." Julie shook her friend's arm. "Everything will be sweet. I only want to see him again. See if he's as stunning as I thought. Probably he'll sound like a redneck as soon as he opens his mouth."

Marcy looked up as the two young women entered the pub. She knew who they were, or she knew the cute little blond one, always laughing, shoulders bobbing, staring around her with wide blue-eyed interest. She was the daughter of the rich couple, the Maitlands, the people who had built a luxury retreat out at Aurora Bay. Marcy, who liked to give people private nicknames, called her Blondy. The other one was Sable. She'd seen her a couple of times around town. Hard to miss her. Where the little blonde was pretty, her friend totally eclipsed her. Mane of darkest brown into black hair like a luxurious fur pelt so thick it formed a swirling hood around her face. Light, luminous eyes like a river in the rain, polished skin. She was tall and very slender, but healthy-looking, vibrant. The two of them were dressed almost exactly the same. White cotton jeans so tight they looked like they'd been poured on, little-nothing tops that made the most of high young breasts and delicate shoulders. The heads were already turning, as well they might.

To have looked like that even for a day, Marcy thought. "Can I help you, girls?" she greeted them with her wide infectious smile.

"Yes, please." Sable approached. For all her classy look she wasn't uppity. Nice and friendly. "I'm Cassie Stirling. This is my friend, Julie Maitland. We're staying at Julie's parents' place on the point."

As though I don't know everything that goes on in the town, Marcy thought. "Yes, I know, luv." She nodded pleasantly. "Aurora Bay. Big terracotta place on the point."

"That's it!" Julie moved up to join her friend at the counter. "We thought we might do lunch." She had an appealing slightly breathless delivery, but there was a touch of patronising there absent in her friend.

"Glad to have you," Marcy said. 'You're not looking for anyone are you?" Blondy was all but standing on tiptoes looking around.

"You have to understand this is confidential." The girl bent to Marcy with a stage whisper. "We're hard on the track of a gorgeous-looking guy with hair like a dark flame and burning blue eyes. We had an idea he might have come in here."

"Well, you had the idea." Cassie coloured, wishing Julie would shut up.

"That would be Red. Red Carlyle." Marcy told them matter-of-factly, picking up a cloth and wiping off the already spotless counter.

"You know him?" Julie asked hopefully.

"Twenty years and more."

"Not married, is he?" Julie asked.

"Funny you should say that." Marcy gave them a rather sardonic smile. "He's advertisin' for a wife."

"Then that's definitely not the one," Sable said.

"There's only one Red." Marcy shook her head. "Matter of fact, the ad is in the local paper."

"You're having us on, aren't you?" Julie pulled a little face.

Sable smiled, too, but in a special way, kind of tender, Marcy thought. For some reason Marcy associated smiles like that with people who carried an inner sorrow. Red had a smile like that. Dazzling, lighting up his whole face, but with something that tugged at the heartstrings. At least that's what Marcy had always thought.

"What's wrong with the women of this town?" Sable was asking with a humorous tilt of her brows.

"A man like that on the loose!" Blondy rolled her eyes.

"Works too hard, that's his problem," Marcy told them. "How's he ever gonna find a wife when he spends all his time on Jabiru?"

"And may I ask what Jabiru is?" Blondy spoke in a facetious fashion that didn't do her justice. "Make sense to you, Cass?" Looking amused, she turned her head.

"I'm sure it's a property of some kind. A cattle station probably." Cassie gave Julie a little quelling shake of the head.

"Right in one," Marcy announced cheerfully. "Red runs Brahmans. Very hardy breed. They do very well right throughout the North where the British breeds can't survive."

"How interesting," said Julie. "And this—Jabiru, is it *big?*"

"Up here, girlie, we take vastness for granted," Marcy said bluntly. She was starting to tire a little of Blondy, something that wasn't lost on her friend.

"Would you have a table for two free?" Cassie intervened. By now she really wanted to get out of the pub but she was loath to offend this nice, cheerful woman with the smile lines creasing her vibrant green eyes.

"Sure, luv." Marcy reached under the counter and retrieved the local paper folded over to the page that carried Red's astonishing advertisement. She was still trying to take it in. All Red had to do was turn up Saturday night when the pub was full and holler. Chances are he would get knocked down in the stampede. "The one with the ring around it." She stabbed the paper for emphasis. "You can read it while you're waiting for lunch."

The courtyard expanded magically, wonderfully, a cool and shadowy place with masses of flowers in pots, great baskets of ferns suspended from the rafters, latticed walls dripping with a dusky rose bougainvillea, circular tables, green and white bordered cloths, garden chairs. There was a lot of laughter, a lot of talking, with everyone dressed very casually, tourists and locals. It was almost full. Every male to a man gave the girls long appreciative looks. One around their own age raised his hand indicating there was plenty of room at his table. But Marcy ignored him, showing them towards the rear with its green-gold bars of light for all the world like the sun pouring through stained-glass panels.

"This is enchanting," Cassie said, gazing around her with real pleasure.

"We think so, Luv." Marcy was pleased. She and Bill had put quite an effort into getting it right. She stopped at a table for two centred like the others with a bud vase holding a spray of the lovely Cooktown orchid, the State flower. "Anything to drink?"

Both girls chose mineral water with lime.

"You'll find the chef's suggestions posted on the board." Marcy waved a plump arm towards the blackboard. "I'm sure you'll find something you fancy. Coral trout. Red Emperor, straight from the trawler. Gulf prawns big as bananas. We could make up a lovely seafood platter for two if you like. The crab is superb."

"I know, heavenly!" Cassie's mouth started to water.

"Think it over. I'll be back in a few minutes to take

your order." Marcy started to move off, then turned. "By the way, Red will be in shortly. He has some business down the road."

The Lord works in strange ways, Marcy thought. The girl, Cassie, with the eyes clear as diamonds and her obviously privileged background, was at a crossroads in her life. There was something missing. Someone. Marcy had a sure instinct about such things. Bill often told her she had the second sight inherited they both thought from her Scottish grandmother. Besides, there wasn't anything she wouldn't do for Red.

Less than ten minutes later as the girls exclaimed over the delicious seafood platter Marcy was setting before them, Red Carlyle appeared at the entrance to the courtyard, instantly creating his own force field. He was greeted on all sides with shouts and waves, lifting an all-encompassing hand in acknowledgment. His gaze ranged over the courtyard for a moment until he caught sight of Marcy's short plump figure. Immediately he began to stride towards her, moving with such grace and pent-up energy, Cassie felt a thrust of excitement in the pit of her stomach. He had such a blaze about him she felt like ducking her head. He was heading towards them, abundant dark red hair swept back, touching the collar of his blue denim shirt. No short back and sides for him. The remarkable eyes glowed turquoise, sweeping over the girls as Marcy moved her body to follow the girls' stare.

"Red!" She greeted him with motherly pleasure.

He smiled and Cassie found herself gripping the arms of her chair. This was the man who was *advertising* for a wife? Why, he was so handsome, so vibrant, it made her eyes smart to look at him. The dark blue gaze was on her now, a long measuring scrutiny, then on Julie, who had her pretty pink mouth open like a fish.

"Well, I see you made it safely into town." He softly shook his head as though he was surprised.

"You know these young ladies, Red?" Marcy executed a double take.

"We passed one another back on the road. Didn't get to names."

"I'm Julie Maitland," Julie piped up, giving her best Drew Barrymore smile. "This is my friend—"

"Cassandra Stirling." Cassie wanted to identify herself.

"*Cassandra?* As in, daughter of Priam King of Troy?" He looked at her with those amazing eyes, the same long steady assessment.

"You'd better believe it," Julie quipped. The original Cassandra had been condemned by Apollo to prophetise correctly but never be believed.

"A beautiful dangerous name for a beautiful, dangerous woman," Matthew responded, seeing a woman he could want badly but was hopelessly out of reach. Her eyes put him in mind of a silver river, the lining lashes as thick as inky-black ferns. Skin like magnolia silk, lovely long neck. Dire consequences were attached to wanting a woman like that and he wasn't a man to long for things beyond hope of fulfilment.

"Red Carlyle." He introduced himself. "I wasn't christened that. My ma called me Matthew after my grandad in England, but it look less than a week to be rechristened up here."

"Gorgeous hair, that's why!" Marcy grasped a handful, fixing him with an affectionate gaze. He towered over her by a good foot. "I was telling the girls, here, you've been advertising for a bride."

Perhaps he would be embarrassed! He wasn't. Unflappable. A touch speculative.

"Sure have. Saves a lot of time. Only *one* thing. The frivolous needn't apply. A serious offer demands a serious response."

Julie raised her eyebrows, plainly dumbfounded. "It's hard to believe any woman could resist you."

He glanced at her and shook his head. "We're talking about a full partner in my business. Cattle ranch, name of Jabiru. I'm talking about a woman who can share my vision. A woman who's strong in her own right. A woman who can give me children we'll both love and enjoy. I'm not talking about a chick who wants to move in and play house. I'm talking about much, much more."

Julie coughed. "So this brings me to my application." She was only half joking.

He laughed. Warm and deep. His voice far from being country hick was educated, very attractive, with curiously an English accent.

"Write it down," he invited. "No need to send along the photograph. I know what you look like. Pretty as a picture. I know, too, you're joking. You're the daughter of a very successful man and you've been looked after all your life. *Pampered.*"

Julie sighed. "That's exactly the way my folks raised me. What about Cassie? What do you see in her?" Julie had already gained the impression of some undercurrent.

He turned his attention to Cassie of the billowing hair. "Oh, someone who's had sadness in her life at some point. But a person who won't let herself be overwhelmed."

"Say that's spot-on. Tell us more. Sit down," Julie invited. "Talk to us."

He shook his head as though he had already said too much. "Love to. Some other time maybe. I'm on a pretty tight schedule."

"You have to grab a bite to eat, Red," Marcy jumped in. "I can easily move you all to a larger table."

"Really, please join us," Cassie said with so much feeling it shocked her. In all her life she had never met anybody to match his shattering impact. Though he was acting friendly, she was smart enough to realise this was a man with a dangerous edge. There was an inner core of aloofness in him, as well, almost an arrogance. Maybe it was just a fiery pride.

"All right, then." He came to a quick decision. "I'm pretty hungry for Marcy's roast lamb. And vegetables, Marcy. Lots of them. I haven't cooked for days."

"You mean, you do your own *cooking?*" Julie, whose pièce de résistance was an overcooked omelette, asked.

"I'm an expert," he answered with no sense of false modesty.

"He is, too." Marcy gave him a proud smile. "His mum started him off and I took over by handing over a few cookbooks. Red, here, lives like a feudal lord."

Pleased with the way things were going, Marcy busied herself setting up a larger table two places down. Matthew, obviously used to helping her, picked up the girls' seafood platter arranged beautifully on a colourful ceramic plate and carried it down. He even went back and picked up the bud vase seeing there wasn't one on the new table. Finally, he seated both girls with a stunningly elegant flourish, before he flung himself into a chair with lavish pent-up grace.

"So, what are you doing up here?" he asked. "Holidaying?"

"Julie's parents have a hideaway up here," Cassie explained, turning her head to face him.

"Hideaway? I bet it's big enough to get lost in," he mocked.

Both girls nodded their assent. "It's on the point at Aurora Beach."

"Hell, I love that place," he said. "I haven't been there in a long time." Although he appeared to be addressing Julie, his eyes kept regarding Cassie as though he sought to commit her features to memory. He even moved his chair to a better angle.

Cassie found it as disconcerting as it was thrilling. She felt overexcited: racing in top gear.

"Jabiru keeps you very busy?" She allowed herself to look into his bronze face and saw chiselled features, a beautiful sensuous mouth, good jaw, cleft chin.

He nodded his handsome, flamboyant head. "It's taken years of my life. Years of backbreaking work to develop it."

"But you treasure it?"

His eyes glittered turquoise. "My Promised Land. The place I feel truly at home."

"Then you're a lucky man."

"I figure I am." He stared at her. So why did he catch

that little note of sadness? It didn't make sense. Both of them were undoubtedly young women who lived in a style he could only imagine.

"But to advertise?" Julie had been avidly following their dialogue. "I bet you could get any woman you want."

"I'm thinking you're too kind. Getting the right woman might take a miracle, but I'll keep trying. I live an exhausting life, but soon I hope I can slow down. I'm not getting any younger. Thirty-four. Time to get a life."

Julie laughed. "But surely you know all the local girls?"

"As in saying 'good day,'" he admitted. "I haven't invited them all out to the ranch." The turquoise eyes glinted. "You'd be surprised that local rag goes far and wide."

"So how are you going to *know?*" Cassie asked quietly. She turned her head, pinned by the charge he sent out like an electric thrill. Maybe he even *saw* it, because of what he said.

"A thunderbolt from Heaven." His tone was sardonic. "What do the French call it, a *coup de foudre?*"

"Does it *really* happen?" Cassie asked from the depths of her soul. She hadn't meant to. She wasn't used to being fascinated by a man. Generally it was the other way around. She the object of desire who turned away.

"I'm *sure* it does," he answered in a strange, harsh voice. "Just as I don't think acting on it would be wise. I'm looking for something less extravagant than a dangerous passion."

"You have to see you're just the person for it?" Julie shot him a playful glance.

"No, ma'am." Not only did he shake his head emphatically, he waved a dismissive hand. Elegant, long-fingered, darkly tanned, calloused on the fingertips and palms, Cassie noted.

There's a story here, Julie thought, convinced of it.

"Headlong passion can be very destructive. Wouldn't you agree?" he continued. "I wonder just how many people have been swept into an ocean of grief. I know it happens."

"So you're planning a marriage of convenience?" Cassie asked, a flicker of something very like antagonism in her voice. What was the matter with her? She felt as tight as a spring.

"Hey, it must be convenient, that's for certain. Perhaps something in between. Many cultures have arranged marriages. Had them for many centuries and they seem to work out. Have true worth."

"So you're saying falling in love isn't the answer?" Cassie was persisting and didn't know why. If only he'd stop looking at her like that.

"I'm saying many, many love matches end in divorce," he retorted, his enunciation clear. "I've seen plenty of relationships flounder. The woman is generally left to make a home for any children involved."

"Yes," Cassie agreed, then abruptly changed the subject. "So, you're English."

"I'm as Australian as you are." His beautiful eyes stared her down.

"I only meant you have an *English* accent." She had

to strive to smile. Her mouth felt dry. "Where did you pick it up?"

"My mother was English," he explained briefly.

"Oh, I see." Cassie realised it wasn't a subject he was going to talk about.

"Actually you sound great," Julie soothed. She could have sworn Red and Cassie were attracted to each other. Attraction with a dash of hostility. No, not *hostility,* she decided, something rather complex.

Marcy returned at just the right moment with Red's roast lamb and a large side dish of vegetables. For a while conversation stopped as they enjoyed their meal. He ate ravenously for a while, Cassie noted. No bad table manners, indeed not, just a man who was totally concentrating on good food. A man who probably had only in recent days been able to grab a meal on the run.

"This is wonderful." He looked up and reached for his glass of beer. "We've been out on a four-day muster. Didn't stop for long. Pushed too damned hard. The floods have held us up but the country's in fine form now the waters have abated."

"It's like another world!" Cassie gazed at the stupendous hanging baskets of ferns. "I've never seen anything like the vegetation up here. Or the colours! The extraordinary depth and brilliance of the sky, the rich red and emerald earth, the endless white beaches, the sparkling blue sea."

"The Tropics, ma'am," he drawled. "I expect you know many of the islands of the Great Barrier Reef?"

"We know Hayman well," Julie volunteered, daintily downing a creamy rock oyster.

"Of course." Momentarily his lids came down. Hayman was one of the great resorts of the world. A resort for the wealthy.

"Actually I cruised the Whitsunday's with friends," Cassie said, smiling in remembrance of one of the most beautiful and peaceful holidays of her life. "We visited many of the lesser known islands and cays, explored the wonders of the coral reef, the gardens and grottoes, swam in beautiful lagoons. A heavenly blue world of infinite distances."

"Yes, it's glorious," he agreed, spearing the last morsel of roast potato. "So close yet I haven't been able to get away in years."

"You mean you haven't been able to take a *holiday*," Julie asked.

"More important things to do," he laughed. "I'm not complaining. Jabiru's mine and I love it. On the other hand it's good to have the company of two beautiful women." The dazzling eyes flashed over them, brilliant but impenetrable. "Do you know anything about ranching, as the Americans say?"

"Some." Cassie nodded. "I was invited once to a race meeting on Monaro Downs. A huge affair. The place belongs to Sir Jock Macalister," she said casually. "Being a cattleman you're bound to know of him. Monaro Downs is the Macalisters' flagship in the Channel Country."

"I know where it is," he interrupted, startling her with the curtness of his tone.

Colour moved under her high cheekbones. She spoke quietly. "What's the matter? Have I upset you in some way?"

A muscle in the clean line of his jaw jumped erratically. He nearly said yes. Such was her magic. "Not at all. Anyone in the Outback would know of Macalister and his empire. So you were impressed?"

"I sure was," Cassie replied, regarding him with an odd half smile. "I've never seen anything like the homestead. The finest mansion you could imagine set down in a million wild acres. Nothing except for endless miles of plains and towering sand hills. I missed the miracle of the wildflowers. It was the middle of the drought. My parents were lucky enough to witness the spectacle. They said it was unbelievable."

"So you weren't along on the trip?"

"I was at boarding school at the time."

"Boarding school?" One black eyebrow shot up. "I figure your parents must be on the land, as well?"

"My father is a Sydney businessman," she told him quietly. She didn't dare mention his strong business connections with Macalister.

"Nobody heard about day school?" The sensual mouth quirked. "I'm sorry." He gave Cassie a smile that heated her blood. "I have to watch my tongue. You have brothers and sisters?"

"I'm the only one."

"Tell me about it." He shrugged. "I was the only one, as well. And you, Miss Julie?" he addressed her with a light-hearted mockery.

"The only daughter, which I'm happy with. Two big brothers. Cass has been my best friend since our first day at St. Catherine's. A posh school for young ladies."

"You mean you were bundled off, as well?" he asked in amazement.

"No, I was a day pupil. Cassie's parents travelled a lot," Julie informed him.

"And when was this? How old?"

"Not yet eight." Cassie reached over to take Julie's hand affectionately.

"Really." Carlyle shook his head. "It hardly seems possible any parent could part with you. Even *now* the unhappiness is in your eyes, Cassandra."

It was like being caught in a passionate embrace. "Surely not," Cassie managed.

He regarded her with the kind of intensity she was just barely getting used to. "You've got the kind of shimmering eyes that's a heart's beat away from tears."

She took a deep breath, feeling a very real panic. "I can see I'll have to protect my gaze from you."

"Too observant?" he asked with a mixture of sympathy and challenge.

"No one else has mentioned it." She thought she was losing a layer of skin.

"I'm sure they've noticed." His smile was twisted. "Luminescent, isn't that the word? I didn't get past high school—" this with a touch of self derision "—whereas you two got to go to university I'll bet."

Julie nodded. "I did what I was told. I struggled through. Cassie is the brain. We both work for my father. He's a stockbroker." She didn't add "big-time" but she got his full attention.

"That's interesting. I've made quite a bit for myself playing the market. It's amazing what you girls are doing these days. Showing us guys up. All you need is the chance."

"So, no chauvinist?" Cassie asked, feeling another great surge of attraction but struggling against it.

He tossed back the rest of his beer. "No way. Women have resources to call on we guys don't. I know a woman took over the running of a big station when her husband was killed, as tough and intelligent as the best of 'em. Actually I have an intense admiration for a woman's strength. And an intense sympathy for the soft little vulnerable ones some man always treats badly."

"You're going to make a wonderful husband," Julie sighed.

"I'm going to give it my best shot. A commitment is a commitment. Isn't that right?"

Neither young woman was about to argue. If the truth be known, they were spellbound.

A moment later Matthew shoved his chair back, coiled ready to spring into action. "That was great!" he said with satisfaction. "Marcy knows exactly the way to a man's heart." He pushed his chair in, a smile deepening the curve of his mouth. "It's been a great pleasure meeting you, Julie, Cassandra." His eyes moved from one to the other. "But I've got to get cracking. I hope you enjoy the rest of your holiday. Before you go back to your world of luxury."

"No chance of seeing Jabiru, I suppose?" the irrepressible Julie asked.

He was about to shake his head, but suddenly relented. A split second's impulse. "Why not, if you're really interested," he found himself saying, much against his better judgment. "I can't come for you, much as I'd like to. This is a bad time. But by next week the pace should slacken off. If you'd like to make the drive, you're very welcome. But I think that'll put you off," he mocked.

"So, what day next week?" Julie persisted, wanting to follow it up by helicopter if she had to. This guy was something else.

"Ring me," he said, his voice deep and sonorous. "Marcy will give you my number."

God, how dumb can a man get! he thought as he made his way out onto the street. Little Julie with her wiggle was having a bit of fun, he could see that. But what the hell! He was sick of the quiet life. The other one—Cassandra—though she listened to her friend with a mixture of amused affection and dismay, was sending different signals. She didn't look like she wanted to come. There was even a kind of anxiety in her. He had sensed it. Anyway, she was way out of his league. A woman from a world he could never get into. A woman, it now seemed, from Jock Macalister's world. That alone suffused him with a chill, helpless anger. Nothing could be gained from even seeing her again. He regretted, too, ever looking into her eyes. There was a woman he could badly want but never have.

CHAPTER THREE

"WHAT in the world is goin' on, Red?" Ned Croft, his old mate from town, asked him. They were sitting on the veranda enjoying a cold beer and a quick lunch of the fresh bread rolls Ned had brought from the town's bakehouse, stuffed with his own ham, cheese and pickles.

Ned, all of seventy-five, but very fit and wiry with a long bayonet scar on his right arm from the Second World War, often made the trek, lured by his old bush life and the fact that he and Red had struck up quite a friendship, kept glancing down at the swag of mail he had assured Mavis at the post office he would deliver to Red.

"Bloody advertisin', mate. I can't accept that," Ned said, scratching his balding, freckled scalp. "A big handsome fella like yourself could have any girl you wanted. Especially now you've become so successful. It's a great life out here and you've made the homestead real nice."

"I need a wife, Ned," Matthew said, straightening up to pick up another roll. Was there anything better than freshly baked bread and butter?

"You did mention that. But *advertisin'*, mate? Seems utterly wrong for a bloke like you."

"The way I see it, Ned, it will save me a load of time."

"Goin' on that." Ned pointed downwards with a gnarled thumb. "But what about love, boy? Haven't you given a bit of thought to that?"

Matthew's eyes blazed. "Hell, Ned, I know what love is. I loved my mother. But I've found this romantic love business is a bit of a trap. Sometimes it's over before it's begun. Then there's my background. The past. At least everyone around here knows all about the skeleton in my family closet."

Ned shook his head. Given to lengthy considerations, he didn't say anything for a while. "Don't talk skeletons to me, lad. You're as good a bloke as any girl could get. Better. I know you take this illegitimate bit real serious, but no one else does. You was the victim. The unlucky one. It's Macalister who's the bastard."

"And no argument from me." Matthew grinned. "But some people place a lot of store on family. I remember life with Mum. Moving from place to place. Never having anyone. No relatives. No support group. No damned identity. Even some of the kids at school gave me hell until I found a way to shut their mouths. I have to find an ordinary girl who knows the truth and won't shy away from it."

"Why, did you have someone *else* in mind?" Ned asked shrewdly, turning his bony silver head.

"No," Matthew lied.

"You don't sound sure," Ned replied. "I don't know

about this ordinary bit, either. There's nuthin' ordinary about you, Red. Don't you understand that?"

"I'm a realist, Ned. I've come a long way, but now I want to put down roots. Marry a good woman who'll give me a family. I want to build a relationship that will hold us together."

"That's some ambition," Ned, long divorced, said. "That girl, Fiona, didn't you like her?"

Matthew laughed. "Ned, Fiona left town ages ago. She went to Brisbane to find herself a nice solicitor."

"Don't know what she's missin'. Are you gunna read all of these?" Ned leaned down to loosen the neck of the mailbag.

"Every last one."

"Gunna take a while," Ned snorted, rubbing his jaw. "Want me to help you?"

"Thanks, Ned, but I have to look after these myself," Matthew declined. "You know, respecting a girl's confidence."

"'Course. Fine," Ned nodded in agreement. "Looks like pretty hard work to me all the same." He finished off the rest of his tea. Good tea, too. Red made a nice cuppa. "Reckon I can stay overnight?" He was hoping Red would say yes, and he did.

"You know you can, Ned." Matthew gathered the few plates together, put them on the tray. "Listen, we're doing a little muster at Yanco Gully. Want to ride along?"

"Count me in!" Ned said with enthusiasm, jumping to his feet. "This Jabiru is a great place. And haven't you made it work!"

Red mightn't want to know it but he had surely inherited Macalister's legendary drive. It was an absolute tragedy when a man rejected his own son, Ned thought. Moreover, *such* a son! And his *only* son. Macalister for all his millions and his empire must have plenty of bad moments.

"I'm serious about this," Julie called as Cassie walked out onto the magnificent upper deck with its breath-taking views of a glorious blue sea and the offshore islands that adorned it like rings of jade. "That guy's fantastic."

Outside the wind off the water was whipping through Cassie's hair. She hesitated a moment then returned to the huge open-plan living room. "I've told you before, Julie, this is one dangerous-edged man. He won't take kindly to any little jokes. He strikes me as a man with a real temper. He could confront you about it."

"Well—" Julie was seated at a table trying to answer Red's advertisement. "You're not *listening,* sweetie. I'm dead serious. I need some excitement in my life and he's offering."

"You're talking absolute rubbish." Cassie took a chair at the circular table. "And what about Perry?"

"You've got no idea, have you? I said I want *excitement.* Perry's nice, but no one could call him macho. Red is real *man!*"

"And too powerful for you. I wouldn't want to be the woman who tried to make a fool of him. You'd be left with a very sorrowful tale to tell."

"He's not a guy to beat a woman up," Julie scoffed. "He seemed very different from that."

"Well, what do you actually know about him? Zilch."

"I know the best already. I can work my way to the worst. It could just work out." At this Cassie shot out of her seat and Julie fired off, "If you weren't such a control freak you'd admit he got to you, too. I thought that was real sexy the way he kept calling you Cassandra. I wonder what happened to his mother?"

"Something bad," Cassie snapped. "It wasn't a subject he was about to discuss. You did see that."

"Simmer down, Cass," Julie begged. "I'm not clever like you. I want to find myself a *man*. So far, Red's it."

The shrill voice of the vacuum cleaner cut through their conversation. Molly Gannon who with her husband Jim, acted as caretakers for the Maitlands' very expensive retreat appeared from the hallway. "Not going to bother you am I, girls? I can come back later."

"No, come in Molly," Julie beckoned. "You might be able to help us here." Julie turned in her chair. "You know everyone around here. What do you know about a guy called Red Carlyle. Owns a cattle station in the hinterland."

"Red?" Molly switched off the vacuum cleaner and straightened up, pressing a hand against her aching back. "'Course I know Red. Everyone knows Red. He's a big success story around here."

"Ah," Julie cried in satisfaction. "Pull up a chair, Molly."

"Can't we leave this?" Cassie was exasperated and more upset than she knew why.

"It's not Red's ad?" Molly settled herself in an armchair.

"You know about it?" Cassie asked.

Molly gave her rich, rumbling laugh. "We *all* know about it. If I didn't have Jim I'd be applying myself. Mavis at the post office reckons she's flat out handling his mail."

"So they're answering already?" Julie bit her lip.

Molly just looked at her. "You've *seen* Red, haven't you?"

"Yes we have," Cassie told her quietly.

"Talk to him?"

"Just a few words."

"That'd be enough, I reckon." Molly nodded her head. Up and down several times. "He's really somethin', isn't he? He came here with his mum when he was about twelve years old. Wild kid then and for a long time after. A real hot temper. Typical redhead. Used to zip into anyone who said anything about him or his mum. His mum especially. He was very protective."

"What could they possibly *say?*" Cassie asked, some-how fearful of what was coming.

"Aa-ah!" Molly retorted, shaking her head from side to side.

"Come on, Moll," Julie urged. "You can't leave us up in the air. If you want to know, I'm thinking of answer-ing his ad."

"What?" Molly couldn't hide her shock. "You're not *serious* are you, dear?"

"Sure." Julie gave her a challenging look. "I'm real interested."

The odd, shocked expression was still on Molly's face. "Deary, deary, be *warned*." She gave it such emphasis.

Cassie turned to Julie. "Isn't that what I told you?"

"He hasn't spent time in jail, has he?" Julie demanded, her eyes turning steely.

"No, no, nothing like that." Molly scratched her springy grey head, locking eyes with Cassie, who she thought was far the more sensible of the two. "I said that badly. Red is a fine young man. He's worked very hard to get where he has. We all admire him, but he's got a bit of a cloud over his name. If you know what I mean. Doesn't mean anything to us up here, but it would to *your* folks. Take my advice, girls. Enjoy yourselves and go home. Your life's not up here."

"Is that today's lecture?" Cassie smiled to take the edge off her words. What Molly had said had only made her defensive. On Red's behalf.

"I'm only trying to give you good advice," Molly maintained, now staring at the floor. "Your parents wouldn't thank me, Julie, if I didn't put you straight."

"Why don't you?" Cassie invited. "What's Red's dark secret?"

Molly thought for a moment then sighed. "No *secret* in these parts. He's the flamin' image of his father at the same age, that's why. The colouring. The red setter hair, the blue eyes, the black eyebrows. You've got no idea, have you?"

"Obviously not," Cassie said, and Julie made a snorting sound.

"He's Jock Macalister's son," Molly announced like he was royalty.

Julie sat up, chin up. "For crying out loud!"

"Wait a minute." Cassie frowned. "Sir Jock doesn't have a son. He has three married daughters and as far as I know their children are little girls."

"How come you know so much?" Molly gave her a puzzled stare.

"My parents are quite friendly with Sir Jock," Cassie confided. "They've visited Monaro Downs a number of times. I've been there years ago when I was a child. I don't remember Sir Jock having red hair. It was thick and tawny, as I recall. But I do remember his black eyebrows and brilliant blue eyes."

"He's Macalister's son, all right," Molly said in such a stern voice her double chin trembled. Her disapproval of Macalister was very evident. "Won't acknowledge him though."

Cassie felt heat spread all over her skin. "But that's appalling!"

"It is, too." Molly gave another vigorous sideways jerk of her head. "I can't begin to tell you how that boy suffered. And his mum. The prettiest little thing you ever laid eyes on. Rather like you in style, Julie. Petite, blond. She was English. Posh accent. We all wondered about her background. Red sounds like a Pom to this day."

"But how did they meet?" Cassie asked, clamping her own hands together. "Red's mother and Macalister?"

Molly blew out a long, whinnying breath. "Appears she was employed as a governess, nanny, some such thing, on one of his stations."

"So he took advantage of her?" Cassie said, seeing the tragedy.

"Sure. Don't they all?" Molly retorted caustically, though sadness spread over her kind, homely features. "Little thing was killed a few years back. The whole town turned out for the funeral. Seems like yesterday.

It was rough on Red. He really loved his mother. Did everything he could to look after her."

"How was she killed?" Cassie felt a little sick. Julie sat slumped in her chair as though all the wind had been knocked out of her.

"Road accident," Molly said vaguely. "Red's carrying a lot of baggage."

"One can understand that," Cassie mused.

"He'll make a good husband and a good father, mind you," Molly said loyally. "But don't you two young ladies go thinkin' of answering any advertisements. That would rock your folks to the core."

By mutual consent both girls left the house and headed for the beach, walking barefoot in the fine-grained white sand that ran like hot silk.

"Let's move down to the water's edge," Cassie murmured. "Easier going. We'll walk up to Leopard Rock."

The water at the edge was crystal, a beautiful aquamarine that deepened into brilliant blue.

"Well, that sure put a lid on it," Julie groaned. "Poor old Red. It must be awful to be illegitimate."

"It's not the social stigma it once was," Cassie said steadily. "And rightly so. The innocent can't be victimised. They can't pay for something that happened before they were born. Anyway, plenty of couples are having children without getting around to marriage."

Julie nodded, flipping a blond curl out of her eyes. "But it's not *our* way, is it? Our folk's way."

"I guess not. I don't really believe it's any woman's preferred way. Women want security, permanence, the best possible life for their children. There are enough hurdles surely?"

"But what an extraordinary story." Julie bent to pick up a very pretty sea-shell. "Your parents so friendly with Macalister yet they've never heard the rumours?"

"They could have for all I know." Cassie shrugged. "It seems to be common knowledge."

"Yet the family, the Macalisters, ignore it. Ignore Red. He's got a big family with tons of money yet he's an outcast."

They stopped to watch a flock of disturbed seagulls take to the air.

"You haven't met *Lady Macalister*." Cassie shuddered, turning to Julie with a theatrical expression. "Even my mother said she's a woman with a very cold heart."

Julie would have laughed at the irony if it weren't so sad. "Well, she'd know." She put an arm around Cassie's waist. "Why don't we go and look at this place? Jabiru. It can't do any harm. I'd really like to see it, wouldn't you?"

Of one accord they walked into a foaming little breaker. "Actually I *would* but it'd be against my better judgement. We might be getting drawn into something here, Julie. Something about Red Carlyle scares me."

"Afraid of his attraction?" Julie gave her friend a shrewd glance. "I'd say you're even more interested in Red than I am."

Cassie frowned. "That's the part that bothers me. I can just imagine telling my parents I was interested in Jock Macalister's illegitimate son."

"Can't wait for that one," Julie quipped. "They'd give

you a very hard time. Your dad would probably zap you out of his will."

"I don't care about that." Cassie threw back her head, letting the sea breeze whip her hair into a silk pennant. "I've had a good education. I can make my own way. Besides, there's Grandma's money."

"That's right!" Julie brightened. "Tell you what, we'll have a swim on the way back then I'm going up to the house to leave a message for Red. He did invite us and we've got the time. We could take care of his mail for him. Help him pick out the right bride."

In the end Red organised everything himself. He enlisted the help of a friendly neighbour, Bob Lester, a well-established cattleman, to ferry the girls back after his business meeting in town. Red himself would drive them home. But it meant an overnight stay.

"What do you think, Marcy?" Cassie whispered across the counter. They often came into the pub now and each time they had a conversation with a willing Marcy.

"Safe as houses," Marcy maintained stoutly.

"What a pity. I thought he'd grab me," Julie giggled.

"Not Red, I swear. He'll treat you like the fine young ladies you are. Bob and Bonnie Lester are pillars of the community. You'll be safe with Bob. You'll need riding gear. Big shady hats. Red has organised with me to send a few supplies out. You'll take them along on your trip. Bob doesn't mind. I think you're going to have a very good time."

I'll pray for that, Cassie thought.

Bob Lester turned out to be a tall, hale cattleman with a thick shock of prematurely snow-white hair and a full white moustache, handlebars and all. He picked them up at the house and entertained them with lots of stories on their long journey into the hinterland.

Cassie had thought it might be endless but the time flew. The scenery was remarkable. Under a cloudless cobalt-blue sky the countryside waved a lush emerald-green to the horizon. The spurs of the Great Dividing Range stood in stark relief above the plains, their colour the most wonderful moody grape-blue into purple. Small white and lavender-blue wildflowers floated on this sea of hardy green grasses and scattered all over were pools of tranquil water, relics of the floodwaters Cyclone Amy had brought down.

"You can consider yourselves fortunate, girls," Bob Lester told them. "Red don't have many visitors. He's been pretty darn content on his own. Leastways up until now. I'm blessed if I know if he's serious about this advertisin' for a bride. There's already bagsful of mail arriving from all over. He'd be well advised to be serious, I reckon."

"So how's he going to handle it?" Julie, in the back, piped up.

"I don't rightly know," Bob admitted. "What I *can* tell you is the woman who lands Red is one mighty lucky woman. Even I never imagined he could work the wonders he has. Jabiru was terribly rundown and the old homestead was in such a state it had to be demolished. Red built the new place with his own hands. It's a credit to him but you'll be able to see for yourselves. 'Course he's a chi—"

"Chip off the old block?" Julie promoted.

Bob gave a wry grin. "Everyone knows around here. Macalister ignoring his own son. Makes ya wonder!"

"There's no room for doubt?" Cassie asked.

Bob gave her a brief telling look. "None, unless a man has a double."

It was a paradise of the wild.

Flocks of magpie geese flew overhead and a solitary jabiru stood in stately silence at the edge of a silvery pool. A big sign above the iron gate announced the entry to Jabiru Station. Another sign on the fence carried the warning: This Gate Must Be Shut At All Times.

Cassie jumped out to open the gate, waited until the Land Rover had passed through, then swung the gate back into position. The metallic sound caused an amazing number of brilliantly coloured parrots to rise out of the magnificent gum that stood to one side of the gate, screeching their arrival. Not that Red would have heard. They had to travel a good mile up an unsealed drive before the homestead came into sight. A long, low-slung building that seemed completely at home in its verdant surroundings.

"Say, this is nice," Julie breathed. "But very isolated. He must find it hard out here all by himself."

"Well, he's aiming to change that," Bob said. "Probably he's had no time to feel lonely. He's slaved to get this place back to what it was."

Red was on hand to greet them, all taut and terrific male grace, coming down to the vehicle and opening up the front and back doors. "Right on time!" He looked beyond Cassie for a moment to smile at Bob. "Thanks a lot, neighbour. You'll stay and have a cup of tea?"

"Love to." Bob grinned. "Lots of supplies in the back, Red. Cold stuff in the esky. Marcy sent it along."

"Good. I'll take care of it. You hop out and stretch your legs. Well, now, Julie, Cassandra, I'm very pleased you could come."

The blue eyes made Cassie feel hot and helpless, but Julie answered for both of them. "It's great to be here. Worth working hard for, Red?" She swept out her arms.

"What do *you* think?" Suddenly he turned his head and pinned Cassie's eyes.

For a moment she forgot to breathe. "A paradise of the wild," she managed at last, her voice faintly husky.

"I'll accept that." He smiled. "Come on, come on up. Bob—" he turned his head "—leave those things I'll get them."

"Just the esky, then," Bob answered, reaching into the vehicle for the cold stuffs. "I'll have a cup of tea, then I'll be off."

Inside the bungalow both girls were astonished at how attractive Red had made it. It was rustic, admittedly, the furnishings were old, inexpensive, but comfortable-looking with several sofas, one good leather armchair in a rich burgundy. The scatter rugs on the polished floor were colourful, as were the fat cushions on the sofas. There were prints that looked like they'd been selected carefully, hung around one large main room with a whole wall taken up with books, books, books. Heaps too many to count. There were even two big planters containing luxuriant golden canes and sprays of yellow orchids in a copper pot in the middle of the dark-timbered old dining table that had been polished to quite a shine.

"Come on, a decorator did this," Julie cajoled. "What's her name?"

"This was put together by a man." Cassie looked around. "It's comfortable and relaxed and it has a great feel of home."

"Glad you like it." Red sketched a bow. "While you look around I'll bring your things in. My guestroom is to the left. Two single beds. Clean sheets. I hope you'll be comfortable."

What have I let myself in for? he thought as he lopped down the front steps. The cute little Julie didn't bother him. She was pretty, never giving herself a moment to get bored, but Cassandra of the luminous eyes. He was far from immune to her. In fact for a moment there when they had arrived he had hardly dared to look at her. But still, he had. Stared at her oval face, her skin, her eyes, the luscious tender curves of her mouth, the way her gleaming hair went into deep soft waves over her shoulders.

It was one hell of a risk to have her here, he thought as he reached into the Land Rover for the luggage. Why hadn't he just let it go? Last night when he wasn't cleaning house in preparation for their visit, he had sat reading a score of letters from young women who had given serious consideration to spending their life with him. Some of the letters moved him. Those were from young women from unhappy homes, desperate to find security and a new life. Some of them he even knew. Couple of kooks. One he put down fast. Dirty talk, for God's sake. He realised he might expect it.

Now this beautiful porcelain creature who stood inside the rough house he had built had said it had a great feel of home. She wasn't just saying it, either. He could see the sincerity in her lovely features. The princess he could fall in love with. The princess he couldn't wait to be gone. Jock Macalister's bastard he might be, but he wasn't any fool.

CHAPTER FOUR

BECAUSE Julie couldn't ride, he drove them around the station until late afternoon, stopping to watch the glorious tropical sunset from Warinna Ridge. Fiery reds, glowing rose, brilliant streaks of indigo and gold that illuminated the whole world.

"We'd better not delay," he murmured at last, "dusk will set in fast and we have to get down the ridge." They had left the Jeep at the bottom, making the fairly easy climb on foot. It would be easier still going down. Red went ahead, holding any low-slung branches out of their way, moving with his special rhythm that had Cassie's eyes glued to his wide back.

That was when it happened.

As Julie padded past her just a little out of breath, the ground seemed to move under Cassie's feet. Pebbles and small rocks rolled down the slope. She gave a little shriek as she lost balance, skidding forward, a sharp rock slashing at her ankle as she seemed all set to take a fall. Except it didn't happen that way. Red whipped around in a lightning flash, grabbed her body and hauled her to him, holding her strongly as she fell crushed against him on legs as wobbly as a new born foal's.

"Lord!" she gulped on something that sounded like a sob, her heartbeat driven up into her mouth.

His body was so beautiful. Beautiful! The male scent of him so clean and warm and so erotic. She felt wildly aroused in an instant. Sinking in a well of sensation. And he knew it. He *knew* it. She was more alive than she had ever been. More afraid.

"Cassandra." He bent his head, his mouth touching her hair. "You okay?"

While Julie called out anxiously, "You're not hurt, are you, Cass?"

"I might have hurt my ankle." She spoke breathlessly, betrayingly, feeling the shame of it.

"Here, let's have a look," he said with measured gentleness. "Rest your hand on my shoulder."

She had to get herself under control, glimpsing something wonderful but afraid to follow.

"You've gashed it," he told her. To a man he would have added, "No big deal." But this was a princess with a fine delicate ankle. "Have you got a clean handkerchief on you?"

He gazed up into her face, finding her pale with sexual feelings briefly glimpsed before the veil fell.

"I have." Julie came to the rescue. "Say, that looks nasty, Cass."

"It won't be when I clean it up," Red retorted, fixing a makeshift bandage. "Bad luck. Want me to carry you?" he asked, powerfully aware of his desire to hold her.

Her beautiful hair bounced loose all around her flushed face. "No, I'll be fine." She denied what she longed for. "It just shook me a little."

Understatement of the year. Inside she was burning

hot. Imagining herself alone with him in the night. What it would be like?

When they returned to the house, Red insisted on cleaning up the gash straight away.

She protested again, jittery, not knowing what to do with her hands. She couldn't believe she could feel this way. So soon.

"I think I should. I'm your host. While I'm attending to it, maybe Julie would like to pick the makings for a salad while it's still light?"

"Will do," Julie answered obligingly. "Just so long as you don't ask me to cook the dinner."

"You mean to tell me you can't cook?" He turned on her with sparkling eyes.

"No." Julie grinned. "I guess that means I can't respond to your advertisement."

"Cooking is pretty important. Bottom line." He smiled.

"Where are we going to do this?" Cassie asked as Julie picked up a basket used for the purpose and moved out of the back door to the vegetable garden.

"This way, please." He gestured towards the bathroom which was surprisingly spacious. Built to accommodate a big man, she supposed. Here again, on a limited budget and doing most of it himself, it was bright, attractive with floods of light in the daytime and timber screening. Privacy for guests, she guessed, because there was no one around for miles. There was a long bench in the shower recess and Red told her to sit down there while he hunted up his first-aid kit which lay behind the mirrored wall cabinet.

"This is silly. I can do it." Cassie swept her hair

out of her eyes, determined not to let her guard down completely.

"Why so nervous?" His tone was moving them into a new zone.

For a moment she had a dazed, mindless feeling, knowing herself to be transparent. "I think you know the answer."

He stared at her for a moment, a stare as intimate as a kiss. "And what's that?"

Cassie set her delicate jaw, not rejoicing in her vulnerability. "I know you got a lot of mail, Matthew, but don't let it go to your head."

His eyes flickered. "Why not, with a highly desirable woman like you? Anyway, some of these letters would break your heart."

"I suppose." Somehow she wasn't surprised by his sensitivity. "Most of us are looking for something. Someone."

"*You* wouldn't have to look far, would you?" he asked ironically, filling a basin of water and tipping in antiseptic. "I bet you have a string of guys standing in line."

"Well—" A shadow crossed her face. "No one I care about. It takes time to find the right person."

He wanted to touch her cheek, stroke it, run a finger across the lush pad of her mouth. Have that mouth open to him. "And sometimes that person enters your life when you least expect it. The element of chance that can make or break a life. Who said you could call me Matthew?" he asked belatedly on a soft growl.

"It just seemed natural. You don't like it?"

"Maybe too much," he said with a trace of self-derision. Very gently, he removed Julie's blood-stained handkerchief, set it aside, then began to bathe Cassie's ankle. "You have very delicate ankles. Pretty toes." He traced his finger this way and that, slow and steady. Along her instep, over her ankle, down her toes, which she thought gratefully were as nice in their way as her fingers.

"Stop that, Matthew." Her voice was silky soft. Shaky. She knew how much she was giving away.

He paid little attention. "I just thought a little massage." The compulsion to draw her into his arms was becoming unbearable.

"It's not clear to me but, but are you flirting?" Best to sound a little angry.

"Flirting!" He threw back his handsome head and laughed. "Oh, Cassandra, I've never flirted in my life. Never had the time."

"All the same, I think you're dangerous to me."

"You're not going to interfere with my plans, either," he said with a taut smile, picking up the tension.

"If you want to put the bandage on."

"Bandage? Maybe a little Band-Aid?" he lightly mocked, his eyes sliding over her.

"Sure. Make fun of me."

"I'm not like that, Cassie." He held her foot gently and dabbed it dry. "In fact I'm going to kiss it better."

She didn't move. She didn't make a sound. This was seduction itself. Her eyes closed as he bent his glowing ruby head and kissed the smooth skin of her ankle.

"You devil!" she said softly. "No."

"No, what?" He smiled back at her.

"Mocking me again?"

"You know exactly what I'm doing, Cassie." He

clipped his words, but his sapphire gaze held her with intensity. "Maybe you'd better make allowances for—"

"A pretty complicated guy?" she suggested, strong emotion leaping from him to her.

"Is that how you see me?" He rose from his haunches and stood up, towering over her, causing her to eye him with trepidation.

"I'm sure of it."

"Why did you come out here?" he challenged very quietly.

She clasped the bench with her two hands, fixing her gaze on the white duckwood floor in the shower. "You invited us. We had nothing else to do. And we genuinely wanted to see the place. Which I must tell you I love."

"For a visit of two days?" he asked cynically.

"What do you want me to say, Matthew?"

His eyes held hidden currents. "Nothing. Heaps. What does it matter?" He looked down at her, his attitude as intense as hers. "How does that feel?"

"Fine." She transferred her gaze to her ankle. "You're very competent in everything you do."

"A top guy."

"You really expect something to come of this advertising?" she burst out spontaneously, revealing part of her turbulent feelings.

"I'm sure something will."

"What about love?" What did it have to do with her, anyway?

"Love can be poisonous, Cassandra. I know that." He looked through and beyond her.

She stood up abruptly, pushing the heavy fall of her

hair behind her ear. "You can't let what happened to your mother affect your life."

Too late, she realised her mistake, but she was hopelessly off balance in his presence.

His eyes burned into her like a blue jet of flame. "So the lovely Lady Cassandra has been gossiping?" His expression turned into hard arrogance.

She held up her hands, almost in supplication. "Sorry, Matthew. Please don't call it gossiping. It came out."

"Sure." He shrugged a shoulder. "Who did you ask?"

She could feel the hot blood suffusing her face. "I'd prefer not to say, but someone who's on your side."

"Not Marcy, surely?"

"No, not Marcy. I'm such a fool. I can't believe I blustered that out. But you unnerve me." Just how much she didn't want to fathom.

"If it comes to that, you unnerve me," he said in a grating voice. "So you know the other bit, as well."

She backed away, leaning against the far wall. "Jock Macalister is stuck with his wrong, Matthew. You aren't. You've made a successful life for yourself. You don't have to account to anyone."

There was a voice in the hall. Julie's.

"Hey, you guys, what's happening?"

Red straightened but there was tension in his lean powerful body.

"Coming, Julie," he called in a perfectly calm voice. "I've been attending to Cassandra's ankle."

"Want to tell Red about how I hurt myself skiing?" Julie called. "Boy, that's some vegetable patch, Red. It was hard not to pick the lot."

"Take some home with you tomorrow," Red said, leading Cassie back into the main room. "I'm not the market gardener, by the way. One of my men, Charlie, part Aboriginal, part Chinese in another life, handles that."

"Well, it's a credit to him," Julie said, beaming at them over a basket laden with lettuce, fat red tomatoes, shiny green and red capsicums, shallots and a few lemons she had pulled off a tree. "Say, everything all right here?" Her bright smile faltered after a moment.

"Of course it is," Red assured her so smoothly she was put at her ease. He held out his hand and took the basket. "The ankle is giving Cassandra a bit of gip."

"Well, sit down girl." Julie hurried over to her. "Take the weight off it. Read a book. Red's got a whole library. Meanwhile he's going to give me a lesson on preparing— What's on the menu, Red?"

"What about peppered steak, Jabiru eye fillet, melt in your mouth. Salad and some little new potatoes. Just dug up. Nice bottle of red. White, if you prefer. Cheese for later. One thing I haven't gotten around to cooking is a cake."

Julie went on in her vivacious fashion. "Then let Cassie show you. She makes a wicked chocolate cake."

Red's two cattle dogs, Dusty and Jason, had returned at sundown and he went out and greeted them affectionately introducing them to the girls but not letting them through the door. They stayed out on the veranda, growling gently in the dark when some movement or sound alerted them.

"They're superb working dogs. Watch dogs, as well," Red said.

In the end they stayed up late, their conversation covering a wide range of topics. Cassie folded herself into the corner of a sofa while Julie took the armchair opposite Red and laughed delightedly at all his stories. And he, like Bob Lester, had a fund of them. In turn she regaled him with funny episodes from hers and Cassie's shared life. Which he appeared to enjoy.

"Now that I've run out of stories," she announced over a nightcap, "what about if we help you to run through a few more of your letters? You'll have to hire a secretary anyway."

"I don't think so, Julie." Red rubbed his forehead, starting to debate with himself. "Maybe I should. I never expected anything like this, I have to tell you. I won't have the time to get 'round to all of them.

"We'll help you," Julie repeated.

"But they're *personal*," he stressed.

"They won't know."

"That's not the point, is it?" He gave her a wicked smile.

"We'll take the task very seriously, Matthew," Cassie promised. "Assemble the ones with the most appeal."

"All right. All right." A little exasperated, he rose to his six plus, went to a cabinet, selected another twenty letters and slammed them down on the old cedar wood chest he was using for a coffee table. "We won't speak and we won't dare laugh. We'll just set aside what seems to come from the heart. Ah, yes, the photograph, too," he added with humour. "I'm not aiming to ruin my life. I set the limit at thirty."

"The old biological clock, eh?" Julie muttered, select-ing one from the pile.

"I want children." Red snatched up one, making short work of opening it up.

And I wouldn't mind mothering them, flashed into Cassie's head.

She woke from a sound sleep for a few moments almost completely disoriented. The clouds of mosquito netting, the narrow bed, the strange room, the incredibly fresh and balmy air that wafted through the windows. Where was she? Then full consciousness set in. She had chosen to visit Matthew Carlyle on Jabiru.

It was early. Very early. The predawn sky was a trans-lucent pearl grey. She slipped her feet out of bed and reached for her robe. Julie, the night owl, was still fast asleep, her two hands tucked sweetly under her chin. Cassie found herself smiling. Julie had slept like that since she'd been a little girl.

Cassie walked to the tall window looking out over the green valley. There was a radiance on the horizon, a radiance that would turn into an explosion of light as the sun burst over the top of the range. Such a beautiful place! It made her feel rejuvenated, more at peace with herself than she had been for a while.

The dawn wind was stroking rustling sighs out of the trees that surrounded the homestead. Gums and acacias, a magnificent poinciana that would be something to see when in flower, numerous bauhinias, the orchid trees and a pair of tulip trees covered with opulent coral-red flowers. From this angle she could see an old tank stand smothered in cerise bougainvillea that cascaded right to the ground. She was truly fascinated by Matthew's world. No wonder he loved it.

Matthew. Matthew Carlyle. Red Carlyle. She tried the names over silently on her tongue. What exactly did he mean to her? How had she reached this stage of involvement—no, "involvement" didn't say it—in such an impossibly short time? True, he was stunningly handsome, bore himself like a prince, was uncommonly well read, highly intelligent. Those attributes hadn't blinded her before. Her ex-boyfriend, Nick Raeburn, with whom she worked, was all of these things as had been a few men before him. What they lacked, or significantly what they lacked for her, was Matthew's brand of magnetism. It penetrated to her very depths. She had been drawn headlong toward him at first sight. Up close and personal he stirred her even more, a combination of the physical and spiritual. He had such *power*.

She was twenty-four. She was moving along in her career, well paid, successful, but something vital was lacking in her life. She thought of it as her dream. To be blessed with the right man. To create a good future together. To love and above all to *share*. Was she crazy to think she could put her needs down on paper? Show them to him. Offer to become his wife.

She wasn't that brave. He would throw back that dark gleaming red head and laugh. A hard ironic laugh. He saw her, she knew, as someone who came from a different world, she didn't dare mention her parents weren't merely acquaintances but friendly with the man who had fathered him only to spend a lifetime ignoring his very existence. Thanks to Jock Macalister, Matthew trusted no one on earth. He wouldn't trust her, either.

Cassie turned away from the window, opened the bedroom door very quietly and listened for sound. Nothing stirred. The dogs weren't on the veranda. She padded down the hallway to the bathroom, found it empty and shut the door. Her towel was there in its allotted place, her bath things. She would have a quick shower and maybe cook breakfast. The truth was Matthew could fend for himself. The steaks last night had been cooked to perfection, the salad, which he'd insisted on making though she'd offered, at its simple best, crisp and fresh tossed in a good olive oil and red wine vinegar.

She was touched by the way he lived. Admired it, too. A man alone, yet keeping everything spick-and-span. He'd allowed her to set the table using an attractive cloth and napkins, good quality dinnerware, stainless-steel cutlery. He was a civilised man with innate good breeding. She wondered what his English mother had been like. A road accident, Molly had said. Leaving a lot more unsaid.

She knew what Matthew's mother looked like. There were several photographs atop an old pine chest in the living room. Photographs of a very pretty blond woman with a bubble of soft curls and a lovely smile, looking unselfconsciously at the camera. Others with her arm around a little boy so handsome he would bring tears to any woman's eyes. Matthew as an older boy, already inches over his mother's head, then an arresting young man, holding his petite mother in front of him, two hands resting on her shoulders. It was evident they were very close.

Cassie was returning very quietly to the bedroom when suddenly a door snapped shut.

Matthew. And no way to avoid him. It brought her close to trembling. Matthew Carlyle, a random element in her life but so compelling it seemed like he was everything she had ever wanted in a man. Cassie stood arrested, the blood coming up into her face.

At that moment Matthew, moving across the living room towards the kitchen, caught sight of Cassie in the hallway.

For a minute he felt like someone had struck him high in the chest. It was a terrible shock to discover he wanted this woman, this near stranger, so very badly. How had this happened? He wanted to touch her, to feel her touch him. She was wearing a blue robe with some sort of lustre, her hair, that wonderful crowning glory, billowing around her shoulders, the outline of her body, sloping shoulders, the small high breasts, delicate hips, just barely concealed by the satiny fabric of her robe.

"Hi there!" he managed when inside he felt hot and heavy, his heart squeezed by emotion. She started to walk towards him as if at a silent call, looking at him with luminous eyes.

She might have been a sleepwalker or someone in a dream so directed was her progress. He found himself putting out a hand, spearing his fingers through the long thick mass of her hair. It came to him he would love to brush it. Have her sit there while he brushed through its deep waves, listening to the electric crackle, revelling in the sable flow over her shoulders.

She should have been startled but she wasn't. She just stood there mesmerised letting him take control.

"How beautiful you are," he said very quietly, lost

in the pool of her eyes. "I didn't want you to come, Cassandra," he told her.

"Why?" She knew the answer, her own heart quaking.

"Not difficult to explain. I'm trying to sort out my life, not get in way over my head."

"Of course, I understand that." Still she watched him.

"So why are you looking at me with those river eyes?"

"I thought you *knew*," she said at last.

He nodded. "Sometimes things happen that should never happen." Despite himself his hand moved to her flawless flower skin. His desire for her was growing to the point he knew he should move away, say something about getting breakfast. Anything but pander to his own unparalleled sexual need. Something about her struck such a painful chord. The memory of love. *Real* love. The great love he had had for his mother. The sense of desolation and loss he had endured. His feeling for this woman, Cassandra, was undreamt of. In pursuing it he could cause great unhappiness for them both.

He heard her draw in a little shaken breath and his eyes dropped to her mouth, dwelt on its smooth cushiony curves. Her lips were parted and he could see the pearly nacre of her teeth. Did he imagine it or did she sway towards him? Her long-lashed eyes were wide open, yet so dreamy, so rapt, she might have lost all orientation.

It seemed to work both ways. He found himself taking her oval face in one hand and then he bent his head, caught up her lips with his own, kissing her so deeply, hungrily, it even seemed he was trying to eat her.

The scent of her! The wonderful woman fragrance mixed with the freshness of a lemony soap, and the talcum powder reminding him of a baby.

Quite slowly she wound an arm around his neck like a tendril, knowing what that would do to him. No stopping him now. He pulled her into his arms with a low cry, gathering her tightly against him, ravished by the imprint of her beautiful body on his hard frame. What was happening had never happened to him in the past. He had taken women thankfully with gentleness, glad of their responding pleasure. Now his longing was so harsh he felt the arms that closed around her turn to iron. She was afraid and excited at the same time, he could tell. Her head draped back over his arm as she offered up her mouth, kissing him back, exchanging this almost unbearable rapture. It drove him to half lift her from the ground, desperate not just for kisses but to go all the way. Spread her out on his bed, that beautiful hair fanning around her head.

It was outrageous. He knew that. He barely knew her. She was, after all, a rich girl from the city. A guest in his home. He should be treating her with respect. He had begun to run his hand across her breast, aware of an arousal that matched his own. Now, before another towering wave of heat broke over him, he reeled back, releasing her so abruptly her knees started to buckle and she clutched at him like a child.

"I'm sorry." His breath came out like a bitter gasp. This was fantasy. A dream. Not his rough-and-ready world.

"Wait a moment, Matthew," she answered, very gently, very sweetly. "It was my fault as much as yours."

"So what do we do now? Pretend it didn't happen?"

She saw the high mettled set of his head, the blaze in his eyes. "I'm not the girl you'd pick to marry?"

"You're way out of my league, Cassandra," he said, a nerve beating in his temple.

"How can you possibly say that?" She really meant it. He was the kind of man with the vital force to make a mark in the world. The fact of his birth meant little to her beyond the deep well of sympathy she felt for his abandoned mother and a fatherless child.

"Would you introduce me to Daddy?" he asked in a very crisp, confronting way.

"I'd be happy to." None of the young men her parents had lined up could match Matthew.

"Doesn't it upset you, knowing my background?" He frowned, black brows drawn down.

"It upsets me only in the sense it upsets you," she answered simply. "You're your own man, Matthew. You're an achiever. You can take your place anywhere."

"Sure, I know that," he shrugged, "but it doesn't mean your parents mightn't hate me."

It was possible. Matthew Carlyle was very different. "Matthew, I want to tell you my parents have put me through hell. My father is a very successful, clever, overbearing man. My mother lives a highly social life. That's all she cares about."

"Be that as it may, they wouldn't want their daughter to throw herself away on a guy like me. I know without your telling me they've got someone lined up for you. Someone they're accustomed to. Someone with the same background as themselves. Hell, he's probably already chosen."

She couldn't deny it and it showed on her face.

"You'd have to be totally mad to settle for a small-time cattleman, a beautiful creature like you, to spend your life hidden away in the wilds." He laughed ironically. "Now, what about if you get dressed," he suggested, starting to put distance between them. "I'll make breakfast. Orange juice. Pawpaw. Bacon and eggs."

"You'll make someone a wonderful husband," Cassandra said, suddenly feeling humiliated. Put back on some pedestal. Shut away.

"Good of you to tell me," Matthew said with a suave bow. "All I will admit to is that was the best kiss I've ever had in my life. It's quite possible I'll remember it as an old man."

CHAPTER FIVE

"You're fascinated by him, aren't you?" Julie said, her pretty face betraying her anxiety.

"No," Cassie denied, adjusting her sunglasses.

"You can't fool me, girl. I've been your best friend for sixteen years." Julie shook her head.

"You sound worried, Julie." They were sitting out on the deck enjoying the earthly paradise that surrounded them.

"I am." Julie reached for the sun cream, rubbing some more on her tanned legs. "I'm not such a fool I can't tell you and Red are wildly attracted to one another. You haven't been the same since we arrived home, even I'm getting out of my depth. I know I started all this, but you must know your parents have their own hopes for you. It has to be someone they approve of, Cassie. Someone who will fit in."

"That's right. Aren't you relieved, then, Matthew wouldn't dream of considering me? He actually told me to my face."

Julie laughed nervously. "He *did?*"

"Meeting Matthew Carlyle was like having an abyss open up in front of me," Cassie said.

"Lord, Cassie." Julie sighed deeply. "Not that I can blame you. Red is just amazing. Bright, breezy, arrogant, fun. In truth, quite a guy. I could have fallen in love with him myself but it was perfectly plain he had no interest in me. It was you who caught his gaze that first day on the highway. I can't think why when I'm far more beautiful." She laughed softly then sobered. "I'm sorry, Cassie. I could have spared you the heartache. You're usually so sensible." She shook her head again.

"You think it's a disaster to allow myself to fall in love with Matthew."

"Oh, boy. *Yes!* I know you've shown plenty of spirit but in a way you're still a mite afraid of your parents. Your father especially. Goodness knows he's a regular despot though he's been a little more human of late."

"Well, that's because he thinks finally I'm going to toe the line."

"In a sense my own parents aren't that different," Julie admitted. "They'll want a say in my marriage. That's the only way, according to Mum, I'll get the perfect match. I'm still a kid in the classroom to her."

"You poor thing! Anyway, it was quite an experience. I'm none the worse for it."

"You must excuse me if I don't believe that," Julie burst out. "Red's the one person I've ever seen get to you. It would have to be someone totally unsuitable."

"Ah, yes—" Now the about-face. "I've thought a lot about it," Cassie said. "I'm going to answer Matthew's advertisement."

Horror and a kind of admiration broke over Julie's pretty face. "But he'll think you're trying to make a fool of him. Heck, Cassie, didn't you warn me not to think of upsetting Red?"

"I'm dead serious."

This affected Julie so much she jumped up and went to the balustrade, looking out sightlessly over the glorious blue sea. Finally she turned with a sympathetic frown. "There *is* such a thing as love at first sight obviously."

"The poets say so." Cassie had a clear picture of Matthew's face. "I just didn't think it could happen to me."

"Usually I'm the mad, impulsive one," Julie moaned, "and you're so calm and controlled." She came back, dropped a kiss on the top of Cassie's head, then sat down. "This is like a romance novel. It can't be real. Do you realise your parents would blame *me?*"

"Well, I'll tell them you advised me against anything so crazy."

"A wise move for me." Julie sounded wry. "What is it you want, Cassie?" she asked. "Adventure, a rip-roaring life? Can't you have a good old time? Get Red out of your system."

"I want him," Cassie said very carefully.

"Then it's not just sex?" Julie looked hard at her.

Cassie drew off her sunglasses. "We didn't get into that, Julie."

"Oh, yeah, no time?"

"Surprise, surprise. Matthew goes a long way towards being a very chivalrous guy."

Julie shrugged. "I find myself agreeing. You can see his mother's story has affected him deeply."

"Sad but no bad thing," Cassie said with a slight

hardening of her tone. "We've both met guys with a callous hand for all their so-called eligibility."

"You're absolutely right. But I should stop you," Julie said.

"Sorry, kiddo," Cassie answered staring up at the sky. "Too much time has passed. I've already written the letter. In fact Matthew should have it by tomorrow."

The morning had barely dawned before Julie took a call from her mother telling her of the sudden death of her great-aunt.

"You don't have to come with me," Julie said, seeing the torn expression on Cassie's face. "Aunt Sarah lived a good life. At some point in her eighties she decided she didn't want to go on. All the family knew it. I'll have to go to the funeral, show my respects, but you can stay on. We still have to the end of the week."

"But your parents will expect me to come home with you," Cassie said.

"Not in the least. They're very happy to have you enjoy this. Molly and Jim are here to look after you."

"We both know the reason why I want to stay, Julie." Cassie met her friend's eyes.

"It might come to nothing, Cassie," Julie warned. "You said yourself Red is one complex man."

"I know, but I have to hear what he has to say."

"It could be painful," Julie stressed, "and I won't be here to offer comfort."

"He could simply ignore me," Cassie said as calmly as she could.

"I don't think that's possible." Julie's answer was wry. "Different backgrounds or not, you both seem to *identify.* It's more than chemistry, I can see that. Just as I can see it might involve a lot of trauma."

Cassie sipped at her coffee meditatively. "I think I know, Julie, who I am and what I want. I've been drifting unsatisfied, unfulfilled. We've talked about it often enough. I want commitment. A mature relationship before I'm too much older. I want children. I want to share all the pleasure and the pains of my life. I want a husband to love. I want to be able to tell him I love him. I could never say it to my mother and father. Maybe that's one of the reasons I'm drawn to Matthew. I know he wants commitment, too. Family. The stable relationship he never had in his childhood."

"I know, and it's just beautiful," Julie all but wailed, "but your parents will kill you when they find out."

Two hours later Julie was on her flight to Sydney, pretty flustered by all that was happening, but vowing not to say anything at all about Cassie's reason for staying on. "You'll ring me just as soon as you get Red's response." She gave Cassie instructions. "I'm really desperate to know how this turns out. This is your *life,* Cassie. Your future. I thought you were the one who had wisdom."

Cassie didn't protest. "I have to pin my faith on my deepest intuitions, Julie." She kissed her friend on the cheek and walked her to the departure gate. "There are no guarantees in life. I've only known Matthew a very short time but I feel in my bones he's a fine human being."

The same fine human being arrived on Cassie's doorstep late afternoon, eyes flashing blue fire under a fine head of steam.

"What's this supposed to mean?" he demanded of Cassie without preamble, waving her letter in the air.

"Are you going to come in?" she invited.

"No, I'm not," he returned bluntly. "How do I know Julie isn't in this with you? Two cruel little city cats having a bit of fun."

"It's not like that at all, Matthew. No way. I promise. Anyway, Julie has gone home. I drove her to the airport this morning. A member of her family died suddenly."

"That's awful." His anger dimmed briefly. "I'm sorry. Death hits even the rich. In the meantime, you're staying on. What are you hoping for? An outback adventure. Some fantastic sex?"

She almost laughed then, sobering quickly, said, "No!"

"Come on, Cassandra. I'm a realist. You're playing a game. Well, I'll tell you, lady, with the *wrong* man."

There were heavy footsteps in the hall. The next moment Molly hove into sight, carrying a huge vase of tropical lilies she had picked that morning. "Cassie, I thought I heard you talking to someone," she exclaimed. Then, when Cassie moved, "Ah, Red, how nice to see you. What brings you to town?"

"Business, Molly." He managed to sound casual. "How did Jim get on on his fishing trip with Deputy Dan?"

"Hear about that, did you?" Molly smiled broadly. "There's nobody knows more about what's goin' on than Red," she told Cassie, placing the spectacular floral arrangement on the circular table. "Don't know how he does it so far out of town."

"You'd be surprised, Molly, who drops by."

"The girls certainly enjoyed themselves," Molly stood back to admire her handiwork. "Had a lovely time. I suppose Cassie's told you Julie had to fly off home."

"Well, yes, but I've just arrived."

"Come in and have a cup of coffee, then," Molly invited. "Expect you're staying overnight at the pub?"

He nodded. "I'll start back before dawn."

"So, are you comin' in or what?" Molly looked from one to the other, her broad smile fading as she picked up on the atmosphere.

This time Matthew shook his head. "No, thanks, Molly. I have a problem to address."

Molly moved uncomfortably. "Oh, sure, right."

"Don't mean to be rude, Moll. I was hoping Cassandra, here, would come back into town with me. We have something to discuss."

"A date, is that it?" Molly asked cautiously.

"Not at all. A *discussion*," Matthew said impassively. "Coming, Cassandra?" He transferred his hard gaze to Cassie's face. Her beautifully sculpted cheekbones were tinged with colour, but her eyes were calm and level.

"If you wait just a moment I'll grab a shirt." Some sort of cover-up. She was wearing a sleeveless indigo top with matching drawstring trousers, but it felt right to put something over the top. For one thing, she wasn't wearing a bra. Matthew's gaze was like a lick of flame.

Molly was staring at them both with a hint of puzzlement. "Everything okay with you two?"

Red flashed her his beautiful smile. "I promise I'll bring Cassandra back safe and sound."

Inside Matthew's Jeep all was quiet but for the knocking of Cassie's heart. Matthew was silent driving on down the coast road, stopping at a point where the beach became accessible.

"Let's go for a walk," he said in a clipped voice, putting the vehicle into Park and switching off the ignition.

"All right." She opened out her door and sprang onto the grassy verge.

Everywhere was radiant light, the cobalt-blue sea stretched to the horizon, floating coral cays and emerald islands surrounded by blazing white sand. The throbbing heat of midday had cooled off and the breeze swished through the tall coconut palms and the dense vegetation that gave life and colour to the cascading slopes. Armies of little wildflowers in scarlet, vermilion, deep blue, and gold embroidered the foliage while all about an array of bougainvillea blossomed prolifically.

It was ravishingly beautiful, tranquil, the golden sand shifting beneath Cassie's feet. The water near the edge was so crystal clear she could see all the pretty little shells lying on the seabed. She turned her head, seeing the long stretch of beach to the headland was deserted. There was no one around but the flocks of gulls that took to the air at her unexpected appearance.

Matthew, vigorously crunching his way across the sand, caught up with her and took hold of her arm. She was forced to stop.

"What do you expect to come of all this?"

Her breath caught in her throat at the severity of his expression. She remembered then the stories about his temper.

"Is it so incredible to believe I meant it?" She spoke,

emotionally seduced by his gaze. "After all, you've had dozens of letters."

"Dear God." He turned his handsome head towards the sea where a shoal of small fish were leaping from the waves. "I want the truth, Cassandra," he gritted.

"I meant every word." She gave a choked little cry and tried to break away.

He held her hard. "Sorry. I'm not buying it. I suppose the two of you laughed yourselves sick at your boldness."

"Did you think my letter bold?" A stab of deepest anxiety pierced her. She had tried so hard to get it right.

"It would have been a beautiful letter. From a stranger. Not from *you*." He stood proudly, unsmilingly, cleft chin upthrust.

"That's it? Not from *me*." Her spirits lifted. *A beautiful letter.* "I'm like you, Matthew. I want a life. I want a husband, family. I'm longing to live my dream."

"So you said in your letter," he cut her off. "The brutal fact is, you'd hate every moment of living Outback. Even the town is only a very small community. There aren't any theatres, nightclubs, concert halls. No flash department stores and boutiques to go shopping. No luxury. Only peace and quiet and the land."

"You don't think I feel its tremendous attraction?" She looked at him, challenging him to deny it.

"I feel you and I have something utterly different going," he said with hard meaning.

Cassie bent her head in acknowledgment. "I only know I've never felt like this before."

His hands took her shoulders. "How do I know you're

not some consummate actress? Why don't you level with me? What do you want, a quick affair before you vanish?"

She blushed. "Do you intend to talk to all the other women who wrote to you like this?"

He ignored her. "Hell, don't you realise you could have been taking a big risk?"

"I trust you, Matthew," she said, and she really did.

Something flashed in his eyes and he grasped the long fall of her hair with one hand.

"What sort of a future could *we* have?"

"A good one if we work at it. I'm not so very different from you. In my own way I was abandoned. That's not going to happen to my children."

He reflected on this with a daunting frown. "You're dreaming," he said at last. "Fantasising. All on the basis of one kiss." Even then there was residual passion in his voice.

"You felt what I felt," she returned simply. "You can't deny it."

"So? It's only because you're so beautiful." He spoke coolly. "A magnolia who shouldn't be uprooted. You don't know anything about loneliness or isolation. Doing it hard. This idea about living happily ever after isn't enough. It takes much more than sexual fascination to make a marriage. Or is it like I said, you're just plain bored?"

It seemed to her she might never convince him. "The first moment I saw you I sensed some part of what was going to happen," she offered.

"Are you going to call it Fate?" His voice was tight.

"Is that so strange?"

"Don't you dare cry," he said sharply, uncertainly.

"It's the salt air in my eyes." She blinked and her voice began to falter. "I promise you, Matthew, my letter was written in all sincerity. I know how you might think it was some kind of a joke. I know I'm as much a mystery to you as you are to me, but I'm not like that. Cruelty, insensitivity, is something I've had turned on me most of my life. The more I see of you, the more I want to learn."

"This is so damned crazy," he muttered in a low voice. "Dangerous. Aren't you scared?"

"Of course I am." She spoke nervously. In reality she was intoxicated, out of balance. It was wonderful just to be with him again. Even if he was angry. He was like some marvellous ray of attraction with his intensely male sexuality, his power and vigour, the eyes of a visionary. Who needed safety?

The sky above them began to fill with long billowing clouds to set the sun to rest. Broad golden beams of sunlight were pervaded by a pink mist. Sunset was approaching to silence them with its beauty.

"You know nothing about me, nothing at all." He raised a hand to his temple, a gesture of uncertainty, exasperation.

"Some things we take on faith without *knowing* it." Cassie was disturbed by her own headlong behaviour.

"You want to escape. You're not happy."

"I haven't been happy for a while now," she said after some moments, staring up at the splendour of the sky.

"I'm surprised to hear that. You're beautiful, rich.

Ah, I get it, you've had an unhappy love affair." His tone was dry. "You're trying to forget."

"I don't give a damn about anyone." She faced him, catching at her skeining hair. "There is no one. Do you want a wife or not, Matthew?" she challenged.

"Stop it. Damn it, Cassandra," he said as though she was making him feel desperate and trapped. "You're not the right girl to come into my life. You don't understand what you're letting yourself in for."

"So, I'm rejected?" She felt a weight of terrible dismay.

"Listen, why don't we go into town?" His eyes creased against the setting sun. A glory of crimson rose-pink and gold. "Have something to eat."

She hated herself for agreeing. Tormented now by her vulnerability to the man. "All right," she replied almost curtly.

"I'm sorry, Cassandra, if I don't respond to the shots as you call them."

"I'll keep trying."

"Why would you? Why *should* you?"

"Because it's important," Cassie said with surprising conviction.

By mutual accord they sought something more private than Marcy's, choosing Francesco's, an excellent small restaurant run by a local family with strong Italian roots. Arriving early as they did, the place was almost empty, but as they took their time over a pre-dinner drink other customers began to arrive, some with children, their voices bright and cheerful as they greeted their host and different members of the family, all accomplished cooks, who took turns manning the restaurant. Cassie felt too intense to be hungry but delicious aromas kept wafting from the kitchen whenever the swinging doors opened and shut.

"The ravioli here is wonderful," Matthew mentioned, himself infected by her mood. His face uplit by the blossoming candlelight was all planes and angles. "A simple enough dish yet plenty get it wrong. Frank uses the finest, freshest ingredients. They speak for themselves. Come to think of it, I've never been here when the food wasn't good. We'll eat whenever you're ready, Cassandra. Maybe after that you'll be ready to talk."

Cassie laughed wryly. Not a terribly good beginning, she thought, but from the first bite of a beautifully tender pillow of pasta with a delectable filling of eggplant and a marvellous sauce which turned out to be melted zucchini flowers, Cassie began to unwind. If only there was no...issue between them, this would be a joy.

Matthew ordered a bottle of red wine and for the space of the meal, which included the classic *vitello tonnato,* they simply savoured the food. Francesco came over to the table smiling broadly, complimenting Cassie on her beauty while they in turn complimented him on a memorable meal.

"How have I never seen you before?" Francesco asked Cassie with a wide grin which embraced Matthew.

"This is my first time." Cassie smiled. "I sincerely hope it won't be the last."

"Not the first time for Red." Francesco clapped his hand on Matthew's shoulder. "But the first time I see such a light in his eyes!"

"Hell, Italians are such romantics," Matthew said in

a throw-away voice after Francesco had moved on. "I can see what the candlelight is doing to your face, let alone my eyes."

"What is it doing?" Cassie looked at him, her wine-glass cupped like a chalice between her two slender hands.

He didn't answer for a moment. "Your skin has turned to pale gold," he began. "Your eyes are no longer silver-grey, they've taken on the violet of your shirt. Your mouth is as tender as a child's but very much a woman's. You're powerfully beautiful, Cassandra. I don't know how to describe what you've got. On the one hand it's all sensuality and plenty of it, on the other, there's high intelligence, a flame of purity, goodness, sensitivity. It's enormously intriguing. Tell me about your childhood." He gave her a straight, interested look.

It touched her that he didn't just consider her a body. She sipped at her wine then put it down. "Not uncommon, Matthew." When goodness knows it was. "As I've told you, my father is a very successful businessman. Making money is his life. My mother, in her own way, is devoted to him. He provides her with just the sort of life she craves. They travel a great deal. My father never embarks on a business trip without my mother. Their marriage works for them. It's solid."

"So, material success and high social position are at the heart of it?"

"Very much so," she said softly, like a sigh. "A great many people feel that way."

"You seem a little traumatised by it all." He reached across the table, unexpectedly putting a hand over her own, a gesture that made tears sting her eyes.

"I probably was when I was very young. I was a sort of formless little kid. I didn't quite know what my place was in the scheme of things. I wasn't the light of my parents' eyes. I couldn't fail to know that even if I didn't understand it. I had a nanny from birth until I was seven. I loved her and I continue to see her. Then when she left, I was sent off to boarding school. It was there I met Julie. We looked into one another's eyes and were friends. Just like that. Julie's a lot of fun."

"Yet on the face of it, you don't seem to have a lot in common?" He said it as he saw it, from his own observation.

"Actually we share a great deal of affection and loyalty. Opposites attract." She gave him a slight mocking smile. "Maybe being opposites is essential to balance. You have a dark side to *you*, Matthew."

He nodded his red head. "So I have. We've both lived our little dramas. You seem to have found out about mine." This with a tinge of bitterness.

"It wasn't simple curiosity." She held his gaze. "I wanted to see into your heart and your mind and your soul."

The muscle along his taut jawline worked. "How in earth did it happen?" He ran his fingertips across his wide brow.

"You mean, our attraction? It's not just me, is it, Matthew?"

His handsome face was so still it looked carved. She didn't move, either, waiting on his reply.

"On the basis of one kiss? A couple of days together? Showing you all Jabiru has to offer?"

"It's possible." In the soft warmth she felt a little chill.

"I believe there is a connection between events no matter how seemingly random. I don't remember you being so hard on the writers of your other letters."

Still he said, "With a couple of exceptions, they weren't trying to make an ass of me."

Her quick flush answered him. "You know I'm not."

The hardness inside of him softened at her expression. "All right, I accept that, but I have this troubled feeling about it, Cassandra." He looked at her levelly with his piercing eyes.

"You know what it is?" She felt the two of them were locked in a bubble. "You're scared of loving someone, Matthew, and you're trying to protect yourself. You want a woman who'll accommodate all your needs but won't get under your skin. Really falling in love hurts."

A harsh protest rose in his throat. "Not only that, it can muck up a life." He turned his head, looking for a waiter. "Let's have coffee."

"I don't mind." She lifted the heavy fall of her hair at the back of her neck. The restaurant was entirely filled now, people around them exclaiming at the food, the children tucking into thick crusty bread, mopping up the remains of spaghetti.

"And you'd have to give up your very comfortable life in Sydney, your very good job, the prospects of promotion Julie was talking about, to settle down on an Outback cattle station?" Matthew said eventually. He stopped talking as the waiter arrived with their short black espresso coffees, then left.

"I don't know all that's coming, Matthew," she conceded. "How could I? I thought I wanted a career. It seemed to be important to be a success as my father expected. And I am. I'm well regarded in the firm. But I wouldn't give my life to a career. I told you what I want. Love. Family. Husband. Children. The full traditional bit. I've given a lot of thought to this. I've enjoyed the adrenaline rush of my job, the rock beat of big business, getting all the calculations right, but it's not the full picture. The *right* picture. I could love you if you let me. I could love your way of life. I want to share your vision. I admire you so for all you've achieved."

"Have you ever been in love?" he suddenly shot at her. "Tell me *now* before you have time to think."

"No." She paused.

"Is that the truth?"

She looked up at his handsome face and found it taut and hawkish. "Once I thought I was."

"Thank you," he said dryly, his handsome mouth twisting.

"The feeling didn't last."

"So where is he now?" The brilliant eyes stared into her face.

"Actually, I work with him," Cassie admitted, wondering if she should have told a white lie.

"So in a way it *is* flight?" A little cloud of hostility had set in, breaking up the fragile rapport.

She shook her head and said in a neutral tone, which was actually a quiet challenge, "I've no more argument to present, Matthew. I can see your unease. We've only had this short time together, I know, but either you accept me or push me out of your life forever. I have to go home Friday." Either way I've been burnt badly.

"You started this, Cassandra." The words burst from

Matthew with the force of pent-up passion. "Now we both have to live with it. I'm damned well not going to give you an instant answer. I know what it's like running around with a ring through the nose. I'm a cattleman remember?"

Francesco came to see them off, exclaiming again at Cassie's beauty, bowing over her hand, giving Matthew another thump on the shoulder, making it look like happy, earthy congratulations. Matthew thought it was time to get out before Frank started teasing him unmercifully. He and Adelina, Frank's wife, were always encouraging him to get married.

"Get someone to wait on *you*," Frank often said, and laughed. "No good, a man being on his own."

He could run off with a beautiful princess. Be totally enraptured until the princess decided she'd had enough of the back blocks and left him sick of heart and forsaken. Both of them lapsed into a silence while he drove back to the luxury hideaway on the headland.

"I haven't asked you what Julie thinks of all this," Matthew said finally into the fraught silence.

She didn't turn her face to him. "She's concerned."

"Well, hell, she isn't a fool, exactly."

Her own anger surfaced. "Let it alone, Matthew. I hear you loud and clear."

"Meanwhile we lust after each other." That when the beginnings of love were flowing into him and with it a lot of unexpected stress.

It must have hurt her because she dropped her head, giving a little smothered cry to which he responded powerfully.

He braked and scanned the road he knew so well.

A minute later he turned the Jeep off the road, pulling into a scenic vista bordered by white timber rails. The sea was shining all around them, the sky fantastic, glittering with stars, the air smelling so sweetly of the sea and the thousands of little wildflowers that rioted across the vegetation and down the sandy slopes.

"Ah, Cassie." Beyond composure, finding himself with her in the melting dark, he moved to clasp her face between his hands, feeling the trembling that broke over her as he lowered his head.

She had no standard by which to measure his enormous fascination. It was enchantment, emotion running so deep she could feel the heat of it on their skin. There was a buzzing in her ears, in her veins. She wanted him with all her body. Very nearly so with all her heart. But she knew he was a lot tougher than she could ever be. She knew he was a man who could make hard decisions. Who would do anything to arrange his life.

His hands moved to her shoulders and stopped there. The bones so delicate, so elegant, he felt steam was actually coming off him, his desire for her was so powerful, burning him up. She wasn't wearing a bra. How could he not notice? That pretty little top all that was between her and her bare skin. The filmy shirt that changed the colour of her eyes fell back like a shawl so all evening he could see the tender, shadowed cleavage, imagining the rose-pink of the nipples that peaked so erotically against the indigo-blue fabric.

The beauty of the night, the scents and the burning diamond-white of the stars were increasing his feelings of wildness, of going out of control.

It shouldn't be. He had worked hard at being his own

master. He wasn't going to let go of it for a woman. She was right. It scared him. This feeling of being spell-bound like she had stolen his soul.

Her eyes were closed. He knew there were tears behind her eyelids. He kissed them, staring down into her beautiful, luminous face. Was this the woman to take to the rough bush? She deserved the finest mansion. A man who had no stain on his background, not Jock Macalister's bastard son. He thought he had risen above it. Now, with this woman, it was a source of exquisite pain.

"I want you," he groaned. He thought he had his life in near perfect order. How things had changed! He tried to pull her closer but the console was the stumbling block. A tiny barrier yet it seemed insupportable. "We have to get out," he said very urgently, feeling the fine tremble in his hands.

"Hold on." She shook her head frantically, trying to whip herself back to some sort of control. "What *is* it you want of me, Matthew?" she pleaded. This man in some ways was as wild as a falcon.

He let out a shuddering breath. "You haunt me too much. I want to make love to you. Can't you just accept it?"

"No." If she did she would never be free of him. Her body began to arch and she held up her hands defensively. "I've been trying to convince you I could make you a good *wife* and you've been pushing me away. You refuse to take me seriously. You're a man who likes to keep control. I'm too—what do you say?—*exotic* to take a place in your life, but I'm plenty good enough to make love to."

"My God! You are," he rasped. "Actually, Cassandra, you're a first for me."

"You could tell me what that means. A first? You're not taken with the idea? Does it disempower you," she taunted.

Abruptly he reached out and gripped her shoulders. "Already you've got the power to wound." He sobered up at her small cry, softened his grip, apologised. "I didn't hurt you?"

"No." Her head fell forward with a mixture of help-lessness and yearning. "There's nothing safe about us. *Nothing.*"

"Not from where I'm sitting." His voice was laced with self-derision. "There's no insurance we can take out."

Now she felt his hand on her long hair, fisting it, drawing it away from her face.

"Matthew." She began trembling, her hair spilling everywhere like silk, but already his mouth came back to hers, so passionate, so sizzling, she could feel her whole system turn molten, then…melt. He was willing her to risk everything, to move down to the beach, allow his hands and his mouth to race over her, her life's blood beating hot and wild beneath her skin. So easy to get her out of her clothes, so light, so fine. He was already slipping her voile shirt and her camisole top from her shoulder, baring it to his mouth that nevertheless spoke a kind of silent love.

"Matthew," she began again before things got totally out of hand.

"I'm so glad you call me that. I thought I would be Red for the rest of my days." He pressed his mouth into the hollow above her collarbone. "Damn you for making a fool of me, glorious Cassandra. Damn you for coming here looking like a princess on a royal visit."

"I really didn't have much say in it," she whispered. "It was Fate."

"So we don't know what we're up against? This could pass for you, Cassandra." He released her edgily and sat back in his seat. "Like a bout of fever. Once you're back in the city among your own kind. Not the least of it the guy in the office who's in love with you. I bet he considers himself among the high fliers. You could talk it over with Julie. Blame it on the tropics."

"That's absolutely wrong." She protested with her first real despair. Didn't he know she couldn't think of anything else *but* him? She drew away trying to straighten her shirt. "Maybe you should stick with a sweet little hardworking country girl, after all. A good cook with a green thumb. One who won't let it bother her you don't really love her. That's life. She answered an advertisement. She's not about to complain. There'll be babies, a home, financial security. She knows how to count her blessings."

He nodded, indolently, looking unbelievably handsome and thoroughly arrogant. "Well, hell, Cassie," he drawled. "Any man in his right mind wants a peaceful life, not a woman who befuddles his brain and gets between his ribs and his heart. 'Course I didn't stay long at school. Never went to university. No money for that. We were very very poor. How's that for Jock Macalister's only son?"

Cassie shivered at the bitterness. All the deeply entrenched pain.

"Of course, he's the *only* one who's not certain of who I am," Matthew added.

"He'd know it in two seconds if he ever laid eyes on you," Cassie burst out, and wished more than anything she hadn't.

"That's a damn odd thing to say, Cassandra." He placed a finger under her chin and turned her face to him. "Explain."

"I told you. I met him once."

"When you were a child?" He raised his distinctive black brows. Macalister's brows.

"I was clever even then. Very observant."

Still cupping her face with one hand, he ran a very shivery finger behind her silky ear.

"You wouldn't be lying by any chance?"

"No way," she said, colouring, glad of the glimmering dark.

"He could very well do business with your company," Matthew continued suspiciously. "He's into everything. Real estate. Freight, oil, energy."

"I met him once in my life." Cassie told the truth, still lacking the courage to reveal the rest. The scent of danger was all around the Macalister name. "I told Molly I wouldn't be out long." She turned her face away, perturbed by her own passion and her slight control. "Why don't you drive me home?"

"I guess that's best." What he felt for this woman was almost against his will, but still he asked, "And our unfinished business?"

"Sleep on it, Matthew," Cassie advised. "Weigh it up."

CHAPTER SIX

HE DIDN'T contact her at all before she went home, knowing it was cruel; just as sure it was necessary. He wasn't
quite ready to make the most important decision of his
life realising his attitude was coloured by his own early
sufferings.

Yet the thought, *What have I done?* raged constantly
through his mind. For the first time he found it difficult
to sleep, his work-weary body twitching in bed, often
until dawn when the soft grey light streamed into his
room and he got up to stare out the window. Even the
sky reminded him of a pair of luminous eyes.

She would have made the journey back to Sydney
thinking him a callous brute. This gave him tremendous
concerns. If he was so disturbed, so, he was sure, was
she.

But she had to return to her own life, friends and
family, her own community, to view what had happened
with any detachment. Everyone had heard of a holiday
romance. People going on boat trips, having a fling.
Flings weren't his nature. He'd had an eternity to ponder
on what had happened to his mother. An eternity of
bearing the brunt of a rash, ill-advised liaison. It was

entirely conceivable once back among her own kind, Cassandra would come to believe their headlong attraction, so wildly at variance with their normal behaviour was just some powerful aberration to be put right. But then, a man of action, he had to *do* something.

It came to him during the night, so the next morning he rose early, got the men together, allocated them their respective jobs then organised a trip to Sydney. Maybe Cassandra wouldn't be thrilled to see him. Maybe she'd refuse to see him. It had been all of three weeks but he had learned something as frightening as it was thrilling. Right or wrong, he didn't want to live without her. She filled him with passion, with energy, a longing to carve out a great future. He knew he had it in him to give her a fine life.

Back in Sydney, Cassie had two priorities. To forget Matthew Carlyle. To keep her mind on her job. She was up for promotion. Julie's father waxed lyrical about her capacity for cutting to essentials, her coolness in tight situations. It was early days, she was a bit young for it, but she was a serious contender for Phil McKinnon's job now that he was moving up in management.

Cassie spent many long hours at her desk, tapping away at her computer, threading her way through innumerable facts and figures. All to prove her prowess. She was very good at tracking and cross-tracking numbers. It was a language she had got to know and understand. She didn't fare anywhere as well trying to forget Matthew. He smiled at her from behind her eyes.

Julie was shocked but relieved at her return.

"Obviously he was deeply attracted to you but he

must have realised, Cassie, it would never have worked," she pointed out gently.

"Who the heck knows what is or isn't going to work?" Cassie fired back, upset and exasperated. "There couldn't be an institution more subject to risk than marriage. Falling in love and getting married isn't a guarantee of bliss. It's like being infected by a fever. Neither person can run out and buy insurance."

"I know. I know, but couldn't you love Nick?" Julie pleaded. "He worships the ground you walk upon. Even your father spent quite a deal of time talking to him at our Christmas party, don't you remember?"

Cassie made a dismissive gesture with her hand. "Nick has mastered the knack of buttering up to VIPs."

"True," Julie agreed with a wry grimace. "But he was especially nice to your father for a reason. He's hoping to be looked on as a prospective son-in-law."

"But it's over, Julie, and it can't be resurrected," Cassie said. "It's Matthew who's captured my heart."

A kind of despair settled on Julie's face. "But he was always a wild card, Cass. And he has a very problematic background. What a fight you would have trying to get your parents to accept him."

"Don't I know it." Cassie felt the old familiar knots in her stomach.

"Don't think my heart doesn't bleed for you," Julie said quietly, "but the connection between your father and Red's. Did you ever tell him the *full* story?"

Anxiety seethed in Cassie's soul. "I regret to say, no. I wanted to, but I couldn't. Matthew would have exploded if I'd said Jock Macalister was my father's *friend* as well as sometimes business associate. Anyway, what does it matter now?" She sighed and picked up the phone to ring a client. "Matthew completely rejected me."

"I could kill him," Julie muttered darkly, seeing Cassie's deep hurt.

"That's okay." Cassie looked at her friend with shadowed eyes. "Given time, I'll get over it."

Cassie had dinner with her parents on the Saturday night, asking Nick along for company, because these supposedly quiet family dinners usually turned into a gathering.

Fourteen in all sat around the gleaming mahogany table, elaborately decked out with the finest china, crystal, silver, exquisite white linen and lace place mats with matching napkins. There were two low crystal bowls of white lilies flanking a filigree silver basket of luscious summer fruits and table grapes. Tapering candles in Georgian sterling silver candlesticks were placed meticulously down the table length.

The overhead chandelier was on the dimmer and candlelight threw a flattering light over the faces of the women. Everyone, with the exception of Cassie, was middle-aged but beautifully preserved through a strict diet and beauty routine. Cassie's own mother, in deep burgundy silk, could have passed for ten years younger, or as Nick put it outrageously on arrival, "I have to hand it to you, Mrs. Stirling. You look more like Cassie's sister with every passing day."

So what does that make me now? Cassie thought wryly. I must be showing the strain. In fact she looked beautiful in white silk crepe scattered with sequins, her mane of hair drawn into an elegant chignon and secured with a bejewelled clip the way her parents liked it. These dinners were invariably black tie. No backyard barbeques for the Stirlings. Her mother, in fact, would not have been caught dead in a pair of jeans.

Now Cassie looked down the table at her father, scrutinising him over the waxy petals of the lilies. He had a wonderful profile, his handsome head turned as he tossed off a joke to one of the women guests. He was a big man. Tall with broad shoulders but not heavy. He looked what he was: a rich, influential man, his personal wealth understated, not commented on.

He really needed a son to carry on the wonderful business empire he had built up, Cassie thought. A son in his own image. Not me. Women didn't really count to her father beyond the basic and obvious pleasure of their beauty, the charm of their conversation, the buzz of their admiration and artful flirtatiousness.

He turned, caught Cassie's eyes on him and raised his glass to her in a smooth, studied toast. She knew she was looking good. It was definitely about pleasing him. She was wearing the jewellery he had given her for her twenty-first birthday. A necklet of large South Sea pearls, with matching pearl earrings set in a basket of gold studs with diamond points. A glorious present as befitting the sort of patrician father he considered himself to be.

At least the gift had impressed everyone at the celebration when her mother had invited every young man she considered suitable for Cassie to fall in love with. That had included Nick. This was far from being his first time inside her parents harbour-side mansion.

Her father, who did approve of Nick, wouldn't like

Matthew. She knew that in her bones. Even if Matthew weren't Jock Macalister's son. Her mother wouldn't hesitate to call Matthew uncouth. The fact was, anyone who didn't have money, dressed carelessly, or drove a battered car would be considered a boor. A terrible sense of loss continued to bear down on her. She had only known Matthew such a short time but he had captivated her utterly.

While the conversation eddied around her she absorbed the familiar scene, trying to place Matthew somewhere in it. Dressed in a costly dinner suit like her father's, his wonderful dark red hair brushed straight back from his wide brow, maybe an inch or so off it at the back, Matthew would easily eclipse any man at the table. Including her father.

No one had the blazing intensity of Matthew's blue eyes, that electric air. Matthew, she had found, could be witty, charming, clever. He mightn't have gone to university but she was prepared to bet he could hold his own in any discussion going on around this table. He was totally his own person. He was a true achiever. He was also the last man in the world her parents would regard as an excellent match.

"Where did you go off to?" Nick asked much later as he escorted Cassie to his car.

"Why make it sound like I've been orbiting Mars? I've been to too many of these rituals, Nick, I can't take a seat at my parent's table without grieving."

"About what?" Nick asked in genuine puzzlement.

"Family togetherness," Cassie said. It was the simple truth.

When they arrived outside Cassie's apartment block,

Nick begged to come up. "I don't think that would help, Nick." Cassie pulled away from the hand that had moved caressingly around her neck.

"What's happened to you since you went away on holidays?" Nick demanded, his handsome face perplexed. "Where *are* you really?"

"Right here."

"Was it someone you met up there?" Nick persisted, a frown appearing between his brows.

"If I did, they turned me down," Cassie said in a wry voice, preparing to get out of the car.

"Are you serious?" Nick caught her arm, restraining her. "Let's get this cleared up. You met some guy and he turned you down?"

"They don't do that often," Cassie joked.

"So now you know what it feels like," Nick said. "I love you, Cassie."

"And I love you, too." She reached back and kissed his cheek. "But as a dear friend. Not someone I want to spend my life with. We've had all this out, Nicko."

"Ah, a *pal!*" He stared into her face. "That's not too bad for now. I'm going to give you time, Cassie, to get over your fantasies." Nick stepped swiftly out of the car and came around to Cassie's side, helping her out onto the street. "Marriage is a big step. We've both got plenty of time to think about it. A big thing I've got going for me is your father approves of me."

"What about *me?*" Cassie asked laconically.

"Your father is very proud of you. He told me," Nick said in a tender voice, but Cassie only smiled.

"I don't suppose you noticed I left home as soon as I was able. I think it was close to six months before anyone noticed. Anyway, thank you for coming with me, Nicko. You're always so supportive."

"Can't I come up for ten minutes?" he begged, the old desire pumping. "I promise I won't overstay my welcome." Nick reached out and tightly held her to him. Such a beautiful girl but so vulnerable. Of course her parents adored her. It was simply they led such a high-powered life.

Matthew, watching from the shadowed interior of a hire car, was witness to this tenderly passionate scene. Now the guy was kissing her, his whole body language yearning. In the lights from the well-lit exterior of the swish apartment block, Matthew could see the man was roughly his own age, maybe a year or two younger, tall, dark-haired, dressed in an outfit Matthew had never worn in his life nor ever expected to. An expensive dinner suit. He wore it with easy grace. He couldn't stop kissing Cassandra and Matthew felt a momentary delirium, an intense rush of jealousy, raw and pure. The thought of another man touching her. He felt his hands clench on the steering wheel. His breathing stopped as he waited for the next move. He didn't care if it was right or wrong, he was going to stop it.

Cassandra broke away.

The relief he felt was so acute it actually hurt. She was shaking her head, saying something.

"'Bye-bye, Nicko," she called.

Then she was almost running. It was time for him to move. He'd been waiting in the visitors' parking lot for over two hours. He had found both her parents' address and hers simply from running a finger down the phone book. He got a recorded message when he rang

Cassandra's phone, thrilling to the sound of her voice again, tongue-tied for a moment when it came time for him to speak after the beep.

He'd even driven past the Stirlings' mansion, impressed despite himself at its sheer size and imposing structure, the magnificent position overlooking arguably the finest harbour in the world. The mansion, one simply couldn't call it a house, was all lit up. Obviously some kind of party was in progress. Though the frontage was walled to a man's height, he could see several luxury cars parked around the driveway through the massive wrought-iron gates. Probably Cassandra was there, celebrating some event at the family home.

Finally he drove back to her apartment block and waited. And waited. That was hard. He wasn't a man for much waiting about.

Now here she was. He could feel the instant heat, the adrenaline rush, that flooded into his body. What's his name—Nicko—was back in his car, driving away.

Matthew acted, leaping a small beautifully manicured hedge to meet up with Cassandra before she activated the security door and went inside.

"Cassandra," he called once. Then louder. "Cassandra." This was what he preferred, action.

She turned and saw him, the shock registering on her beautiful face. She was wearing a white dress that sparkled, a dream of a dress, her wonderful hair drawn away from her face and knotted at the back. He could see some ornament that held the gleaming masses. Diamonds, crystals. It glittered.

Then he stood before her, a kind of anguish on his

face, his high cheekbones flushed with the sudden torrent of emotion. "I need to see you," he said.

"What can you possibly want to say?" Anger and passion overlapped. Hadn't he put her through hell for weeks?

"Hello, beautiful Cassandra," he said, his vibrant voice a little unsteady. "It's wonderful to see you again."

"God, Matthew."

She struggled to come to terms with her warring feelings. Pride demanded she send him on his way.

"Let's go inside. Talk," he urged.

Such was his powerful fascination, Cassie let him in. "How did you know where I lived?"

"The phone book, what else?" He was desperate to touch her. Didn't.

"You didn't call Julie?"

"Let's keep Julie out of it." He only wanted to talk about *them*. "I even drove over to your parents' house. Be it ever so humble."

"I was there for a dinner party."

"With Nicko?" He had another powerful urge to sweep her into his arms, kiss her, but he didn't want to appear the reckless wild man. They were in the elevator that took them to the tenth floor where Cassie had bought her apartment with some of her inheritance from her maternal grandmother.

Every nerve in her body was jumping. She felt like she was being deliberately teased.

Matthew Carlyle.

They were inside the apartment that she had made as attractive as she knew how, listening on one level to Matthew saying how much he liked it, the English floral upholstery, the couple of beautiful antique pieces, the three remarkable paintings, all left to her by her grandmother. The objects, the porcelains, two bronzes of a boy and a girl she had loved as a child. Having her grandmother's things around her comforted her. She wished she had her grandmother now to give her advice.

"Would you like something?" she asked, dropping her evening purse onto one of the sofas, trying to ease the enormous mounting tension.

"Just to look at you." He had been standing admiring one of the paintings, a magical landscape, now he turned, his blue eyes ablaze against his copper skin. "You look radiant. A goddess come straight down from her pedestal. Is Nicko the guy in the office?"

"Does it matter?" It shamed her to realise how very much she was in his power.

"He is, isn't he?"

"Are you going to tell me why you're here?" Irked, she almost snapped.

"Like I said. To see you." His eyes appraised the large lustrous necklet of pearls, the fancy earrings, the unfamiliar hairstyle. "I've never seen your hair like that."

"Classical style," Cassie explained. "My father likes it this way."

"So the dutiful daughter wears it like that." He came across the room and closed in on her. He put out his hand, freed her hair of the jewelled pin, then the clips that secured the chignon, dropping them into the top pocket of his jacket, a navy blazer which he wore over an open-necked sapphire-blue shirt and a pair of dress jeans. His body was simply so tall, so perfectly proportioned, so elegant, he looked like a Calvin Klein ad.

"I've missed you, Cassandra." He felt turbulent in an odd blissful way, revelling in the scented weight of her loosened hair.

She drew in a sharp breath, at the same time impaled by his hand. His fingers were moving against her scalp, gently massaging, dropping to her nape, encircling it.

"Don't be angry at me," he muttered, intense desire in his eyes.

"I am angry." She was, and furiously aroused.

"Of course you are. Why wouldn't you be?" He sounded shaken and humble.

"Why didn't you even come to the airport?" She said, a tear glittering along her lashes.

He couldn't bear to see her wounded. "Because I'm a stupid, stupid, man. I don't believe it now, but I wanted to make it as hard for you as I knew how."

"You brute!" Her face flamed with feeling and her mouth, rose-tinged and velvety, shaped an exquisitely sensual pouting cushion.

The crackle in his blood rose to a roar. There was no time for her to refuse him. He hauled her hard against him, plunging his mouth over hers, a wild beating in his ears while he waited for her to yield to his onslaught. He knew it was wrong to force her. He believed, he hoped, he would never do that, but this fever inside him was making him dizzy.

He had never wanted any woman like this. The sheer power of that want had come as a terrible shock.

Gradually under that rage of passion, the hand that had been pushing with such futility against his shoulder, now slid across his chest, her fingers finding a button, working it free. She was caressing his bare skin, her fingers moving through the tangle of hair plying that taut flesh. If she continued to do that, all his precious control would surely crumble. My God, he was so hungry for her. Starved.

They were kissing open-mouthed, desperately, avidly, as if each couldn't get enough of the other. His hands moved down over her body, skimming the beautiful white dress that clung like a second skin, cupping her provocative small bottom, holding her tighter against his own throbbing body. The pleasure was dazzling, driving him on. Cassie's knees must have weakened because she was sliding limply against him, an invitation for him to pick her up and carry her through to her bedroom. Overwhelming desire tore the breath from his lungs. He felt as fierce and focused as a caveman. This woman he wanted. She was unbelievably alluring to him, the long hair, the silky skin, the slender limbs. He could almost feel himself entering her beautiful body.

But what would happen then? He who prided himself on his judgement. He *cared* about her too dammed much. Blindly he broke away. He hadn't come prepared for a sexual encounter, and he realised she had gone beyond the point where she was strong enough to resist him. He wasn't playing the good guy. He was mad for her, his whole body one compulsive, powerful dangerous machine, but it was more than probable he could make her pregnant. He felt virile enough. Insatiable. Making her pregnant was something he wished for with all his heart, but she had to crave it, too. In her own time.

"Cassandra." He scooped her up and sank into the

plush depths of a sofa. Her short skirt had ridden up, revealing her slender legs pale and gleaming in the sheerest stockings. Past the shimmering hem of her skirt was the apex of her heart-shaped body. To touch her there would be glorious and a potential disaster. She was so vulnerable, so vulnerable.

It took Cassie many moments to find her voice, sensation still shooting through her body making her limbs tremble. "You're good at making me lose my head." Her words were huskily given.

"I couldn't go any further." His voice was deep, agonised, intimate. "I had to stop."

"Why?" When she was desperate for him to devour her.

"Why?" He searched for the answer, amazed at his control. "Because it's the right thing to do." His nerves were as tight as wire. "What sort of man do you think I am? A man like my father? A man who takes what he wants without a thought for the woman. I know what that sort of behaviour brought to my mother."

Cassie sobered, under a flood of understanding. "But I'm not your mother, Matthew. I'm not even like her. I'm one of the generation educated to looking after themselves."

"You're on the pill?" His fingers that were playing with agitation through her hair, stilled.

"Ask no questions, hear no lies." Cassie wasn't going to go into any detail. "I'm not sexually adventurous but I have taken it, yes."

"You had a relationship with Nicko? Is that right?" He slipped instantly into a jealousy that left him shaken.

She pressed her head back into his shoulder. "On

and off for about two years. But it's long over. Does that shock you?"

He stared away, his eyes glowing like coals. "I wish it hadn't happened."

"But you've had relationships, Matthew." She felt and sounded upset. "I know nothing about them."

"They *were* nothing," he countered. "Nothing compared to you."

"Then it's the same with me. I thought I was in love with Nick. He means a lot to me as a friend, but my emotions lacked deep involvement. I tried but I could never see myself as his wife."

"Did you live with him?" Matthew fought to overcome this dark jealousy, so new to him. It was something he hadn't been prepared for.

"No. It wasn't best for either of us. Neither of our families would have approved, anyway. Marriage, yes. Live-in relationships, no. My own space has always been important to me. Up until now."

"But you still see him?" He wanted to learn everything about her. Discover her secrets.

"I *work* with him, Matthew," she retaliated. "Our romance is finished but he's still my friend."

His hand slid around her face, dangerously electrical, forcing her to meet his eyes. "Watching you, I thought he was a lot more than that."

"No." She gave a little distressed sigh. "Nick could kiss me a thousand times and it would never add up to one kiss from you."

He released her then, giving his heart-wrenching smile. "Fine. Can I talk to you now?"

"I want you to." She lay breathless in longing while he pushed a cushion behind her head.

His heart thudding crazily, he tried to repress the passion the sight and nearness of her aroused. For the first time it struck him his hands were terribly rough. Okay, so they weren't a bad shape, but the inside of his fingers and his palms were calloused.

Amazingly she took his calloused hand and held it to her breast. "We'll work it out, Matthew. Neither of us could say goodbye easily."

"I should never have let you leave." His fingers moved to link with hers. "Why don't you come back with me to Jabiru for a few weeks? I want you to experience Outback life at first-hand. Living in the middle of no-where. Then we can both be certain it's where you're going to thrive. Too much emotion has happened to us too fast." His voice deepened as he looked very earnestly into her lovely face, sensing she was both excited and troubled.

"You're asking me to live at the homestead with you? The two of us alone?"

God, it would be *perfect*. An answering excitement was like a blaze within him but he tried to bank it down. No use being hard and hungry. This was a princess. "I'm not asking for a trial marriage, Cassandra, though it's a powerful temptation."

"But you're *human*, Matthew." Her eyes sparkled like diamonds.

"You're telling me! I'm no saint." His vibrant voice rasped. There was a swift rise of colour beneath her velvety skin, a sure indication of her imaginings, her lying spread out on his bed, him deep inside of her, fevered with desire, glorying in possession. "I swear I would never take advantage of you, Cassie, even if it kills me. I care about you too much to sabotage my chances. Obviously it can't be the two of us *alone*. If you agree, there's an old mate of mine, Ned Croft, who could play chaperone or something very like it. He'd be right there, at any rate. He'd love to come. Ned's a real character and a good person. You'll like him."

"So we play house?" Cassie's lips parted on a shaky breath.

"Don't you want to?" His blue eyes smouldered.

"Oh, yes." Suddenly all misgivings fell away. She reached up to link her arms around his neck. "It sounds great."

CHAPTER SEVEN

CASSIE lay in her narrow bed, the mosquito netting billowing around her, eyes closed but ears alert for the early morning sounds. This was her third day on Jabiru and she was settling in beautifully. Ned was a real sweetie, with eyes as bright and innocent as a baby's. They had taken to each other at once.

Ned was never happier than roaming the station doing little jobs here and there, drinking billy tea with the men. It seemed to Cassie he idolised Matthew, and Matthew clearly looked on Ned as family. It had worked out well. Ned had a droll sense of humour, as well, and he was well aware he was there to keep a "sharp eye" on the household arrangements as he once told her in his spare funny way.

It was decided, on Cassie's insistence, she would take over the cooking, something that appeared to make both men happy, so that meant she had to be up at dawn to make breakfast. And a full breakfast at that. Juice, fruit, steak and eggs, lashing of tea and toast. No hardship. Matthew and Ned appreciated her efforts and she was coming to realise she was quite domesticated.

She loved the early mornings. Especially the predawn.

Picaninny dawn, the Aborigines called it, a time of magic, so wonderfully peaceful and still when nothing moved except the stars as they picked up their swags of diamonds and left the velvety sky one by one.

In a few more minutes the dogs would begin to stir, then Ned, who had his bunk out on a veranda silvered by the moon. Cassie opened her eyes, threw back the mosquito netting and got a little gingerly to her feet. Her muscles were a bit stiff and sore after so much riding. She had never been on a horse for such long periods in years. But she was loving it, riding between Matthew and Ned as they toured various camps on the station. It was an exciting life, so open and free, but she could see at times brutally hard and dangerous. Terrible accidents weren't unheard of.

Matthew came behind her as she was slicing pawpaw and mango into a bowl, bestowing a heart-stopping smile upon her, allowing himself the luxury of nuzzling her cheek.

"Sleep well?" The intimacy of his tone lent great charm to his voice. There was the pleasant scent of a herbal soap. More luxurious, the scent of *him*.

"Did you?" she parried, thinking her whole life had changed.

"Think of it this way, Cassandra," he drawled, "I'm a man on a knife edge. Rapture lies into the future."

"I'm thinking it will have to with Ned around!" Cassie answered, excited and amused. Ned took his job of chaperone seriously.

They ate at the big pine table, Ned contending he hadn't eaten so well for years.

"And here I was thinking you enjoyed my cooking," Matthew teased.

Ned nearly choked to set him straight. "So I *do*. I do, but it's lovely having a woman around. One as sweet and beautiful as Cassie. She's a man's dream."

"I think that earns you another cup of tea, Ned." Cassie got up to fetch the teapot.

Later in the morning she sat in the leafy shade of a paperbark with a marvellously textured trunk, watching Matthew, stripped to the waist, repair a section of fencing at the Twenty Mile. The cattle had trampled it down in their efforts to break out into the wild country. Now when time presented they would have to be brought back.

What a beautiful man he was! Cassie thought, feeling her heart thud. He could have posed for Michelangelo, some heroic work of young male virility. She began to fan herself with her cream akubra, trying to cool her blood. Such a play of muscle across his tanned back. He had the body of a natural athlete, wide-shouldered, tapering into a narrow waist, lean, long, muscled flanks, strong straight legs. He was, she had found, possessed of an enormous energy and the wonderful vitality of an absolutely fit and healthy man. Even after rain the earth was as hard as a rock, but he was wielding the crowbar and shovel like he was slicing through cake.

"That should do it," he called out sometime later, walking towards her with his elegant stride. The fan of hair across his dark copper chest cut to a narrow trail down his taut torso and disappeared into his body-hugging blue jeans.

Cassie's tensed fingers bit into her arms. "Well, you

promised me a swim, didn't you?" Feigning casualness, she stood up and smiled.

"Absolutely right. I dreamt about you last night," he said very softly.

"Want to tell me the content?" Cassie stared back at him, mesmerised. This hands-off seduction focused every one of her senses. Sometimes, like now, unbearably.

"For some reason we were on a yacht together." His eyes drank deeply of her. "The Whitsunday's. Turquoise-blue into cobalt water, a fifteen-knot wind strumming against the sails, you in a bikini."

"What colour?" she asked on a shaky breath.

"Yellow. I remember that distinctly. Yellow like a hibiscus." He placed his right hand so gently against her cheek she closed her eyes. "This is hell. And heaven," he breathed. "Arousal without ever cutting loose."

"It's not the *worst* experience of my life," Cassie told him in a wry, husky voice. It was sexual excitement on a short leash. Breathless with just a touch.

"What a super day!" a cheerful voice called to them, breaking the spell. Ned riding towards them. "Just great! I've got a surprise for you two lovebirds. While you have yourselves a swim, I'm going to cook the damper. Got the coals just right. We can wash it down with a panniken of tea. How's zat?"

Matthew smiled his beautiful smile. "We won't say no, Ned."

They rode light-heartedly towards the nearest billabong, a long curving sheet of water, surprisingly deep, watching a brolga flap its great wings in what appeared to be slow motion. Cassie hadn't as yet witnessed one of their stately dances. She had been told all about them, now she was hoping she'd be privileged to catch a performance. The water in the sunlight glittered a metallic dark green, jade in the shallows, with stands of water reeds and small cream lilies lining the banks, the whole framed by magnificent gums. It was the most wonderful natural swimming pool remote from anywhere.

It was as Cassie was slipping out of her cotton shirt and jeans—she was wearing her two piece swimsuit beneath—that the brolgas arrived, flying low above the chain of billabongs in a bluish-grey cloud. Thousands of budgerigars flew above them, a bolt of emerald silk against the burning blue sky.

"Oh, Matthew, look!" Cassie cried out in delight, running down the sandy slope to join him where he stood near the shallows.

"Quiet now!" Matthew turned quickly and caught her around her hands' span waist. "If we make any noise, they'll take off."

She rested against him, his splendid male body clad in black swimming briefs, his arm ringing her as the brolgas turned into the wind and began touching down with a series of running steps like stones skimmed across the water. "How beautiful!" Cassie was enchanted. Now the budgerigars flashed low in formation over the water, their chittering filling the air. "Do you suppose they'll dance for us?" Her eyes shone in anticipation.

"Not while we invade their territory," Matthew said carelessly, himself well used to the spectacle. "It's *our* turn for a swim after all that labouring. There'll be plenty of time, Cassie, don't worry." He clapped his hands and immediately the cranes took off again, racing forward on their long spindly legs, they gained enough buoyancy to spread their great wings. The air vibrated with the swoosh of their flight. They stood and watched the birds until their shrieks faded and the quivering sheet of water became calm again, the surface silvered by the sun.

"They'll move to another water hole further down." Matthew transferred his gaze from the cloudless blue sky to Cassie beside him. His heart juddered at the sight of her, near naked and beautiful. Her swimsuit, a tiny little bra and bikini pants, to his desire-drugged eyes barely seemed to cover her, the brilliant tropical print accentuating her smooth-as-satin skin. This woman... this woman...was the great revelation in his life.

"Matthew?" She felt her blood catch fire at the look in his eyes. "What are you thinking?" On impulse she fingered the cleft in his chin.

"Why don't we make love on the sand?" His voice was tauter than he intended. Hell, this was fabulous, but he was continually on the edge, his passion for her like a hurricane that could obliterate his moral stand.

Even Cassie's little laugh fizzled out. "I was thinking the same thing."

"I suppose Ned wouldn't look," Matthew said very dryly.

"He might consider it an infringement of our deal."

"I guess so." Matthew pulled a contrite face. "So, let's swim. Cool off."

Despite the crystal-clear coldness of the water, the heat between them continued to sizzle and spark. Taking her hand, Matthew tugged her into deeper water, beginning to kiss her with passion and a flicking tongue that licked the droplets of water from her open mouth and her flawless skin. He felt unbearably frustrated, the two of them curling their limbs together until they sank beneath the emerald waters still kissing with abandonment.

When they had to surface again for air, Ned was pacing back and forth along the golden sand. "Are you two okay?" he yelled, gnarled old hands framing his mouth.

"Yes, yes." Cassie began laughing, scooping up handfuls of water and throwing them up in the sparkling winelike air.

"Gawd, you gave me a bit of a fright, that's all."

"Sorry, Ned, my fault." Beneath the water, Matthew's hands cupped Cassie's small breasts, the silky tantalising flesh. The provocation to strip the bra from her was powerful but he had made a commitment. He had to be crazy. But then he knew beyond doubt. He loved her.

Time didn't seem to have any meaning for her. The days just flew, never enough time for all the jobs that had to be done. Matthew as the Boss worked like a Trojan, never asking more of his men that he was prepared to do himself. He needed more staff, Cassie thought, even though they all appeared to be tireless. Everyone on the station recognised her now and seemed to accept her. She was a good rider, getting even better, and wasn't afraid of a bit of hard work herself, though she always wore gloves to protect her hands.

Matthew, delighted with her interest and enthusiasm and confident in her organising abilities and intelligence, allowed her to organise choppers and cattle trucks for the current muster, and selling, giving her a sense of teamwork, of belonging. Ned took it upon himself to instruct her in the art of survival in remote country and how to recognise good bush tucker. Everything fascinated her to the extent she gloried in life. She and Ned were the easiest of companions, so much so, Cassie felt she had known him all her life.

That day was spent herding cattle along the Pardoo Trail which led to the highway and the cattle trucks after two days' drove off. Matthew's foreman and three of the aboriginal stockmen were to continue walking the cattle in, but Matthew had other priorities.

They were sitting around the dinner table relaxing after a long day when Cassie introduced a topic that had been on her mind. "What you really need is wings of your own," she told Matthew, her face bright and animated.

He smiled at her. "Don't I wish. But I can't come up with that kind of money, Cass."

"I'd be honoured to contribute," she burst out without thinking.

All of a sudden, Matthew's handsome face closed. "No, Cassie," was all he said, but it sounded absolutely final.

Ned licked his lips, a little dismayed by Matt's tone. He had great respect for this girl. If she was out here to prove herself, she was doing fine. "Why not consider a compromise, Matt?" he suggested. "You could do with a helicopter. You could run the show from up there."

"I can't afford it, Ned, you know that. Not yet, at any rate."

"But Cassie has offered to help out. Aren't you two getting hitched?"

For a minute it looked as though Matthew was going to react hotly, but he laughed, an edgy sound. "I'm giving Cassandra a chance to make up her mind, Ned. I'm not taking her money."

"Face it, son, you're too proud for your own good." Ned scratched his head.

Matthew gave another grin. "That's the way I am, Ned, but it was very generous of Cassandra to offer."

Things were different now. Cassie stared at him. Back to *Cassandra* when he had slipped into the shorter Cassie or Cass.

"All right. Sorry I mentioned it." Cassie felt her mouth go dry. She hadn't intended to hurt or offend him. His fiery pride was explained in part by his damaged past.

Now Matthew abruptly changed the subject. "I've been wanting to talk about tomorrow. We start drafting the horses. The cleanskins have to be branded and the stallions castrated. It's not a job anyone who cares about animals enjoys, but it has to be done. You won't need to come." He shot a glance at Cassie's face. That beautiful bright light had gone out. He cursed himself for that, but he couldn't take money off her.

"But it's all part of station life, surely?" she protested with a renewal of spirit.

"Of course."

"Then you're on." She wasn't giving up even if he did look strung up.

Matthew went to shake his head but Ned intervened. "Ar, Matt, so far Cassie's acquitted herself well. She was great today, holding the line. I didn't expect her to be so good. It ain't pretty, I agree, but like you said, it's a job that has to be done. Besides, it gives the ringers a chance to show off."

"I'll think about it," Matthew clipped off, his eyes still on Cassie's lovely sensitive face. It was a source of some wonderment to him she had fitted in so neatly, like a piece of a jigsaw puzzle. A princess passing life in the bush with flying colours. But he was worried about taking her along to the draft. Tough as *he* was, he hated the spectacle.

"Well, I'd better get the washing up done." Aware of his withdrawal, Cassie rose from the table.

"Let me help you, love." Ned leapt up in his sprightly fashion, aware she was hurt.

"You have a bit of a rest, Ned." Matthew shook his head, reminded of Ned's age and their full day. "Cassie can wash, I'll wipe."

"Might have one little snort of whisky," Ned said gleefully. "Help me sleep."

"Go right ahead." Matthew walked around the table only to break into a mild curse as all the lights suddenly went out.

"Damn it, the generator."

Cassie was astonished by the blackness. It was total. "We're not out of fuel. I checked." Her voice sounded a little shaken.

"Probably a blockage in the fuel line," Ned guessed correctly.

"Gosh, it's pitch black." Cassie put her hand out uncertainly, feeling swallowed up in a dark canyon.

Even in the dark Matthew's hand closed around it. "Everything's okay," he said soothingly, his thumb caressing her palm. "Ned, the torch is just a few feet behind you. On top of the cupboard."

"I know. I know," Ned grunted as he stubbed his toe against the leg of the coffee table. "Got it."

A ray of light beamed through the blackness. "You stay here with Cassie, Matt, I'll fix it. Shouldn't take more than ten minutes or so."

"You don't need to do it, Ned. I can go." This when he wanted to pick Cassie up and carry her to his bed.

"That's okay. Cassie might be a little scared, I reckon. City folk are used to the lights." Ned sounded like he'd arranged the whole thing.

They stood in fraught silence for a few seconds after Ned had gone, taking the dogs for company.

"You're *not* scared, are you?" Matthew asked.

"Of course not. Not with you around. I'm a bit surprised by the degree of blackness, that's all."

"Come here to me." His arms reached out, made contact with her warm woman's body and encircled her. He was so hungry for her. In such need. But starkly aware of his power over her.

"I'm sorry if I offended you before. I feel terrible." She was aching for comfort.

"Offended me." He brushed that aside. "Of course you didn't, but I can't have you making those kinds of unbelievable offers."

"I do have money, Matthew. Money my grandmother left me." She felt a fierce need to help him realise his vision.

"That's for *you*," he said in a voice that brooked no argument and seemed to put her in her place. A step behind him.

"Why are you so angry with me?" she demanded. Sexual hostility rushed through her blood. How could she ever aspire to be his wife when he wouldn't allow her to help him?

"I'm not angry with you," he repeated, realising his own voice was stormy.

"You are." She was every bit as aggressive as he when she was nearly fainting with desire.

"Because I'm half mad with wanting you. I'm sorry," he gritted his teeth, "people don't really do this, do they?"

"Do what?" she asked hotly, clutching at the front of his shirt. Her vision had adjusted somewhat. They were very close, touching, but he was just a towering presence in the dark.

"When are you going to sleep in my bed?" He hanked the ribbon that held the gleaming wealth of her hair at the nape, speared his hand into the freed masses. "I believe I'm doing the right thing. I'm certain it's best for both of us, but, God, there couldn't be anything worse." Furiously, the hand at her back hard and possessive, he began to kiss her in the intoxicating dark as though keeping his distance was far more than mortal man should have to tolerate. "Cassie, Cassie, I ache for you." He dragged his mouth from hers and moved it on a turbulent journey down to her breast.

"What do you think it's like for me?" Her whole body trembled violently under his plundering hands. But she wanted it. Loved it. "Just because I'm a woman doesn't mean the turmoil isn't the same."

"We can break our agreement anytime you want." His voice was harsh with the force of his passion. "Is that what you want? Just tell me." Her skin was hot, glowing. He could feel the tight, lovely buds of her breasts.

"I…" When it came to it, overwhelmed by the avalanche of pent-up emotions and the emotional cost of it, the words dried up in her throat.

"All right, then." His hands released her so abruptly she started to fall backward and he made a grab for her, groaning in bittersweet regret. "I'm sorry, Cassie. It's my fault. I'm wild in more ways than one."

She had to wipe that slate clean. "No, you're a man I trust absolutely. That's vitally important." Her voice was strained but steady.

"Even so, I make you frantic." He was an expert now at gauging her body's signals.

"Why not?" She let her head drop forward onto his chest. "Why not!" It was heartfelt.

"It might be better, Cass, if we cut short this experiment," he said a little harshly as knots of frustration tightened in the pit of his stomach. "I know it was my idea, but I'm not sure I can take it."

"I need to know what you *think,* Matthew. Her voice had an edgy desperation to it. "Haven't I proved myself?" She lifted her hands, tracing the strong bones of his face in the dark, blinking rapidly, as like a miracle the lights in the homestead came on again. Unnaturally brilliant. She wanted to retreat from them, wondering if she was anywhere close to convincing him she had found what she was searching for. This was a world previously unknown to her yet its wild beauty and grandeur brought peace to her soul. She wanted to make Jabiru her home. She wanted Matthew for her husband, for the father of her children. Even if the old secrets forced them apart, she would never forget this place or these few fleeting weeks. The understanding she thought had grown between them.

"Cassie," he murmured, drawing a lingering hand down over the soft curves of her breasts. "You have such strength inside you. But can you be strong enough?" He knew because she had told him, her parents had been outraged when she had come up to join him. She had never, ever, done such a thing before, so they knew now the strength of the relationship. Both of them were feeling too much, wanting too much. It was a tremendous experience falling in love, but soon outside forces would begin to gather.

On the morning before it was agreed Cassie would return to Sydney, she rode with Matthew and Ned to one of the holding yards where several hundred head of bullocks had been mustered and penned. These were some of the biggest cattle Cassie had seen, big and wild from their long sojourn out in the scrub country. Four of the Aboriginal stockmen, wonderful horsemen, were on hand to release the bullocks through the yard gates into pasture, all riding good, sound, working horses, geldings of a nearly uniform bay colour. Cassie herself was on the beautiful little chestnut mare Matthew had selected for her to ride.

It all started off well. The bullocks were strong and frisky but a few looked positively dangerous. Cassie decided she wouldn't want to meet them in a bullfight. This was a big mob and it would take some time. "Steer clear of this lot, Cassie," Matthew warned her. "Stay on the sidelines." He wheeled his horse to ride into the throng.

"These are wild brutes, luv," Ned told her. "Some of them rogues."

Cassie wasn't about to argue. Her sweet-tempered mare was in fact dancing sideways as red dust rose from the holding yard and the bellowing of the cattle grew to an ear-splitting roar.

"You, too, Ned," Matthew had to shout over the noise.

"I'm not that stupid." Ned chuckled. "Some of those fellas are right bastards." He doffed his old battered hat. "Excuse the language, Cassie. Why don't we trot over to that ring of gum trees? Matt, he's a wonderful cattleman. Scared of nuthin'."

They watched in a companionable silence for some time, admiring the skill of Boss and stockmen as they contained the beasts' rush holding them in line. Finally when all danger seemed past and only thirty or so head remained in the holding yard, they rode out to join Matthew and the men, taking up their place in the line. Cassie had tried this operation a number of times before and acquitted herself well.

Yet danger was the very stuff of life on a cattle station.

As one of the stockmen was momentarily diverted by a dive-bombing nesting bird, a huge bullock crashed out of the yard and thundered off at breakneck speed towards freedom. The same stockman, thoroughly disconcerted, wheeled his horse to go after the tearaway, leaving a break in their well-organised line. In a flash, the remaining cattle seized on the escape route so offered and started a stampede to get clear of the yard and out into the scrub.

Without even thinking, Cassie, next in line to the stockman who had broken ranks, made a desperate attempt to baulk the mad flight, oblivious to Matthew's agonised shout. "For God's sake, Cassie!" Matthew's blood curdled in fear and his heart began a hard pumping action as adrenaline flowed into him. This woman was precious to him and she was in terrible danger. Curse the mare! Though it was scarcely to blame. With good thoroughbred blood in her, the mare was not used to stock work and consequently startled easily. Now she was bucking with increasing vigour, ignoring Cassie's valiant attempts to control her. The men were desperate to get to Cassie, as well, but blocked by a heaving wall of bullocks. Matthew could have cheerfully killed the lot of them. As they picked up speed, Cassie was plummeted out of the saddle and momentarily disappeared from his sight in the great spewing clouds of dust.

For a split second all was chaos; not a one of them not sick with fear.

Don't let this happen. Don't let this happen, Matthew prayed to his God. With no thought for his own safety he plunged into the crushing throng, flailing his stock whip, cracking it over heads and backs. Finally he reached Cassie who had had the sense to curl herself up into a ball. While she cowered, fully conscious, he stood his big black gelding over her prone body, spitting hell and brimstone with whip and fierce shouts. The men, too, were closing, old Ned's tortured face filthy with red dust, all of them holding themselves together with great courage.

The mob, intimidated by Matthew's mounted figure and the thundering crack of his whip fanned out, their momentum broken, passing harmlessly with the blue sky above them full of nesting birds, shrieking in outrage at the tremendous din.

Matthew, grim-faced, was off his horse in a flash, handing it to Ned while he bent to Cassie huddled on the ground. It came to him with dread she could have broken bones, and he shook his head to clear it of confusion and the odd anger that gripped him now that the danger had passed.

"Cassie, oh, sweet Jesus," he groaned. No blasphemy, a prayer, half terror, half thanks. She looked so fragile, her narrow woman's shoulders, slender frame, her pale blue shirt and jeans coated all over with red dust, as was her face and beautiful hair. "Cassie, are you all right?" He touched her shoulder as gently as he knew how, thinking if he had been robbed of her he would have been robbed of his life.

There was a moment of complete silence then Cassie straightened slowly, put out a finger and touched Matthew's beautiful mouth in the centre. "I reckon," she managed laconically.

Sick at heart a moment before, Ned shouted with laughter. "Good on yah, me little darlin'," he cried in trembling delight. "Good on yah. Yah a little trimmer."

But Matthew's frown was like a thundercloud. "That was the most foolish thing I've ever seen in my life," he reproached her, swirling the dust out of her hair. "I couldn't live if you got hurt. Here, let's have a look at you."

The men standing around with vast relief in their eyes, gave her the thumbs-up of approval. This Cassie was a regular bloke. She had acted instinctively as they all would have done. Only for the mare, everything would have been all right.

"You've got a bloody elbow there." Matthew sighed, and sighed again, unable to drive those moments of horror from his mind.

"And knee," Cassie observed, touching it gingerly. "I've torn a hole in my jeans."

"We'll get you another pair." Ned patted her like she was his favourite niece.

"Let me help you up," Matthew said, still in that taut voice that covered his agitation.

"Give me a minute." Cassie put a hand to her face and found it caked in dust. "Is the mare okay?" she hastened to ask.

"She's in disgrace," Ned told her cheerfully. "You put up a good fight, luv, before she tipped you off."

"A proper work horse would have made the difference," Cassie said in a matter-of-fact voice. "I'll never make that mistake again."

"You'll never get the chance," Matthew rasped, not looking up from his task of checking her limbs. This woman was his future.

"Don't get mad," she cajoled him gently, seeing inside him. "You couldn't have taught me better."

"All experience, luv." Ned was studying both their faces. Instinct told him Matthew's heart was badly twisted inside him. He really loved this girl. It had to work out.

"I'm going to take you back to the house and throw

you in the tub," Matthew announced, getting his arms under her and lifting her like she was no more than ten.

"The outside shower will do. I won't have red dust all over the bathroom." She tightened her arms around his throat and looked into the blue flame of his eyes.

"So it's your bathroom now?" For the first time he found a quick smile.

"You saved my life, Matthew Carlyle. My home is your home. You can't get rid of me now."

CHAPTER EIGHT

AFTER that, there was no looking back.

Matthew returned with Cassie to Sydney, bent on speaking to her parents. "It's the right thing to do," he told her. "Your parents mightn't like me, but I'll have to take my chances. No sidestepping it. Just remember nothing and no one can come between us." It was said with such passionate conviction, Cassie felt the swift tears sting her eyes. She loved all of Matthew. His heart, his mind, his proud spirit, the sculpted face and body had left her weak at the knees. Here was a man strong enough to overcome every obstacle.

They were embarking on a life-changing journey, but she knew in her bones her parents' opposition would be the ultimate test of their love. Matthew had made the careful decision to stay in a city hotel. Both of them agreeing the celebration of their marriage and the ultimate union of their bodies would be the more wonderful for the wait.

"As long as it's damned soon," Matthew murmured into her creamy neck. He had almost become accustomed to battling the demons of desire but they had to cut the waiting time before he ran off the rails.

When Cassie rang her father at his office, shrinking a little at the severity and deep disapproval of his tone, he told her he was too busy to speak, he deplored what she had done, but if she wished to speak to him and her mother she should call at the house on Saturday afternoon. "At two."

How utterly predictable, Cassie thought. She was just another appointment. She had summoned up the courage to tell her father Matthew would be coming with her, but her father had already hung up.

Matthew, for his part, was quite ready to face the discord and get it over. Cassandra was a grown woman. She made her own decisions. Her parents had to accept that.

He hardly ever glanced at his own reflection, but that Saturday afternoon he took a good hard look at the man in the mirror. A strange face really. Very distinctive features.

He'd had his hair trimmed. Not much. The guy in the barber shop told him to stick with what he had. He'd always left it long to combat the burning rays of the sun on his nape, anyway.

He scarcely knew himself in the new clothes. Smart casual, they said. *Casual* at that price? Grey jacket with some sort of pattern in it, trousers a shade deeper, a blue shirt that felt incredibly soft against his skin. New socks, new shoes, the works. All for Cassandra. He smiled at the thought, catching the stark white flash of his teeth. Hell, he looked theatrical. To combat the feeling he gave a low growl in his throat.

Before he left the room he took a small green velvet case out of the top drawer of the bureau. He hoped with all his heart Cassandra would like it. Only one way to find out. Put it on her finger. Third finger. Left hand.

"You look wonderful," Cassie said when they met, so stunningly handsome he robbed her of breath.

"All for you, my magnolia love." She was wearing an ivory silk shirt and a full skirt that set off her small waist, sandals on her feet, her long hair caught back with a turquoise silk scarf. She had such magnificent hair he wondered how anyone could possibly prefer it confined. He was shaken by the rush of fierce protectiveness. No one would ever hurt Cassandra. Not while he was around.

As they were nearing their destination, Matthew pulled over to a beautiful little park with an adjoining marina, helping Cassie out. The afternoon sun was dazzling, casting patterns on the ground through the light canopy of trees. Flower beds showed riotous displays of poppies and day lilies, a small boy was flying a splendid Chinese kite, watched over by his father, a young couple sat close together on a park bench beneath the welcoming shade of a blossoming gum. A truly peaceful scene.

Matthew took her hand, strolling to the water's edge. "The harbour is unbelievably beautiful," he said.

"We think so."

"Sure you won't miss it? Sydney has so much to offer."

"We can visit now and again."

"We can," he agreed. "And you can always take time to visit your parents and friends, Cassandra. I'm not going to keep you a prisoner." He reached out to brush her cheek. A shivery possessive gesture.

There was something immensely exciting about being Matthew's prisoner, Cassie thought.

"So much has happened," Matthew mused, his expression serious.

"I know it isn't easy for you, Matthew, meeting my parents."

He slipped a supportive arm around her waist. "I'm not concerned for myself. It's *you* I don't want to see upset. I don't know that I would take to that too well. You've given me a picture of what your home life has been like. But you're a woman now. In charge of your own life. Your parents will have to realise that."

"I hope so." The cold clear part of Cassie's mind told her that they wouldn't.

"What you need is an engagement ring." Matthew delved decisively into his breast pocket. "That will make a statement like nothing else can. Hold out your hand." His voice was low and rich with emotion.

Cassie's bones seemed to dissolve. She stood without moving, almost without breathing, a pulse beating heavily in her throat.

"I hope you like it," Matthew said, opening up the box to reveal an exquisite solitaire diamond ring set in gold.

Looking at the ring, a full carat or more, Cassie realised with a throb of anxiety how much it would have set him back. Could he afford it? But the eyes blazing into hers held only the realisation of a dream. "Matthew, it's so beautiful. I love it." She struggled not to cry. "Please, put it on my finger."

He took her wrist in one warm possessive stroke. "I want it to be a part of you. Of us. This reminds me of a star," he said with such brooding emotion it made her shiver. "Of your eyes. I want you to know before we speak to your parents, *you're* the star in my firmament. I want you to promise me for *always*." He slid the beautiful ring down her finger, lifted her hand and kissed it.

"*Always,* Matthew," Cassie promised with an answering depth of feeling.

Yet the afternoon that had started so brilliantly was to end badly. When they arrived at the Stirling mansion, a maid showed them through the luxuriously appointed house filled with magnificent furniture, paintings, antiques, so much it was impossible to know where to look first, to a large informal living room at the rear. It had a breathtaking view of the harbour. The whole area was flooded with light from the great expanse of glass and the French doors that led to a covered terrace with a deep pink bougainvillea climbing the columns. All this Matthew saw with a sense of appreciation not untouched with awe. It gave him a blinding perspective, too, on what Cassandra was giving up.

She had grown up in this splendid house when he and his mother had tasted real poverty in those awful years before they had found their way to North Queensland, where people like Marcy had reached out to help them.

The light was just so brilliant for a few moments he had only a dimmed view of three people seated very companionably on the boldly upholstered sofas on one side of the very large room. All heads were turned, two men and a woman. The men, tall, well-built, imposing in demeanour, stood up and for a split second Matthew thought he was going mad.

How could it be? As his eyes adjusted to the dazzling light it seemed to him the devil himself had materialised.

Jock Macalister.

At long last. Jock Macalister with a dazed expression on his damnable face. It matched his own, but Matthew felt only a terrible hush fall all around them.

Beside him, Cassie went white with shock. Couldn't her father have at least told her Jock Macalister would be there? But that was the curse of their family. There had never been communication.

Her father started to speak, looking aghast. "For heaven's sake, Cassandra, what *is* this?" For once his voice had lost its customary aplomb.

Her mother was speaking, too, rushing in, unable to believe her eyes. How in the name of all that was holy was Jock Macalister's terrible secret right here before them? With her *daughter.* She found it impossible to understand. Was it possible Cassandra had done this on purpose? If she hadn't been so shocked, Anita Stirling would have been enthralled. The young man of the dark red hair and blazing blue eyes was the living image of the Jock Macalister in a portrait painted long ago. It held pride of place in Macalister's study at Monaro Downs. She had admired it many times. Now the living, breathing double?

Macalister himself reached out for the back of an armchair, clinging to it as for support.

"Cassandra, would you mind telling us the name of your friend?" Stuart Stirling barked. As if he didn't *know.* This was Jock's son. The astounding resemblance made it an uncontroverted fact.

"Don't tell me you don't know, Mr. Stirling?" Matthew's vibrant voice challenged, resounded around the room. His commanding physical presence was such, he was impossible to not heed. "I go by the name Matthew Carlyle. My mother's maiden name. I never knew my father." This with a flashing glance of contempt at the imposing, tawny-haired elderly man who stood in an agonised silence, looking ill.

Stuart Stirling turned to Macalister with the face of acute embarrassment. "Be certain, Jock, we had absolutely no idea of a possible connection. Cassandra has given no hint of any such thing. We've never laid eyes on the young man."

"Well, now, that makes all of you," Matthew drawled. "My father never laid eyes on me, either."

Until now.

He might as well have declared it from the roof tops.

Anita Stirling, looking whiter by the minute, closed the distance between herself and her daughter, her eyes wild. Stuart was bound to Jock Macalister in friendship and business.

"You'll pay for this, Cassie," she said in a furious undertone. "I always said you were a very strange girl."

"It was meant to happen." The gravity of Cassie's tone stole her mother's breath. Cassie was certain now it was so. She was as pale as her mother and all eyes. "Don't you see, it was *meant* to happen. I had no idea. Father never said Sir Jock would be here."

"Do you think I believe you?" Anita Stirling gave a brittle laugh. "Are you stupid, crazy?"

"While you're casting around for insults, Mrs.

Stirling," Matthew interjected, disliking this thin, elegant woman on sight, "I want to tell you I would *never* have come here had I known the identity of your guest."

Stuart Stirling moved to join his wife, anger leaping in his eyes. "Look here, young man, don't expect us to believe that. Somehow you and Cassandra got wind of it. Sir Jock calls on us often when he's in Sydney. Many people would know. Her boss, for one."

"You're good friends, I take it?" Matthew gave Cassandra's father a hard smile.

"Twenty years and more, if it's any of your business," Stuart Stirling returned curtly. Arrogant young devil, but with the unmistakable stamp of authority.

"Why did you never tell me, Cassandra?" Matthew suddenly transferred his attention to Cassie, who was quaking inside.

"The moment was never right, Matthew." She lifted her head resolutely, feeling his trust in her begin to unravel.

Jock Macalister, who had been silent so long now, found voice. "I don't know if this means anything to you, Matthew Carlyle, but I've suffered for my wrongs." Carefully he walked across the room.

"You know nothing about suffering." Matthew stared back at him. "It was my mother who knew all about that."

The blood drained entirely from Macalister's face. "I swear one day I'll make it up to you."

"Don't try to be human, sir," Matthew warned, drawing Stuart Stirling's fire.

"I'd appreciate it, young man, if you'd leave my house," he said, throwing his head back angrily.

"No, no, Stuart, it's me who should leave," Macalister managed painfully. "Forgive me, Cassandra, my dear." He addressed her almost sadly. "What a beautiful young woman you've grown into. Could I ask where in the world you met...Matthew?"

"Ah, you know as well as anyone where we lived," Matthew broke in, full of a good, cleansing anger. "I bet you had us followed from place to place."

Macalister looked shaky and old. "And I've always been ashamed. So terribly ashamed. But in the beginning your mother simply disappeared."

"The hell with that!" Matthew spun on his heel. "May you live with your lies and your guilt forever."

Cassandra caught urgently at his arm. "Don't leave, Matthew, *please*."

He stood riveted. But only for a moment. This was the woman who had stolen his soul. Now she had betrayed him. Anger flooded him. Anger and outrage.

"I'm sorry, Cassandra. I'm shocked beyond words."

"I'll come with you." She drew closer, trying to align herself with him. Something that outraged her mother.

"Perhaps you can tell us first why you're *here?*" cried Anita Stirling, her voice ragged with dismay.

"Tell her, Cassandra." Matthew sounded indifferent to the reason.

"We came to tell you we're engaged," Cassie replied with dignity, lifting her hand and turning it so the light hit the sparkling solitaire diamond.

Her mother shook her head vehemently. "I've never

heard such nonsense. Engaged? Why you only met this young man when you were on holiday, you've known him no time at all."

"Yet he's the man I'm going to marry." Cassie faced her parents with utter conviction.

"Good God!" Stuart Stirling's face went craggy. "This must be a terrible joke of some kind. None of this can be happening surely."

The heat and bitterness of Cassie's anger surprised her. "You've never taken much interest in my affairs, Father. I was trying to tell you on the phone but you were too busy to listen."

"Why don't you all sit down and talk this out?" Jock Macalister suggested, trying to contain the terrible damage. "Life is so strange. A man ought to see his only son before he dies."

Anita Stirling went to him, staring at him with anxious dark eyes. "Whatever are you talking about, Jock? You're a wonderfully fit man. How do we know he really is your son?"

"I know." Macalister spoke slowly, sorrowfully. "You didn't doubt it for a second, did you?" he challenged her in a quiet, pained voice. "He's the image of me as a young man."

"But you couldn't bring yourself to meet me?" Matthew said with profound scorn.

"You're not familiar with all the aspects of my life, Matthew, just as I'm not familiar with yours," Macalister answered.

"*Nothing* could excuse you."

"I can't forgive myself." Macalister bowed his head.

Matthew didn't respond, his handsome face carved in bronze.

"I'll see myself out, Anita," Jock Macalister said. "Maybe, Matthew…" he pleaded, his eyes seeking those of the young man with hair like dark flame. He saw the way it sprang from the wide forehead, the blue eyes, black brows, the chiselled features so exactly like his own.

For a powerful man, how uncertain he sounds, Matthew thought without pity. How miserable. Like a man who had sold his soul to the devil. "It's all too late." Matthew wheeled away, such a cold, prideful expression on his face. Terrified, Cassie went after him, but he put her away from him with his strong arms, anger exploding like an erupting volcano.

"I'm not ready to hear your explanation, Cassandra."

"You're not leaving without me?" Cassie was appalled at the turn of events.

He looked straight at her, his handsome mouth thinned to a straight line. "You know I fell in love with you, Cassandra. You watched me do it. You've been the greatest thing in my life, now hell, you probably set me up," he accused her heavily.

Cassie lost all colour. "No, Matthew, never!" She caught at his taut arm. "Can't you at least listen to what I have to say?"

"I believe not," he retorted curtly, removing her hand. "I'm pretty well disenchanted with your whole damned family."

He wasn't back at his hotel for hours and hours, causing Cassie to fret dreadfully. She had had the most terrible row with her parents and her head was spinning like a top. Where had he gone? She didn't know, but she was painfully aware in not being absolutely honest with him she had hurt and disappointed him, damaged her standing in his eyes. She had really come down from her pedestal. But then, she had never wanted to be on a pedestal in the first place.

Matthew's feelings ran very deep and his feelings were all centred around her. That was a big responsibility. Surely when he had time to think about it he would reject any idea she had set him up. Set him up for what? To bring a father and son together? It complicated matters dreadfully.

Jock Macalister was a millionaire a couple of hundred times over. Matthew surely couldn't believe she had connived to bring them together? But then neither could she forget his pride nor the way he had rejected her offer to help him financially out of hand. She felt sick with anxiety. One thing in her favour, he hadn't booked out of the hotel. She would just have to keep ringing.

Finally she went over to the hotel and waited, sitting in the lobby until she saw him alight from a taxi and swing through the entrance, a handsome vibrant force of nature. He didn't even see her, tucked away as she was, but made directly for the lifts. One of the desk clerks had given her the number of his room earlier, now she gave him a few minutes before she followed.

"Oh, God, please help me," she breathed. "Tell me how to handle it."

He greeted her at the door, stunning, raffish, jacket off, shirt undone by several buttons, a tumbler of whisky in his hand.

"Well, if it isn't my beautiful fiancée," he drawled in a deep slow voice.

"May I come in, Matthew?"

He gazed down at her, his eyes drinking in the poignant cast to her beauty. "As a matter of fact, no." He wasn't what he wished to be, totally in control of himself.

"I want to be with you," Cassie insisted, her heart in her eyes.

"I bet you do." His breath was warm, fragrant with the Scotch. "Maybe we can have a little adventure in bed?" He gave her a devilish wink.

"I thought we had a plan. A design for marriage?" Cassie said, realising this wasn't his first drink of the day.

"But you're a player now, Cassie, and you can spin tales. I'm not sure I like that. Or whether I can forgive you."

"Please let me in, Matthew." She took another step towards him, for some reason feeling tiny against his swaying height. "I don't want to hover out here."

"Hell, is that what you're doing?" He put his head out of the door and looked around in an exaggerated fashion.

"Of course I am." With smooth deliberation she ducked under his arm, walked quickly into the room and stood near the small circular table and chairs.

"What do you need from me, Cass?" he asked her in a hard voice, shutting and locking the door.

"I love you, Matthew," she said quietly, standing her ground. "We became engaged today, remember?" Tears glinted like diamonds in her eyes.

"Ah, hell, no need to cry about it, sweetie." His vi-brant voice was faintly slurred. He reached out and pulled her down on the sofa, wedging her into the corner with his lean powerful frame. "The thing is, Cassie—" he turned his face to her "—you did the worst, worst thing you could ever do."

"I didn't lie to you, Matthew," she said swiftly, but he put a finger to her mouth and brushed it across her lips.

"'Course you didn't, sweetheart. You just didn't tell me the whole truth. *Big* money. Is that why you tried to bring me and dear old Jock together?" He lifted a hand to his eyes and rubbed them fiercely. "God, Cass. I would give my life for you in a second, but that doesn't matter. The fact is I can't give you what you've always had. What you really want."

"You can't be talking about *money?*" She turned to him in extreme agitation.

"Oh, darling, *pleez.*" He kissed her forehead, kissed her cheeks. "That's one hell of an enormous house you were raised in. Chock-a-block with first-class paint-ings and antiques. On Sydney Harbour, for God's sake. Who the hell has a hope of living in a house on Sydney Harbour? Cassie, girl, you were born rich."

"So what?" Cassie was quivering all over, her whole body responding to being pressed against his. "It didn't make me happy. While my father was making so much money I was almost completely cut off from him. My mother lived for him and her social life. I might as well have been an orphan. Money isn't important to me, Matthew."

He smiled at her, a beautiful white sardonic grin.

"No, darling, because you've never been without it." On a surge of anger he put a hand to her neck, and kissed her furiously on the mouth.

She couldn't seem to fight free of him. Didn't want to. He tasted wonderful when she had never had the stomach for whisky or spirits of any kind.

"Oh, for God's sake." He released her abruptly, turned away as if with self-disgust.

"Matthew, will you please let me speak?" she implored, her mouth pulsing from his kiss.

"Sorry, Cass." He shook his marvellous red head. "Right now I'm workin' on gettin' drunk. Would you like something yourself?" His eyes mocked her.

"No, I'm fine."

"Tell me, when did Macalister leave?" he asked in a harsh voice.

"Not long after you."

"Have you the slightest inkling what it meant having you drop him on me?"

She leaned into him and covered his hands with hers. "Matthew, for the last time, I had no idea Jock Macalister would be there, any more than my parents knew about your relationship to Jock. I simply didn't tell them as I wanted them to be free of preconceptions. Surely you can understand that? Even angry as you were, you must have registered their shock when we turned up?"

He laughed. "I thought you were all absolutely superb. Academy Award stuff. It's obvious to me, Cassie, your parents are manipulators of the highest order. All three of you could have set it up. All you needed was to bring Jock and his long lost illegitimate son together. For all I know, Macalister could be on his last legs. He didn't look too clever. Money always seeks to marry money. There can't be enough of it in some circles."

"I wonder why my father has threatened to disinherit me if I go ahead and marry you, then?" Cassie asked.

"Ah, come on, Cass!" He lifted his glass to her and drained it to the last drop.

"I'm perfectly serious," she said.

"You poor little soul," he mocked.

Still, she persisted, loving him, forced to endure his distrust. "I feel terrible about not telling you the whole truth about Sir Jock and my father, Matthew."

"So what was your big problem?" he asked bluntly, his whole body emanating a tightly controlled anger. "You're not a teenager, Cassandra. You're not a poor little kid from the wrong side of the tracks. You're a princess. Hell, a Madonna. I'm half crazy to have sex, but I hold off. All for you. I want everything to be perfect for you, you adorable little liar."

"Oh, well, if you're not going to believe me." She tried to rise, her own temper flaring, but he held her down easily, without exerting any real strength.

"Enough's enough, Cass. Level with me and I might forgive you. You all thought marriage with me wouldn't be so bad if Macalister at long last acknowledged me. Better yet, felt moved to compensate me for a lifetime of rejection. I think he's worth around 300 million, isn't he? I'm sure I read that sometime back. It made me mighty mad. The distinguished Sir Jock Macalister, who kept his bastard out of sight, out of mind."

"I know how angry and hurt you are," Cassie repeated. "At him. At me." Without warning, overwrought and feeling the crisis of confidence she had created, she began to cry.

"You think that will make me soften?" His voice and eyes suggested he was losing control.

She twisted away from him and dashed her hand across her eyes. "I'm just beginning to realise you're a very hard man. I'm not a saint, Matthew. I'm a woman with flaws. I regret not confronting the issue of Sir Jock and my father, but all my life I've hated confrontations. I've had so many of them. With my parents...."

"Well, of course you were scared stiff of me." Angry, affronted, he cut her off.

"No, no." She shook her head. "But you're the one person in the world who would have made the telling hard, Matthew. Can't you understand that?"

"No. I'm not buying it, either."

"Do you want to break off the engagement?" she asked emotionally, her eyes sparkling with unshed tears.

"Listen, honey, I thought I made it very clear to you. You're *mine*."

"Then you'd better reach deep inside you for the grace to forgive me," she countered with some spirit.

"Maybe I will. Sooner or later," he drawled.

"You're behaving badly, Matthew," she accused him, tossing her long hair over her shoulder.

"*I* am? That's splendid, coming from you." He was angry now. Really angry. Wanting to pull her into his arms. Punish her.

"You have a dark side." She gritted her small teeth.

"We all have a dark side, Cassie," he informed her. "You couldn't look more beautiful, more luminous, or pure, but all along you've had an agenda of your own."

She wanted to hit out at him. Her captor. "You'd better stop that now, Matthew. I don't like it."

"Well, let's do something you do like," he said almost cheerfully, reaching for her in one powerful movement and dragging her across his lap, holding her so her head fell back and her long abundant hair fell across the arm of the sofa. He had the crazy illusion his blood was lava. "Come on, Cass. Wouldn't you rather make love than argue? How do you get to know so much about it, anyway?"

"About what?" she said furiously, trying in vain to get up.

"About turning a man on."

He sounded hopelessly cynical, but looked wonderful.

"Go on, you need to vent your anger on someone," she said shortly, vivid rose colour in her cheeks.

"You bet!"

He should have stopped there, but the tumult in his blood was too fierce. One hand beneath her back, he raised her to him, his mouth closing over hers so voluptuously, so hungrily, he might have been eating her. Her sweet lips. He silenced her in a way she was never likely to forget. However much she had shocked him that day with her parents, the hated presence of Macalister, this woman was in his blood. He kissed her over and over until the breath was rasping in her soft throat.

"Matthew!"

"I'm here and I'll never let you go."

"I never lied to you."

"Hush." He spoke harshly but he wanted to believe her. Even her small struggles added to his sexual excitement. He wound his hand possessively into her long hair. Wonderful hair. Hair like a woman should have, thick, silky, fragrant. He revelled in holding her body against his in an intimacy she couldn't escape. She knew he was terribly aroused. Hot with hunger. He had talked so much about waiting for their wedding night. Hell, it was too far away. He was inflamed by a flood of desire so monstrous its power was taking him under.

She was wearing some skinny little top like a silk sweater. It outlined her tantalising small breasts. He rolled it up, pulled it over her head. Her bra was a scrap of lace. That went, too, as he fell into a mindless well of pleasure. Her breasts were beautifully shaped, spreading to his hand. He ran his calloused palm in quick friction up and down over her nipples, hearing her soft moans. Her face was so beautiful, eyes closed, mouth opened to her sighs, her expression akin to ecstasy. And agony. That was what it looked like. Her skirt was the same colour as the shucked-off top. The same intense violet-blue of the morning glory on Jabiru. He wanted to run his hands up and down her slender legs. Did. It was a matter of wonderment to him, the soft satiny feel of her skin. The exultation in him was growing fierce.

He was momentarily distracted when she cried out like a wild bird.

"Cassie! Who do you belong to?" he asked her tautly.

"Love me. Love me," she responded, her eyes intent on him but somehow unfocused as though she was centring her own overpowering desire, acknowledging it freely. "Now, Matthew. *Now.*" Her whole body was aflame.

He lifted her high in his arms and held her. "You want this, Cassandra."

"Yes, yes, a million times over."

"Then come to me."

CHAPTER NINE

OWEN MAITLAND showed no surprise when Cassie handed in her notice. He had in fact been waiting for it.

"So Jock has finally admitted Matthew is his son?" he asked, studying her with sympathy, seeing the sadness in her eyes.

"Yes, he did," Cassie answered huskily.

"It will all come out in any case, Cassie. You must be aware of that. Not that most people haven't heard the rumours anyway. They've been circulating for thirty years. I know Jock socially. Not half as well as your father. Jock's ruled over his empire with an iron hand, but to put it bluntly, in some respects Eleanor Macalister wears the pants. She's a Mondale, you know, which is to say, an aristocrat in her own eyes. Old money. Not a whiff of scandal has ever touched the Mondale family. As a matter of fact, Eleanor was considered to have married very much beneath her when she married Jock. He could buy and sell them now."

Cassie's expression was grave. "Are you saying Lady Macalister was the reason Sir Jock never recognised Matthew?"

Owen Maitland nodded. "Don't you think it highly probable? Eleanor Macalister is not a woman who could ever be taken lightly. She has a great stake in everything Jock does. He can have his mistresses. I'm sure he has done over the years, but he'll never leave Eleanor. The alliances, the mergers. She knows where all the bodies are buried."

"So he's a coward?" Cassie spoke like a woman who had weighed everything up carefully and given her decision.

"Coward?" Owen Maitland pressed against the warm leather of his armchair. "No one could ever think that of Jock."

"Then what would you call abandoning Matthew and his mother?" Cassie challenged.

"I've never understood that." Owen Maitland frowned a little. "But I don't believe it was as simple as you think, Cassie. Jock might tell a different tale. Not that he's ever opened his mouth. But I do know he's carried a lot of unhappiness. I don't know the exact state of his marriage but I do know in many respects Eleanor cracks the whip. Many the occasion I've met him and I've come away thinking Jock Macalister's a very lonely man. Of course the terrible irony is, he's never had another son."

"It's very hard not to judge him," Cassie said. "Matthew is understandably bitter. Especially in relation to the treatment of his mother. He loved her. They were very close."

"I understand she died?"

"Yes."

"How sad. She couldn't have been very old."

"It was an accident," Cassie said, not wanting to be pressed.

"Julie told us Matthew has a fine property of his own?"

"Yes, he has." Cassie's eyes lit with pride. "Matthew's a fighter. He's had to triumph over a lot of obstacles. It's built strength of character."

"I would have liked to have talked to him," Owen Maitland said. See if the young man passed the test.

Cassie looked at her boss keenly. "I can arrange that. Everything has happened so quickly. In many ways its been overwhelming. We'll be married in North Queensland. I expect Julie has told you already. She'll be my chief bridesmaid. We have a mutual friend, Louise Redmond, I'd like to ask, as well."

"May I enquire what your parents think?" Owen Maitland uneasily awaited the answer.

"My father has threatened to disinherit me if the marriage goes through," Cassie said, apparently unfazed.

But Owen Maitland looked and sounded shocked. "Cassie!"

"He means what he says."

"Surely not," Owen Maitland exclaimed. "Parents often say what they don't mean when they're upset."

"Mr. Maitland, you know my father," Cassie pointed out gently.

Too well. Owen Maitland shrugged. "What exactly is it he's holding against you, Cassie?"

"The fact Matthew is Sir Jock's son." An irony when Matthew had briefly believed her father could have been party to the contrived meeting between himself and Macalister.

Owen Maitland gave a grim smile. "Whose side is he on anyway?"

"Not mine," Cassie said instantly. "Father believed if he offended Sir Jock or Lady Macalister in any way it would affect their business relationship."

"Well, yes," Owen Maitland was forced to agree, "it might, but it has to come down to *your* happiness in life, Cassie. You must love this young man?"

"With all my heart," Cassie said with such fervour Owen Maitland was touched.

At the same time Cassie was meeting with Owen Maitland, Stuart Stirling was moving on a plan to get rid of Matthew Carlyle from their lives. The whole point of being a rich man was that he could afford to buy out his opponents. Cassandra could have anything she wanted. *Except* Jock Macalister's illegitimate son. Getting rid of Carlyle was an imperative.

At home on Jabiru, Matthew worked himself to the bone so he and Cassie could have a clear ten days for their honeymoon on Angel Island, a small exquisitely beautiful island on the Great Barrier Reef with thirty private pavilions set in a magical rainforest garden, each villa overlooking the heavenly blue ocean.

Matthew, who had been there only once, remembered it as being the most romantic and tranquil place on earth. It had stood out like a beacon in his mind as he began planning this very, very, special wedding. He and Cassie had talked daily on the phone and they had worked out forty guests in all. The Maitlands had offered their luxury retreat for the reception, which was nice and supportive of them, but Matthew thought he needed to make it up to Marcy for all she had done for his mother and him.

He drove into town as soon as he was able, thinking it was high time to speak to Marcy about their plans.

Marcy spotted him as soon as he walked in the front door, greeting him with pleasure, throwing her arms around him and giving him a big motherly hug. "I've been expecting you to show up." She looked up at him, deciding he looked wonderful. Blazing with life and energy. "How's Cassie coping with all the excitement?" she asked.

"She's due here next week," Matthew told her with a feeling of powerful relief. "I can't bear her out of my sight. Now there's something I want to talk to you about, Marcy." Matthew took her by the arm and sat her down at an empty table. "You've been like a second mother to me."

"True." Marcy eased herself back in the chair, beaming with pleasure. "And I want to tell you right now, it's been an honour."

"I want you to handle the reception, if that's okay?" Matthew asked in a voice that hid a well of emotion. "Not a big crowd. I was hoping we could have it in the al fresco dining area, perhaps retract the roof. Around forty. Invitations are due to go out. The weather should be perfect so we could have it under the stars."

Marcy leaned forward and clasped Matthew's face in her ruddy hands, her mind working overtime. "This is going to be so exciting," she cried. "I know just what to do. You leave it to me, son. I'm going to give you and

Cassie the best flaming reception this town has ever seen."

"I don't think we could ask for more." Matthew grinned.

"Oh, this is marvellous!" Marcy enthused. "By the way, luv," she suddenly remembered. "There's a guy looking for you. Arrived earlier this morning. Staying upstairs." She gave a jerk with her thumb. "City guy. Wears a tie."

"Name?"

"Simon Parker, on the register," Marcy said. "Seems a nice bloke."

"Never heard of him."

"You will now," Marcy pronounced. "That's him coming in the door."

Matthew shot the new arrival a quick look, feeling pinpricks of premonition. This was someone with something to say. Something he didn't want to hear about, he was sure of it. Nevertheless with a backward word to Marcy he walked straight up to the stranger with his graceful fast-moving gait and held out his hand.

"Matthew Carlyle. Marcy tells me you've been asking for me?"

The man, middle fifties, dapper, overdressed for town, thinning dark hair worn straight back, smooth, intelligent face, nodded cautiously as though suddenly conscious of Matthew's ranging height and lean, powerful body. "Simon Parker, Mr. Carlyle," he introduced himself. "I'm here to represent my client, Stuart Stirling." He produced a card bearing the name of a major law firm above his own. "Perhaps we could find a quiet place to talk? My room, if you've no objections?"

"Why don't we just go for a walk?" Matthew suggested in a brisk voice.

It came to Parker he now dreaded having to say what he had been instructed to say to this dynamic-looking young man whose physical appearance had shocked him rigid. But his firm had been acting for Sir Jock Macalister for many long years.

They were outside in the brilliant sunshine, walking down the leaf-canopied main street of the picturesque little town, palm trees soaring, brilliant lorikeets flashing rainbows of colour from hibiscus, jasmine, oleander, bougainvillea. A village, really, on the edge of the rainforest but a prettier place it was hard to imagine. "This is very difficult for me, Mr. Carlyle," Parker admitted with a genuine feeling of regret, "but my client has instructed me to discuss a proposal he thinks might interest you."

"Fire away," Matthew said a little brusquely, understanding it wouldn't be good.

Parker did something he hadn't done in more than twenty years. He blushed. "What about if we sit down on that park bench over there?"

"You sound nervous, Mr. Parker." Matthew Carlyle gave him a half smile that nevertheless lit up his handsome face.

Parker shrugged. "I confess I am. You're not what I imagined."

"And that was? Some upstart cad trying to make off with the rich, snobby Stuart Stirling's daughter?"

"Something like that," Parker agreed, studying Matthew for a time, liking what he saw.

"Well, I'm happy to tell you, Mr. Parker, I love

Cassandra. And she loves me. Stuart Stirling is just a damn big windbag."

Parker couldn't help it. He gave a whooping laugh which he quickly choked. "It has to be said that he and Mrs. Stirling have genuine concerns about the important step their daughter is taking."

"Indeed?" Carlyle looked down his fine straight nose in a manner that instantly brought Jock Macalister to Parker's mind. "I'm sure you've been told it has something to do with my family tree."

"Would I be impolite in saying you're the image of Macalister?" Parker managed, thinking it was a bit scary.

"I'm not completely happy with it." Matthew gave an ironic laugh. "After all, he has disowned me from birth."

Or decided he needed a quiet home life, Parker thought. "You've never met Lady Macalister, I take it?" he asked.

"Sorry," Matthew said without a trace of regret. "He must be a real wimp to be dictated to by his wife."

"Lady Macalister is *Establishment*," Parker said as though that explained it.

"Better get on with it, Mr. Parker." Matthew flashed him a glance.

"Mr. Stirling is my client, Matthew. I hope I may call you Matthew," Simon Parker waited for the younger man's nod. "I'm merely acting for him. Passing on his proposal."

"I'm not dangerous."

But he could be under certain circumstances, Parker thought. Although he had a very engaging laugh. "To get to the point, Mr. Stirling has offered a sum of one hundred thousand dollars if you would ease yourself out of his daughter's life."

Matthew made a parody of scratching his cleft chin. "You're serious now?"

"Dead serious," Parker confirmed, thinking Stuart Stirling had a poor understanding of this young man's psychology.

"Have you ever done anything like this before, Mr. Parker?" Matthew shook his head in wonderment.

"I'm happy to say, no."

"Just how many hundreds of millions has Stuart Stirling got?"

"I'm sure you realise I'm not at liberty to say."

"Perfectly all right. It must be around three hundred, four? And he thinks Cassandra is only worth *one hundred thousand dollars?*"

Parker looked at him for a moment aghast. "Would you be wanting more? I have that amount in a cheque."

"I'm a gentleman, Mr. Parker, so I won't respond to that. May I see the famous—infamous—cheque?" The sunshine caught Matthew's dark red hair, making it flare. Like his temper.

"Why, yes, you can. As it happens I have it in my wallet." Parker stood up in a flash, delving into the pocket of his trousers. He withdrew an expensive light brown leather wallet, nicely engraved with his initials, S.A.P., Matthew saw with narrow-eyed amazement.

He smiled without humour. "Let's have it."

Parker sighed deeply. It was hard not to.

"What kind of a man is he?" Matthew asked quietly after a while.

Simon Parker shook his head. "A man who thinks his money can buy him in and out of every situation. Mostly it works."

"It's not working this time," Matthew said with disgust, and very neatly tore the cheque to shreds. "Take this back to Mr. Stirling and tell him that was a very bad move. Bad. Bad. Bad."

"I have to tell you I knew that the moment I laid eyes on you," Parker said.

"Why don't we go back to the pub?" Matthew suddenly invited, like that particular exchange was well and truly over. "Marcy does a great club sandwich. We could wash it down with a cold beer."

Stuart Stirling's envoy felt both relaxed and relieved. "Sounds great. Nice little town you have here."

Matthew looked down at him from his superior height. "You should come and see my place before you go. Cattle station by the name of Jabiru. I don't know what it's worth exactly these days but it's a hell of a lot more than one hundred thousand dollars."

Of course he said nothing about it to Cassandra when he spoke to her that night. One day he might, but for now he didn't want to add to the stress that all the inevitable changes to her life were creating. And yet, though he tried to put it out of mind, Stuart Stirling's plan to buy him off had inflicted yet another wound. Did Stirling really believe he was nothing more than an opportunist looking for a rich wife, or did he genuinely fear Jock Macalister, friend and business associate for so long, would desert him if Cassandra went through with the marriage. It was so easy to misread situations. Hadn't he done it himself until he came to his senses.

CHAPTER TEN

THE week before the wedding was a lot more eventful than Cassie ever anticipated. One morning when she answered the door of the Maitland hideaway where she was staying, she found Nick Raeburn, looking tired and haggard, staring back at her.

"I got your little letter telling me how you were going to get married," he said without preamble, as though accusing her of some crime.

This shouldn't be happening, Cassie thought. "'How are you' might work better, Nick," she returned a little hardily. She wanted to turn him away but he looked ill. On the other hand Matthew was driving into town to be with her and discuss final arrangements. She just knew he'd turn up before Nick could be persuaded to leave and, as she knew, Matthew had a temper.

"Is it possible you're really going to go through with this?" Nick demanded, far more aggressively than Cassie had ever heard him speak.

"Stop shouting, Nick, and come in." Cassie was satisfied now someone had got to him.

"This will kill your parents." Nick walked behind

her while she headed to the sunroom overlooking the spectacular view.

"I didn't know my parents were your big favourites," she said with some irony.

"Lord, Cassie, why are you doing this?" Nick groaned.

"Would you believe I'm in love." Cassie turned to face him, indicating he should take a chair.

"You can't be, not like *this*." Nick sat down heavily on the sofa, looking utterly dejected.

"I'm sorry, Nick, I really am." Cassie spoke briskly. "We were over long ago."

"We weren't completely over and you know it," Nick protested hoarsely.

"I don't believe this." Cassie fell into the armchair facing him. "Your only excuse is you're not terribly well."

"Fatigue and shock." Nick gave her a disappointed look. "I feel as though I'm walking through glue. I've spoken to Julie. She explained the whole thing."

"That was decent of her," Cassie said dryly.

"I hope you know Julie loves you." Nick held up a hand. "She only wants what's best for you."

"Are you telling me that's *you?*"

"I *used* to be. Once." Nick pulled an unhappy face. "Honestly, Cassie, I can't believe this. It's not real. You of all people to respond to some damned silly advertisement."

"Julie told you that, as well?" Cassie felt somewhat disenchanted with her friend.

"No, not really," Nick said fairly. "It just sort of

slipped out. Who is this guy crazy enough to advertise for a wife?"

"Someone who's serious and doesn't have a lot of time," Cassie tossed off. "Anyway, for whatever reason, I'm in love with him and we're getting married on Saturday."

"Believe me, you're going to regret it." Nick leaned closer.

Cassie put her hands over her ears. "No more, Nick, please. A plane leaves around 2:00 p.m. I think you ought to be on it."

"I'm not going until I get some answers, Cassie," Nick said stubbornly.

"It would be an awful pity if Matthew had to throw you out."

"How could he?" Nick squared his sagging shoulders. "I'm pretty damned tough. Anyway, is he here?" He whirled his head.

"I'm on my own, Nick, except for the caretakers, but Matthew is driving into town right now. If you think you're tough, believe me, he's tougher."

Nick dropped his dark head into his hands. "If anyone had told me only a short time ago you could do a thing like this, I wouldn't have believed them. Your mother and father are tremendously upset."

"You've spoken to them?" Why should it be a surprise?

"Your mother has been a wonderful support," Nick said gratefully.

"I bet." Anger leapt and flared. "Did she advise you to come up here?"

Nick lifted his head to stare at her. "She has every

right to try to protect her daughter. The very first thing she said was, 'Nick, you have to help me.'"

"You know how old I am, Nick?" Cassie asked.

"Of course. You're twenty-four."

"So stop talking to me like I'm under age."

"I'm willing to do anything to stop you, Cassie, if you can't stop yourself. You're infatuated with this guy. Julie tells me he's really something, but hell, you've got nothing in common. What do you know about living in the Outback? You think it's going to be great? It'll be as lonely as hell. What about the cyclones? The floods? You know you've never had to cope with anything like that."

"Think positively, Nick. I'll survive. Besides, I'll have Matthew."

"I see this guy as a sinister figure," Nick cried. "He's taken you over like some damned Svengali." He was so agitated, his hand spearing into his wavy dark hair, it was standing in corkscrews. "I never thought I'd ever say this, but I feel like crying."

"I wish you wouldn't." Cassie crossed to him and put her arm around his shoulder. "I'm very fond of you, Nick. I want us to remain friends."

"You're just saying that to shut me up. Why, you didn't even invite me to the wedding."

"Listen, it didn't seem like a good idea." Cassie gave him another hug.

"He needn't think he's getting a rich bride," Nick said tightly. "I hope you were able to convince him of that. There'll be *nothing* for you. Your mother made that perfectly clear."

"And you agree with parents disinheriting their only child?"

Nick bit into his bottom lip. "If it's the only way to make you change your mind."

"But I'm not changing my mind, Nick." Cassie shook her head. "Not for you. Not for anyone. I love Matthew. You don't know him."

"Neither, it appears, does his own father," Nick retorted bitterly, burned up with jealousy.

"You've learned that, as well?" Cassie sighed.

"Oh, yes. God, Cassie, you're not going to be able to keep it a secret," he groaned. "The whole thing's bizarre. This Matthew could be setting you up. He could have known all along your father and Macalister are business associates. Maybe he's having a crack at the big-time. You could be part of the master plan."

Cassie shook her head. "I'm sorry, Nick. Too many scenarios. Most of them wrong. Matthew despises Jock Macalister."

"Maybe so, but that doesn't stop him recognising a pot of gold."

"You don't know him, Nick," Cassie said in a clear voice. "If you did, you'd know what you're saying is all wrong."

"Don't count on it." Nick turned on her. "I hate the guy. He's not one of us."

"I see that as a bonus," Cassie said a little wearily. "I know my mother got you all fired up to come here, but she was only using you."

"Maybe." Nick's eyes stung at the thought. "But I still love you, Cassie."

"Lord, Nick." Cassie tried to straighten him as he fell

forward and half collapsed against her. "I think you're coming down with something."

"I had a virus in Singapore. High fever, but the hotel doctor fixed me up. I'm all right, I'm over it. I just can't take this in."

"Why don't you lie down? You're not well." Cassie wasn't at all sure how to deal with this.

"Just let me hold you." Nick tried to clutch her.

"Listen, Nick, we can't sit here like this." Cassie was profoundly rattled. "Matthew could walk in."

"Don't mess up your life," Nick implored. He raised his head, his handsome face distorted. "I'm here to get you out of trouble. Take you home."

"Only one problem, she's not going," a hard voice behind them clipped off. "I don't know what in hell you're doing trying to hug my fiancée, but you've got half a second to stop."

Cassie could have wept with relief. "Matthew, I didn't hear you."

"Obviously not." His tone was as dry as ash. "I think you'd better introduce your pal. From where I'm standing you look like an old married couple."

Nick rose a little groggily, gulping at the sight of Matthew Carlyle in person. "I'm Nick Raeburn," he announced with as much self-assurance as he could muster. "I've known Cassie for years and years. I'm her friend and I love her."

"Wait up, here," Matthew grated, moving like a wild-cat into the room. "I can tell by looking at you you're none too bright, Nick. I'm Matthew Carlyle, by the way, Cassandra's hillbilly fiancé. We're to be married on Saturday. It is still Saturday, isn't it, Cass?" He shot her a coldly dazzling glance.

In one springy movement Cassie was on her feet. "Nick doesn't really know what he's saying. He's not well."

"So?"

"I think he should lie down."

"And what am I supposed to do? Carry him up to your bed?" Matthew added with totally false affability.

"Don't be an idiot!" Cassie flared.

"I'm no match for your friend."

"I'll always treasure the lovely times Cassie and I shared together," Nick muttered mournfully.

"I just bet you will," Matthew said in a slow, deadly drawl.

"You're not going to hit him, surely?" Cassie rushed to grab Matthew's arm but he fended her off.

"Go ahead," Nick invited stoically.

"I have never hit a defenceless man, but I could make an exception."

"Why, hello there, Red!" said an entirely different voice. It was Molly, who hadn't seemed to notice anyone else.

"The front door was open so I walked in." Matthew nodded to her.

"Molly, meet a friend of mine, Nick Raeburn," Cassie interrupted quickly. "A lightning visit; he's flying back to Sydney this afternoon."

"Actually I have time to put him on the plane." Matthew consulted his watch.

"Pleased to meet you, Molly," Nick said. "I'm trying to talk Cassie into coming back with me."

Molly gave a snort like a horse. "I don't see how that can be."

Nick reeled on his feet, hoping against hope his faintness would go away.

It was Matthew who caught him, taking his weight, pushing him back onto the sofa and lifting his legs so Nick lay back groaning. "Blessed if I've ever done that before."

"To hell with this!" Matthew exploded. "What's wrong with this guy?"

"I'd better get a doctor," Cassie said worriedly.

"No one can patch me up," Nick proclaimed. "Not now."

"Poor Nick!" Cassie took the wrong path to sympathy, not seeing Matthew's face darken.

"Get on to Doc Sweeney, Molly. Tell him Cassandra's ex-hero is suffering from a virus, exhaustion, whatever. Just get him here," Matthew ordered.

"I haven't had lots to eat," Nick said in a low, heart-tugging voice.

"You sound like a real asset, Nick," Matthew said, a dangerous light in his eyes.

"I've done a lot with my life." Nick looked up at the other man with a faint flicker of challenge.

"That's the go. But if you want to survive, you'll keep your nose out of my affairs. You see, Nick, it's quite simple. Cassandra loves me and I love her. You don't come into it. Understand? You're history."

"You're making a lot of people unhappy," Nick squeezed out.

"That's a shame," Matthew softly jeered. "Maybe if they were big enough they could change that."

* * *

Tom Sweeney finished examining the patient, then looked up at Cassie. "Nothing much wrong with him that good food and rest won't fix."

"Maybe I could stay for a few days, if that's okay?" Nick asked hopefully after the doctor had gone. He was soon jolted out of it as Matthew turned to look at him.

"You can't stay here, Nick, much as you were hoping to."

"Just for tonight perhaps?" The soft-hearted Cassie suggested.

For answer, Matthew took Cassie by the hand and propelled her out of the room.

"You're a lot of woman, Cassie." Matthew held her by the shoulders. "Tender. Compassionate. But having your old boyfriend stay over isn't on."

"But he seems to be heading for some sort of collapse, Matthew," she tried to speak reasonably.

"He's making that pitch, yes, but *I'm* making the decisions here. It's not a good idea."

"Heavens, Matthew, you don't think I *want* him here, do you?"

"You'd never guess when you're in your comforting mood," he answered tautly.

"You can't be jealous?" Her eyes went huge. Matthew was everything to her.

"I'll be damned if I'm going to allow your old flame to sleep over. If you're not going to protect yourself, I will. You're my girl. Hear that and hear it well."

"But this is absurd," Cassie said, looking straight at him. "It's only a kindness."

"Is it?" There were vertical lines between Matthew's black brows.

"And general stupidity on your part," Cassie said, with a little answering huff of anger. "I was just feeling sorry for him."

"It's one helluva step from your point of view to mine." Matthew slid his hands from her shoulders to her waist. "Raeburn goes."

"Okay. Fine. You're the boss."

"And what's he doing here, anyway?" Matthew was shocked by his own jealousy. "Apart from trying to persuade you to go back to Sydney with him?"

Cassie's anger turned to an ache. "It's mainly my mother's fault," she sighed. "She spoke to him. Got him all riled up."

"So who *else* is going to run interference?" Matthew flashed. This was to have been a wonderful day together, not playing nursemaid to Raeburn.

"What do you mean?" Cassie stiffened instantly.

"Ah, forget it." There was self-disgust in his eyes and he tugged her close.

"The hell I will!" She broke away. "You were going to say something, Matthew. Who *else?*"

Off balance, he exploded. "Your father sent one of his legal guns to buy me off."

"No." It caught her like a blow.

Matthew recovered, appalled. "Me and my big mouth," he groaned. "I wasn't going to say anything at all."

"You were going to keep it from me?" She fisted one small hand and punched it into his hard muscular chest.

"I didn't want it to hurt you, Cass." He caught her hand and held it still against him.

"When *was* this?" She felt furious.

"A few days ago. Before you arrived." He reached deep inside him for calm, wanting to kiss, to soothe.

"It's just the sort of move Father would make," she said bitterly. "How much was I worth?"

Matthew was determined she would never know. "I could name my own price."

"Why didn't you take it?" she lashed out in humiliation.

That rocked him to the core. He hauled her back into his arms. "You dare to ask me that?"

The tenderness and passion he had felt turned to steam. His strong arms trapped her so she couldn't move. She shouldn't be thinking of anyone but him. His mouth came down over hers, hard and furious, persuading it into a ragged surrender so her petalled lips opened and he could taste the seductive velvet of her tongue. No one could make him feel like this. His need for her had grown even keener, wilder, since he had so eagerly consummated their love. Capturing her in one long, rapturous night when all the love he felt for her came pouring out like a torrent. Could he ever forget it? Hell, he loved her so much he couldn't think straight. Now, damn it, she had insulted him.

Cassie had already come to realise it with distress. Frantically she tried to make amends, responding with a passion that matched his, running her hands possessively over the taut muscled ridges of his wide back, straining to give him what he needed.

"I didn't mean what I said, Matthew," she gasped between kisses, pulling her head back.

"I can't get enough of you. Hell, I can't even get close to you." He pressed his mouth to her neck.

"Soon." Cassie's voice shook with emotion. "Soon we'll be together again."

Irresistibly, her mind, like Matthew's, raced back to that one fabulous time they had come together in a delirium of passion. A night that still fuelled her dreams and made her desperate for him to claim her again.

"I want it to be Saturday *now!*" Matthew groaned in frustration. "When you're mine forever."

"Our wedding day." Joy welled in her.

"I don't want anyone else loving you," he muttered, putting a hand to her breast. "No one but me."

"There's never been anyone like you, Matthew," she answered him.

"So, Raeburn has to go?"

"God knows, I didn't ask him." Cassie rose to him and kissed his mouth. "Why don't we both take him into town? Marcy can keep an eye on him."

"Why not?" Matthew gave his first laugh of the morning. "Marcy's had a lot of experience taking care of people."

Back in Melbourne at the old Mondale mansion, Eleanor Macalister was sitting in her father's study, a dark-panelled room full of leather-bound, gold-tooled books, waiting for her husband to arrive. Eleanor spent most of her time here now, to be near her grandchildren. She had inherited the very large house from the father she had adored. Now the home was used as a grace and favour residence by their eldest daughter, Tessa, her husband, Graham Downes, a young Liberal MP, and their two children, Amanda and Laura. Beautiful children. But all girls, girls ran in Eleanor's family.

Hardly a matter of concern for loving parents and grandparents, Macalister thought, but there was no male heir for the cattle empire he had built up. He couldn't die before putting that straight. His daughters wouldn't be resentful as long as they got their share of the money. None of them, husbands, either, were born to the land. They wanted the glamorous city life. Only Eleanor would stand firm against him. As she had done from the beginning.

It occurred to him, iron-fisted cattle baron he was purported to be, he was bracing himself for the coming ordeal. Damned if Eleanor couldn't make him feel perpetually in the wrong. She was five years older than he. Thirty-five when he had married her without anyone else asking for her hand despite her father's wealth and social standing. Not that she was plain. Then or now. It was her autocratic manner that put most people off. Not him. He had always been an adventurer. And wonder of wonders, she had fallen in love with him. It wasn't a love match for him, of course. But it suited him well. At the time. He had places to go. Eleanor would help him.

There she was waiting for him in her father's favourite wing-back armchair, beautifully dressed as she was every day of her life, fully made up, a handsome woman with sharp refined features, an immaculate snow-white coiffure and piercing light grey eyes, her thin hands glittering with diamond rings. The immense emerald-cut diamond that had belonged to her mother, the lesser rings, still very valuable, he had given her through the years. His engagement ring at the time, a modest sapphire, had been put aside many long years ago as unworthy to join the collection. Which in fact it was. Seventy-five this year and Eleanor was still as sharp as a tack, her hearing acute, her vision excellent. She enjoyed splendid health. She would see him out.

"Well, Jock, what have you to tell me?" A stern mother to a naughty boy, he thought tiredly. Eleanor didn't beat about the bush. She had her spies. Just like him. She knew how he longed for that son of his. She knew of their meeting in Sydney at the home of Stuart Stirling. She knew all about the bitter quarrel that had caused Stuart Stirling to disinherit his child.

"I think it's time, Ellie, we confronted the fact I have a son," he began sadly, taking a seat opposite her. He was longing for a cigar, the very poison that was killing him, but Eleanor for many years now had never permitted him to smoke in front of her.

"*You* have a son, Jock," Eleanor returned icily, "*we* do not. I will never acknowledge your bastard in any capacity until the day I die. You have a family. Your daughters and your beautiful grandchildren. Isn't that family enough?"

Macalister drew a deep, harsh, rattling breath. "To put it bluntly, my dear, *no*."

Eleanor glared at him. "I know what's on your mind, Jock, but you can't bring disgrace on us all. I won't have it. Not now. You've ignored the boy's existence for the last thirty years. Why this pitiful last stand?"

He actually laughed. "Because I'm dying, Ellie. You know that."

She stared at him, never forgiving him for that terrible

defection, but still loving him in her way. "You've got years left in you yet."

"No one better than you, Ellie, for hiding your head in the sand. You've been a good wife to me." Another wry laugh. "You've always stood by my side, but you came between me and my son."

"How do you know he's your *only* son?" Eleanor demanded, her voice as sharp as a knife. "Are you going to search the countryside for them, too? I know how many women you've had in your bed."

"Ah, Ellie. That mightn't have happened if you hadn't hated it so."

She had the grace to blush. "You know I did everything you wanted in the early days, Jock."

"I know you always found sex awkward," he answered her, almost kindly.

"Well, it *is*." She frowned. "Why you had to get mixed up with a child, that nanny, I'll never know."

"So long ago, but it doesn't seem like that," he said. "I've never forgotten."

"How dare you say such a thing, Jock," Eleanor said through clenched teeth. "It's water under the bridge."

"It's the most shameful thing I've done in my whole life," Macalister answered with enormous regret. "You threatened to ruin me, Ellie. Well, maybe I deserved it. But you can't stop me now. I'm honour bound to make amends before I die."

Eleanor Macalister looked shaken and aghast. She had wielded considerable power in her own right. Now *this!* "The press will pick it up, Jock," she warned. "You realise that. A disgraceful scandal and that Stirling girl involved."

"They've threatened to disinherit her."

"They couldn't do better." Eleanor leaned back in her chair and closed her eyes.

"You're a hard woman, Ellie."

The ice-hard eyes flew open. "Of course you would say that. I have standards, Jock. My whole life has been devoted to you, though I know I was only a ticket to where you wanted to go. But you have daughters. Do you think they will permit you to bring this young man into our midst?"

"Their half brother, Ellie, but he won't want to come. Wild horses wouldn't drag him here. He's proud."

"I know human nature all too well." Eleanor tried to rally but she was in shock. "He's after the money."

Macalister sighed. "You *all* are. It's my intention to leave Monaro Downs to the boy, together with two or three other stations in the chain. He'll need them. But there's not going to be any knock-down, drag-out fight."

Eleanor who never cried was almost in tears. "We'll fight it after you're dead, Jock."

"Fight all you like and stop looking like you'll all be out on the streets. The one who decides to contest the will stands to lose their inheritance." Now he sounded tough and grim.

"You'll never get away with it, Jock," Eleanor warned.

"I think I will." Calmly, with finality, Jock Macalister stood up and walked to the door. "This is one fight, Eleanor, you're not going to win."

Cassie remained absolutely motionless with shock when she saw Sir Jock Macalister approaching her in town.

For a moment she wondered if she was hallucinating. The sun that had been flooding the world so brilliantly seemed to slip behind a cloud. She'd finished her shopping and now she was enjoying a quiet cappuccino at an outside table of the local coffee shop.

"Sir Jock, what a surprise!" It fact it was like a blow.

"Wonderful to see you, Cassandra," he answered courteously, tipping the grey akubra he wore. "May I sit down?"

"Please."

He seemed to be out of breath and even thinner than the last time she had seen him, but still a man of immense presence. Already customers at the other tables were whispering quietly behind their hands. Everyone knew who he was. Sir Jock Macalister, the cattle baron. Maybe he was about to put an end to all the rumours.

"You look enchanting." Macalister gave her a smile that was still dazzling.

"Thank you." It was impossible not to smile back. Besides, it was Matthew's smile even to the heart-breaking quality. "Was it Matthew you wanted to see?"

"Ah, Cassandra, you've read my heart."

This was Matthew's chance to reject him. Cassie found herself shaking with nerves. "You know we're getting married this Saturday?" Nothing must mar the great day.

"I've heard." Macalister nodded. "As far as I can make out, the whole town is jumping for joy."

"It's wonderful." Cassie's smile trembled. "Everyone's treating our wedding as a grand occasion."

"Which it is," Macalister said warmly. "The most

important step of your life." His own marriage mocked him now.

"You know my parents haven't replied to our invitation," Cassie told him, glancing away.

He touched her arm. "That makes no sense."

"My father is a very stubborn man. He has strong notions about what's right and wrong."

"And he thinks it's wrong for you to marry Matthew?" Macalister's voice hardened, but he stopped himself.

"He thinks it will cause a great deal of trouble."

"He surely couldn't think it would offend me?" Macalister frowned.

"What you think is very important to him," Cassie told him quietly.

Macalister considered that with a lurch of the heart. "How ironic! As it happens, Cassandra, I'm absolutely delighted you're to marry my son."

"So you admit it? He *is* your son." Cassie mourned for Matthew, all he had lost. Now it was spoken. Ineradicable. "You've never acknowledged him before."

The ghost of Matthew's mother rose before Macalister's eyes. "To my eternal shame. I can't bear it anymore. I can't bear Matthew's anger and hatred of me."

Cassie couldn't speak for a moment, then she murmured, "I'm sorry. I can see you're very unhappy. But there are such reasons for it, Sir Jock."

Macalister moved the jar of raw sugar slightly but deliberately, as if he were making a chess move. "Of course. No excuses from me. It was a one-time encounter with Matthew's mother, Cassie. She was so sweet, so pretty, so loving, I simply lost my head. The next time I visited the out-station she was gone. Just like that. Disappeared like the wind blew her out of my life. It was a few years before the rumours began to reach my ears."

"You didn't follow them up?"

"Oh, yes." A sick look came into his eyes. "My wife learned about them, as well, and threatened to walk out on me and take the children. She and her family wouldn't tolerate a breath of scandal. But the real trouble was, Ellie knew everything that went on behind the scenes. You understand? The deals. She struck a hard bargain. I deny my son, or she'd ruin me."

"You really believed she would?" Cassie was dismayed.

"I've never been more certain of anything in my life. None of which excuses me. With your help, Cassandra, I have to meet Matthew again. I look on this as my great mission."

"You make it sound as though Matthew's eating out of my hand," Cassie said in a distracted way. She recognised this could cause trouble.

"Isn't he?" Macalister replied simply, thinking at least his son was a lucky man.

"Matthew is his *own* man. He loves me, as I love him, but he makes his own decisions," Cassie declared. "I don't think I could persuade him."

"All I want is a half hour," Macalister was reduced to begging. "Just long enough to beseech him to forgive me."

Surely he deserved that chance. "Sir Jock, I *want* to

help you," Cassie began, "but I can't promise anything. I feel bound not to upset Matthew before our wedding. Matthew feels very strongly about this."

Macalister said nothing at all for a few moments as a hard dry cough racked him. "If you could just intercede, Cassandra," he implored when he had recovered. "It means everything in the world to me." I don't want to face my Maker with this on my conscience, he thought. He had decided not to speak of his failing health let alone the unvarnished fact he had six months at the most. "I need to reconcile with my son, Cassandra. To offer him my deepest remorse."

His appearance and the way he was speaking told Cassie a good deal. She stretched out a sympathetic hand, looking into Macalister's suffering eyes. "Let me speak to him. He's very proud. I'm sure you saw that."

"There's compassion there, too, Cassandra," Macalister insisted. "If it's at all possible I'd like it to be today. If you'll come with me, I'll organise a helicopter flight. That will save the long journey and a lot of time."

Cassie couldn't raise Matthew despite several attempts, so in the end she agreed to their taking the helicopter to Jabiru on the other side of the purple range. She was acutely conscious of Sir Jock's exhaustion. He seemed so tired, as if this was his last chance. She only hoped Matthew would understand. Sir Jock needed her beside him. She was sure of that.

The landscape seen from the air was an eternal green. The miles and miles of cane fields, the great crop of the tropics, then as they crossed the rugged spur of the Great

Dividing Range that ran the entire length of the east coast, the vast savannas, home of the great Queensland cattle stations, the biggest holdings in the world. Macalister himself controlled a chain that stretched from the Channel Country in the far southwest, through Outback Queensland into the Northern Territory. Now they could see the glittering lakes, the great flights of birds that banked sharply over the water. Thousands and thousands of them. An astonishing sight.

"Here we are, Jabiru." The pilot lifted his voice above the noise of the rotor and pointed below.

Cassie's stomach lurched as they dropped altitude.

"I'll try for a landing close to the homestead."

On the ground the heat assailed them and the pilot grabbed Sir Jock's elbow, speaking cheerfully. "Steady as you go, Sir Jock. Let's get you into the shade. Reckon Matthew will have heard the chopper. In fact, if I'm not mistaken, that's a puff of dust."

The puff of dust materialised into a rider on horseback, covering the ground at a full gallop.

Even with sunglasses on, Cassie cupped her hands against the glare, staring at the horseman until his image became clearer.

It was Matthew. No mistaking his topnotch riding style or the set of his lean, wide-shouldered body. He stopped only a few feet away, his beautiful bay mare trembling ever so delicately. Matthew dismounted, his expression so tight nothing was revealed of his feelings.

"Hi there, Matthew." The charter pilot waved, walking down the steps towards him, holding out his hand. "How's it going, mate?"

A few words were exchanged and the pilot moved off to the yellow helicopter a small distance away. He had a call in the region. It had been arranged he would come back for Macalister and Cassie in a little over an hour.

As the pilot lifted off in a flurry of dust, Cassie stepped down from the veranda and out into the sunlight. She ran towards Matthew, holding out her arms.

He caught her. Held her. His quietness more daunting than anger. He wore his normal working gear, blue denim shirt and jeans, red bandanna around his neck, high riding boots, a black akubra pulled down over his eyes.

"Cassie," he said, his voice clipped hard. "What's Macalister doing here?"

He stared over her head to where Sir Jock was standing in the shade of the veranda, a portrait of dignity.

"I tried to reach you several times," Cassie said with a quick, frustrated shake of her head.

"I've been out since dawn," he told her, raising his chin in a high mettled gesture. "He approached you. Of course he did."

Cassie laid a placating hand against his chest, feeling the strong pump of his heart. "Matthew, he's a sick man. I'm sure of it."

"And how does that piece of information justify his presence here?" His eyes were stormy.

"He wants a chance to speak to you." She appealed

to him for understanding. "Won't you allow him the opportunity?"

Matthew shook his head. "I really don't think so. If my mother had lived, maybe. Not now. Why is he bothering us? Can't he leave us in peace?"

"He has no peace himself, Matthew, don't you see?"

Matthew's handsome mouth compressed. "He's never spoken a word to me in my entire life, now he's here wanting some sort of forgiveness?" He gave an angry, baffled laugh.

Cassie's breath came on a long sigh. "I want you to give it to him for me. It's a big ask, Matthew, but I think he's been punished enough."

His gaze softened. "You know what? You're compassionate to a fault."

Cassie swallowed on tears. "It's *you* I want to see at peace, Matthew."

He studied her lovely upturned face, torn between his love for her and the tremendous hostility he felt towards his father. There were tears in her beautiful eyes that bothered him. Cassie won. He looked towards the tall man standing on the veranda. There was a slump to the fine head and shoulders, as though a once powerful persona had lost his great vigour.

"Only for you, Cassandra," Matthew said quietly, "only for you. I really love you."

Her lips curved with the most beautiful smile. "Oh, thank you, my darling Matthew." Cassie felt a wonderful calm. "Let's put an end to all the long years of bitterness and pain. Reach out to him. I fear the life force is slipping away from him."

Matthew didn't really understand it but he felt a sudden tightness in his chest, an odd pity. He raised his hand, acknowledging the man who was his father.

CHAPTER ELEVEN

IT WAS one of those glorious blue and gold days just made for a wedding, the world flooded with sunshine and soft breezes that spread the perfume of the beautiful heady tropical flowers and lifted the heart. Cassie woke early after the most wonderful of dreams. All she could think of was by the end of the day she would be Matthew's wife.

Matthew's wife! It filled her with such joy and excitement. She didn't feel in the least nervous, rather her sense of anticipation was like a bright light inside her, causing her whole body to glow.

Her dress, made by a Sydney designer, was a ravishing sheaf of delicate white silk lace, the long skirt forming a slight train. The sleeves were long, too, to show off the exquisite beauty of the lace, the gossamer confection worn over a slender white silk slip. She and Julie, when they had shopped for it, had thought it perfection and wonderfully appropriate for her rainforest wedding.

Her hair she was wearing full and loose, long strands woven with tiny orchids, a delicate headdress of seed pearls and crystals worn like some medieval fantasy diadem down on her forehead with her hair streaming around it. Her bridesmaids, Julie and Louise, were to wear delicate, summery, silk gorgette dresses, Julie in a misty green, Louise in a soft gold. All three would carry a simple spray of lilies and orchids.

Matthew's two attendants, best man and groomsman, she had only just met. Cattlemen like Matthew, one the son of a Northern Territory pastoralist, the other managed a large Central Queensland property.

Matthew, Cassie knew, was wearing a cream linen suit with a Nehru-style jacket, as were his attendants, the difference being different coloured shirts with the same stand-up collars. With eyes like Matthew's, his had to be sapphire blue. Matthew had arranged that they would spend their wedding night in a suite at the very beautiful Port Douglas Marina Mirage, leaving the next day by helicopter for one of the most magical places in the Great Barrier Reef, the secluded Angel Island, a guarantee of romantic bliss.

Cassie felt like she was drowning in pleasure. She hadn't heard from her parents. She simply had to accept it. Just as she was planning to get up, the bedside phone rang.

"I have to see you," a vibrant voice murmured into her ear.

"You can't wait for this afternoon?" She lay back against the pillows.

"It has to be *now,* my darling bride," Matthew said. "Not at the house. I want you to come down to the beach."

"You'll have to give me five minutes," Cassie said. "I'm still in bed."

"You'll have me right beside you tomorrow."

"You don't know how good that sounds."

She was out and running in just under ten, willow

slender in a tight pair of jeans and a mulberry camisole top. Matthew was waiting for her at the base of the long winding stairs to the beach, looking so vital, so handsome. God, so beautiful, she threw out her arms to him in an ecstasy of love.

"My beautiful Cassandra, my delight and pride." He caught her to him, whirling her about in a circle as though her weight was no more to him than a child's.

The pleasure was so heady, so sweet. She went to speak, but he slid his arms around her and bent his head, kissing her with such heart-rocking desire Cassie felt humbled. At last, at long last, someone to love her as she loved him. Someone with whom she could realise her dream.

"Matthew!" Dreamy-eyed, she stared up at him. "The gods have smiled on us."

"I know exactly how you feel."

He smiled and reached into his breast pocket for a small package wrapped in tissue paper. "I'd love it, Cassandra, if you could wear these today," he said in a low intense voice that throbbed with emotion.

"Here, let me see?"

"They belonged to my mother," Matthew explained. "The only things she had of value. I'd like you to wear them in memory of her. It seemed to me they would suit beautifully."

Cassie touched the long pendant earrings with a reverent finger. "Oh, Matthew. They're lovely." Her eyes filled with tears at the association.

"My mother would have loved you to wear them, too, Cassandra." Matthew battled his own deep feelings. "Do you want to try them on?"

Cassie blinked to free her long lashes of teardrops. "Of course. They'll be perfect with my dress."

"And I can't wait to see you as my bride." Matthew watched as she swept her hair back from her face, screwing the earrings to her small earlobes. She wasn't wearing makeup, not even lipstick, and she looked as beautiful as a magnolia. There was no other word for her. That perfect matt creamy skin, the very soft mouth he loved to kiss, a natural velvety rose. The earrings were "family," his mother had told him. He had only seen her wear them on special occasions. Now they were swinging from Cassandra's ears, a delicately worked combination of silver, corals and pearls.

"They're Victorian, mid-Victorian, I think," Cassie said with interest and pleasure. "How do they look?" She tossed up her head for his inspection.

He was shaken by his love for her. The force of it leaping out of his eyes. "Perfect."

All at once she was back in his arms, mouth on mouth, both of them murmuring passionate endearments between kisses. Temple. Cheekbone. Chin. Oh, the mouth!

"My goodness, you two," a laughing voice called down from the overhead terrace, causing them to at last break apart. "Can't you stop kissing?"

"This woman is mine!" Matthew shouted exultantly, locking Cassie in his arms.

"You've got a great way of showing it, Red." Julie felt their deep emotion as if she could catch it on the breeze. "Come on up. Molly is making breakfast. The wedding day has started."

On the edge of the rainforest, a beautiful bright and sunny place, myriads of butterflies greeted them, flitting around and between the bridal party like a fairy tale. Even the breeze blew showers of confetti from the great billows of lantana interwoven with bougainvillea that grew along the rainforest borders, attracting these flying kaleidoscopes of colour.

Permission had been given for them to enter the rainforest, everyone moving delicately along a track carpeted with fallen leaves. The procession was led by a young girl barely into her teens but already a fine musician, playing the flute for them. Flowers garlanded her head and she wore a floating ankle-length dress of cream organdie. It was like having a head full of the most wonderful singing birds, Cassie thought.

Eventually they reached the spot she and Matthew had chosen. A small clearing before a magnificent rainforest giant with buttresses soaring some fifteen feet high, creating deep, woody caverns. Luxuriant masses of intertwining vegetation ringed them round, heavy evergreen crowns of the forest trees formed an interlocking canopy a hundred and fifty feet and more over their heads.

On the forest floor it was like a mysterious luminous jade-green twilight as quiet and calm as a cathedral. There was barely any breeze but it was beautifully cool, the air redolent of mosses, ferns and herbs, the magnificent cycads, the staghorns, the elkhorns and the orchids that grew from large clumps high up in the trees, sending down cascades of richly scented flowers in colours of cream, gold, deepest pink, coral and deep mauve. The air was like incense as befitting Nature's great cathedral.

The celebrant, a woman dressed in silver brocade, waited until everyone was assembled. Then the marriage service began, the celebrant's expression serious but entranced as were they all by the beauty and power of this most ancient place.

Cassandra's headdress, delicate as a silvery spider's web, sparkled in the green light as did her lovely pendant earrings and the white-gold bracelet set with two pave diamond hearts that encircled her wrist. Matthew's gift to her. She turned to him, so heartbreakingly handsome, a loving smile curving that beautifully shaped sensuous mouth. Softly she made her responses, her voice flowing like music. The wonder of it! It was flawless. She would remember every moment down to the tiniest detail. Once she put her hand briefly to her throat as emotion threatened to overwhelm her, but in truth she had never been happier.

Matthew, for his part, wanted to shout his love for his Cassandra to the treetops, hearing it echo through the forest, scattering the brilliantly coloured birds that were feeding on the starbursts of flowers across the canopy. It seemed to him life had been aimless until now.

The marriage ritual over, Matthew bent his head to his bride for their ceremonial kiss, sweeping her slender lace-covered body to him, both of them drowning in the magic of the moment. Now they had joined forces to face the world. Mr. and Mrs. Matthew Carlyle.

But the deepening forest had one final surprise for them. As bride and groom turned to face their guests, the great canopy appeared to split open, allowing a momentary single ray of light to enter this wonderful, mystical, luxuriant terrain. It seemed to enfold Matthew and his bride like some marvellous beneficent force before vanishing like a bright puff of smoke.

"Maybe it was your guardian angel," Ned whispered to Cassie later. "Whatever it was, it was most extraordinary."

The street barbecue was already in progress by the time they were all driven back to the reception. Seemingly everyone in the town, including tiny babies, cheered the wedding party as they arrived, offering their best wishes. It wasn't the grand, sophisticated affair Cassie knew her parents would have given for her had she married a suitable man of their choice, but it was so wonderfully friendly and heart-warming.

Marcy and her team had made the al fresco dining area as romantic and celebratory as possible, flowers everywhere, a combination of cream, white, and dark green foliage, luxurious big cream silk bows tied to the chairs dressed with cream slip covers. The tables were covered with sugar-pink linen cloths over full-length cream, with matching napkins, the tables topped by posies of white orchids interspersed with feathery green twigs of baby's breath and tiny white roses. The bride looked like an illustration from a fairy story, her attendants like moonbeams.

As Matthew and Cassie walked into the reception room, delighted and grateful to Marcy for all her hard work, their eyes were instantly drawn to three people who stood before the long bridal table draped in cream linen and tulle. All looked resplendent in their wedding finery, Sir Jock Macalister, grey-suited with a white flower in his buttonhole, beside him delivered by his private jet, Cassie's mother and father, their expressions for once, anxious and a little torn.

"Matthew!" Cassie whispered, her hand tightening

within her husband's clasp. No matter what, these were her parents. She wanted them here.

"Go to them, darling," Matthew urged, his own happiness opening his heart. "It's what's called absolution."

Weddings are times of high emotion, of hope and reconciliation. This was no exception.

Many hours later while the wedding celebration continued into the night, Cassie and Matthew arrived by limousine at the luxurious Port Douglas resort. They were shown immediately to their suite, the sitting room scented with the incomparable perfume of two dozen velvety red roses. Champagne in a silver ice bucket waited, two crystal flutes beside it.

"Twelve o'clock, the witching hour!" Cassie began to twirl in pure pleasure, stopping to look out on a night made radiant by a huge silver moon. "Time for bed," she cried, causing Matthew to burst into a rapturous laugh.

"I'll turn back the covers, shall I? I can toast my little mail-order bride between the sheets."

"You can toast her *after!*" she called.

In the dressing room she quickly removed her chic little going away suit, then, in her lace bra and briefs, creamed off her makeup before the mirrored wall in the spacious bathroom. This was it! Their Shangri-la.

Everything had gone so splendidly but now they were alone. They had earned it. Under the shower she let the perfumed foaming bubbles slide all over her satiny-smooth skin, her excitement intense. She felt alight with desire. Her body dry from a big fluffy white towel, she rubbed her favourite body lotion over her breasts and limbs, imagining Matthew's caressing hands. Next her nightgown that had cost almost as much as an evening dress. The softest, tenderest, pale peach, thin as a veil, with tiny empire sleeves, the ruched front secured by tiny pearl fastenings. She reached for a brush and dropped it in her excitement then let her hair crackle and stream over her shoulders. The way Matthew liked it.

Matthew!

In the bedroom with its huge king-sized bed, she found him. His pintucked blue shirt was undone to the waist, and her bones seemed to melt.

Matthew turned and saw his bride with the light from the dressing room behind her. It streamed through the exquisite nightgown he had heard so much about, clearly illuminating the beautiful naked body beneath. At least he got to see her in it before it would fall in a pool at their feet.

Slowly, tantalisingly, he walked toward her, his eyes gone darkest blue. "I'm going to make love to every little inch of you," he warned in a voice so thrilling it made her heart hammer. "Every bone, every bend, every curve, every crevice. Right down to the last little atom."

Cassie trembled, ravished by anticipation, her body arching in delight as Matthew began to undo the tiny pearl buttons...one by one....

* * * * *

HUSBAND BY INHERITANCE

Cara Colter

PROLOGUE

"I'M SURE it won't be much longer, Miss Blakely."

"Thank you," Abby murmured.

She looked around the lawyer's office uncomfortably. The furnishings were so rich—the coffee table in front of her dark walnut, the sofas soft, toffee-colored leather, the burgundy rugs deep and velvety, the lights muted.

Abby had never been in a lawyer's office before, and if a plane ticket hadn't been sent to her, she doubted she would be in one now.

Who would give a gift to her?

But that was what the registered letter had said. That she had been named as the recipient of a substantial gift, the donor anonymous. Her phone call to the law firm had gotten her no more information, just an invitation to be in the office of Hamilton, Sweet and Hamilton, in Miracle Harbor, Oregon, today, on February 15, at 10:00 a.m. precisely.

"Miss Blakely, are you sure you won't have coffee?"

The receptionist smiled kindly at her, and Abby knew she was doing a terrible job of hiding her discomfort. She knew she did not look like the kind of woman who belonged in these rich surroundings. Her wardrobe these days ran to things that washed easily. Clothes that she could wear in the sandbox or the playground, clothes that stood up to small handprints and grass stains and drool. And so she was wearing a casual skirt of stain-disguising navy blue, a matching tunic and a sweater jacket. She had made the ensemble herself for less than fifty dollars.

She caught her reflection in the highly polished wood of the coffee table, and patted her short blond hair self-consciously. Even the cut was about low maintenance rather than style.

She had been away from her just-turned-two daughter for less than twenty-four hours, and she felt as if a hole inside her heart was opening and getting wider by the minute. It was now almost ten-thirty.

"Is there a problem?" Abby asked. She looked wistfully at the door, sorry she'd been tempted to come here, sorry she'd accepted this odd invitation, knowing somehow her life was about to take an unexpected turn. Why now, when what she wanted most was a life without unexpected turns? A life of stability for her baby, Belle.

But that is why she had come here, too. Yes she was skeptical, but some small part of her hoped the gift would be something that would enable her to give her daughter exactly the life she wanted for her. A little house of their own, instead of the apartment. A nicer neighborhood, closer to a park. A new sewing machine so Abby could take in more work.

Counting her chickens before they hatched, she reprimanded herself. Still, she had been sent a plane ticket worth several hundred dollars. She had been picked up in Portland by a limo and deposited at Miracle Harbor's most luxurious hotel. And the letter had promised the "gift" was substantial.

Hope was what had made her cross the continent, from Illinois to this small hamlet in Oregon. Miracle Harbor. The town, built in a half moon on the hills surrounding a bay, was a place of postcard prettiness—neat rows of beautiful old shingle-sided houses behind white picket fences, rhododendrons growing wild, the air delightfully warm and scented of the sea.

"Is there a problem?" she asked, again.

"No, of course not. We're just waiting for the arrival of the other parties."

"The other parties?" Abby asked, baffled. This was the first she had heard of other parties.

The receptionist suddenly was the one who looked uncomfortable, as if she had revealed more than was professionally acceptable.

So when the door swung open, both she and Abby looked to it with relief.

A woman stepped into the office, in dark glasses and a short fur jacket. A long skirt, shimmering jade-colored silk, swirled around her slender legs as she moved with a breezy self-confidence into the room. Her hair was beautifully coiffed, and yet a hint of something wild remained in the way it swung, electric, around her shoulders.

There was something so familiar about her, Abby thought, frowning, and then realized the woman must be almost exactly her own size and height. Even her hair color was familiar, tones of wheat mixed with honey.

"Hi. I'm Brittany Patterson. I—"

As she caught sight of Abby out of the corner of her eye, her voice froze. She swung around and stared. Her mouth opened, then closed, then opened again. Slowly, she lifted the sunglasses off her eyes, and Abby felt the blood drain from her face, thought for an awful moment that she was going to faint.

Because the face she was looking at was the very same face she looked at in the mirror each day.

The makeup was bolder, the eyebrows more carefully shaped, this woman lovelier somehow, and yet identical to her in every way.

The door swung open again, and Abby turned to it in relief, needing a distraction from the intensity of emotion, the confusion welling up within her.

Another woman entered the office, breathless, as different from the woman in the fur jacket as night from day. She was in jeans and a jean jacket, both faded nearly white, her long hair swept back off her face in a careless ponytail.

Different from the other woman, except in one way.

Her face was identical. And so was her shade of hair. And the striking hazel of eyes nearly blue, except for a star of brown around the pupil.

As if in a dream, Abby got up from the deep sofa. Moved toward the other women, and then began to shake. She sat back down. Silently, the other women came and sat down, too, looking at each other with an astonishment deeper than words.

The receptionist was bringing them all coffee now. Abby might have laughed to see each of the other women get their coffee ready just as she did—a tiny splash of cream, three sugars, and then a soft blow on the hot liquid—except that it was too bizarre to be funny.

"Well," said the one in the fur, finally breaking the

stunned silence, "unless we're on *Candid Camera,* I'd guess we're related."

"More like *The Twilight Zone,*" the one in the jean jacket said, and then all three of them laughed. The two young women's voices, though they had different regional accents, were identical in tone and pitch. Abby recognized her own voice when they spoke.

And then they were all talking at once.

"Did you have any idea? I knew I was adopted but—" Abby's voice was shaking.

"I knew I was adopted," the one in the fur coat said, "but I didn't know I had sisters."

"I was never adopted," the jean-clad woman said, her voice hesitant. "I lived with my Aunt Ella until I was ten. She said my parents—our parents?—were killed in a car crash."

"It's clear we are more than sisters. We must be triplets," the one in the fur coat announced, and they stared at each other, thrilled and shocked and astonished. "I'm Brittany."

"Abigail. Abby." She could hear the catch of emotion in her voice.

"Corrine. Corrie."

The receptionist interrupted. "Mr. Hamilton will see you now."

They followed her down the hall into an office, glancing at each other with speculative delight, with wonder.

Mr. Hamilton was a dignified man, his manner and dress authoritative. Silver hair and deep wrinkles around his eyes made him look as if he should be retired. He looked genuinely amazed as the three identical young women entered his office and took seats across from him.

"I'm sorry," he said. "Pardon me for staring. I—I didn't know. You all had different last names. I had no idea—"

He looked down at the papers in front of him, struggling for composure. When he looked up he studied them each in turn.

"Triplets," he finally concluded. "Had you ever met each other?"

When they shook their heads, he looked very grave. "I'm sorry. I would have never popped this kind of surprise on you without warning you. I can't imagine what she was—" His voice faded, and then he cleared his throat. "As you know from the letter you received, I have asked you here because my client wishes to bestow a gift on each of you."

"Who is your client?" Brittany asked, and Abby noted she seemed far more comfortable in the rich surroundings than either of her sisters.

"I'm not at liberty to say. I have been given a letter to read to you." He took a paper off his desk, held the letter way back and squinted at it.

"Dear Abigail, Brittany and Corrine," he read in a rich baritone, "Many years ago, I made a promise to your mother. She died within minutes of extracting that promise from me. To my shame, it was a promise I was unable to keep. I have reunited you with your sisters in the hope this gesture will begin to make the amends I owe your mother and each of you. I have also given you each a gift that I hope will turn out to be the very thing you most need in your lives. My attorney, Mr. Jordan Hamilton, will outline the nature of each gift, and the conditions I have attached to it. My wish is for your every happiness."

"What was the promise she made to our mother?" Abby asked, hungry to know any detail that would help her come to grips with this overwhelming set of circumstances.

"I'm afraid, aside from the gifts, and the attached conditions, I don't know any more than what is in the letter," Mr. Hamilton said.

"Conditions?" Brittany asked skeptically. "You might as well get to that first."

"All right. In order for you to receive your gifts, permanently, you must remain here in Miracle Harbor for a period of one year." He cleared his throat uncomfortably. "And you must marry within that year."

Abby stared at him. So, it was a joke after all. It had to be. But he looked perfectly serious.

She shot a look at her sisters.

Brittany looked indignant, Corrine was looking out the window, her thoughts masked. Except for some reason, Abby knew exactly what she was feeling. Corrie was scared to death.

"The gifts?" Brittany said, narrowing her eyes at him, and folding her arms across her chest. "And this had better be good."

He gave her a stern look, rattled his papers, then, beginning with Abby, he told them about the most astonishing gifts....

CHAPTER ONE

AFTER ALL THESE years, he still slept as though there was a possibility of someone sneaking in the room and putting a gun to his ear.

Even in Miracle Harbor, Oregon, where such things were unheard of.

He lay awake, now, listening, every muscle tense, ready, wondering what small noise had startled him awake in the deepest part of the night. The green glow of his clock told him it was just after 3:00 a.m.

The foghorn, he decided, not the creak of his front gate, badly in need of oiling. He allowed himself to relax slightly, and then slightly more, closing his eyes and willing himself to go back to sleep. He hated this time of night the most because he was unable to exercise his customary discipline over his mind. For some reason this was when the memories wanted to visit.

The sound came again.

The quiet crunch of someone's muffled footsteps moving up the walk. He listened for and heard the scrape of the loose board on the second step up to the porch.

It was when he heard the soft groan of his front door

handle being tried that he moved, fast and quiet, out of the his bed and to the window.

An old car, hitched to a U-Haul trailer, was parked out on the street. Thieves? Planning to clean him right out?

They'd be disappointed. He had no interest in "stuff." His apartment was Spartan. No TV, no stereo, just his computer.

Had he once had an interest in "stuff"? He had trouble remembering small things like that. Though he had a flash now of his wife, Stacey, standing in front of something in a store, looking back at him, laughing at the outrageous price, but there had been something wistful in her eyes, too.

He flinched as if he'd been struck when he remembered what they had been looking at that day.

A bassinet.

A blackness that did not bode well for his intruder, descended over him. Wearing only the boxers he slept in, he made his way down the steps and through the darkened house, the of movement—stealthy, cautious, icily calm—second nature to him.

He slid out the back door, not opening it enough to let it squeak, his plan already formed. He'd use the walkway alongside the house and follow it to the front. The prowler would be trapped on the narrow porch. He'd have to go through him to get away.

Fat chance of that.

This intruder had picked the wrong house.

Home of Shane McCall, agent, Drug Investigation Unit. Retired.

The mist was thick and swirling, the cement of the sidewalk ice-cold under his bare feet, the rhododendrons so thick along the side path that his bare skin was brushing the rough shingles of his house on one side, and getting soaked by the rubbery leaves on the other. These details barely registered, he was so intensely focused. He came around the side of the house, stopped in the shadow of the fog and dense overgrown shrubs, and watched.

He saw a shape bent over the door; the night too dark and the fog too thick for more than vague impressions. A baseball cap. A build too slight to be threatening to him.

A kid, he thought, and felt his anger wane as he watched the intruder jiggle the door handle again. Was he trying to pick the lock? Shane should have just called the police. Maybe Morgan was working tonight. When the business was done they could have exchanged war stories.

Vastly preferable to going back up those stairs to bed when he'd finished here, to the memories that were waiting for him.

Knowing that calling the police was still an option, and knowing he wouldn't take it, he moved quietly out of the shadows to the bottom of his steps.

It occurred to him that maybe he should have taken his service revolver out of retirement, that someone without the physical size to handle a confrontation might attempt to even out his odds with a weapon. A knife, a handgun. That was probably especially true of the kind of kid who would break into a house at three in the morning.

His mind working with that rapid, detached lightning swiftness that came naturally to him, Shane decided on a course of action—keep his distance, make it seem like he was packing a gun himself.

Hard to do, considering he was standing out here in his undershorts. But not impossible.

He went to the bottom of the stairs, and with the cold authority that came so easily to him, he said, "Put your hands up where I can see them. Don't turn around."

The figure bolted upright and then froze.

"You heard me. Hands up."

"I can't." Fear had made the voice high and girlish.

"You can't?" he said, his voice cool and hard. "You'd better."

"I might drop the baby."

The voice was so scared that it was quivering. *The baby?*

Shane went up the steps two at a time, put his hand on intruder's shoulder and spun him around.

Her.

Two hers, a full-grown her, and a baby her, both looking at him with the same saucer-huge blue eyes. Blue eyes tinged with a hint of brown.

He dropped his hand from her shoulder, ran it through the dampness of his hair, and swore.

When her foot connected with his shin, he was reminded, painfully that he had forgotten rule one: never let your guard down *ever.*

"Fire," she screamed. "Fire."

Without thinking he clamped his hand over her mouth before she managed to roust the whole neighborhood, something he was not exactly dressed for.

She was beautiful. Blond hair, very short and straight, poking out from under a Cubs ball cap and framing a face of utter loveliness—perfect skin, high cheekbones, a shapely nose. Her eyes were her dominating feature, though. Huge, the color partly a sea blue he had only seen once, a long time ago, off the coast of Kailua-Kona, in Hawaii, and partly brown. The combination was nothing short of astounding.

Those eyes were sparkling with unshed tears.

He swore again. She was shaking now, and the baby looked anxiously at her mother, screwed up her face and began to howl.

The noise seemed to reverberate in the fog, and he glanced uneasily at the neighbor's houses again.

"Promise you won't scream," he said. "Or yell fire." Fire. All right. She was beautiful, but obviously deranged.

She nodded.

He moved his hand fractionally, and she backed away from him until she could back away no more, her shoulder blades right up against his front door, her eyes wide, her arms folded protectively around the baby. It wasn't a small baby. In fact, she was quite sturdy looking, possibly two.

"Stay away from us, you pervert."

"Pervert?" he sputtered. "Pervert?"

"Hiding in the bushes in your undershorts waiting for a defenseless woman to come home. That's called a pervert."

"Home?" He stared at her. Her voice was shaking but her eyes were flashing. She probably weighed less than him by at least eighty pounds. And he knew she was going to take him on if he came one step closer.

She nodded, licked her lips nervously. Her eyes darted by him, looking for an escape.

He folded his arms over his chest. "This happens to be *my* home. I thought *you* were a prowler."

Her mouth fell open, and then her eyes narrowed with suspicion.

He could *see* what she was thinking: that perverts were damnably clever. But he could also see the confusion in her face, her eyes searching for and finding the black iron house number over the wall-mounted porch light.

He was not sure he'd ever been quite so insulted. A pervert? Him? And she didn't seem really deranged. Just exhausted. He could see dark crescents bruising the skin under those beautiful eyes.

She studied him a moment longer, and then he could see some finely held tension ease slightly.

"Oh, God," she said. "I've made a mistake. I'm very tired. I—"

To his horror, little tears were slipping down her cheeks now, too. She wasn't wearing any mascara, which he liked for some foolishly irrational reason. Her shoulders were shaking under a jacket that looked too thin to offer any kind of protection from the penetrating chill of the night.

The baby's howls intensified when she saw the tears dribbling down her mother's cheeks.

Striving for dignity, the woman pulled back her shoulders, lifted her chin. The gestures wrenched oddly at a heart that he would have sworn, only moments ago, had been cast in pure iron.

"Could you just direct me to a motel?"

"I could, but you won't have any luck." This did not seem to surprise her. "Why fire?"

"Pardon?"

"You yelled fire," he reminded her. "Are perverts scared of it? Like holding a cross up to a vampire?"

She laughed nervously. "I read once that nobody listens when a woman calls for help. But they will if someone calls fire."

She wasn't from around here, he decided. Not even close. Survival tactics of a big city woman. Her voice was intriguing. It wasn't sweet, like her face. It had a little raspy edge to it.

"Why aren't there any motels? There were 'No Vacancy' signs on every motel for the last fifty miles it seemed." She wiped impatiently at her eyes with the back of her sleeve, and then wiped the baby's face, and kissed her on the nose.

A magical effect. The baby, an exact replica of her mother, except with blonder hair that was, wildly curly and unruly, ceased howling. The girl turned her head enough to look solemnly at him out of the corner of one eye, but apparently the glance failed to reassure, and she began to cry again, louder than before.

"There's a major resort going up on the edge of town. We have contractors, carpenters, plumbers...you name it they're here."

He doubted there was a room to be had anywhere this night.

Unless you counted his empty house. Three bedrooms. One up, two down. The place had been a duplex until a few months ago when, with his landlord's permission, he had turned the upstairs kitchen into a workroom.

Don't, he told himself.

But he did, feeling slightly put out that he'd frightened

her so badly, but even more put out that the baby was going to wake up the whole bloody neighborhood.

"Look, maybe you better come in for a minute."

He reached past her for the door. Which was locked. The baby's crying was affecting him so badly, he considered a well-placed kick to the old wood, but contained himself.

"No," she said, firmly, her suspicion leaping back in her eyes. "I'm leaving. It's all right. Really. I'm tired. I drove too long. I must have the wrong address."

She went to move by him and then stopped, the porch opening onto the stairs too small for her to squeeze by without touching him. It was when he saw the delicate blush rising in her cheeks that he remembered he was in a state of undress.

"Wait right here," he said sternly, using his no-nonsense cop voice, a man to be taken seriously, even in his underwear. Boxers, thank God. The plaid kind that could be mistaken for a pair of gym shorts in a thick fog. Maybe.

She was scared still, it was written all over her face.

Scared that if he was not a pervert that had been hiding in the bushes, she had accidentally knocked on the door of Miracle Harbor's only axe-murderer.

"I'm a cop," he said reluctantly, "Retired." He knew she'd see it. The stance, the look in his eyes, the cut of his hair.

Her eyes wide on his face, she nodded, then as soon as he stepped back, she flew by him, and scurried down the walk. He let her go, listening to the snap of the locks on her car doors when she was safely inside it.

Then he listened to the unhealthy grind as she turned the ignition.

Not his problem, he thought, at all. Thank God.

He went back down the sidewalk, and in his back door. He ordered himself up the steps and into bed. He made it up the steps, but his mind, never disciplined at this time of night, listened for the sound of the car pulling away. Nothing.

He opened his window, took a look out, and heard again the grind of the starter.

"Hell," he said, and picked up a pair of jeans off the end of his bed. "Double hell."

Despite a shin that should have told him otherwise, the woman had a vulnerable quality in her eyes. He wanted to leave her to her fate, and couldn't. She wasn't dressed warmly enough to be sitting out there in a freezing car, and the child probably wasn't, either.

Minutes later, snapping up his jeans, he turned on the porch light and flung open the front door.

She could come in if she wanted to.

But she didn't.

Stubborn. That was written all over her face. Beautiful, yes, but stubborn, too. He snuck a glance out the door.

The wind lifted the fog enough for him to see her. She had her forehead resting against the steering wheel. She was probably crying. But she wasn't going to ask for his help. Not him. The pervert.

Sighing, he pulled a jacket over his naked chest. He'd taken an oath, years ago, to protect and serve. And retired or not, that oath was as much a part of his makeup as anything else. It ran through his blood, and he found himself almost relieved at the discovery that his personal tragedy had not stolen that part of his nature from him.

He was not capable of leaving her out there in the cold.

She didn't see him coming, and started when he tapped on her window. There, he'd managed to scare her again, which should warn him to give up any notion of a new career in the damsel-in-distress department.

She opened her window a crack. "Yes?"

"Do you want me to call somebody for you? Have you got road service?" Old habits died hard. Her license plates said Illinois. There was a parking sticker on her windshield for a lot in Chicago. He'd been right when he guessed this woman was a long way from home.

"I'll be fine," she said proudly. "In Chicago this is picnic weather."

"Yeah," he said. She was shivering. "I can see that. Is that baby as cold as you are?"

She gave the child a distressed look, and turned back to him. "Are you really a police officer?"

"I was, yes."

"Have you got a badge?"

"Not anymore."

"Why aren't you a policeman anymore?"

His aggravation grew. It occurred to him it was the most he'd felt of anything for a long, long time. He actually felt alive. Aggravated, but alive.

"Lady," he said, "are you going to make me beg you to come in?"

She seemed to mull that over, then with a resigned sigh, she undid the lock and reached for the baby. She followed him up the walk.

He held open the door for them. The baby was nestled

into her mother's chest now, sucking her thumb. When she glanced at him, she scrunched up her face again, and opened her mouth so wide he could see her tonsils.

The baby was wearing a knitted sweater with a little pink hood and pom-poms.

A memory niggled, so strong, so hard, he nearly shut the door.

Their baby was going to be a girl. The amniocentesis had told them that. Stacey had begun to buy pink things. Little dresses. Booties.

"Are you all right?" the woman asked him.

No. He wasn't. Two years, and he still wasn't. He had accepted it now. That he was never going to be all right. That time would not heal it.

But he lied to her. "Sure. Fine. Come in."

She stepped hesitantly over the threshold. The baby craned her neck and looked around.

"I'm Abby Blakely," she said, and freeing a hand, extended it. She was small, but in the full light, she looked older than she had outside. Mid to late twenties. Not the teenager the Cubs cap had suggested. Her figure was delectable—slender, but soft in all the right places.

He took her hand, noting for a hand so small, it was very strong. "Shane McCall."

"And you really were a policeman?"

"Why do you find that so hard to believe?"

"It's not the policeman part I find hard to believe. It's the retired part."

"Oh."

"You don't look very old."

The mirror played that trick on him, too. He looked in it and saw a man who looked so much younger than he felt.

"Thirty," he said.

"Surely you're a little too young to be retired, Mr. McCall?"

"Shane. Uh. Well. Semi, I guess. I'm a consultant on police training, now. Look, do you want to come in and sit down?"

Her eyes found his ring finger, and he saw her register the band of soft, solid gold that winked there. "Are we going to wake your wife?"

"No. I'm a widower."

"I'm sorry." After a moment, "You seem young for that, too."

"Tell God." He heard the bitter note in his voice, and would have done anything to erase it. "Look, are you coming in or not?"

She hesitated, looked like she was going to cry again, wiped at her face with her sleeve. "I don't know what I want to do. I'm so tired." She brightened. "I know, I'll call one of my sisters."

He liked the way she said *sister,* somehow putting so much love into the word that he knew her sister wouldn't mind her calling at this time of the night. But why hadn't she thought of that before?

She thrust the baby at him and bent to undo her shoes. It seemed to him he'd been in a better position when she didn't trust him. He wasn't good with babies.

He held the chubby body awkwardly, at arm's length. "Uh, just leave your shoes on."

"On these floors. Are you crazy?"

He looked at the floors, not sure he'd ever noticed them before. Wood. In need of something. Tender loving care.

The baby was regarding him with a suspicious scowl.

Like mother, like daughter. "Me, Belle," she finally announced warily.

"Great. Hi." He still held her out, way far away from him.

She wiggled and he could feel the lively energy, the strength in her.

Abby straightened, and he went to hand the baby back. "Could you just hold her for a minute? Just until I use the phone?"

It would seem churlish to refuse. "The phone's through here," he said, leading the way, past the closed door that went into the empty main floor suite, and down the hall to the kitchen. The baby waggled away on the end of his held-out-straight-in-front-of-him arms.

"She won't bite you."

"Oh." He made no move to change his position. Belle wiggled uncomfortably.

"Does she smell?" Abby asked.

"Belle no smell," the baby yelled indignantly.

"Uh," he managed to unbend his arms a little, draw the baby into him. Sniffed. She did smell. Of heaven. Something closed around his heart, a fist of pain.

And whatever emotion it was, it telegraphed itself straight to the baby, because she stared at him round-eyed, then touched his cheek with soft fingers, took the collar of his jacket in a surprisingly strong grip, and pulled herself into him.

"That's otay," she told him, nestling her blond curls under his chin and her cheek against his collarbone, and beginning to slurp untidily on her thumb. Drool fell down the vee of the jacket he hadn't taken off for fear of reoffending Ms. Blakely's sensibilities with the view of his naked chest.

"The phone's right there."

His intruder gave his kitchen, which was as Spartan as his bedroom, a cursory glance, went to the phone and picked it up. He could hear her calling information. How come she didn't have her sisters' phone numbers?

When she hung up she looked discouraged again.

"They're not here yet. My sisters."

"Here yet?"

"We're all moving here. It's a long story." She looked exhausted and broken.

"All? Like how many dozen are you talking?"

She laughed a little. "Just three. I'm one of triplets."

Three of her. That was kind of a scary thought for a reason he didn't want to contemplate. The baby was sleeping against his chest, snoring gently. He registered the warmth of her tiny body, the light shining in her curls, and braced himself, waiting for some new and unspeakable pain to hit him.

"I'll call a road service for you," he said, tight control in his voice, "But I wouldn't count on anything happening right away. This isn't Chicago."

She looked at him, startled.

"License plates," he said. "Parking sticker on the left-hand side of your windshield."

"You really are a cop."

"Not now," he corrected her.

Still leaving him with the baby she began to fish through a bag nearly as big as she was. She came out finally, triumphant, with a piece of wrinkled paper.

She handed it to him.

He awkwardly shifted "Me-Belle" to the crook of his arm and took the piece of paper. He stared at it. Blinked rapidly. Looked again. His own address was written there in a firm, feminine hand.

"There's some mistake," he finally said.

"Why?"

"This house is number twenty-two, Harbor Way."

She looked deflated. "I must have written it down wrong."

"You must have."

She slumped down on a chair, took off her ball cap, ran a hand through her straight hair. It was sticking up in the cutest way. "Now what? I have to go. Obviously."

That was obvious all right. Her hair was tangled and damp, and her face was pale with weariness. And still, all he could think, was that she was damnably sexy. She was wearing jeans that were way too big for her, accentuating the fact she was as slender as a young willow. She couldn't stay here. Obviously.

"Look, for what's left of tonight, you can stay here," he heard himself saying. "The house actually used to be two self-contained units. It also used to be a summer rental. It's all furnished. There's linens in the closets. I've never even used the bedrooms down here. They're across the hall."

"You're a complete stranger!"

"I admit it. Stranger than some."

She managed a small, tired smile.

"There's a lock on the door. Not that I'm in the habit of attacking people. In my underwear."

He could tell that clinched it. The lock. Not his reassurances. The lock and the fact that she was tired beyond words and probably close to collapse.

"Thank you," she said softly.

"Whatever. In the morning, I'll help you get your car straightened away, and find your house."

"Shane?"

"Yeah?" He wished she wouldn't have called him his first name. He didn't want to be her friend. He didn't even want to be her rescuer. He just didn't have any choice.

"You're making me very sorry I kicked you so hard."

From behind the locked door, Abby listened to Shane go up the stairs, and wondered if she'd lost her mind. Not only had she packed every earthly possession that she cared about and trekked across a whole country with her baby, now she was under the same roof as a man she knew nothing about.

Well, not nothing exactly.

He had been a cop.

And she had never in her life seen eyes like that. It wasn't the color, precisely, though the dark choco-latey brown was enormously attractive; it was the look in them. Intense, the gaze steady and strong and stripping.

It was those eyes that had kept panic from completely engulfing her when he had come up behind her as she tried to make her key fit in the front door. *His* front door.

While part of her had been screaming in pure panic—*near-naked man lurking in the bushes at three in the morning*—another part of her had registered those eyes and told her that the hard beating of her heart might not have a single thing to do with fear.

Naturally, she wasn't going to listen to that part of

herself. She was resigned to the fact that she was not a good judge of masculine character. Belle's father being a case in point. Still, even when she'd been desperately trying to think of how to get by that formidable man who had trapped her there on that tiny porch, some traitorous little part of her had been staring at him in awe.

Registering every detail of him. His height, the width of his shoulders, the smooth unblemished skin, the clinging night mist showing off his impressive physique as surely as if he was a bodybuilder, oiled.

Because he had been tense, geared for action, he had seemed to be all enticing masculine hardness. Mounded pecs, the six-pack stomach, the ripple of sinew and muscle in his arms and legs.

She shouldn't have been so surprised when he'd said he used to be a cop, because he had policeman hair—the cut short, neat and very conservative and the color of cherry wood. And there had been a certain authoritative hardness in his face, too. A look of readiness in the taut downturn of his mouth, the narrow squint of his eyes. He was a man who was prepared to do battle.

It was probably that strength, a core-deep thing, that had convinced her to take a chance and trust him. Her instincts told her that of all the places she could choose to stay tonight, admittedly limited, she would not find one safer than this.

Her adopted mother would, of course, be horrified. Poor Judy wanted life to be so neat and tidy. She had worked so hard to give Abby a decent home, even though she herself had been a single mother.

Judy had thought it was insane to go to the lawyer's office, even more insane to accept the gift. What would she think of this latest twist?

The situation tonight, Abby reminded herself, had been desperate. What else was she going to do? Sleep in her car? If it was just herself, that might have been okay. But with Belle? It was a terrible night out there, damp and cold. Even her mother would understand why she had chosen to stay here. Wouldn't she?

Abby went unseeingly through the plainly furnished apartment, found the first bedroom, lay her sleeping daughter in the center of the big double bed, and went to pull the drape. As she did, she realized she was facing the street. Miracle Harbor didn't look at all like it had looked when she'd been here a month ago. It had looked so beautiful then, with its quaint, weathered houses lining steep, narrow avenues that all led to the ocean. The main street had redbrick shops, with colorful awnings, big picture windows looking out on the beach and the ocean they fronted.

Tonight, with the swirling mist, it looked more like a scene out of a horror movie, set in the fog-shrouded streets of Gothic London.

How could she have written down the address of the house she had inherited incorrectly? How could she?

And how could a town that had looked so cheery and welcoming in the light of day look so distinctly formidable at night?

And how could her traitorous car just give up like that? Of course, it was old, and she had asked a lot of it, carrying her across the country dragging all her earthly possessions along behind it. Maybe it was a miracle that it had made it this far before it had quietly quit.

Miracles, she thought, and turned from the window. She checked the corners and under the bed for spiders or webs, and finding none, tumbled into the bed beside her daughter, too tired to find the bedding. Miracles, she thought again with a sigh. Isn't that why she had come here, really?

Some part of her wanted to believe, more than anything else, that this old world could still work a miracle or two.

She thought of the conditions of her inheritance, the inheritance that would allow her to give her daughter everything she wanted for her. A home, a safe place to grow up.

If you didn't count perverts in the bushes. She giggled tiredly at the thought.

Of course, there were those conditions. One to live here in Miracle Harbor for at least a year. No problem. But two?

Preposterous. How could someone get married just for personal gain? What kind of marriage would that be? And given her history with Ty, Belle's dad, she simply knew she couldn't trust herself in the all important department of mate selection.

So, why had she come, uprooted her whole life, knowing she had no intention of fulfilling that second condition?

During her brief visit with her sisters, she had learned they had been separated at about age three. She had no memory of them, but Corrine said she had foggy memories of something. And Brit's adoptive parents had told her she was three when she came to them.

Abby had come because she wanted to know her sisters better, *had* to know them, had felt as soon as she had seen them, a deep sense of having found herself.

And maybe, in some small, lost part of herself, she really wanted to believe in fairy-tale endings, wanted to believe in a place with a name like Miracle Harbor, maybe she could expect anything to happen.

Maybe it had already started, with her at the wrong house, and the car not starting, all things linked together, part of a larger plan.

For her.

And what about him? How would he fit into that plan?

He wouldn't. He'd done the decent thing tonight, she suspected because his training would allow him to do nothing else.

By tomorrow, he would be part of her history, somebody she could nod to when she passed him on the street.

There had been mile-high barriers in that man's cool eyes, and she felt no desire to try and penetrate that mystery.

But even if she did decide to try and fulfill that ridiculous condition placed on her gift, she would never pick a man like him. She wanted someone sweet and kind. Someone who would make a good father for her daughter.

A little pudgy fellow with glasses, who took lunch in a paper bag to his office.

Upstairs, she heard the groan of a bedspring, and felt the oddest little stir in her stomach. A stir that a little pudgy fellow with glasses would never be able to create.

Which was just as well. That stir, she knew, led to nothing but trouble.

CHAPTER TWO

A STREAK OF sunshine had crept through a crack in the drape, and lay in a stripe across her face, making her blink lazily awake. Abby stretched luxuriously, looked around the room. Even in the full light of day there was not a spiderweb in sight.

The furnishings were plain, in keeping with what Shane McCall had said about the house being a summer rental, but the room itself was lovely. High, plastered ceilings, wood floors, wide oak window casings.

Would the house that had been given to her as a gift by a complete stranger be as beautiful?

She thought of last night, and Shane McCall, and she felt, again, that funny little shiver of pure awareness.

"Abby," she told herself. "You are now rested. You are immune to that man. You know the truth about another pretty face. Isn't that right, darlin'?"

She reached out to pull her daughter to her, reached further, patted the mattress, and as the awful truth sank in, she sat bolt upright in bed. Only a little dent remained where her daughter had slept snugly beside her last night.

"Belle," she called, leaping from bed, "where are you?" She fumbled for buttons on her homemade blouse that had sprung undone during the night, trying to keep the panic out of her voice. This place wasn't child-proofed like her modest apartment in Chicago. "Belle?"

She raced into the next room. A chair had been pulled up to the door, the kind that had the twist style of lock on the handle. The door was now open into the hallway that led to the outer door and the kitchen they had been in last night.

Did the door to the outside have the same kind of lock? Abby tried to think from last night. She was sure the lock she had tried to fit her key into was a deadbolt. Even her precocious daughter would have trouble with that.

But, as she scrambled into the hallway, her heart sank. The front storm door wasn't locked. It wasn't even closed, a brisk, sea-scented breeze coming in through the screen.

"Belle!"

"In here."

Only it wasn't Belle who answered. It was him, his voice loaded with irritation.

She catapulted into the kitchen, and skidded to a halt.

Immune, she reminded herself.

But really that rush of relief that her daughter was here and not happily exploring the streets of Miracle Harbor, getting closer and closer to the ocean, seemed to have lowered her defense system again.

She was suddenly not sure she had registered his full impact last night. Just looking at him made her feel hot and flustered, like a woman who had a sign flashing on her forehead that said: I Need A Husband. Desperately.

He was a man who didn't seem to like much clothing. This morning he had on navy blue running shorts that showed off tanned, muscular legs, and a flat, hard fanny. A grey sweatshirt with some sort of police emblem on it stretched tight over the broadness of his chest, sleeves cut off at the shoulder so that every inch of his powerful arms were on display.

Could a woman look at that and not wonder what it would be like to be held by him? Only if she wasn't human!

He had a white towel strung around his neck and his hair was dark with sweat, curling at the tips even though it was so short.

His facial features, she decided, were nauseatingly perfect. High cheekbones, straight, strong nose, faintly jutting chin. He hadn't shaved yet today, and for some reason that only made him look better, faintly roguish, untamable.

She knew all about this kind of man. They could have anything, and they took it. And when they were done they threw it back.

Only one thing stopped her from hating him completely—the look of muted panic that was in those amazing dark eyes as he surveyed her daughter.

"What does this kid eat? We're about out of options, here." He snapped this at her, like a military man on a mission that was about to fail.

Abby dragged her gaze away from him. Belle was settled happily on top of a stack of books on a chair, at a kitchen table covered with cereal boxes and bowls.

"You mean she's sampling everything?" Abby asked, aghast.

Her daughter took a regal bite of the offering in front of her, which looked like chocolate covered raisins in milk, swallowed, frowned and pointed autocratically at her next choice.

Which he, heartthrob of the universe, rushed to get for her.

"What are you doing?" Abby said, folding her arms across her chest. As if that would protect her. *From what?*

Her desire to laugh that's what, she told herself firmly. At the sight of one hundred and ninety pounds of one hundred percent menacing, masculine ex-cop being commanded by a baby.

"I'm feeding the kid." He glowered at Abby.

"Why?"

"When I came in from my run, she was just coming out the door of your suite. I tried to stuff her back in, but she wasn't having any of it. She announced she was hungry, and she damn well expected me to do something about it."

"In those words?" Abby couldn't resist teasing him.

"She doesn't need words! All she needs to do is screw up her face and show me her tonsils! When I told her to go back to Mommy, she yelled at me. Loudly."

"Belle!"

"Not a bad girl," Belle said, anticipating what was coming. "Belle bad?" she asked Shane and blinked at him with sweet coyness.

"Yes!" he said, but when Belle blinked again, he said,

"Maybe not bad. Just stubborn, strong-willed, loud and fussy."

"She is not fussy," Abby addressed the only accusation that was not totally accurate. "She's taking advantage of you."

"A two-year-old?" He paused in his pouring of yet another sample into a bowl and drew himself to his full height, which was formidable, at least six feet, and gave Abby a disdainful look. "That seems unlikely."

"Really, you didn't have to feed her. You could have come and got me up."

"I thought of that." He added milk to the bowl, paused thoughtfully, and then added a sprinkle of brown sugar.

"And?" she asked, watching as he pondered for another moment, then dropped another dish of sugar on the cereal.

"You looked done in last night. I thought maybe you needed to sleep. Also, given that I promised you a secure room, I didn't think you'd appreciate waking up with a strange man hovering over you."

The very thought made her mouth go dry, actually. Did he have to be so devastatingly attractive?

Suddenly an uncomfortable reminder of what she must look like shot through her. Her hand flew to her hair. She could feel it standing straight up, and not in those cute little spikes she could accomplish with a tub of gel and a lot of patience. She glanced down at the rumpled clothes she had slept in. The buttons were done up crookedly on her blouse.

Naturally, he looked like he was ready for a photoshoot, even with the shadowed face, and sweat forming dark stains on his sweatshirt.

"One black shin is enough," he told her, with a side-long look from under sooty, tangled lashes.

Abby looked at the leg she had kicked last night. It was sporting a rather large purple and blue bruise. Somehow, she doubted a kick would have been the first thought that would have come to her mind if Shane McCall had been the first thing she saw this morning.

"I hope that doesn't hurt too much." She thought she sounded very stiff, a woman transparently anxious to let a man know she could not be swayed by him, no matter how devastatingly attractive he was.

"To an old warrior?" he growled, then sighed. "Yeah, you bet it hurts."

"Mommy kiss better," Belle suggested wisely.

"Okay by me. What's Mommy have to say?" He said it casually, a man who knew the lines, but there was no emotion attached to the words, not even friendly teasing.

She kept her own features carefully bland. "Mommy's kisses are reserved for Belle. Only."

"That makes me feel real sorry for Belle's daddy," he said.

"A man less in need of your pity, you will never meet," she shot back, and then was sorry for all that she had revealed about herself with that one line. "Belle and I are on our own."

Still something about being in the same room with this scantily clothed man, and that word *kiss* hanging in the air between them, made the most bizarre thought crowd into her head.

I'm looking for a husband.

Her sister, Brittany, had said she was going to place an ad in the newspaper with similar wording after the three sisters had heard about the conditions placed on their gifts. And then Brittany had laughed with devil-may-care ease when Jordan Hamilton had treated her to a look of formidable disapproval.

But Abby wasn't Brittany. Not even if they did look identical.

"I think we've intruded quite enough," she said, the stiffness still in her voice. "We can be on our way now." *Before I make a complete fool of myself, not for the first time.*

Really, she had thrown herself at Ty, Belle's father, bowled over by his good looks and his easy charm, thinking they meant something. No man had ever made such a fuss over her before.

Besides, Ty's attentions had meant something. He wanted something. And as soon as he'd gotten it, the chase was over. Still, pregnant and afraid of being alone, she had stayed with him longer than any woman with an ounce of self-respect should have. He claimed, right up until the end, to love her madly, but still no offer of marriage had been forthcoming.

"I'll have a look at your car," Shane said.

Anybody, she reminded herself, could be charming. Anybody could seem like someone he was not.

"No," she said, watching as he stood there, carefully monitoring Belle's reaction to his latest offering. "That's unnecessary."

Brit would not approve. After all, hadn't she sent Abby that ridiculous book, *How to Find the Perfect Mate?* Abby had vowed not to read it, but found herself reading it anyway, with a kind of horrified fascination.

Had Brit sent one to Corrine as well? Corrine seemed a little clumsy in the man department, just like Abby.

Or maybe clumsy wasn't the right word. Corrine was more—aloof wasn't quite the right word. Reserved?

More like scared, Abby thought, wondering if only a sister would see behind the barriers in Corrine's eyes. Even a sister who had never known her. Well, who could blame her if she was scared? They were being asked, the three of them, to leave everything they had ever known and start over. With only each other.

It still shocked Abby that somebody who looked exactly like her could act like Brit.

Outgoing, bubbly, confident. Brit moved and talked and acted as if she believed she was incredibly beautiful.

And how could Abby look at her sister and see how beautiful she really was, and then look in the mirror and not see it at all in herself? Maybe, she should try her hair like Brit's—grow it out, let those curls go wild. A little more makeup, a little more style—but for what?

To attract that perfect man? she asked herself scornfully.

Abby bet Brit had sent Corrine a copy of that dreadful book, too. The book which had a whole chapter devoted to man-trapping grooming and dressing techniques.

And said absolutely nothing about what to do with wild, sticking-straight-up hair, and a morning-after look that was notably missing the night before. What use was a book that didn't deal with emergency situations?

Unless she just hadn't gotten to that chapter yet.

Abby, she reminded herself, *you hate that book and everything it stands for.*

Her mission was not to attract this man in front of her, even if he was just about as close to a perfect male specimen as she could probably hope to find in this lifetime, but to get away from him, leave him to his own life, and to find her own.

She could afford a mechanic, she reminded herself. Her meager savings were soon to be supplemented, because she had been given a house like this one, divided into two suites.

And her upstairs suite was inhabited by a reliable tenant. He'd been on the premises for nearly a year, and showed no signs of leaving, according to information she had from the management company.

With the income from him, and if she could pick up a bit of sewing, she and Belle would be just fine. Rich, by her standards.

Rich enough to have someone else come look at her car.

"I'll just call a service station," she said. "We've put you out enough."

"That now," Belle crowed, having rejected what was in the bowl in front of her.

"To be honest," he said, in a stage whisper "I think I'd rather look after the car than her."

"You don't have to do, either. I'll take her out for breakfast. We don't need to trouble you any—"

"Nooo," Belle wailed. "Me like here."

"I guess, you would, you little minx. Don't you dare push that away! You love Sugar Pups!"

"Don't," Belle said mutinously.

And while Abby tried to do the impossible, reason with someone who had not yet fully developed reasoning skills, Shane picked her keys up from where she had left them on the table the night before and went out the door, whistling, one of those aggravating men who took control of everything.

Her feminist heart was appalled of course.

But her human one admitted wanting nothing more than to be looked after every now and then.

He felt, as he went down the walk, as though he had been hit over the head with a sack of bricks.

First, twenty pounds of tiny female wrapping him around her little pink finger with complete ease, and then her mother coming in to finish the job.

How on earth could a woman look that good first thing in the morning?

Her hair going every which way, her blouse with the buttons done up crooked, her jeans all rumpled and so ridiculously large they were ready to fall off.

And she looked like a damned beauty queen.

Like with a flick of her finger, she could have had him pouring cereal for her, too.

He recognized this feeling as one he did not like and would not tolerate.

Shane McCall would not be vulnerable. Isn't that why he was here? In a little town where he didn't know a soul, and planned to keep it that way?

Correction: didn't know any girl souls.

He'd known Morgan for years, from when they had worked together on a temporary assignment on a drug smuggling case in Portland. Morgan had moved back here, to his hometown of Miracle Harbor, to get married and have babies. Morgan had invited him to come for dinner one night. Meet his wife, his kids.

The wife he might have been able to handle, but kids?

He couldn't be around kids.

He didn't want to *feel* things. Guys talked about

basketball scores and work. Kids related on a different level entirely. And women, well, he wasn't even going to go there.

An old pal on the Drug Unit, Drew Duarte worried about him, had pulled him back from a life of complete loneliness and despair by begging him to help out with training. So he did specialized training sessions a few times a year, which is why he ran and lifted weights. He wasn't letting any young buck ten years his junior run him into the ground. Now, Drew had him taking it a step further. He was working on a chapter on drug detection procedures for a Federal enforcement agency training manual.

Maybe a life where the thing a man was most grateful for was the spelling checker on his computer had gotten a little too controlled, even for him.

Had he wished for something else, even for a moment? Yearned?

No!

Maybe moving to a place called Miracle Harbor was asking for trouble. Which, he told himself, with annoyance, was not a rational thought at all.

It was the thought of a man whose calm and orderly life had been disrupted.

He'd moved here because he had to get away from where he was. Leave it behind him. Morgan had sent a sympathy card when he'd heard, and there had been a note tucked inside, saying if Shane needed a place to get away for a while, his family had a cottage on the ocean.

He'd come, planning to stay a week, and somehow never left.

He'd moved from Morgan's drafty cottage after his

first winter, and rented both suites of this old Dutch Colonial house, ideally located a block from downtown and the ocean. It was too big for a single guy, but he didn't want any of the neighborly intimacy of sharing a house. Rentals in Miracle Harbor were nearly impossible to come by at anytime, and the situation had worsened with the resort project going up on the outside of town. The house was ancient and somewhat like a cranky old lady, constantly demanding. The furnace was finicky, the windows didn't open, the lights flickered, and he seemed to look forward to each catastrophe with the relish of a person who didn't have enough in his life to care about. The house suited him perfectly.

So, he'd fix the little problem that had come into his neat and tidy life with the same calm determination that he fixed the problems that came up with the old house. In no time, he would be rid of the disrupting pair of little-her, and big-her. Really, he was killing two birds with one stone—doing the Boy Scout thing, something he was reluctantly aware of missing now that he no longer had active duty, and getting rid of them at the same time.

"Win-win, I would say," he muttered to himself.

He opened her car door and slid in, reaching down to pop the hood. There was a book peeking out of a pocket of a travel bag that sat on the front seat. It felt like the title was blinking on and off like a neon sign.

He actually felt the sweat pop out on his brow as he read it.

How to Find the Perfect Mate.

Well, hadn't he known that was what she was looking for from the first moment she had turned those huge, vulnerable eyes on him?

This woman needed a man.

And it sure as hell wasn't going to be him.

It gave him added incentive to get the car going, which he did in very short order.

Whistling, wiping grease from his hands, he went back into his house.

She was on the phone. The baby was playing on the floor with his plastic bowls, but other than that, the kitchen was immaculate. All the cereal had been put away and the bowls were washed and stored. The baby made a beeline for him, grinning from ear to ear.

Was it that easy to make friends with a baby? *Beware the warm feeling in your chest, Shane McCall.* He sidled away from Belle, who lunged after him, undeterred.

He was on this third loop around the kitchen table when Abby hung up the phone and gave him a worried look. "The law office doesn't seem to be open on Saturday. I tried Jordan Hamilton, the lawyer looking after our case, at home, but there was no answer."

"One of his sons practices with him. Mitch." Mitch Hamilton was a friend of Morgan's. "I'll call him." But when he looked for the number in the book, it wasn't there. He called Morgan.

The baby Belle was hugging his knee. He shook his leg slightly. She held on a little tighter. He could hear a kid laughing in the background on Morgan's end. The one holding on to his leg was making little squawking noises, too.

"I bought the kids a dog," his friend told him after Shane greeted him and asked him for Mitch's number.

"I can tell from the noise level that was a big hit."

"It was stupid thing to do," Morgan confided in a low tone. " I've been cleaning up dog poop for six days."

Shane listened to the kids laughing in the background and felt that swell of feeling inside himself. He wasn't quite sure what it was, some form of grief for joys he would not know, but he pushed it back, and reached down and pried the chubby fingers off his knee. Her mother got the hint and came and took her. "That number?"

Mitch Hamilton answered on the second ring, listened to the problem. Shane heard only blessed silence in the background. No little kids running around that house.

"Dad's away on business this weekend," Mitch told him. "I'll run into the office. I was going in anyway."

Good man, Shane thought, going to the office on Saturday, not cleaning up dog poop in a house filled to the rafters with laughter.

"Thanks."

"I'll double-check the address of her house, and call you back. What did she think the address was again? Twenty-two Harbor? And which triplet is she?"

"Abby."

"Does she have long hair?"

What did that have to do with anything? "Nope."

"Okay." Did he sound relieved? "I'll call you within the hour."

Fifteen minutes would have been better, but Shane knew he was in no position to complain.

"It's going to take him about an hour," he said. He noticed her buttons were done up straight now, and her hair had been sternly flattened. He'd liked it better wild. "Have you eaten yet?"

"No."

The kid was back on the floor, tottering around, her

arms straight out from her shoulders like airplane wings. She was laughing at nothing, not even a puppy, that sweet laughter filling up his house, a house that had been blissfully empty until now. Blissfully.

"Help yourself to breakfast," he said curtly. "I've got a ton of cereal. And a ton of work to do. I'll just head up to my office until we hear from Mitch."

"Sure. Thanks. Fine."

"And one other thing, Abby?"

"Yes?"

I'm not the perfect mate. Not even close. But somehow he couldn't bring himself to say it. "The coffeemaker is over there, if you feel like some. Just make yourself at home."

As soon as he said those words he felt an odd shiver go up and down his spine.

He went upstairs, listening to her talk to Belle, then hit the shower. When he came out, the smell of coffee had drifted up the stairs. He *wanted* the coffee, but he *needed* to avoid fraternizing with the invading army. He forced himself to sit down at his computer and turn it on. In the next hour, he wrote two lines, neither of which made much sense when he read them over.

When the phone finally rang, he picked it up with all the desperation of a drowning man reaching for a life preserver.

Only the life preserver turned out to be something else entirely.

Once he hung up the phone he went back down the stairs, stood in the kitchen doorway watching them. Big-her was sitting on the kitchen floor blowing soap bubbles for little-her.

"Was that the lawyer?" she asked over her shoulder.

He nodded, dumbly, like a man who had stood too close to a bomb going off and was still reeling from the shock.

She got up off the floor and wiped slippery hands on her jeans. "Did he find my house?"

"That's the good news." He could smell fresh coffee and avoiding the question in her eyes, he walked over and took some, keeping his back carefully to her.

"Oh-oh. That means there's bad news. Doesn't it?"

He glanced over his shoulder, saw anxiety knit her brow, and swiftly returned to stirring his coffee. Why would he want to wipe that anxious look off her face? As it turned out, he was the one with the problem, the one with things to be anxious about.

His idea that she was leaving soon, nice-meeting-you-have-a-nice-life leaving, had just been blasted to smithereens by that lawyer.

Who had assured him, no mistake. He'd double-checked it.

Out of the corner of his eye, Shane watched his silence make her shoulders slump, so he turned and faced her, took a long sip of his coffee and cleared his throat.

"Just tell me," she said, bravely, jamming her hands into her blue jean pockets. "I should have known. It's probably falling down, right? A wreck. I won't be able to live in it."

"That's not exactly the problem, no."

"The tenant is awful?" she guessed. "He's a filthy old man. He's living in *my* house with three goats and sixteen tomcats, isn't he?"

"No."

"Tell me," she implored. "Please."

"Miss Blakely, it would seem *this* is your house."

CHAPTER THREE

"THIS is *my* house?" Abby said.

"Yeah," Shane said. He didn't miss the way she was looking around with a brand-new kind of interest, seeing the potential for a picture here and a splash of paint there, planning where she was going to put her rocking chair.

There was even a word for the look in her eyes.

Nesting. He knew, because he'd been through it all before. Stacey, when they had bought that falling-down house, had had those stars in her eyes, seeing a castle instead of a catastrophe. Shane was pretty sure he could not survive *that* again.

Of course, he wasn't married to this woman. And she wasn't going to die. Hopefully. Hopefully, she was going to accept, with good grace, that there had been a terrible mix-up, and that *her* house was already inhabited by a most reliable tenant.

Who, according to her lawyer, did not have a legal leg to stand on once his lease expired, in two months.

He looked at her face. And didn't feel very hopeful.

"It's so beautiful," she breathed. "Look at the floors."

Shane glared at her. "They need to be refinished.

Your baby will be getting slivers from them. The furnace doesn't work properly. The doors and windows don't open or shut the way they should. Drafts. Drafts are very bad for babies."

In his own ears, he sounded like exactly what he was—a desperate man.

"Somehow you don't strike me as any kind of expert on babies," she said, not at all concerned, running her hands lightly and lovingly over the stained oak window casing and sill.

"I could refinish this."

For an insane moment he thought he would like to tell her that he had almost become an expert on babies, once, a long time ago. There was something in her eyes that said she would know what to do with that information, would know exactly what to do.

That this renegade thought would slip so easily past the carefully constructed wall of his control, shocked him, though shock was not the exact word that described how he felt. He ordered his mind not to replace shocked with the truth: scared.

"The whole electrical system probably needs to be replaced!" he said, instead. "Not to mention the outside stairs. For starters."

"Have you noticed many spiders?" she asked him.

"Spiders?"

"Yes."

"I can't say I've noticed any spiders."

"Oh, well, then, everything else sounds like small problems," she said airily, dismissing them with a wave of her hand.

That was a woman for you. Major structural problems dismissed. But a spider, that was something else. He suspected if he'd told her the place was overrun with spiders, she'd be gone in a blink. But he didn't have that kind of dishonesty in him. He hoped to get rid of her fair and square.

"You seem to be forgetting one quite large problem," he said, his voice stern and unyielding in an effort to claim her undivided attention and to convince himself his control was not slipping.

"I'm going to paper the front hallway with a pattern that has yellow teacup roses in it," she said dreamily. "And get a handwoven Finnish throw rug for the front door. And I'll make red-checked curtains for this window in here. What do you think of red checks?"

"We were discussing the problem," he reminded her. He thought red checks would be awful, give the kitchen the ambience of an Italian restaurant.

"Oh, sorry, what problem is that?"

"Me." He folded his arms across his chest. As an ex-cop he knew all about practicing *presence,* making himself seem bigger and more intimidating than he was. And at just a hair over six feet he was already plenty big and somewhat intimidating.

She didn't seem the least bit concerned. She was looking thoughtfully at the moldings, even got down on her haunches and ran her fingertips along one. She smiled. "Real oak."

"Me?" he reminded her.

She stood up, regarded him thoughtfully, then smiled. The light in her eyes was damned near blinding.

"It looks like you're an excellent tenant. I think we could work things out."

"Really?" he said uneasily. Somehow he did not think her solution was going to involve simply dropping by once a month to pick up her rent check like a good little landlady.

"Why couldn't we share the place?" she asked. "That would save you having to find a new place to live, and it would save me from having to find a new tenant."

"Aren't you just little Miss Reasonable?" he said.

"I think I'm being very reasonable."

Really, he thought, there was nothing unreasonable about her suggestion, except that it put him under the same roof as her. And little-her. Which was completely unacceptable.

"Shane," she said, her voice soft, her eyes huge on his face, "I don't have anywhere else to go."

She wasn't going to pull that woman-in-trouble stuff on him. She'd already worked that once, and look where it had gotten him.

"Last night," he reminded her coldly, "You didn't even want to come in. Now you want to live here?"

"Now I know it's mine," she said.

"Women's logic has always failed me," he said. He'd known her less than one full day, and already his life was in tatters. Disrupted. His familiar routines threatened.

"Do you have anywhere else to go?" she asked him.

He opened his mouth. He wanted to say he had dozens of places he could go. Dozens. But instead, the truth slipped out. "No." He hastily added, "But I could buy a place."

He didn't tell her the part of that equation that made it unworkable. Buying a house involved a little thing called commitment, a word he had carefully and totally eradicated from his vocabulary.

"But I've already invested quite a bit in this one," he stubbornly said, instead.

"I know we can work this out."

Shane didn't want to work anything *out*. The only context in which he wanted the word out used was toward her—as in out of his hair, out of his house.

Except that it was her house.

He noticed she took over his coffeepot, refilling the mug he had already nearly drained.

"The countertops need a little work," she said.

"The house needs a little work," he said, "and I use the term 'little' loosely. Ten carpenters employed full time for a month—and good luck finding even one in this town for the next year or two—couldn't make a dent in all the things wrong with this place."

"I could trade you. Reduced rent for doing some of the work." She helped herself to a coffee and went and sat down at the table, looking around with plans in her eyes. A countertop here, a cupboard door there.

His life being mapped out for him.

Why hadn't the lawyer come over? He was probably an expert at dealing with these kinds of complicated situations that arose with such frequency when men and women tried to share lives. But most of them had *agreed* to share their lives.

Shane pulled out a chair, and sat down uneasily across from her. He had no sooner taken a sip of his coffee, when he felt a familiar little hand on his knee. Belle, having abandoned the plastic bowls, pulled herself up and stared expectantly at him. He stared back.

"Up?" she asked.

"No." She looked cute as could be. Her mother had dressed her in little red overalls, and had tamed the unruly blond curls into a funny little ponytail at the top of the baby's head. But the thing was if you gave an inch to any member of the female species, the next thing you knew—

"Pwease?"

—your heart was broken. It was not the thought he had intended to have. At all. He stared hard at little Belle, glanced at Abby, and then gave in with ill grace. How the hell did you say no to a baby? He reached down and put the little girl on his lap. Oblivious to his mood, apparently not anymore intimidated by *presence* than her mother, she sighed happily, rested her head against his chest, put her thumb in his mouth.

Still, despite their immunity to his *presence,* the cop in him kicked in. Find out the whole story, and then the solution might be more obvious.

"So," he said, "How did you come to be in possession of this house?"

The whole story was that she was an orphan who had only just recently learned she was one of triplets. She and each of her sisters had been given a gift, by a stranger, that reunited them here in Miracle Harbor.

This house was her gift.

A lot of his questions were answered, but instead of feeling clear, he felt more muddled. First of all the policeman in him did not like it one little bit that a stranger, a person she knew nothing about, had given her a house.

Secondly, hearing her story made Abby Blakely not just an irritating problem who had presented herself on his doorstep, but a human being, three-dimensional, with her own history and feelings. Not the enemy. And if he wasn't careful, all those things were going to work against him. The baby on his lap was part of the same plot.

Shane tried to steel himself. Her tragedy-filled life was not his concern. Still, he had to ask. "How come you and your sisters were split up, anyway?"

She shrugged, but not before he caught a glimpse of intense pain in her eyes. "I'm just starting to get parts of the story now. My sister Brittany says she was adopted when she was about three by her parents. My sister Corrine said her parents were killed in a car accident. So, I'm assuming my parents were killed in a car accident when I was about three, and for some awful reason we were split up. Still, my life is like a puzzle that I don't have all the pieces to. I think as I get to know my sisters, more and more will fall into place. And maybe whoever gave me this house knows something."

Her voice cracked just a little bit, before she composed herself and bravely went on. "The only way I'll ever find out is if I stay here, give this a chance."

"The suites in this house don't even have separate kitchens!" Shane pointed, trying to use practicality in the face of emotion, a ploy he knew would not work. She was just another human being, doing her best with the cards that had been given her, a hand nearly as good as his own.

Still, he saw no self-pity in her, but great courage, a hint of pure steel. Which probably did not bode well for his future living arrangements.

"I do have a lease," Shane pointed out.

"For how long?" she whispered.

"Not for long enough to have any bearing on this conversation, unfortunately," he admitted, slightly ashamed of himself for the anxiety he had caused to appear in her face.

Geez. What was he doing? For him it was a house. A place to live. He had no attachment to it.

She apparently, had hopes and dreams wrapped up in this house. Already.

Belle picked that moment to reach up and insert a finger in his nose, reminding him that Abby's interests probably were a little more pressing than his. Still, he felt the last of his hardline stance evaporating.

He could probably find another place to live if he gave his life over to finding it. Which he discovered he was prepared to do. He wasn't going to live under the same roof as her, indefinitely.

"You can't live with your sisters?" he asked, one desperate, last-ditch effort.

He removed Belle's finger, looked at her face, and sighed.

She wasn't going to live with her sisters.

"You see, Shane," she said softly, "I need to live in this house. I can't really explain it. But it has to do with the fact that somebody cared enough about me that they gave me this place. This house is mine, the first thing that's ever been mine. Besides Belle. Can you understand that?"

"Not really," he said gruffly. Her answer showed him another huge chasm between male and female perception. Or maybe it was cop and civilian perception. Whatever it was, he saw her receiving the house as a gift as somewhat suspicious. She saw it in an entirely different light, like the universe was pouring love on her. He sighed heavily.

"I'll go. As soon as I find a place. That might take a while in this town."

"You don't have to go."

"Yes," he said firmly, feeling the sweet weight of the baby in his lap, "I do."

He wondered, right away, how on earth she was going to get a tenant as good as him. Not his problem, he told himself firmly.

Belle bounced on his lap and sang a little song, that seemed to consist of the words "no-go-away-today."

"You don't have to go," Abby said again. "Shane, you don't even use this ground floor suite. You told me that last night. There's plenty of room down here for Belle and I. And there's no reason we couldn't share the kitchen."

"That doesn't work for me," he said.

"Now I feel guilty."

So was he supposed to feel guilty that she felt guilty? Damn, life became complicated with a woman involved. He bet himself he could have a new place to live within a week, if he really worked at it.

And what if she rented the suite to an old man with sixteen tomcats and a goat?

Not his problem.

Even if she did have to share the kitchen with him.

"I'll haul your stuff in." There. "You might as well stay here until I've found a new place. I guess we can share the kitchen until then."

She'd managed to make him feel guilty, anyway. He'd just had his house pulled right out from under him, and *he* felt guilty.

And that's what women did. Turned your world

upside down and topsy-turvy before you knew what was happening.

If he *really* worked at it, and wasn't too fussy, he bet he could have himself a new place to live in three days.

"Belle," Abby whispered to her daughter, gathering her in her arms and waltzing around the empty kitchen, after Shane had left. "This is our house! Ours! Yours and mine!"

"And man's?" Belle asked, smiling at her mother's happiness, touching her cheek.

"Oh, him. I don't know about him, Belle." The truth was she felt guilty. Why should she feel guilty? He was the stubborn one!

"Me like," Belle announced.

"Only because of what he gave you for breakfast. You shouldn't allow yourself to be so easily bought. A life lesson from your mother."

Belle smiled with absolutely no understanding.

Abby set her down on the floor, and surveyed the room. It needed everything. New countertops. New cabinets. New flooring.

But for now, new curtains, and a coat of paint would make it hers. And, of course, curtains were one of her specialities. And maybe he was right. Maybe she'd better be careful just how attached she became to the place. Because if she wasn't married in a year, it wouldn't be hers.

She decided she wasn't even going to think about that right now. Right now she was going to count her blessings. She didn't even have to worry about that car.

Let it sit there! She could walk to downtown from here. And to the beach.

"Abby!"

She recognized his voice, and the annoyance in it. She already knew a few things about Shane McCall. She could tell by the way he lined things up in his cupboards with military precision and from the fact that there was not a speck of dirt anywhere, that he was a man who liked control.

Loved control.

She thought it was a measure of the kind of man he really was, and not the kind he wanted her to think he was, that he had accepted this unexpected loss of his control with a kind of reluctant grace.

Probably just what he needed, the old sourpuss. When he saw how quietly she and Belle lived, he might not move after all. She didn't want to be looking for a new tenant in a town full of transient workers.

"Abby!"

Of course, she was not at all sure she would be able to handle living with him, either. Maybe, she thought whimsically, she'd just let the universe look after it.

It was not doing a bad job so far.

Tucking Belle under her arm, she went out of the kitchen.

Shane McCall was standing in her front hallway, dressed about the same as he had been last night—in next to nothing. Shorts. She could see his shirt hanging from a rhododendron in the yard.

Her eyes took in the bulge of muscle in Shane's arms as he carried her sewing machine. Her glance trailed to the column of his throat, the little trickle of sweat that chased down from behind his ear.

"Where would you like me to put this?" he asked. She knew where he wanted to put it, right out the door, back on the trailer and out of his life.

"Over by the window would be very nice."

"What is it, anyway?" he panted. "Bricks in a box?"

"My serger."

"What?"

"It's a kind of sewing machine."

Just as she said it, the handle on the carrying case, wobbly for some time, groaned and tore away. He caught the box before it hit the ground, but it glanced off his toe.

He said three words in a row she was not sure she had ever heard before. She set her daughter down. "Belle, go play with those bowls in the kitchen. Shane, really, I don't want my daughter learning that kind of language."

He looked sorry and stubborn at the same time. He glared at her. "It's just as well that you don't get any ideas," he said.

"About what?"

"About taming me."

"About taming you?" she echoed.

"I'm leaving. Soon. And I am not the perfect man."

She eyed him suspiciously. Was it coincidental that he had picked that phrase? It must be. She hadn't brought in that book. Would the lawyer he spoke to on the phone have revealed to him the condition placed on receiving the gift? Warned Shane she was on the hunt for a husband, just like her sisters?

"I don't think you're in any danger of being mistaken for a perfect man."

Now he looked insulted.

"Mostly," she added hastily, "because in my experience, there is no such thing."

"I'm going to start to look for another place to live this afternoon."

"Suit yourself."

"I will," he muttered.

"Though I must admit, I'd feel very safe at night if you were to stay."

He snorted.

"But good luck finding another place," she said cheerfully. "You know what? I love this room. Look at the light. I can have my plants over there, and still have room to have my mannequin here."

"Your mannequin," he said flatly, shoving the sofa against the wall and turning to look at her.

"I'm a seamstress. I plan to hang out my shingle."

"Soon?"

"As soon as possible."

"I can't have a whole lot of noise and commotion while I'm working," he told her. He had folded his arms over his chest again, and planted his legs far apart.

Really, it made him look ten feet tall and bulletproof. They'd probably taught him how to look like that in policeman school. If she ever let him think he'd intimidated her, she'd be lost, and she knew it.

"Shane, do you know anything about sewing?"

"Not really."

"It's not exactly loud. Much of what I do, like hemming, and beading, is by hand. My sewing machine, when I use it, is ultraquiet. I tried out quite a few of them before I found one a baby could sleep through."

"But people coming here? Knocking on the door at all hours of the day and night?"

"I'm going to take in a little sewing, not be running a bootlegging operation. I'm sure you'll find it won't disturb you at all before you go. You won't even know we're here, Belle and I."

"And are you willing to put that in writing?"

Before she could reply there was a loud crash from the kitchen and a wail from Belle. She hurried away, but not before she noticed him roll his eyes, and heard him mutter, "Gee, I barely know you're here, already."

CHAPTER FOUR

"I CAN'T hear you," Shane said into the phone. "It's what? Board and room? That's not what the ad says... reduced rent for what? Can you turn down that noise? I can barely hear you. You can't turn down your kids? Reduced rent for *baby-sitting?*"

He slammed down the phone, without saying goodbye, and put a vicious pen slash through the second-to-last For Rent ad in the morning edition of the *Miracle Harbor Beacon.*

Downstairs, he heard her. Singing again. Obviously when this old dump had been renovated not a single thought had been given to soundproofing. And she had been singing as if her heart were overflowing with joy since he had hauled in the last of her things around seven o'clock last night. He'd heard her unpacking her newly purchased groceries in the kitchen.

If it had been rock and roll, he could have told her to can it.

But she didn't sing rock and roll. She sang ballads, loaded with haunting Celtic lilt.

Even worse than the singing was what he heard once it had grown quiet in her apartment last night, the kid apparently finally asleep in a crib that had been more complicated to assemble than a Chinese puzzle. Just when he had thought his life was going to be returned to blessed silence, he had heard the water going into the downstairs tub. Her tub. And then he had heard what he had to presume was her filling her tub.

He resented the fact that in just a little more than twenty-four hours his whole life had been wrested out of his control. To be honest, he was weary of fate throwing wrenches into the well-oiled machinery of his life.

She splashed and sighed and hummed in that bathtub for long enough that he had to go out for a good brisk walk. He'd succeeded in completely clearing his mind of her, too. Put together in his mind six or seven pretty good paragraphs on proper stakeout technique.

But then he'd made the mistake of coming back through the lane, and had seen the candlelight flickering through the frosted panes of her bathroom window.

A disturbing mental picture had formed. Of her. In that bathtub. Wearing only bubbles. With the candle flame dancing and throwing erotic shadows on the wall.

His body's reaction had been instant, embarrassing in a man his age. Going up the stairs to his suite, two steps at a time, he couldn't help but wonder if his monkish lifestyle was making him into the pervert she'd accused him of being.

What was wrong with him? Adolescent boys pictured women naked. He didn't. Wouldn't. To prove it he had proceeded to throw himself into his work with single-minded fury. At midnight, when he had not heard a sound in her quarters for the better part of an hour, he reviewed what he had just spent three hours working on.

He was shocked to find that he had written sixteen paragraphs of drug-bust gibberish. He'd turned off the computer without saving, gone to bed, and had lain awake.

An hour later, he'd crept down the stairs into the kitchen, a man bent on a bologna sandwich.

His bologna, only two weeks old, had been disposed of. So had an open can of sardines.

His fridge was jam-packed with green things. Lettuce. Broccoli. Asparagus. Way in the back, behind 2% milk and smoked Gouda, he found a can of soda that he knew was his.

He debated trying the Gouda, but decided what his life was going to need, if he was going to survive the next few days, were rules.

Starting with thou shalt not touch the other guy's Gouda. Or bologna, as the case might be.

Still unable to sleep, he'd returned to his section of the house, and begun a list of rules and a schedule for kitchen use. When dawn broke, he went for a run and got a newspaper.

He hadn't prayed for a long, long time, but he sent a little plea heavenward as he dialed the last number in the For Rent section of the classified ads.

Yes, it was a house. No, no, not for sharing. Perfect for a single man.

He began to get suspicious. In his experience, no one *wanted* to rent to a single guy. At least not until they met him.

Small, but clean, he was assured.

The address? That nice little row of cottages on Cannery Street.

He hung up the phone, no goodbye again. There

were no cottages on Cannery Street. There were shacks. Depressing places with Rottweilers chained in the front yards, and cars decomposing in the back. All the houses had an impressive view of the old Jones' Brothers Cannery, closed for at least fifteen years, rotting away at the end of a tilting dock. It was the part of town that nobody in Miracle Harbor wanted to admit was there.

Displeased with the results of his house hunting, he allowed himself to review his kitchen schedule with a flicker of satisfaction. He would take early shift in the morning, before she was even up. And then it would be his again at twelve-thirty. He only needed a few minutes to make lunch. He could have supper late, between seven and eight. An electric kettle should look after the odd urge for a cup of coffee.

The schedule actually might be workable, he thought. The way he had things planned, it was possible he would never lay eyes on her. No more sessions with a baby on his lap. A thing like that could muddle a man's thinking.

He had his own bathroom, so really they were sharing a kitchen and a hallway. Maybe that wouldn't inconvenience him nearly as much as he thought it would.

Her voice, full of merriment, floated up through the cracks in the floor, and the pipes, and the hollow walls.

"The bear went over the mountain, the bear went over the mountain, the bear went over the mountain, to seeee what he could seeeeee."

Little-her cracked up, shouting with laughter.

Savagely, he crossed out the last ad, and retrieved his phone book. At the back was a listing of apartments, and even though he had sworn he would never again live in an apartment building, he began the tedious job of calling them about vacancies.

After an hour, he'd had about enough of hearing people snort at him when he asked about vacancies. Underneath, Do Not Remove Other People's Belongings from the Fridge, he scrawled, No Singing, then recognized that in pursuit of his own survival he was becoming churlish, and crossed it off. His stay here was only temporary. What did it matter if she sang?

The doorbell rang.

He frowned, not sure he had heard the doorbell before. He waited for her to get it, but heard only silence. The doorbell rang again. And then again.

She hadn't even been here a full day. What were the chances that it was for her?

He'd been in Miracle Harbor for two years, and there was even less chance it was for him. He liked what that said about his life. He'd succeeded at removing himself from entanglements of any kind.

The doorbell rang again.

He'd be better at getting rid of a salesman than her, anyway.

He picked up his schedule, and his rules and bounded down the steps. At the last moment, too late, his mind registered the baby gate. Where there had been nothing before, now there was a wooden gate, two and a half feet high, at the bottom of the steps.

He tried to leap over it, but his toe caught and he crashed painfully to the floor, leading with his knee. It felt like the kneecap was shattered. He swore a blue streak, reached down and gingerly manipulated the knee. Not broken. He swore some more, remembered the baby, and satisfied himself with several low and heartfelt growls of pain mixed with aggravation.

The doorbell rang again.

He got painfully to his feet and limped over. Rubbing his knee, he swung open the door, and got ready to blast whoever stood there.

The blast died inside of him.

The sweetest little old lady stood outside his door, her gray hair in a prim bun, her lovely blue eyes, which had somehow remained young even as her face had aged, twinkling merrily at him. She was wearing a hat, with a jaunty red feather in it, and her hands were folded primly over a pocketbook. She looked exactly like the granny who loved Tweety-Bird so dearly.

He braced himself. It was going to be hard to slam the door in her face if she asked him if he'd been saved.

"Hello, dear," she said gently.

Dear. She'd heard him cussing a blue streak, and still called him dear? "Uh, hello."

"You don't look very much like a seamstress." She chuckled. "Is this where the seamstress lives?"

He was so relieved that she wasn't handing him a tract, that he stood and stared stupidly at her for a moment. "Seamstress? There's no—"

Then he remembered his toe, which was as black-and-blue as his shin and now his knee were, and the heavy object he had dropped on it. Some kind of a sewing machine. A seiger? That didn't sound exactly right, but it was in keeping with the fact his life was under siege. "Oh," he said. "*That* seamstress."

The door to the seamstress's apartment opened, and Abby came out, her cheeks flushed and her short hair curling wildly, a damp baby wrapped in a thick white towel in her arms.

It seemed to him a proper seamstress should look more like the little old lady at the door than like Abby. Abby was wearing jeans, three sizes too large, that rode down low on her hips. She had on some kind of sawed-off white top that was wet enough to hint at what was underneath it. Her belly button was showing.

Her belly button, and the secrets under that top both looked like they were even better than he had imagined last night.

"Did you fall?" Abby asked him, her eyes wide on his face. "I heard the most horrible crash."

In answer, he dragged his eyes away from her, and turned and glared at the baby gate.

"Oh, dear," she whispered. "I only put it up an hour ago. I didn't want Belle disturbing you. I thought you'd notice it."

"If I'd had a proper night's sleep I might have."

"A proper night's sleep? But I didn't disturb you, did I?"

"No!" he snapped, knowing a bald-faced lie could occasionally be concealed with uncalled-for aggression. The baby was humming about the damned bear, and he just knew when he tried to go to sleep tonight that tune would be caught in his head, and the bear would go over the mountain again and again and again.

Which was far preferable, really, to his thinking about Abby's wet shirt and belly button, or candles, wet skin and bubbles.

"Are you hurt?" she asked anxiously.

It would be easy to kill her tender concern. All he'd have to do is let her know what he was thinking. He could kill two birds with one stone. She'd probably pack her bags and be out of here in the blink of an eye. Pervert confirmed.

He told himself he didn't only out of deference to the baby, and the little old lady, who was looking back and forth between them with bird-like interest.

His knee was throbbing painfully. He could feel it swelling. "No." He nodded at the door. "You have a visitor."

"A visitor? But I don't know anyone here."

"I'm looking for a seamstress," the old lady said, helpfully.

"Really?" Abby said, delight lighting up her voice. "Come in."

Shane pushed open the screen and held it as the little old gal moved daintily by him. She rewarded him with a lovely smile.

"Thank you, dear. Just when I thought chivalry was dead."

"Yeah, well," he said, and then had a brainstorm. "You aren't in the market for an apartment are you? The one upstairs is for rent."

"Oh, I don't do stairs, dear. Besides, isn't that where you live?"

He frowned at her. How could she know that? She must have heard him coming down them. He muttered, "Not for very much longer, I don't."

Still, he wanted Abby to have a tenant just like this little old lady. Did any little old ladies do stairs? He sighed heavily. He supposed he was going to have to look after that, too. Finding Abby a tenant who wouldn't think evil thoughts every time he heard her bath running.

He turned and picked his kitchen schedule up off the floor.

"These are the hours I'll be in the kitchen. I'm posting a schedule on the fridge door."

Without waiting for her to reply, he went into the kitchen. Little magnets in the shapes of pears and peaches graced a fridge door that had always been plain white.

"How very handy," he said out loud, posting the rules with a little fuzzy peach.

The hallway was empty when he came back out, her door shut. He stepped over the gate, though the maneuver caused his leg to scream with pain, and went back up the stairs and back into his office. He shut the door with a little more force than was absolutely necessary, picked up a piece of blank paper from his desk, and wrote:

"Wanted—tenant for upstairs apartment. Shared kitchen and entryway." He thought about it for a moment, and squeezed the word reliable in between wanted and tenant. And then he squeezed the words female only between apartment and shared. He put down his own phone number, and dialed the *Beacon*.

Abby's visitor moved by her into her suite. She reached out and touched the baby's cheek with a gnarled hand.

"How nice that the young man is posting a schedule to let you know when he'll be in the kitchen," she said, looking at Abby over round wire-rimmed glasses. "He must want you to join him!"

"I don't think that is quite his intent," Abby muttered, noticing that even as she tried to focus on her visitor, her mind kept drifting back to the *nice* young man.

The look in his eyes when she'd come out the door hadn't been nice at all.

Not, she decided, that it had been angry either, which is what she had expected when she had heard that awful crash. The look in his eyes had changed the color of them, made them even darker and more intense than they usually were. The look had been—what?

She became aware of an uncomfortable dampness down her front and glanced down at her shirt.

She flushed, recognizing exactly the look she had seen in his eyes.

Heat.

She gave herself a mental shake, that did nothing for the heat rising, suddenly and inexplicably, up her own neck. She freed one hand from underneath the towel and desperately tried to focus on her visitor.

"I'm Abby Blakely. How can I help you?"

"I'm Angela Pondergrove. For some silly reason people call me Angel. I'm looking for a seamstress. Imagine my surprise when *he* opened the door. It does seem a little early in the year for short pants, but I must say his legs made my heart race in a way it hasn't done for quite some time. Don't you think he has the nicest legs?"

Abby thought she had given the gorgeous legs of her tenant quite enough thought.

"How on earth did you hear about me being a seamstress?" she asked, instead of answering the question. "I just got here."

"Oh, Jordan said something to me," she said vaguely. "Jordan Hamilton. The lawyer?"

"That was nice of him, but I don't remember telling him I was a seamstress."

The old lady held out her frail arms. "May I hold the baby? You must have said something. Perhaps a chance remark. Jordan doesn't miss a thing, you know."

Abby hesitated before passing her Belle. For one thing, Mrs. Pondergrove looked frail, like the weight of stout little Belle might be too much for her. For another, Belle did not always take to strangers, not that it was obvious from her reaction to the man upstairs.

Come to think of him, she felt a certain unwanted *heat* when she looked at him, too. She thought maybe they should come up with a list of rules.

The first one being: Thou shalt keep all your clothes on.

Belle went willingly to Mrs. Pondergrove after all, and the old woman had quite a bit more strength in her arms than Abby would have thought.

"Come sit down," Abby suggested.

Mrs. Pondergrove did, and after making a fuss over Belle for a while longer, she set her between them on the couch and took a picture from the pocket of a gray wool jacket that, though tasteful, had seen better days.

"This is what I was wondering about," Mrs. Pondergrove said softly.

Abby took the picture, and drew in a startled breath. The picture was a line drawing of a wedding gown. It featured a high collar, and a sweetheart neckline shaped like a perfect teardrop. The effect was a dress that was innocent and sexy at the same time. The entire bodice was beautifully beaded and formfitting to the waist, where the skirt was attached in a sensuous vee that would accentuate the soft roundness of a woman's hips. Then the line of the gown fell in beautiful and breathtaking simplicity to the floor. A full train flowed out behind it.

"It's beautiful," she breathed. It was the kind of dress every girl dreamed of. Exactly the kind of dress she had once believed she would wear.

Before Ty. And Belle. And the death of her silly, Cinderella notions. So why, looking at this dress, could she suddenly see herself in it? And why did that picture cause an unexpected yearning, almost like pain, to rise up in her?

It was as if the dress shouted her best kept secret. That underneath all her proclamations of independence, underneath how competently she handled the challenges and rigors of being a single mother, there was this hope, still, that someday love would happen to her.

"Is something wrong?" Mrs. Pondergrove asked.

"Of course not, no," she said hastily, but put the picture down on the couch beside her all the same.

"Could you make that dress?" Mrs. Pondergrove asked her anxiously.

Abby looked again at the picture, without picking it up. Could she make that dress? Of course she could. It would be a dream to make such a dress. She could almost feel the richness of the fabric beneath her fingers, just from looking at the drawing. It would have to be silk. Nothing else would do the dress justice.

She could make the dress, but what of her own dreams? Wouldn't making such a dress make her painfully aware of all the things that had not happened in her life? Of all the things that would never happen? Of course, she might wear a wedding dress one day, but given the fact she was already the mother of a child, a tasteful suit would be more appropriate than the virginal white innocence of the gown in the picture.

She shot a surreptitious look at her visitor, and decided the question of her making the dress was probably, thankfully, largely theoretical.

Mrs. Pondergrove's gray wool coat was tidy and had probably been quite elegant in its day, but now it looked just a little worn at the cuffs and around the collar. The hat, too, was jaunty and elegant, but obviously old.

"A dress like this would take nearly a month of full-time work to make," Abby said, gently. "The fabric alone would cost a small fortune. And to do it justice, you would have to use very expensive beading on this bodice. The beading would all have to be done by hand."

"But you could do it?" the woman asked eagerly, as if she had not heard a single word Abby had said.

"I could sew this dress," Abby said slowly, "but I really think it would make more sense for you to go and buy one ready-made. I think it would be far less expensive."

"My dear, how touching that you would be concerned about an old lady spending her money."

"The truth is that the cost of making this dress would be extravagant."

"Oh, pooh. What is money for, except to make people happy?"

Reluctantly, Abby decided to burst the bubble. She named what she thought the dress would cost to make, including materials and a rough guess on her labor. She expected her visitor to flinch visibly, and was astounded when Mrs. Pondergrove beamed at her.

"When could you start, then?"

"You want to go ahead? At that price?"

"I most certainly do! When could you start on it?"

"Well, I guess I could start right away," Abby stammered.

"Good. Let me write you a check."

"Oh," Abby said. "Are you certain? You've never even seen my work."

"At my age, you can tell what kind of work people do from the look in their eyes. You can tell all kinds of things from that. Take that young man who answered the door. I could tell he was as lonely as a camel on a cattle farm."

"Really?" Abby said, a little weakly.

"Oh, yes. He's heartbroken, that boy."

Abby was not certain she had ever seen a person less likely to be called a *boy* than Shane McCall. And he seemed like about the least vulnerable man she had ever seen.

Though suddenly she thought of him telling her, that first crazy night, that he was a widower, and of the bitterness that had flashed briefly in his eyes when she had commented he seemed too young to have dealt with such a tragedy.

Bitterness? Or was that how a man like him would mask a broken heart?

"He thinks you mend a broken heart by putting a block of ice around it, but of course, nothing could be further from the truth."

"That seems rather a lot to know about a person from one meeting," Abby said, and saw the shrewd eyes turned on her.

"You're right, of course," her visitor demurred. "Now,

how will we proceed on the dress? A check for the full amount?"

"Oh, no!" Abby said. "A down payment would be fine. A third now, and another third part way through, and a third at the end if you are completely satisfied. Who is the dress for? I'll need to contact her to arrange for fittings."

"Fittings? No, I'm afraid that's not possible."

"But—"

"The dress is a surprise, you see."

"I can't make a dress without knowing who it's for! It won't fit correctly."

"Yes it will. Because the girl it is for is your size, *exactly*."

"That's a strange coincidence."

"Isn't it?" Mrs. Pondergrove asked happily.

Abby looked at her visitor. She was lovely, but obviously eccentric. Was it possible she wasn't even all there? Could Abby, in good conscience, take her money? Maybe there wasn't even a bride!

"It must be for someone you love very much," Abby said, probing, hoping to get a little more information.

Instead, she found a check pressed into her hand, and she found herself looking into eyes that were young and strong and imminently sane.

"It's for someone to whom I owe a great debt," Mrs. Pondergrove said. "A debt that cannot be measured. I owe her happiness."

"No one could owe anyone else happiness," Abby protested.

"You are very young to realize something so wise." Mrs. Pondergrove sighed. "Still, one does what one can. I don't think white is quite right for that dress. You know what white represents these days is hopelessly old-fashioned. What do you think of ivory?"

Abby thought it made it a dress she could wear, after all. But she did not want to get attached to the dress, she did not want to think of herself in it for one moment. She suddenly wanted to refuse, but as a single mom she knew she could not base a financial decision that would affect her and Belle's well-being on emotion. Especially romantic, silly, wistful emotion.

"When do you need the dress by?" She heard a certain woodenness in her tone.

"Oh, they haven't set a date yet, but as soon as possible. Would you mind if I dropped by now and then to see how its progressing?"

"I'd be delighted."

Mrs. Pondergrove nodded with satisfaction. "I thought so. I can tell a great deal about you from your eyes, too."

"And what would that be?"

"Oh, I've jabbered quite enough for one day. I don't want you to dread me coming, to think, 'oh here comes that talkative old bag again,' when you see me coming up the walk."

"I would never think that," Abby said, and laughed.

After her guest had left, Abby took Belle across the hall to the kitchen. She realized she still had Mrs. Pondergrove's drawing in her hand, and she set it on the kitchen table. His notice about hours for kitchen use was posted on the fridge.

Neatly typed, it looked like a military itinerary. Underneath the itinerary were a list of rules about use of the fridge, also typed. The first requested her to label her food as belonging to her.

"Hungry," Belle announced impatiently.

She tore her eyes away from the list. "Honey, it looks like we're here illegally."

"Hungry," Belle repeated.

He had posted this time as his time to prepare lunch. Well, it would just have to go into effect tomorrow.

And sure enough she heard him coming down the stairs, but there was something off about the sound of the thumps. She heard him open the kiddie gate, instead of stepping over it.

He limped into the kitchen, and looked annoyed to see her there.

But she barely registered that. His knee was swollen up like a basketball.

"Did you read the schedule?" he asked, through gritted teeth.

"Just now. Is that what happened when you went over the gate?"

"Yes."

"Oh, Shane, I'm so sorry."

"It was my own fault. Could we go over this schedule? Does it look acceptable?"

"Well," she said, "it seems I have free rein of the kitchen, except for about an hour each day. I'm not going to complain, but what if you want a snack? Or a cup of coffee?"

The man's face was white with pain.

"I have an electric kettle upstairs. I don't snack."

"Oh. A man of complete self-control."

"That's correct."

"What are you going to do about your knee?"

"Put some ice on it, and take a pill."

"I think you need to see a doctor."

"Really?" His voice was like ice.

"Really."

"We will get along much better, until I have found new accommodations, if you don't give me advice."

"My apologies," she said with false meekness. "I'll just write that on the notice on the fridge, right under the rules about labeling."

"That would be good of you." His face suddenly went a whiter shade of white, and he limped over to a chair and sat down.

"I'll get you some lunch," she said. "What do you like? I bought peanut butter yesterday. Belle's favorite."

Peanut butter! She was offering this man peanut butter, as if he was two. She had been around her two-year-old a little too much. "I also make a mean omelette."

"I don't want you to get me lunch. I want you to get out of the kitchen, as per the posted schedule."

"It's the least I could do. It's my fault you hurt your knee."

"Thank you. I know."

"I just read the schedule. I didn't know it was your time."

"But you do now," he pointed out.

"Fine. Belle, we're leaving."

Belle was busy taking the bowls out of the cupboards. She looked up at her mother in horror and howled, "Belle hungry!"

"It's Mr. McCall's turn in the kitchen. You and I can walk downtown and get something."

"He feed me," Belle decided. "Sugar Pups." That decided, she went back to her bowls, happily nesting one inside the other.

"Oh, for God's sake, feed the kid," he said with great irritation, and then he sighed. "And while you're at it, I guess you could get me something, too. I have a package of bologna in the fridge."

Was he watching her with a certain humor in his narrowed eyes?

She squared her shoulders. She wasn't about to lie to him. "Not anymore, you don't."

"Really?" he said silkily.

"It was green in places!"

"Kindly don't throw out my belongings."

"You should thank me. I may have prevented you from death by food poisoning!"

"Maybe death by food poisoning was my preference over death by baby gate. I am a free man. I can eat deteriorating bologna if I want to."

She looked at him, and suddenly thought of Mrs. Pondergrove's remarks. Lonely as a camel on a cattle farm. Heartbroken.

"Humph."

"Pardon?" he said.

"Nothing."

So she made an omelette for him, which he thanked her for by scowling. She put Belle in her high chair, gave her some omelette too, and then sat down herself.

She saw the picture of the wedding dress was right in front of him, and that he was glaring down at it suspiciously.

"What is this?" he finally asked.

"My new job," she said.

He actually looked terrified. "Your new job is finding a husband?"

She wasn't quite sure how he had made that leap in

logic. "No, the lady who came, Mrs. Pondergrove, asked me to make that for her."

"She's a little old for this dress," he said, his suspicion not dying.

Abby snatched the picture away from him, and said snippily. "Really? I didn't know people ever got too old to dream."

But suddenly she wasn't sure who she was talking about. Mrs. Pondergrove or herself.

Or maybe even him.

CHAPTER FIVE

"It's a foolish dress for an old woman," Shane said stubbornly. For some reason, when he had looked at the drawing, he had been able to picture Abby in that dress as clearly as if it were a photograph.

It reminded him of another dress, a long time ago, and a young woman coming toward him, the love shining in her eyes stilling the hammering of his heart.

"It's not for her to wear, obviously," Abby said, with a trace of annoyance.

Mrs. Pondergrove looked like the type who could be eccentric, able to overlook what was *obvious* even to him, about a dress like that. A dress like that was about believing in happily ever after.

"The omelette's pretty good," he said, but grudgingly. The truth was that after a steady diet of bologna and sardines, the omelette tasted like a little piece of heaven. And little pieces of heaven were just the things he needed to steel himself against.

Because he knew it was those little things that hurt the most after. Stacey had made banana bread that he thought of now, craved, yearned for. Bologna did not make his mind wander to such memories.

"The secret is to use water," she said, reaching

over and popping a little chunk of omelette in Belle's mouth.

"I thought you used eggs."

She rolled her eyes at him. Oh-oh. Something else that was obvious.

"Water instead of the milk," she said.

He decided he would not admit he had not known milk was an ingredient in an omelette. He'd thought omelettes were made with eggs and cheese. Period. But the omelette did not interest him nearly as much as the dress, and who it was for.

"So, she's not going to wear the dress. I assume she's not getting it made to hang it on her wall and look at it. Who is it for, then?" Really, he should leave it alone. But he could not get over the uneasy feeling that that dress was about Abby, somehow.

"Are you interrogating me?"

"No," he said sharply.

"Good."

"Who's the damned dress for?"

He saw the hesitation in her, saw her eyes narrow, knew she was going to tell him to mind his own business, which was what he deserved. It should, in fact, be posted on the rules. Mind your own business. But that's not what she said.

"Her daughter!" she finally replied triumphantly.

He'd been a cop long enough to be able to tell, most of the time, when someone was lying. Especially, someone like her, who was obviously not accustomed to lying. Her eyes were suddenly everywhere but on him. Getting more omelette into baby Belle suddenly seemed to have become her life's mission.

"Gee," he said, "her daughter would only have to be about eighty."

"Mrs. Pondergrove is not *that* old!"

"Okay, maybe not that old, but her kids would have to be in their fifties. At least." That dress was about hopes and dreams and fairy tales. Even he, an idiot about such matters, could see that.

"Well, maybe its for her granddaughter then."

She was still very busy with that baby, wiping imaginary spots off Belle's face, while Belle flailed, trying to get away from her.

The dress, he thought, was for Abby. His gut had told him that the minute he had looked at it. That, and that book he'd spotted, meant she was on the hunt.

And with a belly button like hers, she should have absolutely no problem. Her top was lifting up and giving him a little peek at it every time she reached over to Belle.

Mrs. Pondergrove had probably come to see her about having a bit of lace put on her hat. Or a slip hemmed, or a button put on her jacket.

Without eating the rest of his omelette, which took considerable discipline on his part, he thanked her coolly for lunch, got up and limped out of the room.

By the next morning he knew she had taken the hint. The cupboards had been reorganized into His and Hers, labeled neatly with masking tape. The fridge shelves been bisected neatly down the middle with white wire dividers.

His side held a brand-new package of bologna and an unopened can of sardines. It made him look pathetic.

It also made him feel guilty that she had spent her

money on the bologna and the sardines when she had a child to support.

Well, he wasn't going to have to feel guilty anymore because he wasn't going to see her anymore. Or hear her, either. He had a brand-new CD Walkman player with earphones. He had bought some rank rock and roll music that he remembered fondly from his younger years. The majority of his fondness came from the fact that neither the music nor the lyrics could be considered conducive to romance.

He ate his breakfast, two pieces of burned toast, while listening to Acid Sam. He was annoyed, and somewhat startled to find he had matured. Acid Sam's vocals hurt his ears. And the lyrics hurt his spirit, which really didn't need further damage.

The kitchen seemed different. He wasn't quite sure how. Sure it was neat and tidy, but all she added was the magnets on the fridge.

No wait. The table had never had a cloth on it before. Bright red checks. Very homey and cozy. Not like an Italian restaurant at all.

He took a guilty swipe at his crumbs.

There it was again, despite all his efforts. Guilt. The feeling he despised as much as any other. The feeling that he had run all the way to Miracle Harbor to get away from. And it had caught up with him anyway. Her fault. Abby's. He took the Acid Sam CD from the player, broke it neatly in half and filed it in the garbage.

The blessed silence that followed was short-lived. He could hear the steady hum of what he assumed was her sewing machine, and she was keeping up a steady patter with Belle at the same time.

He wondered if it was hard to work with the baby around.

And since he was wondering about her anyway, he allowed himself to wonder, ever so briefly, if the top Abby was wearing today would show her belly button.

He heard his phone ring upstairs, climbed over the baby gate, and went to answer it. A prospective tenant he hoped.

And he was absolutely right. A construction worker named Harvey who thought he could talk his way around the "female only" part of the ad Shane had placed yesterday.

On the seventeenth call—all of them from construction workers—he unplugged his phone, and stared grimly out the window.

Little-her tumbled into the front yard in a bright red jacket that made her look as round as a beach ball. Right behind Belle came big-her pulling a red wagon with a few colorful boxes of bulbs in it. Soon the two of them were side by side, digging in the dirt, laughing.

After awhile big-her took off the plaid hooded jacket she was wearing.

His mouth went dry.

In a shirt that fit like that, who needed to see a belly button?

He thought the house needed a new rule: Thou shalt not show your belly button or wear tight fitting clothing of any kind. But then that might apply to him, too, and he was used to running around without his shirt on.

He had the oddest thought. What if his belly button affected her the same way that hers affected him?

Then, he decided, they would be in big trouble. Bigger trouble than he would know how to handle.

With a groan of pure misery, which he knew had nothing at all to do with his still swollen knee, he pulled down his shade and turned his phone back on.

Out of the corner of her eye, Abby saw the shade go down and felt mildly annoyed. She couldn't even put a few bulbs in the ground without irritating him? This was the third day in a row that she had come out into the yard to give Belle a little fresh air, and no sooner had they settled in at whatever project they were working on when his shade would go down.

"Oh, Abby," she chided herself out loud, "what makes you think it has anything to do with you? The sun is probably on his computer screen."

She lifted her face to the sun, and drank in the warmth of it. Spring came so much earlier here on the Oregon coast than it did in Chicago. But then she had learned the weather was always fairly mild here, winter temperatures only dipping down to about forty-five degrees.

"Not like Chicago," she said. When she had left, still it had been very much winter, bitterly cold and nasty.

Yet here, it was only March and the air was warm, tangy with earth smells, mixed with the scent of saltwater. After five days in Miracle Harbor, she was in love.

And not with the man upstairs, though her heart did odd things when she saw him in running shorts, which seemed to be the limit of his wardrobe. Well, so what? He'd had the very same effect on Mrs. Pondergrove. Probably had that effect on every female between the ages of eight and eighty.

One thing she definitely did not need in her life, ever again, was a man who all women found attractive.

Ty had been like a boy in a candy store when it came to women liking him. He grabbed whatever he could. He'd even felt guilty about giving in to temptation, but had been unable to resist all the same.

"Honey, I just don't have any backbone," he told her with that lazy grin after she had found him in a clinch with a woman she had thought was her friend. She'd been six months pregnant at the time.

Well, if she was looking for one difference between the man upstairs and Belle's father, that would certainly be it.

There was no mistaking that Shane McCall had backbone, and plenty of it.

Even so, it was not him she was in love with. She had too much good sense for that.

No, she'd fallen in love with the town and the beauty of the Oregon coast. Her yard had a flowering quince in it, and also a camellia, both of them heavy with blossoms ready to burst. The pussy willow trees were getting fuzzy. The whole town was so quaint and pretty, and the people were friendly and helpful. It was really a town full of people just like Angel Pondergrove.

Twice she had taken Belle to the big town-center beach, which was only two blocks from their house. The ocean was incredible. Huge and mysterious, ever changing, sometimes whispering, sometimes crashing. Belle loved the sand, and though the weather was not yet conducive to swimming, Belle always managed to get good and wet before she was crammed, protesting, back in her stroller to go home.

Abby had worried about the availability of a good fabric store, but she needn't have. There were two, and both of them carried a nice selection. She had purchased a few yards of cheerful red-checkered cotton to brighten up the kitchen, and had whipped up a tablecloth, then hung some cafe-style curtains yesterday.

She had also purchased a bolt of ivory silk, delicate and shimmering as butterfly wings.

She had begun making the pattern for Mrs. Pondergrove's dress. She loved to sew, had been drawn to it since she was a small girl, when she had begun to make her own patterns for dolls, cutting the dresses out of leftover fabric of Judy's. She had been sewing her own clothes since she was a teenager, and had made a decent living making prom dresses and theatrical and dance costumes.

But nothing had ever felt like this dress. When she worked on it, she became so engrossed in it. Time and reality seemed to slip away.

Even now as she dug in the dirt with Belle, her thoughts went to the dress, constructing it step by step in her mind.

Just after one o'clock, she managed to pry Belle out of the dirt. They went into the kitchen for lunch, and she noticed, if he had been in here, there was no sign of it. Not a crumb on the table, or a smear on the counter.

She opened the fridge. The bologna package was nearly empty, evidence that she did share the house with someone else.

And then she noticed the scent in the room, subtle but powerful, and closed her eyes.

It was the scent of a man, wild and heady. Intoxicating.

She thought it would be in her best interests to add a little rule to his list.

Thou shalt not smell so good.

She laughed at her own silliness, made a quick lunch, and then put Belle down for her nap and took out the work she planned to do for the day. Within minutes Belle was snoring and the sewing machine was humming.

Without even knowing that she did it, she began to sing. In her mind, she could see the slender back of the bride as she went down the aisle. Beyond her, at the altar, was the groom. It was *him,* Shane McCall, his eyes softened with the most incredible light. A tender smile playing across his face instead of that perpetual frown.

And then, without warning, the sewing-machine needle faltered, and then froze. The light mounted on the sewing machine flickered and went out.

Abby snatched her hand away from where she had been feeding the fabric and glared at the silk as if it was responsible for her ridiculous flight of fancy.

And then she heard him upstairs, cursing a blue streak. She reached out and flipped the light switch for the fixture above her head. Nothing. Despite the cursing upstairs, she was relieved the power had gone out, and nothing was wrong with her machine.

A moment later she met Shane McCall in the hall. He had a flashlight in his hand, and a familiar frown on his face. As if it was her fault the power had gone out!

Still, he had avoided her so scrupulously for days that she had almost forgotten the impact of him, live and in person.

Of course, he was wearing shorts, grey sweatshirt fabric, and a matching hooded sweatshirt. No emblem. She was too aware of his long bare legs, the muscle standing out in ridges on his thighs and in his calves.

The bruise was almost gone from his shin, the swelling was down on his knee.

But his eyes had that same cool, impenetrable light in them.

"Everything okay upstairs? You sounded, er, upset."

"I yell, you sing."

"You can hear me singing?" she asked, mortified.

"Not often. Usually I have my own music on."

"Really? I've never heard it. I guess that's why I assumed you couldn't hear me."

"I use earphones."

"Oh." Was that a hint? "What do you listen to?"

"I'm trying classical."

"Trying it?"

"In recognition of my advancing age."

She had never seen a man who looked more in his prime.

"Well," she said, "you might want to try some Pachebel. He's my favorite. Good for bad tempers."

"I don't have a bad temper."

She raised an eyebrow at him.

"I just lost my whole morning's work."

"Don't you save?" He'd been listening to her singing. If there was a rock handy she probably would have crawled under it.

"Oh, sure. When I think of it. Which is usually when I'm ready to quit. You'd think I'd get it by now. This house's electrical system is crankier than an old Model T."

She wasn't happy to hear about that. If something major needed to be done, then what?

"I think its probably just a fuse," he said. "Why don't I show you where the fuse box is in the basement."

She had opened the door to the basement once, and decided against going down there. It looked dank and musty. She only had one debilitating fear in life but it was a gigantic one. She was phobic about spiders, and that basement looked, from her quick peek down the steps, like spider heaven.

"I think I'll take a pass on that," she said.

He folded his arms across his chest, and braced those legs wide apart. It made him look every inch a cop, even in the shorts. "No, you won't."

"Pardon?"

"Look, Abby, I'm not going to be here much longer. In fact, I'm interviewing some prospective tenants for my place tomorrow. So you need to know where the fuse box is." He sighed. "And also where the furnace is. And the storm windows."

"Oh," she said, her voice tiny. Somehow she had convinced herself that he would stay. She had glanced through the morning paper every day, and had seen there was not much available for rent. "You've found a new place then?"

"I've got a few places lined up to look at," he said vaguely.

"You don't have to find me a tenant. I can find my own."

He snorted at that.

"Well, I can!"

"Abby, this town if full of construction workers. I don't think you want to expose Belle to too much of that. Swearing—"

"Like she hasn't been hearing quite a bit of that lately."

A fascinating shade of pink moved up the column of his throat. "I'm used to living alone. I say rotten words when I feel rotten."

"That must be often!"

"As a matter of fact, it is."

"Why is that?"

"I have a shin the color of a plum, a toe with a nail about to fall off and a knee that feels like I went a round with someone with a baseball bat. I'm used to blowing off steam by running, and I haven't been out for nearly a week."

She knew he was evading her real question. He suddenly seemed fascinated with the switch on the flashlight.

"Why do you need to blow off steam?" she asked quietly.

"Because if I don't blow it off I feel rotten," he said smoothly, coming full circle.

"I meant, where is all that steam coming from?"

"I knew what you meant."

His eyes were on her face, intent, as if he actually was thinking of telling her something, and then he shrugged it off, rolling his shoulders like a prize fighter between rounds, and said, "Anyway, I feel responsible for you finding a good tenant. I don't want some guy moving in here who will throw wild parties and look lewdly at your belly button."

"My what?"

"Don't you have any shirts that tuck in?"

"Don't you have any pants with legs?"

For a moment, a hot animal awareness shimmered

in the air between them. But then something flickered in his eyes and he said, "Let's have a look at that basement."

She hesitated but he had already moved on, and he shot an expectant look over his shoulder. "Come on."

She didn't want to tell him how afraid she was of spiders. The door to the basement was underneath the stairs. "You first," he said.

"Not on your life," she said. He was big enough to take down at least most of the spiderwebs. She tucked in close to his back, and didn't move her eyes from a spot right between his shoulder blades.

The basement was horrible, she could tell by the smell. She still refused to look at anything but the reassuring broadness of his back. She followed him like a shadow across the basement, registering gloom, spooky shadows and dark places.

"So this is the fuse box," he said, shining his flashlight on it.

"This is not your first trip down here, is it?"

He laughed mirthlessly. "You'd better be prepared to make this particular trip a few times a month."

"Oh." She contained a shudder and looked around cautiously. It wasn't so bad. Plain concrete walls. A few empty wooden shelves. Nothing about this she couldn't handle.

"Have you seen a fuse box like this before?"

"Um-hmm," she said, scanning the walls more bravely now. Maybe she'd been given an old house without spiders in the basement. It was called Miracle Harbor after all.

"You can't see the fuse box from behind me."

She forced herself to step out from behind him. She looked obediently up at the fuse box.

"For this house, it's relatively new. Maybe twenty-five years old."

"That's good," she muttered. Caught in the flashlight beam, right above the fuse box, hanging from the roof, was a web glittering like it was spun of gold. She tried to look just at the fuse box, but her peripheral vision sharpened and noted that the cross-bridging on the ceiling looked like it had been decorated for Halloween. It dripped with webs.

"Now, if you look, you'll see the whole house is labeled. Upstairs bedroom, bath on this one. See this switch that's flipped?"

The spiderweb moved. Running down an invisible cord was the most immense spider she had ever seen—gray, small head, huge bulb-shaped body, hairy legs.

She flung herself against Shane, the scream primal.

"What the hell?"

But even as he said it, his arms tightened around her, and she could feel the strength in them, hear the hard reassuring beat of his heart where her head was burrowed into his chest.

She began to shake. "I—I—I'm s-s-sorry. I—I—I'm s-s-scared of—"

To her humiliation, she began to cry when she tried to spit out the embarrassing truth.

"Shhh," he said, his tone surprisingly gentle, lifting her chin, searching her eyes. She had never seen his eyes look like that, and yet the expression seemed familiar.

Something beyond concern. Tenderness.

Just as she had imagined he might look if she came down the aisle toward him in a gown of pure ivory silk.

Something about the thought calmed her, and she drew in a deep hiccuping breath. She became aware that he smelled wonderful. That same aroma that she caught the occasional whiff of in the kitchen, now enveloped her. A tangy scent, wild, like a pine forest after a thunderstorm.

And she felt wonderful, too. Safe. More than safe. Feminine. Small against his largeness, soft against his hardness, her curvy lines fitting so nicely to his straight ones.

"It's okay," he said, drawing his eyes away from her face, glancing around. "I won't let anything hurt you. Let's just get you upstairs. Thatta girl, take a deep breath."

She did, suddenly realized she was glued to him so tightly a piece of paper couldn't have passed between them, and reluctantly stepped back.

The spider dropped. She felt him land right on her shoulder. The world swung wildly around her, her vision turned red and then cleared and then turned red again. Then she felt the strength leech from her arms and legs.

Don't faint, she ordered herself. Pleaded with herself. And then the world went dark.

She slumped against him like a sack of flour, her body suddenly a deadweight. His arms automatically tightened around her.

His first reaction was that it had to be some kind of trick—something out of her book on man hunting.

But her head lolled back, her lips went slack and her

face turned the whitest shade of white he had ever seen as her eyes rolled back in her head.

He scooped her up in his arms, noting she weighed practically nothing, and sore knee forgotten he went quickly up the stairs, and laid her limp body on the couch. He did a hasty first responder's check—taking her pulse, which was normal.

The girl had fainted, pure and simple.

He went through her apartment to her bathroom, registering, only obliquely, the tidiness of everything, the baskets of toys, the flower arrangements, the tasteful framed prints on the walls. She had created an atmosphere of cheerfulness. He dampened a facecloth in her sink, doing his best to ignore the row of lacy cupped bras that hung on her shower rod.

When he came back, he sat beside her on the couch, and put the damp cloth on her forehead. Her eyes fluttered, and then opened. She looked at him dazed, and then closed her eyes and groaned.

"Please tell me I didn't faint. Please."

"Well, if you didn't faint you had a massive cardiac arrest, so fainting probably isn't so bad."

"I'm not the fainting kind," she said fiercely. "Really."

"You've convinced me."

"It's just that I have this phobia. Spiders. I don't know why. I hate it. It's so weak and silly."

But what he was thinking was who the hell was going to go into the basement and look after fuses and such for her? The prospective tenants he had lined up to talk to tomorrow, after buying an answering machine so he could screen the applicants, were all women.

Still, he reminded himself, it was a brand-new age.

One of them wouldn't be afraid of spiders. And would know all about fuses. And wouldn't be scared to hit the furnace, equally as cranky as the electrical system, in just the right place, with a wrench he kept down there just for that purpose. The successful applicant for his apartment would have to be able to go up the ladder to take the storm windows off and put the screens up, too.

This was a house that needed a man. Unfortunately.

"I feel like an idiot," she said.

When she struggled to sit up, he pushed her gently back down.

"You don't have to prove anything. Lay down for a minute." And she was a woman who needed a man, too. She even had a secret book that attested to that.

"I'm not trying to prove anything." She lay back down. Mutinously.

But she would probably never admit to it.

When he left her, a few minutes later, he felt as troubled as he had felt in a long time. She had, to this point, shown herself to be independent and very competent. She worked hard. That sewing machine hummed away all day, and part of the evening, too. In the face of her daughter's many demands, Abby seemed to remain unbelievably good-humored.

But the thing with the spiders made him very aware of an underlying fragility.

It wasn't that she needed someone to look after her. She would have been insulted at the very suggestion, and he recognized it did not quite fit.

It was something else.

She needed someone, not to take the load, but to share the load.

And he had the sinking feeling he could interview five thousand tenants and never find one like that.

Because she didn't need a tenant.

She needed a mate. A perfect mate.

Thank God he had no illusions about that being him. He had already failed completely and irrevocably in the perfect mate department.

CHAPTER SIX

"So, when is the apartment going to be available? Can I have a look at it?"

Abby didn't dare look at Shane. And she didn't want to be too obvious in her study of her prospective tenant, either, sitting across from both of them at the kitchen table. She and Shane had been interviewing prospective tenants for a week now, during Belle's naptime.

Lola was almost completely bald, except for a purple strip of hair down the center of her head. She had three rings through her bottom lip, and more than Abby could count through her ears. The one through the eyebrow looked particularly painful.

"Did I mention I have a pet?" Lola asked, when no one answered her.

"No, I think you left that part out when I talked to you on the phone," Shane said, his voice cool, a certain dangerous note in it that Lola seemed to miss completely.

"Oh, well, it's not a dog or a cat or anything that smells and leaves hair all over the place. It's an iguana. Iggy."

Abby choked back her laughter. Shane glared at her.

"We don't allow dogs and cats," he said firmly. "Or reptiles."

"That sucks."

"Yeah, well, life does sometimes."

Lola picked up her bag, stood up, glared regally at both of them, and said, "I think you're discriminating against me because of my age. You're just using Iggy as an excuse. I bet legally he doesn't even qualify as a pet. I might sue."

"Actually," Shane said standing up and forming the policeman stance, "it's only because of the iguana. You do share an entryway and a kitchen. Abby has a baby. She's fussy about what crawls around on the floor with it."

"A baby?" Lola said with abject horror. "I can't stand babies. Thanks for wasting my time." And she marched out of the kitchen.

Abby was able to contain herself until she heard the front door slam, and then the first giggle slipped out.

"Don't," he warned her.

She bit her lip. But her shoulders shook. Then she gave up. She put her head down on the table and laughed. She laughed until it hurt, and then suddenly realized he was laughing, too.

"Oh, Shane, when she said the part about smoking marijuana for medicinal purposes I thought you were going to place her under arrest."

"I don't have any jurisdiction in Oregon," he said glumly. "Besides, I still was harboring this hope that maybe you could live with that if she knew what a fuse was."

"And she thought—"

"It was a kind of bong."

"I'm not even sure I know what that is, exactly," Abby said. "Do you?"

"Ten years in law enforcement. Yeah, I know what a bong is. Drug paraphernalia." His stern look melted and he seemed to realize how hilarious their encounters had been. Shane began to laugh.

His laughter was pure, wonderful, like light coming into a dark place.

"And she," he managed to sputter, "was definitely the best of the candidates we've interviewed this week. How many?"

"Sixteen," she said. "And she was not the best one. I could have lived with that lady who coughed so much."

"It might have been catchy! Think about your child!"

"The woman with the cane seemed very nice."

"How the hell was she going to put up storm windows on the second floor?"

"I can do that!"

"Over my dead body."

"I could hire somebody."

"But you wouldn't."

"Shane," she said, "I'm perfectly happy with things the way they are. Aren't you? Where are you going to live if you leave here? In a houseful of people like her? There are worse things than me and Belle."

"I don't dislike you and Belle," he said, slowly. "I never meant for you to have that impression."

"Right! You avoid me like the plague. Except when we're interviewing possible replacements for you." Which she knew by now was going to be impossible, especially since he only seemed to be interviewing little old ladies. With a few wild young ones who slipped by his net and got through the front door by pure chance.

But even if they were interviewing guys, she was beginning to realize she would never replace him.

And how oddly empty her life would seem without him upstairs. And his package of bologna in the fridge.

"Abby, me avoiding you is not about you. At all."

"What's it about then?"

He looked away from her, the laughter gone from the room as suddenly as a rainbow going from the sky. "Me. It's about me."

She waited, knowing that the first threads of a relationship had formed over these past few days while they interviewed possible tenants together. A fragile thing was unfolding in front of her, and she waited, holding her breath.

"Abby, when Stacey died, my wife—" his voice faltered. "I just don't want to be around people anymore. I don't want to feel anymore."

She stared at him, her own heart breaking inside her chest at the look on his face, the strong features, for once, vulnerable. More than vulnerable.

"How long has it been?"

"Just over two years. Don't tell me I should get over it. I don't want to."

"You've made lonely a way of life, Shane."

"I guess."

"What if I promise not to make you feel anything?"

"You can't make a promise like that."

"Why not?"

"Because I'm already feeling all kinds of things."

It took all her courage to ask, but she asked. "Like what?"

"Like this." He got up out of his chair and came over to her. As he bent toward her, she knew it was coming, and she was powerless to move away from it.

Wanted it with her whole heart and soul.

His lips touched hers.

And all her own dark places—wounded places caused by betrayal and by love gone wrong—suddenly seemed to be drenched with light.

She had only seriously kissed one man in her whole life before. But her soul recognized the difference this time. Ty had taken. His kisses had been hungry and about him, about filling some need in him.

But this, her lips meeting Shane's, was something else all together.

It felt like some place within her that had been held in chains was suddenly free, soaring high above all the trials and insecurities and pains of being human. This was the other side of being human, the side every woman dreamed of and hoped for in some secret place within herself. This was the glorious side, the place where all that was human in her took wing and touched the place of the gods.

She twined her arms around his neck, pulled him closer to her, allowed the kiss to deepen. She felt the power in his arms, and the passion in his soul, as he gathered her to him with a moan of surrender and despair.

He pulled away, suddenly, leaving her gasping and looking at him with naked desire that she could not hide.

"I'm sorry," he said, looking away from her and running a hand through his hair.

"Sorry?" she whispered. Sorry was somehow the last thing she was feeling.

"That's why we can't stay under the same roof."

"Oh. Of course."

He looked at her long and hard, troubled, and then he brightened. "Wait, I've got it."

"What?" she asked, though she did not want to know how he had solved what he saw as a dilemma and she saw as a gift from heaven.

"I know where to find you a perfect person to share this house."

"And where would that be?" She felt as if she was getting cold, as if every ounce of warmth had drained from the room, as if she had been swept up in the elating and electrifying power of a sudden summer storm, but was now left only drenched and shaking.

"A church," he said triumphantly. "I can't exactly see Lola hanging out there on a Sunday morning, can you?"

"No," she said woodenly.

Belle, waking up from her afternoon nap, began to cry.

"Pop her in the stroller. St. James's is right around the corner. We'll see if they have a bulletin board or something."

She told herself to say no. But she didn't. She said yes. And then felt pathetic. Was she willing to do anything just to be with him?

Yes.

This was not looking good. At all.

* * *

Shane could not believe what had just happened. He'd kissed Abby. In the kitchen. And her lips had been the sweetest thing he had ever tasted. Ever. He felt like he had been walking in a desert, parched, without hope, and she was an oasis, her lips a sweet fruit that quenched the thirst that had been all-consuming within him.

Which only meant he'd been right all along.

He had to get away from her. From the temptation of her, from the appeal of her. Posting a note at the church was a brainstorm.

Why had he asked her to come along?

He hadn't been thinking. It was completely unnecessary for her to make the trip, too.

Did he want to be with her?

Yes.

All the more reason that notice had to go up at the church and now. She needed someone. He knew that. She wanted to be independent, she was independent, but her life would be easier if she was sharing it.

Belle was a handful.

And so was this old house.

It's just that someone could not be him. She needed someone with a heart that was whole, not torn to pieces. She needed someone who would love only her, not someone who was in love with a ghost.

In love with a ghost. He thought about that for a moment and recognized it was not quite true. He had loved his wife while she lived. And resented her heartily since she died. Resented her for the jumble of emotion inside of him, for the huge cracks in the veneer of his strength. Resented her for showing him that he was not infallible.

But most of all he resented her because of what she had made him. A failure.

He had failed to be there when she needed him.

Failed to save her.

Abby did not need a man with that kind of baggage. A man capable of failure, especially a failure of such a gargantuan proportion. A failure in such a crucial area.

He went up to his desk, pulled his notepad to him and wrote: Wanted: Tenant for upstairs apartment. Shared kitchen. He did not, with great discipline, add what he most wanted to add. Female only. If the last sixteen people they had talked to were any indication, a female who was good with fuses was as rare a find as a gorilla who could tap dance.

But if a nice church-going boy came along who could change a fuse and who did not have a history of not being where he should have been in a life-and-death moment, then that is what Abby deserved.

But it felt to Shane like he was tearing what was left of his own heart out when he tore that piece of paper from the pad.

She was just coming into the front hall when he came back down the stairs. She turned and smiled at him, her eyes cautious.

The caution, he knew, was brought on by his stupid kiss by the new tension crackling in the air between them.

Belle was not nearly so cautious. She stood up in her stroller, she was so excited to see him. Why did she care about him so much? Weren't babies supposed to have some kind of instinct that told them who people really were? Or maybe that was dogs.

"Up?" she crowed, holding out her arms to him.

"Belle, sit down before you fall down," Abby said.
"No, up."

Belle ignored her mother, and he was helpless before
her. He went and picked her up.

"I can carry her. We don't need the stroller."

Belle wrapped her arms around his neck and gave
him a big sloppy smooch on his cheek. Now he'd been
kissed more today than he had in the past two years.

"Are you sure you want to carry her? She's heavier
than she looks."

"Yeah, I'm sure."

Abby went out the door and down the walk first, and
then he directed her which way to go.

He supposed they looked like a family walking down
the street, the baby crowing and pointing at a cat slink-
ing along through the shrubs beside them.

"Name," she demanded.

"Cat," he said.

Abby laughed, a little self-consciously. "It's a game
we play. I name all the animals for her."

"Really? Like what?"

Abby shot the cat a look. "He looks like a...Mr.
Snotgrodden."

"Not you," Belle said officiously. "He." She pulled
at his shirt so he couldn't make a mistake.

"Oh." He looked at the cat. "How about Rags?"

Belle frowned at him.

"The more syllables the better," Abby whispered to
him.

"Oh. How about Bottomsworth?"

Belle smiled, pleased that he had caught on so quickly, while he debated whether or not that was a Freudian slip of the perverted kind.

Who had a worthier bottom, after all, than the woman beside him?

"Walk now," Belle said. After a glance at her mother, he set her down. In short order he became aware the walk to the church was going to take somewhat longer than he had anticipated. Belle crouched down and inspected *everything.* Dried worm bodies, used Popsicle sticks, leaves. All were scrutinized, and explanations demanded.

Out of the blue it hit him, like a punch on his blind side.

If Stacey had lived, this might have been his life. Out for walks. Their baby would have been about this age now. Full of curiosity, and life and wonder.

There it was. That familiar feeling of being crushed under the weight of his own feelings. It wasn't just Abby who needed someone without baggage, it was that baby. She needed a man who could look at her without mourning his own losses.

Belle pointed to something, and proclaimed loudly, "Poop. Don't touch!"

Despite himself, he smiled. They learned all the important things really young. The church was just up ahead, the hall beside it. There was a bulletin board on the exterior hall wall, and he went and posted the notice.

"Do you want to go in for a minute?" Abby asked.

"To the church? Why?"

"I don't know. I like churches. They always smell so good and feel so peaceful inside. Ever since I was little I would ask God to look after my real Mom, wherever she was. And maybe she was up there with Him, looking after me."

Her words reminded him he was not the only one who had suffered losses.

So he shrugged, and followed her up the wide stone steps to the church entry. He hoped it would be locked. The policeman in him thought it should be locked. But, of course, it wasn't.

As soon as he stepped inside, he knew it had been a mistake. He was not a church kind of guy. In recent years he'd only been in one twice. The same one.

He'd married her.

And buried her.

He hesitated as Abby took Belle firmly in hand, and went up the aisle. She stopped at a pew, slid in, looked at the altar. The light from a stained-glass window was falling over her face, and it made her look incredibly beautiful.

She bowed her head and folded her hands together.

Feeling awkward, he slipped into a pew at the back of the church to wait for her. The hush and the smell blended together. He closed his eyes. She was right. It was a peaceful place.

Maybe too peaceful. He could feel his head drooping against his chest. Too many nights of the "bear went over the mountain" running through his head. He hated to think what the additional memory of her lips was going to do to his sleep patterns.

He felt her before he saw her. Stacey.

She looked beautiful, her long dark hair free, wearing a dress that was long and flowing and white. He felt so happy to see her.

But she didn't look at all happy to see him.

In fact she had her hands on her hips in a position he remembered very well. He'd been treated to it on several occasions. Like when, newly married, he'd gone for a few drinks after a hard shift and had forgotten to call.

"You're a real jerk," she said.

Somehow he had not pictured this as being the tone for their reunion. He wanted to speak to her, but couldn't, his tongue lead inside his mouth.

She glared at him. "Look, Shane, I can't stand you like this. Full of self-pity. Full of yourself."

He wanted to protest, but again he found his tongue heavy within his mouth, without words, his lips glued shut.

"That young woman is all alone here in this town. She doesn't know a single soul. Her sisters aren't here yet. She's with that baby all day. That's harder than it looks, you know. It's not all kisses and cuddles. And you won't even be her friend. What's the matter with you?"

He'd somehow forgotten this side of Stacey. Once, he'd come home to find a bust he'd been on had been televised, and she had been furious with him. Said he had been *mean*, unnecessarily rough. When he'd tried to tell her the bad guy had tried to blow his head off, she'd sniffed and said, "So that's all the excuse you need to become the bad guy?"

He'd never forgotten that. It had changed him in some fundamental way, made him a better cop and a better man.

Stacey's look suddenly softened, and with the white dress floating around her, she came toward him. "This isn't the Shane McCall I loved. The Shane McCall I loved always tried to do the right thing."

She turned and walked away from him, tossing her hair over her shoulder. Then she turned back and came up to him, took his shoulders, and shook them. "Wake up," she said.

"Shane, wake up."

"Huh?" He started awake, and saw Abby looking at him, smiling wryly.

"I'm ready to leave," she whispered.

He clambered to his feet. "I must have dozed off," he said, feeling groggy and disoriented. "Sorry."

"You don't have to be sorry."

"I wasn't talking to you."

She gave him a baffled look and he shook his head to clear the last of the cobwebs away. He reached down and picked up Belle, and walked down the aisle of the church. Belle liked what the patterns of light the stained glass threw on the floor.

Out in the sunshine, Abby scanned his face. "I told you it was peaceful," she said with a smile. "I didn't know you'd find it quite that peaceful."

"Yeah." No point telling her it hadn't been all that peaceful for him. "Sometimes I nod off during the day. I don't always sleep very well at night."

"Since I came?" she asked, stricken.

"No."

"Since your wife died?"

"Yeah."

"You must have loved each other very much."

"Yeah."

"How did she die, Shane?"

"She fell down some steps. When I wasn't home." He should have been home that day, but a call had come from work and he'd gone. "She was eight months pregnant."

He wished he wouldn't have added that, because Abby's eyes filmed over with tears, and her hand touched his arm. She didn't say one single word, and he was so grateful to her for that.

He cleared his throat.

Do the right thing.

He thought he had been doing the right thing. Keeping his distance, staying out of her hair, keeping himself free of entanglements.

"Have you, er, met anyone yet? Here?"

"Oh." She looked embarrassed. "I don't get out much. You know, with Belle and everything."

"You haven't even met any other young moms, at the park, or something?"

She looked away from him swiftly, but not before he caught the glitter in her eyes. When she turned back to him she was smiling with false brightness.

"There's always Mrs. Pondergrove," she said, "And my sister, Brittany will be here by the end of the month. I talked to her on the phone the other night and guess what?"

"What?"

"She's scared to death of spiders!"

"You're kidding, right?"

"I can't tell you how I felt when I heard that."

He could see how she felt from the gentle glow in her eyes. Not so damned alone in the world.

"There are worse things than being afraid of spiders," he told her gruffly.

"Name one!"

Being afraid of life. "I knew a cop once who was

afraid of needles. Big guy, too. Bigger than me. We got a call from the hospital one time, after a car accident. Little kid needed a ton of blood. The rare kind. I've got it, so did he. He fainted dead as soon as they stuck the needle in his arm."

"Really?" she said, obviously pleased.

"A phobia is not like a character defect," he told her. "That man was one of the most courageous people I ever served with."

"Thanks, Shane."

"I'm not a complete jerk."

She gave him a surprised look. "Who ever called you a jerk?"

"Somebody who knows a jerk when they see one." He sighed. "Do you want to go and get a bite to eat?"

He wasn't sure what it meant when her face lit up. He only knew he felt completely unworthy of it.

Walking beside him, Belle now on his shoulders yelling her delight at the new view from up there, Abby allowed herself to feel content.

This is what her life might have been. Had she stayed with Ty. The nice family outings. Mommy, Daddy, baby, that grouping of three that she had so come to envy.

Not that she had any illusions about Ty ever being able to fit into that particular picture.

"Monogamy is not in my nature," he had told her, when she'd caught him. "And if any man tells you it is in his nature, he's a liar."

She felt herself pull away from the man beside her at that memory, and then she relaxed. She wasn't having a relationship with Shane McCall. He'd made that very clear.

Could a man and a woman be just friends?

An idea Ty would have scorned.

But what was wrong with just being in the moment? Never mind spoiling it by analyzing what might or might not happen down the road. What about just enjoying the sweetness of this uncomplicated moment?

They walked to a little cafe by the ocean. It was still too early in the year to sit outside, with the blustery wind blowing off the harbor, so they went in. They ordered sandwiches for themselves and a hot dog for Belle, which was a mistake. She removed the hot dog from the bun, took a bite and then threw it on the floor in distaste. She proceeded to squish the bun between her fingers, and soon had relish, ketchup and mustard spread from her forehead to her neckline. Only when the bun had been mashed flat and bore an unfortunate resemblance to roadkill, did Belle take a bite.

"Yum-yum," she declared.

Shane hooted with laughter. It was only the second time Abby had seen him laugh, and she thought the sound of it, the way it stripped the years from his face and the haunted look from his eyes, might make his laughter something she could become addicted to.

After lunch, he bought a kite at a little souvenir shop next to the restaurant and they went to the beach, to fly it.

Running along the beach, laughing, watching that kite, Abby was not sure she had ever felt so carefree, so wonderful, so alive.

Later, walking home, tired, Belle nearly asleep in the crook of his arm, she felt his hand rest on her shoulder, just for a moment.

When they paused at the entryway he handed her the now sleeping child, and looked at her long and hard.

For an exhilarating moment, she thought he might kiss her again, but he didn't.

He smiled, shook his head introspectively, and went up the stairs.

CHAPTER SEVEN

THERE they were, little-her and big-her, out in the yard, earlier today than usual. Shane was watching out his window that overlooked the front yard. Today, Abby had a shovel. At first he found it a little amusing watching her.

She stamped the shovel into the grass with determination, and when that produced no result she jumped on it with both feet. The shovel went into the ground about an inch. She jumped on it again. And then again.

He wasn't sure what she was doing, but it was going to take her a while. Belle had her own little shovel and had plunked herself down near some dirt and was busy digging a hole. She was better at it than her mother.

Abby had already taken off her jacket and wiped her brow. Jeans today, and a man's shirt over a T-shirt, her Cubs hat on backwards. She looked like the teenage boy he had mistaken her for at first. Abby jumped on the shovel again. He hoped she wasn't going to hurt herself.

He shook his head, and turned back to his computer. Staring at the screen, he read over the three sentences he had written this morning, and then looked out the window again. She had managed to loosen a hefty piece of sod, and was trying to tear it off with her hands. Either she shouldn't be bending over like that, or he shouldn't be looking.

He made himself look back at his screen. Hunting and pecking, he typed out the next line of the chapter. Only what appeared on his screen was *You're a real jerk.*

With a sigh, he backspaced over that, saved his hard won three lines and went down the stairs and outside.

"Do you need a hand?" he asked her.

"No," she said, panting, standing on top of her shovel.

"What are you doing?"

She stepped down from the shovel. "I want to extend this flower bed. But the grass is in the way."

"It would probably take me ten minutes to get it out of your way."

"It's all right, I can do it."

He saw now where she had marked a curved line on the grass with something white. It looked suspiciously like flour. She jumped on her shovel again.

"You're going to hurt yourself," he said.

"No, I—Belle, don't eat that!" She dropped the shovel and ran over to her daughter, who was about to ingest a worm.

He picked up the shovel. And started digging, noting his knee seemed to be completely healed. In ten minutes he had the sod stripped, and the ground turned.

"Equal rights aside," he said, handing her back the shovel, "men were made to do certain things."

"I can't believe you could do that so quickly," she said a little glumly. "It makes me feel terribly inadequate."

"I bet there's lots of things you're better at than me," he said.

"Like what?"

"The kitchen smells pretty good after you've been in there."

"It does after you've been in there too," she said.

"What? You like the smell of sardines?"

She blushed fiery red, and turned away from him. "Tell you what. I'll thank you for the flower bed with lunch. How would that be?"

That would be impossible, he thought. They couldn't start sharing that kitchen. But that isn't what he answered her.

He said, "That would be just fine. Do you want anything else dug up while I'm here?" She made him sorry he had asked. She wanted half the yard excavated. A small vegetable garden here, a few herbs right there, a little curving walkway in between them.

"Of course," she said, suddenly embarrassed, "I don't expect you to do that. Really, I don't. In fact, I'd rather do it myself."

"How about if I just see what I can get done before lunch? After that I'll surrender the shovel to you."

She mulled that over for a moment. "That would be fair. Belle, you come with me. We'll go in and make some lunch."

"No, Belle stay with he!" Belle informed her, not looking up from her energetic digging in an existing flower bed.

"I don't mind keeping an eye on her."

Abby's mouth dropped, and then she looked at him narrowly. "It's harder than you think. You can't let her put things in her mouth."

"Trust me. I've protected my nation from numerous bad guys. Very bad guys. I can probably manage a baby."

She smiled and relaxed. "Yes, you probably can. I'll call you when lunch is ready.

He nodded and set to work, watching Belle out of the corner of his eye. After a while he began to feel like a tape recorder because he'd yelled, "Don't eat that!" so often. In the persistence department he didn't think very many bad guys would be able to hold a candle to little Miss Mischief, who in between trying to eat dirt, rocks and worms also made three attempts to escape from the yard. She hooted with laughter each time she made him drop the shovel and come after her.

Finally, he planted her and her shovel right in front of him. "Don't move," he told her, and realized that order was like telling a river not to flow, or the wind not to blow. The kid was in constant motion. He finally realized that what she really wanted was his undivided attention.

He put down the shovel and sat down on the grass. After a moment, she toddled over and sat beside him.

She was eager to show him a worm she had just found, and also a leaf. The leaf looked half-rotten to him, but was endlessly fascinating to her. She garbled away about it for a few minutes, and though he didn't understand a word, he nodded his head and told her it was very nice. Apparently satisfied, she went back to the patch of earth he had designated for her and began to dig again.

And sing. "Bear odor da mowin, bear odor da mowin, see, see, see, seeeeee."

He worked for half an hour or so, enjoying the little

girl's company, and all the strange treasures she brought over for his approval. A rock, a snail, some twigs, an old rusted ball bearing. He turned over each item in his hands, and found for some odd reason, his interest was not pretended. Belle had a way of making him see things in a brand-new way.

And to rediscover old things, too. He became aware of the smell of the freshly turned earth, remembered how much he had always liked that smell, and even this kind of work. The shoveling put a pleasant strain on his muscles, and between that and a mellow spring sun, the sweat trickled down his forehead. He felt content.

Abby opened the kitchen window. It groaned, and she could only get it open an inch or two. Something else that needed to be fixed.

"Lunch," Abby called.

He lifted Belle onto his shoulders. She insisted he gallop around the yard three times before she allowed him to take her into the house.

Abby took her from him at the door.

"Is there a girl under all that dirt?" she asked.

"No!" Belle crowed, delighted to be disguised, but not so delighted when her mother hauled her away to clean her up.

Shane went upstairs and washed up, and as an afterthought, reapplied his deodorant.

A concession to living in a house with a woman.

When he came back down to the kitchen they hadn't returned, though he could hear Belle squealing protests about being subjected to her mother's vigorous cleaning. He acknowledged he felt a little weary, and not from digging. There really was more to raising a child than kisses and cuddles. He wondered how Abby managed it every single day without a break.

The kitchen smelled of heaven—garlic and spices heavy in the air.

The newspaper was open on the table, and he went and glanced at it, then wondered if there was anything in particular Abby had been looking at on this page.

Then he saw it. An full color ad for a red-and-white swing and slide set, with a covered sandbox. Had she been looking at that? Wishing she had it for Belle?

Thinking about getting it but knowing she had no way of putting it together? She probably didn't even have the money for it. Was his rent her only income? Besides sewing flowers on old lady's hats? That couldn't bring in too much.

He closed the paper just as Abby and Belle came into the room. Belle was in a clean denim jumper, with little blue leotards over her plump legs. Abby had removed the Cubs hat and done something to her hair. Gelled it so that it stuck up in cute little spikes. If he was not mistaken her lips were shiny, too. Gloss?

For him? A concession to living with a man? Come to think of it, both of them smelled good too—of soap and soft feminine things that reminded him of spring.

Was he getting himself into trouble here?

The smell of garlic and good things cooking lured him forward even as his mind warned him to go back.

Lunch tasted better than it had smelled, which hardly even seemed possible.

"It's just casual," she said, blushing when he complimented her. "Caesar salad and Tetrazzini."

"Are you kidding? Casual is bologna and sardines."

She laughed. She looked wonderful in that too-large

shirt, tied at the waist and sleeves rolled up, a tight red T-shirt on underneath it. Red suited her. Why?

Did it hint at something red-hot just below that calm "somebody's mommy" surface?

Belle was demanding to know why these worms were okay to eat, but not the ones outside. Because of her limited use of language it took her most of lunch to make her point. He could have lingered forever, entertained by this impromptu game of mother and daughter charades.

Instead, he suddenly remembered the appointment he'd made for that afternoon. He glanced at his watch. The appointment that begins in five minutes.

He prided himself on never forgetting appointments.

Of course, until very recently, he had nothing to clutter up the order of his life.

A young guy had called him and said he'd seen the ad for the suite on the church bulletin board. Shane had decided not even to involve Abby in the interview.

He was looking for something quite different than she was.

He wanted to be assured that whoever took over his suite could help her out with windows that didn't open, and grass that didn't budge until more than ninety-seven pounds of force was applied to it. She would be indignant at the very idea that she needed help.

"Thanks for lunch," he said, "but I've got to run. I just remembered something I have to do this afternoon."

Did she look disappointed?

"Thank you for digging my bed for me"

He could be stripped of the Boy Scout badge he had just earned for the thought that went through his head about what he'd like to be doing in her bed. And it had nothing to do with digging. Or flowers, either.

Still, despite that one renegade thought, he felt strangely good about what had just happened. He knew what he had experienced in the church had just been a dream, but in it had been the kernels of a truth he needed to know about himself. It was one thing to be a hermit, it was another to be a jerk.

Abby was a single mom, and she needed a bit of support. That kid was exhausting without Abby tackling the yard and a job, too. So, he could give her a hand every now and then. Until the new guy took over. The truth was he felt better. Handling that shovel for her had done him as much good as it had her.

Lunch was a bonus.

Because he was running a little late, he drove to the cafe. It was the same one where he and Abby and Belle had had lunch, and he felt like their laughter over Belle and that hot dog still lingered there.

He had just been served coffee when he was joined at the table.

"Mr. McCall, sir?"

"That's me."

"David Hathoway."

The young man looked to be in his early twenties. He was slight and blond, wearing plastic rimmed glasses that made him look like a *real* Boy Scout. He appeared to be clean-cut, wholesome, owlish.

Shane took the young man's proffered hand and shook it, didn't let it register in his face that the handshake was disappointing.

"Have a seat, David. Coffee?"

"Oh, no, I don't use anything with caffeine in it. I consider caffeine a drug."

Perfect. No marijuana for medicinal purposes. Still, Shane took a rebellious sip of his own caffeine-laden cappuccino. "So, David, you saw my ad on the church bulletin board?"

"That's correct. I'm staying with the minister right now, because of the housing shortage. I'm signed up for a bible course he's teaching."

Bible course. Perfect again. He wouldn't be stealing Belle's Sugar Pups from the cupboards, or helping himself to the Gouda.

"Are you handy?"

"Handy, sir?"

"A single woman lives in the ground floor suite. The yard needs some work and she wants to put in a garden. She's got a landscaping plan that she doesn't quite have the muscle to execute." Not that she'd ever admit it.

"I wouldn't mind helping with the yard at all. I'd love to help put in a garden. We always had one at home on the farm."

Shane wasn't quite sure how to tell David he might have to wrestle the shovel from her body. Maybe he'd see how this went, and get to that part later in the interview.

"It's an old house. The fuses blow, the windows don't like to open, the furnace needs a good hard kick every now and then. And you can't let her go in that basement at all."

Shane wasn't quite sure how to make it clear how imperative that was. Maybe he'd get back to that part later, too.

The kid smiled eagerly, "Oh, I'm great at stuff like

that. Our farmhouse was over a hundred years old. My mom calls me a regular Mr. Fix-it."

"And what does your girlfriend call you?" Was that subtle enough? He was interviewing a tenant for Abby, not a potential husband. Which didn't exactly explain why he was so relieved the boy was obviously too young for her. What did he care if David had a girlfriend?

But if David had a girlfriend it might help him keep his eyes off Abby's belly button. Shane was surprised at how much he didn't like the idea of anybody else looking at her belly button, too young for her or not.

Not that he seemed to be able to keep his own eyes where they belonged, not if his life depended on it.

"Well, sir, I'm not currently in a relationship. But if I was, my girl would never see the inside of my apartment. Not until we were married. I wouldn't throw myself on temptation's door like that."

"Oh. Okay." A decent, old-fashioned boy. The boy least likely to sneak a peek, steal the cereal or have wild parties. A boy who looked like he would be eager to help out around the place.

"The rent has to be paid right on time, no excuses."

David looked injured. "I've been saving my money for a year to do this. I plan to get a part-time job, too."

That settled it. Shane had found the perfect tenant.

Why did he feel sick inside? Was it because he really, deep down, didn't want to move? Had enjoyed that day of kite flying, not to mention the little encounter in the backyard more than he wanted to admit? Not to mention Tetrazzini and Caesar salad? And looking at worms in a brand-new light?

"Like I said, your landlady lives downstairs. You'd be sharing a kitchen with her and a front entry hall. You have to be careful with the front door and you have to leave a baby gate up, so that Belle doesn't go outside or up the stairs."

"Belle?"

"Her kid. The landlady's baby."

"Is she married? The landlady?"

Shane looked at him narrowly. David better not be getting any ideas about romancing the landlady. "Why do you ask?"

"I live by a certain moral code." An interesting thing was happening to the boy's face. It was getting all pinched looking around the mouth.

"As a matter of fact, Abby's not married," he said, danger in his voice.

"A widow, I hope."

"That's a funny thing to hope for someone."

"Divorced?" David said.

"No."

The kid missed the warning note completely. "Well, I can't live in a house with a woman of loose morals."

Shane felt like he was going to pick him up and throw him through the picture window at the front of the restaurant.

"Really?" he managed to say, his voice ice-edged.

Again, David seemed to miss the dangerous footing he had moved into, so eager was he to share his self-righteous judgements. "I don't approve of women who have children out of wedlock."

"Is that right?"

"It is."

Somehow, by some thread, Shane's temper held. "I'm not much into this stuff, but I could have sworn there was a part in that book you've come to study about throwing the first stone."

Shane got up and tossed a bill on the table for the coffee he had barely touched. He turned on his heel and walked out. He gave himself a pat on the back for managing not to have that kid's shirt wrapped around his fist, slamming him up against a wall.

Stacey would have called that mean, recognized it as lowering himself to the same level as that creep sitting in there disguised as Mr. Decent. Shane got in his vehicle, then noticed the hardware store was right down the street. Was that the same one that had advertised the swing set? It wouldn't hurt to go check it out.

He came back out with a bulky box on his shoulder. Really, when he thought about it, there was no rush to rent the upper part of the house. He might as well wait until he had found decent accommodations elsewhere.

Which, admittedly, might take a while.

"What are you doing?" Abby asked, coming up behind him as he worked on the yard. He had all the pieces of the swing set lying on the grass, and he'd hauled his tool kit out of the basement. He perused the instructions only briefly, before crumpling them up and rubbing his hands together. Any moron could see what step came first.

"Nothing," he said, confidently bolting the cross piece to the A-frame.

She looked at the box. "A swing set?"

"Cute, isn't it? Kind of like a barber's pole." He fastened the second cross piece, and frowned.

"I think that's backward," she said.

He studied it. Damned if she wasn't right. He didn't

want to uncrumple the instructions in front of her, so he quickly undid it and put it the right way.

"Shane, the swing set is for?"

"I got it for Belle." He dared her to make something of that. "Can you grab that end, and we'll stand this part up?"

Her mouth fell open. "Shane. I wish you wouldn't have. It's too much."

"You wanted one for her, didn't you?"

She looked amazed. "I've never given it a thought."

He frowned and tightened a bolt. She must have been looking at something else on that page of the newspaper.

"Well, do you think Belle will like it?"

"She'll adore it," Abby admitted reluctantly.

"Great," he said. "Could you hand me that half inch wrench?"

For a man who seemed to be digging himself in deeper, he couldn't deny this funny feeling inside himself. It had been so long since he had felt it, that at first he didn't recognize what it was. Happiness. He started to whistle. The swing set took him five hours to assemble and then he had to push Belle, who squealed with glee, for a half an hour. But it made every second it had taken him to put that monster piece of equipment together worthwhile.

He slept better that night than he had slept in years. In the morning he noticed yesterday's paper still sitting on his desk and just out of curiosity, he opened it to the ad for the swings.

On that same page were bridge scores, a supermarket display ad featuring toilet paper, an article and picture about some old gent's hundredth birthday. On the opposite page was a story and picture about the deplorable eyesore the old cannery was. Shane noticed the paper seemed to run that article and picture, unchanged, once a month or so.

And then he saw a very small piece about Friday night being the last night the local theater company was presenting their comedy, *The Hen House*. Had she wanted to see the play?

What would it hurt to ask her? Poor girl never got out.

"A play? On Friday?" Abby said. She put a pin in the cushion she had attached to her wrist, trying to disguise the fact her heart had just tried to leap out of her chest. "Me?"

"Just you."

"I love the theater," she said, and then was sorry. She looked everywhere but at him. "No. I couldn't possibly."

"Why not?"

"I don't have a baby-sitter," she said, which was true, even though any excuse would have done.

"Ask that old gal in the hat. I bet she'd do it."

"Mrs. Pondergrove? I don't know, Shane." Abby thought those were probably the very hardest words she'd ever spoken.

"What's the problem? You said you love the theater. When's the last time you went and did something just for grown-ups?"

"It's been a while," she admitted, and hoped that didn't reveal too much about the pathetic loneliness of her life. Not that she didn't love Belle, not that she'd change a thing, but...

Actually, there was a real reason she didn't want to go. She was working on that dress. The silk, despite being so difficult to work with, especially with Belle wanting so desperately to "help," was coming alive under her fingertips, taking shape each day. Singing to her heart.

About dreams. And romantic notions.

About the man upstairs.

Her thoughts always drifted to him when she sat down with those yards of ivory silk. At first it had been innocent enough. She would hear him upstairs, and try to imagine what he was doing, and what he was wearing and what he looked like.

Was his brow furrowed in concentration? Did he stick his tongue out between his teeth all the time when he concentrated, the way he had when he worked on that swing set?

But then her thoughts would drift a little further, and her tummy would begin to tingle, especially if she thought of how he had looked with that shovel, his muscles rippling, the sweat forming a fine sheen on his skin, the way he'd thrown back his head and laughed when Belle had compared her Tetrazzini to worms.

As she worked on the dress, she remembered how being near him made her feel all quivery inside, as if she had been asked to speak in front of an audience of five hundred.

And then her thoughts would drift further yet, down that river of fantasy, getting further and further from reality. She would rethink that brief kiss, and relive it.

Sewing that dress, she would think forbidden thoughts of what it would be like to be his bride, to walk down an aisle and to see his eyes on her.

And then to go into his bed at night, to feel his lips on her lips, and on her cheeks and on, well, everything.

That dress was like some sort of enchantment.

It made her want to believe extraordinary things could happen to ordinary people just like her. It made her want to do the most dangerous thing of all.

Trust again. Hope again. Believe again.

"Abby, what's wrong?"

The truth crashed down around her. *She was falling for him.* That's what was wrong.

And he was acting like some benevolent big brother who saw she needed help in the garden and the occasional outing. She yearned for his kisses, for his breath in her ears, for the span of his hands on her waist. Not for swing sets.

"Nothing's wrong. I can't go." She went to shut the door, but his foot was in it. "I'd like to have more done on the dress than I have done."

"Mrs. Blundercow's wedding dress," he guessed. "Can I see it?"

"Pondergrove! No. It's unlucky for a man to see a bride's dress before she does." She adjusted the old myth to meet her needs, knowing he wouldn't know any better.

The actual superstition was that the groom should not see the bride in her dress before the wedding day.

She tried to shut the door again.

"Please?" he said. "Come to the play with me."

She closed her eyes, recognizing what it had cost him to say that.

And suddenly she was ashamed of herself. Was this the legacy of her relationship with Ty? *Protect yourself?*

If she really cared for Shane, if it was more than a passing infatuation, wouldn't it ask more of her? Require more of her? Wouldn't it ask her to give, without thought of receiving? Wouldn't real caring want what was best for him?

Shane was a man who had lost everything that mattered to him. His wife. His unborn child. The dreams they had shared together. Their hopes for the future. Everything had been taken from him in the blink of an eye.

His grief had made him turn his back on the world.

And now, here he was at her door, tentatively reaching out.

She thought of the last few days. Lunch. Flying the kite. Digging in the garden. Laughing over Tetrazzini. The swing set for Belle. He was saying he was willing to give life a chance again, even after all life had done to him. She wasn't even sure that he knew that was the decision he had made.

But she knew his heart was trying to mend, trying to grow toward the light, even if he did not, and she knew it wasn't his fault she reacted to his muscles the way she did, to his voice, to his eyes resting on her. It wasn't his fault that she fiddled with her hair for too long each day, in case she caught a glimpse of him, and it wasn't his fault that she tried on twelve different shirts before she settled on one that looked just right—as if she looked sexy just by accident.

She could not say no to him.

Her personal feelings and fears aside, he was holding out a fragile thing to her. She had an opportunity to help another human being. Would she say no because there was nothing in it for her?

Is that what she would teach her daughter about life?

"Shane," she said, taking a deep breath. "I'd love to go."

She opened her eyes just in time to see him smile, and in that smile she saw that she had done the right thing. The only thing.

"I'll come down Friday about seven, then."

"All right," she whispered, already wondering what to wear.

CHAPTER EIGHT

"Oh, my," said Mrs. Pondergrove, her eyes widening behind her glasses, "that is a very glamorous dress."

"Too bold?" Abby asked nervously. The dress was one she had made some time ago, in a reckless moment. It was patterned after one she had fallen in love with while watching the Grammy Awards on television. The dress wasn't indecent. Not in the least. In fact, it had been relatively simple to make.

It had inch wide straps at the shoulders, and an empire waistline. She'd worn a push-up bra that did turn fact to fiction, but in actual fact it was the skirt of the dress that gave it its magic. The skirt was quite full, and two-layered, the top layer a sheer chiffon that swished sexily around her legs.

And of course, the dress was red. Deep true red. The color of blood and hearts and roses.

She had never worn it. Just had a lot of fun making it. And then she had decided it really wasn't the kind of dress someone's mother wore, so she'd filed it away in the back of her closet.

Why had she chosen it tonight?

Because, altruism aside, she didn't plan to be treated like anybody's sister, that's why. If he wanted to be a

Boy Scout, he could go find a granny to walk across
the street. Mrs. Pondergrove would accommodate him
happily, she was sure.

The dress made her feel sensuous and grown-up, not
like someone who spent their days playing patty-cake
and singing "the bear went over the mountain." Not just
a mother. But a woman.

"Is it too bold?" she asked again. If the dress shouted
bold and blazing, what on earth was she going to do if
the signal she was sending out was answered?

Mrs. Pondergrove said, "Oh, no. I think it's just right.
I used to have a dress similar to that. Electric blue. I
used to wear it dancing with my Alf."

"Is that Mr. Pondergrove?"

"It is. The best man God ever created. We had so
many wonderful years together. He's gone now."

"I'm sorry. Has it been long?"

"Several years. Please don't be sorry. When I see the
way so many relationships go, I feel very privileged to
have known the joy of loving a man so completely. It's a
joy I would like for everyone in the world to know. There
is no richness like the richness of sharing a beautiful
friendship and love with your husband." She said this
so wistfully.

So, Abby thought, it really was out there. Not just
the stuff of poetry and novels, but a real thing, that
real people experienced. A love that survived the years,
growing stronger and richer and deeper.

"Do you think you'll ever remarry?" Abby asked.

"Oh, I don't think so. Jordan Hamilton has other
ideas, but really, it's preposterous to think of people
our age falling in love."

"I don't think it is," Abby said gently. She liked the

idea of someone wooing Mrs. Pondergrove. "I think Jordan Hamilton is very handsome, and extremely distinguished."

"Oh, posh," Mrs. Pondergrove said, but she blushed. "Red suits you. Such a passionate color."

"Oh. I'm not sure if that's the signal I want to give."

"Dear, if it isn't, there's something wrong. Perhaps you might want to consider religious life. A nun."

Abby laughed. "I don't know how Belle would fit in at the convent."

"It's not just that Mr. McCall is good-looking," Mrs. Pondergrove continued. "He's decent. Not one of these alley cat kind of men."

"How did you know I was going out with him?"

"Just a guess, dear. I really would have had to have been quite a bit blinder than I am to miss the chemistry between the two of you the last time I was here."

"Chemistry?" Abby squeaked. "You could see it?"

"I've always prided myself on being able to see what others can't always see. Jordan doesn't approve. He calls it meddling in other people's lives."

"How do you know that Shane isn't, um, one of those alley cat kind of men?" She wanted so badly to be able to take her word for it. One thing she did not need was another alley cat kind of man.

"I can tell by looking at him, of course. As I said, I see."

Abby wished there was something a little more solid than that.

"I wish I could see so clearly!" she said.

"Ask your heart."

"Well, I did that once before and I was wrong."

"My dear, you couldn't have possibly asked your heart, because one's heart is never wrong in such matters."

"Well, mine was."

"Something may have been," Mrs. Pondergrove said stubbornly, "but not your heart. For instance, maybe your ego chose the man you are talking about. Maybe he was handsome and dashing and the boy that all the girls talked about. And maybe you thought if he would love you, that would make you feel worth more."

"Good grief," Abby said with the shock of recognition.

"There he is now. Hello, Mr. McCall."

Abby whirled to see Shane leaning lazily on the doorframe. She had not bothered to shut the door to her suite behind Mrs. Pondergrove.

"Mrs. Pondergrove. Abby."

Abby's mouth dropped open. This was not even the same man who ran around the house and yard in his shorts and T-shirt. Shane looked sophisticated and suave in a beautifully cut pair of dark slacks, a white shirt, a silk tie and a dark, expensive suit jacket.

She had never once imagined him in a bigger world, but now that she saw just how he would look in it she felt a little knife of fear. Every woman would react to him just as she was. A sudden quickening of the heart, a sudden slickness at the palms, and sudden hope flickering in the region of the heart.

The question was, how would he react to them?

His eyes rested on her. One of his eyebrows shot up.

"You look stunning," he said, a funny rasp in his voice.

There. She'd accomplished just what she wanted. Only now that she had, it was just as she'd suspected. She didn't have a clue what to do with it, how to turn it to her advantage, how to be the only woman who appealed to him. She doubted if the way to accomplish that was to pick up the white shawl beside her and wrap it primly around her bosom, but that is what she did anyway.

"Thank you," she said stiffly. "Mrs. Pondergrove, if Belle wakes up, she may just want her soother popped back in her mouth."

"You're not to give her another thought," she was ordered sternly by the old woman.

Shane took Abby's hand, tucked it inside his, and ushered her out the door.

"You look gorgeous," he said.

"So do you."

He took one look at her heels, and led her over to his vehicle, a sports utility. "I don't think we'll walk tonight."

She wanted to protest that it would be a beautiful night for a walk, the sea breeze crisp, the light beginning to change to twilight. Besides, it would let her hang on to this moment of intertwined hands for a little longer.

But her own shoes had betrayed her. She was paying a big price to be three inches taller than God had made her.

He opened the door for her, something Ty had never done. The vehicle was very high off the ground, and hard to navigate in the skirt. Suddenly, she felt ridiculous, like she was not even the same person that she had been a few hours ago.

"You don't look like the same person who was pulling worms out of Belle's mouth a few days ago."

When he said it like that, she was able to see it was funny, in a way, and she relaxed. How had he known exactly what to say to make her feel more at ease, more like herself?

"You don't exactly look like the same guy who was on the other end of that shovel, either. In fact, I think this is the first time I've ever seen you with your legs covered up."

"Single men. I'm afraid we're notorious for finding what's comfortable and staying in it. Longing for our favorite sweats when we have to put them in the laundry, like little boys having their security blankets washed."

She laughed at the picture he had created. It was ludicrous to think of him pacing back and forth at the laundromat while his favorite shorts went through the rinse cycle.

They arrived at the theater in very short order. Like most of the Miracle Harbor businesses it was on the town's main street, facing out toward the ocean.

It was obviously a very old building that had been beautifully refurbished. She admired the marble tile and the rich burgundy draperies and carpeting in the lobby as they came in.

She also noticed the cream of Miracle Harbor seemed to be out in full force. The lobby was packed with extremely well-dressed people socializing.

"I didn't know this many suits existed in this town," Shane muttered, taking her elbow and propelling her through the thronged lobby. "Have you ever seen a person in this town in anything more dressy than brand-new Levis jeans?"

Never mind the suits, she thought with a gulp. She was suddenly glad she had put on the dress she had, because there were some gorgeous gowns in that lobby, and some gorgeous women tucked into them. Even so, she was suddenly aware her outfit was homemade and she wondered if it showed.

She found herself stealing a look at Shane's face as a woman went by them in a short, sequined black dress that looked like a tube. It could be made with a single seam, she thought.

He didn't even notice! His eyes were fastened on the draped entry to the main theater, his mission to get there, nothing detracting him from that.

Each time they went by a beautiful woman, she stole another look at him. He seemed oblivious to the looks he garnered. Looks of interest, ranging from mild to plain old predatory, looks that sized her up...and put her down.

Ty would have been in his glory. Saying low pitched flirtatious hellos to complete strangers, sending a wink here and there, stopping to talk, his eyes doing a quick and sultry inventory of everything on display.

Shane got them across the room and into the darkened theater in record time. He had not returned one smile.

"I'm sorry," he muttered, when he'd found their seats. "You probably guessed I don't like crowds much."

It touched her that he had overcome this aversion to escort her. What had made him think of the theater if he didn't like crowds?

"Don't you enjoy seeing all the different ways people are dressed?" she asked. In their short dash across the lobby, she had seen fifty dresses that she would just love to attempt to sew. She reminded herself, sternly, that since this was the first occasion she'd had to wear the one she had on, she didn't need anymore fancy dresses cluttering up her closet.

He actually looked surprised at the notion. He gazed at her thoughtfully. "Well, the men are all dressed pretty much the same. And why would I find the women interesting? I'm with the most beautiful woman in Miracle Harbor. And I knew that before you put on that dress. I'd like to see how many of them looked great just goofing off in the garden."

He said that matter-of-factly, then picked up his program and began to read it.

She stared at him, flabbergasted. He had just told her she was beautiful, the most beautiful woman in Miracle Harbor, and now he was reading his program.

At first, she didn't know what to think. If he really believed that, why wasn't he engrossed in her?

But then suddenly it occurred to her that it just confirmed what she already suspected about him.

He was not a man of superficial passions. How things—or women—looked would not sway him. He had a different kind of strength than any she had ever seen before, deeper, cleaner, infinitely more appealing.

It was, she knew, with sudden insight, that very strength that held him prisoner right now. He believed, with his whole heart and soul, that he had let down someone who loved him. Failed her. And he could not forgive himself for that.

Sighing, she took his hand in hers, ignored his eyes on her face, and looked to the front. His hand in hers felt right. It was that uncomplicated, and that beautiful, and that frightening. She belonged with Shane McCall.

Would he ever see that?

* * *

The play was a light, competently produced comedy if Shane judged it by the amount of laughter around him. The truth was that he had trouble concentrating on it. He liked the way her hand felt in his. He liked the way the shadows in the darkened room played with the blond of her hair. He liked the view he had out of the side of his eye, especially after she took off the shawl and put it in her lap. Her shoulders were even better than her belly button.

The dress seemed to him to be an engineering marvel far worthier of his attention than the play.

Damn. He'd gone and told her she was beautiful. The most beautiful woman here. It was only the truth, but somehow he'd wished even as those words were slipping off his tongue, that he could pluck them out of the air and stuff them back in his mouth.

Until he'd seen the light come on in her eyes, and known, somehow, he had stumbled onto what she most needed to hear.

Why would she doubt that about herself?

He had not missed her anxious looks every time one of those ladies in the slippery dresses had glided by. What had caused that kind of insecurity in her?

The whole play had drifted away while he contemplated these weightier issues.

"Did you like it?" she asked, slipping the shawl back over her shoulders, and rising as the last of the applause died down.

"Sure," he said, hoping to hell she wasn't referring to his enjoyment of her décolleté. Why was it, more than any woman ever had, she reminded him a pervert was alive and well and living inside him? "Did you?"

"It was fun."

On a hunch, he asked her which part she had liked best. Ha. She couldn't answer him, and she didn't even have an astonishing red dress to use as an excuse.

The crowds had pretty much dispersed when they got outside.

"Do you want to go for a quick bite to eat?" he asked. "A drink?"

Her hand was still in his. Something about that felt so right.

"No," she said. "Shane, look at the moonlight on the waves."

He looked across the street to the wide stretch of beach. Beyond it, the ocean was restless.

"The waves look like showgirls," she said, "in frothy feathery hats."

Not saying anything, he guided her across the street. She kicked off her shoes as soon as they hit the sand, wriggled her stocking clad feet, tilting her head back to look at the heavens. He wanted to kiss her throat.

He wanted to kiss the living daylights out of her.

Instead he said, "What's the story with Belle's father?" Once a cop always a cop. There was a mystery about that insecurity she felt, and he damned well intended to sniff it out.

She pulled her hand from his and wrapped her shawl around her, headed down the shoreline. He walked beside her. After awhile he took off his shoes, too. Just when he thought his question had been far too personal, she answered him.

"He was never interested in Belle. To be truthful, he was never that interested in me. I mean he was interested in all women, but not me in particular."

"Snake," Shane said. That explained it, all right.

"There seems to be lots of snakes in the woods," she said.

"Yeah, that's true."

"And along comes Little Red Riding Hood."

"I think it was wolves she had to be worried about. But you got the color of the dress right."

"You're not one of them, are you Shane McCall?"

"One of those wolves or snakes young ladies in red dresses have to be so wary of?" he asked carefully

She nodded, her eyes huge on his face. Moonlight did wonderful things to her eyes. She looked away from him at the waves breaking on shore.

In this moment, he wanted to be everything she wanted him to be. But he knew he was not. "Not the kind you're talking about, anyway."

"I don't believe you are any kind of a snake."

"And what about a wolf?" he asked, trying to kid, wanting desperately to steer her away from where he knew this was going.

"No, Shane, not a wolf, either. I think you are the rarest of things—a man worthy of a woman's trust."

Suddenly the truth about him was there, clawing at his throat, begging to get out. Well, why not? That should kill the light in her eyes quick enough. Destroy her illusions.

"I think maybe you've got me wrong, Abby."

"I don't think so." She said it stubbornly, as if she could know these things.

He knew he was going to tell her the truth, whether to kill her illusions or to get it off his own conscience he wasn't quite sure.

"Remember I told you my wife died falling down the stairs?"

"Yes, I remember."

"I was supposed to be home that day. I got called into work. She didn't want me to go. She was so nervous about having a baby. She was scared to death something would happen to me. She was worried I'd get into a situation that wouldn't be easy to get out of, and that the baby would be born without me being there. We'd taken those classes together. Prenatal." He laughed softly. "I can't tell you how much I hated them.

"Anyway, I didn't take her seriously. I told her I could be home in the blink of an eye, if I needed to. But we weren't expecting the baby for another full month. I thought she was being silly."

He watched out of the corner of his eye as she put her shawl in the sand, then sat on it. She patted the place beside her, and he hesitated and then sat down. His shoulder grazed hers.

"If I'd been there," he said, "if I had stayed home, if only I had recognized she wasn't being silly. Maybe she'd had a premonition. Maybe she *knew* something was going to happen, and tried to tell me, and I wasn't listening. Not in the right way."

She leaned her head into him. He could feel her trembling, and he glanced down at her. She was crying, silently, silver tears washing down her cheeks.

"It won't help if I tell you it wasn't your fault," she whispered.

"No."

She was silent.

"I even regret that I hated the stupid classes. If people knew the clock was ticking, they'd treasure everything. Every breath, every *cleansing breath*."

"Oh, Shane." She picked up a corner of her shawl and wiped her eyes on it.

Well, once a jerk, always a jerk. Here he had a beautiful woman on the beach, and he'd made her cry. His intention tonight had been to make her laugh, to lighten her load.

"I can only tell you what I see now," she said, her voice composed, soft, lovely with the swish and crash of the waves as a backdrop. "Not perfect. Capable of making mistakes. Strong, too. Maybe strong enough to forgive yourself, one day. I hope so."

She was crying for him. Because he was hurt, and she could feel his pain, almost in a way he had not allowed himself to feel it.

"Don't cry."

"It's just so sad, Shane. You would have felt the same way if she had been hit by a car, or if it had happened while she was having the baby, wouldn't you?"

He thought about that. "Yeah. I guess."

"You see, it's why you picked the job you do. You want to protect. Be in control. Be in charge."

It was making him very uneasy that she could see him so clearly.

"But you see, Shane, there are some things human beings are not in charge of, no matter how much they want to be. And life and death is one of those things."

"I guess that's true, isn't it?" But he could feel the reluctance in him to admit the truth of it, even though he knew his heart could not begin to heal as long as he blamed himself.

"Shane?"

"Hmm?"

"Would she have wanted you to feel like this?"

"Good God, no. She would have been madder than hell at me."

"Then maybe the only thing you have left to give her, the only way you can truly honor her memory is to be the man she would have wanted you to be. If she loved you, she wanted you—wants you—to be free. And happy. And open to all life has to offer you."

"And now I'm chained by cynicism, and unhappy and closed."

She didn't have to say anything. He recognized the truth about himself. And knew she was absolutely right.

What had he done in his life to deserve two women who were capable of seeing him so clearly?

And what had he done to deserve this second chance? To feel again, the exhilarating ride of falling over a cliff into a woman's eyes?

He touched his lips to the top of her head. Her hair was soft and silky and smelled of meadows ripe with buttercups.

She tilted her head up.

And he took what she offered. He took her lips and tasted them. Really tasted them. The sweetness, the innocence there, despite her having borne a child, that was like nothing he had ever experienced before.

The thundering of the sea faded, replaced by the thundering of his heart.

He could taste a hint of salt on her lips.

He let his calloused hands explore the sweet curves of her shoulders, the exquisite softness of her skin, the tender curve of her neck.

He wanted to pull her down in the sand with him, to

let go completely of this demon called control that had run his life.

He wanted to be free and happy and open.

Above all things, he wanted to make love to her.

But not here on a public beach in the sand.

At home, where he could take that dress from her and drop it to the floor, look at her, taste her, feel her, tumble her backward into his bed.

"Let's go home," he growled.

She stood up, took his hand, and they went together across the sand toward a brand-new future.

A future that twinkled with hope as surely as the stars twinkled in the sky.

CHAPTER NINE

THE drive home gave him time to sober, to pull back from the intoxicating nearness of her, from the heady feel of her skin beneath his lips.

On the way home, reality knocked.

Had he made his bed this morning? Left his dirty clothes on the floor? A friend, well meaning, had sent him the "Swimsuit Issue" of *Sports Illustrated* last month. He had no patience with things like that, but suddenly he wondered where he had tossed it. He didn't want her to see it. He wanted any thought she had ever had of him being a pervert to be completely banished.

Reality knocked, and asked him how the hell he planned to slip her by Mrs. Pondergrove, and how he felt about that. Sneaking her into his room as if he was a college freshman in a dorm instead of a full-grown man, mature and respected.

Reality knocked, and asked him if this is what he really wanted, not just with his body, but with everything. His mind. His soul. It told him she was not the kind of girl a man should act out an impulse with. She had been the victim of such behavior once before. He wanted to rip the guy apart with his bare hands, so how could he rationalize what he wanted to do tonight?

The voice of reason calmly asked him about what he was planning to do about tomorrow. Move in with her? Buy her a ring? What?

But as soon as he stopped the vehicle, turned off the key, shifted in his seat and looked at her, he didn't care about any of those things. She wouldn't care if the bed was made. They'd send Mrs. Pondergrove home. He hoped to hell he didn't have to drive her.

And tomorrow? Wasn't there a saying that tomorrow never comes?

He came around and opened her door.

She slipped out and into his arms, her lips finding his, famished.

Kissing, their hunger that of two people who had had nothing to eat and suddenly found themselves at a banquet, they went up the walk.

They stood in the darkness of the porch for the longest time, her giggles breathless as his lips touched the places where that dress ended, growing bolder, the fire in him leaping up, threatening to consume him, and her. The voice of reason had already been consumed.

And then suddenly the light came on and bathed them in a glow that seemed too harsh. The door was thrown open with much more vigor than he would have expected of an old lady. And it was not an old lady who stood there, smiling wickedly at them.

"Hi, honey," she said, "I'm home."

Geez. It was her. Abby. Only slightly different. The hair long and wild, the makeup sophisticated, the eyes dancing with a certain devilment that Abby would never be able to manage. And Abby would never dress like that. The rich white silk blouse, cut low at the front, clinging. Expensive jewelry dripping from every earlobe and finger.

Abby shot him a stunned look. He stepped back from her.

"Brittany," she said, trying for enthusiasm and failing miserably.

She gave him one more look, loaded with regret, before she slipped from his side, opened the screen door that separated her from her sister, and hugged her tight.

"Brittany," she said, collecting herself, "I'm so glad you are here."

He wished he could say the same, only it was impossible. He was not glad she was here, at all.

"Well," Brittany said, squeezing her sister, but raising an eyebrow at him over her shoulder, "my timing seems to be a little off, doesn't it?"

"Oh," Abby said awkwardly. "Brittany, this is Shane McCall."

"And to think I sent you a book on hunting men! Girl, why didn't you tell me you didn't need any help from me?"

Abby's mouth worked soundlessly and she sent her sister a pleading look that the girl managed to ignore entirely.

"Is that what that wedding dress in there is all about? It's gorgeous."

"No!" Abby wailed.

"Gorgeous, just like him. So, is he the one? Give."

Abby was looking at her feet, now, a dejected slump to her shoulders.

Shane felt like he wanted to kill her sister for being so bloody insensitive.

But the sister's next words caught him like a slug to the chin.

"Is he the one you're going to marry so you can keep this darling house for good?"

"Brittany, please," but her voice was faint and fading.

"Oh, God, doesn't he know?"

Heavy silence followed.

"Know what?" he asked.

"Nothing," Brittany said swiftly.

"Abby?" he asked, noting she was trying to become invisible, an impossibility given the style and color of that dress.

Shane suspected she was praying. But he knew no matter how much she hoped the floor was going to rot away and let her fall through it, no matter how preferable dropping into a bed of spiders was to the situation she now found herself in, it was going to happen. She lifted her chin and looked at him.

"This house was given to me as a gift. But it has a condition attached to my keeping it."

Her eyes were pleading with him not to ask.

Why the hell start being a nice guy this late in his development? His honorary halo, awarded to him for his past few days of being Mr. Nice Guy was getting too tight anyway. "What condition is that?"

"I would never get married just to keep a house," she said to him. "Never."

"Married?" he breathed. "Somebody gave you this house, but told you you had to get married to keep it?"

She nodded, embarrassed, looking anywhere but at him.

"Who did that to you?" He felt furious. Not just with her, though he felt that, too.

"I don't know. A stranger."

"Well, I think its a pretty crummy thing to do to someone with a kid to look after." Looking at her, he felt she had been boxed in. What choice did she have? She had Belle to look after, and he'd seen her with Belle. Her child was her first priority. And he admired her for that.

Until now. What if her only interest in him was gaining this house? Dear God, if those kisses had been lies, he would never be able to trust himself, or a woman, again.

Mrs. Pondergrove had edged out into the hallway, and was looking at them anxiously, feeling the tension. "What's a crummy thing to do?" she asked Shane, making him realize he must have raised his voice.

"Give someone a house, but attach a string to it that she has to get married."

"Oh gracious," Mrs. Pondergrove said, obviously shocked. She put her fist up to her mouth and looked at them with worried eyes. "Wouldn't that person have meant well?"

"I doubt it," he snapped. "It's kind of a mercenary thing to do. A marriage for a house." He felt like he was going to explode, and it must have showed judging from all those anxious female eyes fastened to his face.

"Mrs. Pondergrove, I'll drive you home."

"Thank you. That's very kind. But I don't mind walking."

"Just get in the truck." She didn't want to go with him, and he didn't blame her. He realized his tone was more appropriate to a drug bust than a little old lady. Mind you, that's kind of what this was, wasn't it? A bust. The real live motivations coming to the surface. That little number in the red dress wrapping him around her finger so she could have a house. Not that that had anything to do with Mrs. Pondergrove who was now twittering nervously, like a bird without a nest.

"Please allow me to drive you home," he amended. "I've been a policeman my whole adult life. Women are vulnerable at night."

Especially little old ones like her, though he didn't want to frighten her by adding that.

"Oh, all right," she said timidly. "Just let me find my coat. Oh dear. Where's my jacket?"

In a moment her jacket had been found for her, and he had helped her into it, and was escorting her down the walk. This was so far from how he'd planned for the evening to end that he could have laughed. Except that he was so angry.

"Please don't be angry at her," Mrs. Pondergrove said quietly as he pulled away from the curb. "It's not her fault about the condition."

"She could have told me."

"I would think maybe she's a little embarrassed about it."

That dress was not the dress of someone who would be embarrassed by a little something like that. That dress was the dress of someone setting a trap.

"She's so naive," he said. "Whoever is behind that gift will probably come knocking on her door, woo her for a few weeks, drop the question, and that will be that."

He realized his mind was contradicting itself. Seeing her as conniving one minute, and naive the next.

He did not think he had felt so hopelessly confused since—ever.

"I don't think that's what will happen," the old lady said.

Something in her voice made him look at her narrowly. What did she know about it? But she was looking through her handbag, a befuddled expression on her face. She came out with a worn looking package of gum.

"Would you like some?" she offered brightly.

"No."

"Turn left here, dear. There's my house. Right up there."

He pulled to a stop in front of a well-kept little Victorian, and got out to help her out of the vehicle. He ended up practically picking her up to help her down.

Which allowed him to see her face very clearly under the glow of the streetlight.

The old gal looked guilty as hell.

But about what? Well, that was one of his specialties. Finding out things people didn't want him to know. He was writing a whole chapter about prying secrets from people, about investigation. And he intended to get to the bottom of this whole thing. Tomorrow he planned to start asking some tough questions.

For Abby's protection.

Even if she didn't deserve it.

By the time he got home, his resolve was fading. He felt like the black weight was descending on him again. Like he had been allowed to be free of it for a few hours, but now its coming back was all the more painful.

He opened the outer door to the house. The door to her suite was slightly open. He tried to slip by, because he had this awful feeling that even looking at her might disturb his ability to think, his investigative powers.

"Where are you going?" Brit demanded, appearing suddenly in the doorway.

"I live here," he said coolly.

"You live here? With my sister?"

"I'm her tenant. I have an apartment upstairs."

"Her tenant," Brit said, then laughed, and called over her shoulder, "I get a stupid bakery as a gift, and you get a house with him in it? I wonder where I register my complaint?"

She closed the door to Abby's suite.

He went slowly up the stairs, feeling like fifty pound weights had been attached to his ankles. He went into his suite, sought refuge in the familiar order of everything but found none. Of course the bed was made, his laundry was in the hamper, and that magazine was filed somewhere. He closed the door, sank to the floor and stared at his hands.

Come on McCall, he told himself. What was the big surprise? He'd seen that book in her bag on the front seat of her car the first day she'd been here. He'd known she needed someone.

The big surprise was that she had cold-bloodedly been hunting for a husband.

The big surprise was that he thought he was the last person on earth anyone could ever succeed in pulling one over on. Too cynical. Had seen to much, both in his professional life and his personal one.

Ha, ha. Big tough Shane McCall.

But it seemed to be true. The bigger they were, the harder they fell.

He closed his eyes, rested his head in his hands, and tried not to think at all. Not even a little bit.

Now there was something he was good at.

"My, God," Brittany said, the door closed behind her, leaning against it. "That man! He's stunning. I'm so jealous, I could spit."

"There's nothing to be jealous of. We're just friends." Had been friends, Abby thought. She didn't even know if she had that anymore. "Could we change the subject?"

"All right. I love your dress. That shade of red is so *va-room, va-room*. Where on earth did you find it? It's exquisite."

"I made it," Abby said woodenly. She wanted desperately to be happy to see her sister. But all she could think of was the look on his face when he'd found out the truth.

"Can you make me one? Say in peach? I look stunning in peach." She laughed. "Of course, what I look stunning in, you look stunning in."

Abby smiled weakly.

"My niece is gorgeous. She seemed to know me. The old gal didn't think I should wake her up, but I didn't think it would hurt. What was her name, Mrs. Poundcake?"

"Pondergrove," Abby corrected her, half-heartedly.

"Oh. Right. I guess I'm just thinking of cakes because I got the bakery as my gift. Not exactly my cup of tea, but wait until I tell you some of my plans. I'm actually excited about taking it over."

"That's wonderful," Abby managed to say.

Brittany looked at her closely, and then hit herself on the forehead with the palm of her hand.

"Oh, God, I should have kept my big mouth shut, right? Oh, Abby, I'm sorry. I was trying to make an impression. He's *so* good-looking, I just kind of started to run off at the mouth. I wasn't even thinking what I was saying, just babbling away. I've hurt you."

"No," Abby said, "Really you haven't. Weren't we going to change the subject?"

"I'm terrible in the sensitivity department, Abby. I am. When my parents kicked me out last year, they said I was a spoiled little rich girl who didn't know the first thing about life, and that it was time for me to learn."

"Your parents kicked you out?" Abby said, managing to rise out of her own pain and confusion. Right underneath Brit's breezy tone, she detected pain.

"After I wrecked my car. They overreacted, I'd say, even if it was the second one I wrecked."

"Wrecked how?" Abby asked.

"Too fast into a corner. I love going fast. Don't you?"

"No," Abby said.

"Well, you wouldn't know it to see the progress you've made with the Hunk of Miracle Harbor. How long have you known him?"

"Not very long," Abby said, but the words sounded oddly false. Because she felt like she had known Shane McCall forever and beyond. "You were telling me about your car."

"Oh, yeah. I wrecked it. Second one. A red Corvette, almost the same color as your dress. Mommy and Daddy had a fit. Sat me down and told me they realized they had been guilty of giving me too much, and that the free ride was over. They cut the purse strings, just like that."

Again, this was delivered in a breezy, I-don't-give-a-damn style, that Abby sensed hid a more sensitive person, after all.

"Anyway, I was getting a little desperate. I've sold some jewelry to make ends meet. I'd applied for all kinds of jobs, but I never got asked for an interview."

Abby detected hurt and confusion in the words.

"But remember when we got our gift, and the lawyer who read it said it was supposed to be the thing we needed most? Well I guess what I needed most was a job. And I got one. And really, I am grateful, Abby. But can you see me icing cakes?"

Abby had to smile despite the terrible pain in her heart. Honestly she could not picture her sister icing a cake.

"But that's enough about me. I want to hear all about you. Start with my beautiful niece. No, start before that. Have you found out why we were split up yet?"

"No. I talked to my Mom—my adopted Mom—several times since all this happened, but if she knows anything she's not saying."

"Well, she has to know something. She didn't find you under a cabbage leaf."

"She said my Aunt Ella made all the arrangements."

"Ask her then!"

"She's been dead for thirteen years."

"Oh, sorry."

"My mother was a nurse at a hospital in Minnesota. She said I was there and she fell in love with me, and found out I needed a home. She had wanted a baby forever. I wasn't exactly a baby, though. I was three when she got me."

"My Mom and Dad said I was just about to turn three when they got me, too. How come you were in the hospital?"

"I don't know about the hospital. I've been wondering about what Corrine said, about our parents being killed in a car accident. Maybe I was in it, too. Do you know how your adopted parents got you?"

"This is awful, but I think my parents bought me."

"What?"

"No kidding. Black market baby. They're not too anxious to talk about it, so I figure something is fishy. I do know they wanted a child desperately. They're not the kind of people to wait for anything if money can buy it. Not that I want to give the impression that they are bad people, because nothing could be further from the truth. But they know money is power and they are not afraid to use it."

"Whatever the reasons we were split up, I'm so glad we were brought together," Abby said. "I can't bring myself to believe that whoever went to all this trouble to get us together had some ulterior motive."

"Well, I'm more than a match for anybody with an ulterior motive. But I don't know about you. Gosh, you're sweet." She laughed. "You're the sweet one. I'm the wild one. What do you suppose sister Corrine is?'

"I don't know. I've only talked to her a few times on the phone. She seems—"

"Reticent?" Brittany suggested.

"Exactly." Abby didn't add, *or scared.*

"She told me she was burning the book I sent her. Didn't even want to donate it to the library. Said that would be like spreading poison in drinking water. Do you think that's a little strong?"

Abby found herself laughing, which was amazing, because fifteen minutes ago she had sworn she would never laugh again. "Actually, I don't think that's too strong. Did she tell you when she's coming?"

"She's got commitments that will take her a while to tie up. She's written and illustrated a book. Isn't that adorable?"

"I can't wait to see her book." Abby said. "She's sending me one."

"I have the most wonderful idea," Brit said, Abby realized she was going to have to adjust to these lightening swift changes of topic. Brittany's eyes caught on the wedding dress, being worn by the mannequin in the corner. "Could I try that on?"

Abby turned and stared at the dress. The sewing of the dress was completed. She had begun the arduous job of hand beading the bodice a day or two ago. Yet she didn't want her sister to try it on. Why not? It would give her her first real chance to fit the dress, something that was difficult to do with herself. So far, she had been making the dress from her own measurements. But for some reason she had not tried it on, avoided that with her whole heart and soul.

"Please?" Brit said. "Abby, it is so beautiful."

Abby went and took the dress gently from the mannequin. "Come here," she told her sister.

Without a bit of self-consciousness, Brit had stripped down to her bra and panties in a blink. Abby noticed they were exactly the kind of underthings she never wore. Lacy, and brief, sexy.

They slipped the dress over Brit's head. Abby had

not yet done the buttons on the back of it, so she pinned her sister into the dress.

It fit perfectly, almost as if it had been made for Brit.

"How do I look?" Brit asked, her eyes shining.

Abby couldn't bring herself to look at her. Instead, she went and got her stand-alone full-length mirror and set it up in front of her sister.

Brit gazed at herself, but her smile became fixed and then faded. Her brow dropped thoughtfully.

"Isn't that funny?" she said. "I love this dress. I mean it is an absolute dream. But I don't like it on me. It doesn't feel right, somehow. I don't know what it is. Too sweet, maybe. You try it."

"Oh, no," Abby said, and felt her cheeks flush.

"Come on. It's just a bit of dress-up. The kind of thing we would have done if we had grown up together, up in the attic going through old trunks. Don't be such a stick."

"A stick?"

"A stick-in-the-mud. Try it on. It'll be fun."

Somehow, Abby found herself with the dress in her arms. She wasn't anywhere near as uninhibited as her California sister, so she went into the bathroom to put it on.

It felt like she was slipping into her own skin. There was such a sense of belonging to that dress, as if it was made for her.

She didn't want to look at herself in it, but Brit was outside the door demanding she come out.

Taking a deep breath, she did.

"Oh!' Brit said. "My sister is an angel. I feel like I'm going to cry. I have never in my life seen anything so beautiful." She took Abby's hand and pulled her over to the mirror.

"Open your eyes, silly girl."

Abby opened one eye. Just a peek. And then she opened both of them.

The dress was everything she had known it would be, and more. It fit her perfectly, falling in exquisite lines and making her look like a princess.

It wasn't just a dress. It was a dream come true. It was an enchantment. In her eyes was the deep and contented glow of a woman in love.

But she reminded herself, this dream took two.

And her last look at Shane tonight had not boded well for her future. Certainly not her future in terms of a dress like this one.

She turned and darted back toward the bathroom, feeling like she was going to cry. The dress made her feel so right. So womanly, so full of hopes and dreams.

But that wasn't reality.

Reality and fantasy had just collided and it was terribly painful.

When she emerged from the bathroom, her face scrubbed free of any remaining signs of tears, her sister was waiting.

"This was my wonderful idea, before I got sidetracked by the dress. Lend me some of your pajamas. I left my bag at the hotel. We'll have a pajama party and talk all night. Just like sisters. I just can't wait to find out every single thing about you."

To Abby that sounded far preferable to spending the evening by herself going over what might have been if Brittany had not flung open the door.

Brit wrinkled her nose at the flannel button-up pajamas she was handed.

"Girl, have you ever heard the word sexy?"

"I'm from Chicago," Abby reminded her. "It's cold there at night. You can't sleep in lace baby-dolls."

"I didn't realize you slept outside in Chicago," her sister teased her, unselfconsciously throwing off her clothes once more and donning the pajamas.

Soon they were in Abby's bed talking, and whispering, laughing.

"I can't believe you're afraid of spiders," Brit said. "I just can't believe it."

"Ever since I can remember."

"Me too. I fainted at my high school grad because a spider walked across the collar of the boy in front of me. I blamed it on the heat, of course. Imagine a girl as notorious for her reckless spirit as me being afraid of something so silly."

"Do you think something happened to us? Before we were separated? Do you think Corrine is afraid of spiders?"

"Let's call and ask her!"

"No! It's late, Brit."

"Oh, she won't care."

"We'll call her tomorrow."

"Well, all right, but I'd rather know tonight."

Abby realized her sister was a person who had never once considered the possibility of putting someone else's needs ahead of her own.

And yet despite that she was so likable. So irrepressible. So spirited, so funny. Abby felt like she had known her forever. Loved her forever.

What Abby didn't know was that the register above

her bed was not a heat duct. That many years ago, a hole had been cut in the floor to let more heat up into the chilly upstairs. The register was strictly for cosmetic purposes.

Shane McCall, lying sleepless in his bed, heard every word of her life story.

CHAPTER TEN

AFTER a long time, their voices, Abby's and Brittany's, wafting up to him from that register right under his bed, grew husky and then faded.

He should feel guilty. Listening in on them. But what was he supposed to do? Pound on the floor with his foot?

Why should a man feel guilty for lying in his own bed?

The truth was he had felt guilty since Stacey died. Felt he should have been there, could have stopped it.

He remembered Abby's voice on the beach soft in the velvet of the night, as she found the truth; that he would have felt he had failed no matter how his wife had died. And then Abby had found that other truth.

He had not honored who Stacey was, or the love they had celebrated together, by turning his back on life.

He could only honor what had been, by allowing the man Stacey had helped him to become, to come out.

And that man had, among other things, always known the truth, and always acted with complete integrity.

There was a truth in this dark bedroom with him tonight.

It was the truth of his own loneliness.

The truth of the life he was leading, bereft of human emotion.

It was the truth that she had changed that. Abby. Abby had carried sunshine into this cave he had ensconced himself in.

There, in the darkness of his room, with the clock ticking off the minutes after three and the foghorn penetrating the thick white mist outside his window, he admitted the one thing to himself that he found the most difficult to admit. The thing he had been trying to outrun since she had first landed on his doorstep in the middle of a foggy night just like this one.

The thing he had not recognized even when he had taken Abby in for the night, and then offered to look after her car, and then offered to dig the garden, and find her a tenant.

He'd been looking after her.

And it wasn't that she needed looking after.

It's that he had wanted to do it. It had made him feel alive again to have her to care about, her and Belle.

With his whole heart and soul, he wanted to look after her, care for her, protect her, be there for her.

And there was a word for that one thing that he didn't want to admit.

But he wasn't going to say it.

Ever.

He woke the next morning feeling like he had not slept, feeling groggy and out of sorts. He glanced at the clock beside his bed. According to *his* schedule, which was about to be reimplemented in a big way, he had ten minutes left before the kitchen was hers.

He pulled on his running shorts and a T-shirt and headed down the stairs.

After a quick breakfast drink he planned to run. And run and run. To run until his thoughts ran clear of her, like rust clearing from a tap that had not been turned on for a long time. And when he got back he was going to begin making inquiries.

If he found out someone with an evil motive had given her this house he was not sure if he could be trusted to deal with it maturely.

Even if the motive was not evil—just a little off-color—he was not sure what he would do.

Still, it was puzzling. Her sister had mentioned a bakery. Was marriage a condition on that, too? Her sister had looked like about the least likely person in the whole world to run a bakery. And if marriage was a condition for her, too, it would mean that Abby had not been targeted.

Her sister would be more suited, it seemed to him, to a little fashion shop, or a cosmetics business. Were there fingernail shops? Her sister's fingernails had been long and spangled with bright nail polish.

He slammed to a halt at the kitchen door. *She* was in there. Abby. Even though she knew it was his time. Her back to him she was dressed in that backward ball cap and those too big jeans and the white sweater which was too small and showed the slender line of her back to him before it disappeared inside the waistband of her jeans.

Was she trying to push him over the edge of his control?

If so, she had succeeded.

Because that word that he had been avoiding so stringently, suddenly flashed across his brain in neon, ten-foot high letters.

Love.

He loved her.

Damn it all. He loved her. She may have tricked him and manipulated him, and it didn't seem to make a damn bit of difference.

He ordered himself to turn away. To go down the hall and out the door. He could pick up breakfast at the cafe. And get a newspaper at the same time. He didn't care if he had to rent a motel. He was getting out of here.

But his mind disobeyed his order.

He crossed the space of the kitchen on tiger-quiet feet, came up behind her, grabbed her shoulder and whirled her around.

He didn't even really see the look on her face.

He kissed her—hard and long, a kiss loaded with all his frustration and humiliation, a kiss that punished as much as anything else.

Punished her for his own weakness. Punished her for making him hope again.

It was penetrating his senses that something was very wrong here.

Very wrong.

It didn't feel right. He didn't feel that overwhelming sweetness Abby made him feel. He didn't feel like he was in a meadow full of buttercups.

This kiss felt like a lie.

He felt like he was kissing a tiger. He noticed the fingernails digging into his biceps.

Wrong girl his brain shouted at him.

Just a moment too late.

Because he heard the cry of dismay from behind him, fought his way loose of the arms that entwined him and whirled.

To see Abby standing behind them, her fist stuffed in her mouth, tears shining in her eyes. She whirled and was gone in the blink of an eye.

He swore, then looked at her sister. "How dare you?"

"How dare *me?* I wasn't the one who started that, buster."

"Well, you sure didn't finish it. I thought you were her."

"And I was supposed to know that?"

"You're wearing her clothes!"

"Mine are at the hotel."

"What would I kiss you for? You're a complete stranger."

"That didn't matter a fig the last time she found herself a guy. And just for your information, that's why I didn't slug you. I wanted to know if you were like him. She couldn't survive another him." The anger suddenly faded from Brit's face. "But you aren't like him, are you?"

"Like who?"

"That creep she tangled up with. Ty something. She told me all about it last night. He preyed on her innocence. When you started kissing me, I admit, at first, I kind of thought—Wow! Nice way to start the day. Even though it was exactly like that wedding dress, and didn't quite fit me. When you started kissing me, I thought she'd done it again, poor thing. Found a man who couldn't be happy with just her."

"That man would be a complete fool," he bit out.

"I think maybe you need to tell my sister that."

"All your sister wants from me is a house."

"Now who's being the complete fool?"

He stiffened under the criticism.

"You want to believe that," Brit said softly.

Truth, another truth, hitting even harder and closer to home this time. Loving was a risk. A risk that could end in a moment, that held no guarantees, that could leave a strong man in tatters. He was looking, almost desperately for one last out, before he threw himself over that cliff again.

Brittany wasn't letting him off the hook, either. "Do you believe a woman who just wanted a house would have reacted to you and I having a little wake-up kiss the way she did?"

It felt like the sun was coming out, piercing the dark clouds that had inhabited his soul for so long, piercing them, and then evaporating them. He ran out of the kitchen.

"Abby!" He pounded on her door. "Let me in."

Silence.

He considered kicking the door down, but tried the handle instead. The door whispered open. "Abby?"

No answer. He ran from room to room looking for her. But the feeling of emptiness, his voice echoing back to him, told him she was gone.

He ran out into the street, looked both ways. He could see her, pushing her stroller, practically running, nearly two blocks away.

He ran after her, sprinting, finally pulled up beside her, puffing.

The tears were streaming down her cheeks as she walked quickly, her chin tilted at a haughty angle.

"Abby!"

"Get away from me."

"Let me explain."

"I have heard all the explanations in my life I ever want to hear. I saw what I saw."

The baby was crying, too, her head crooked around the side of the stroller, looking back at her mother.

"Abby!"

"Get away from me you, you pervert."

This was so much like their first meeting it was sending shivers up and down his spine. Belle was absolutely howling now, attracting all kinds of attention.

"I thought she was you. I thought your sister was you."

She faltered for the first time, shot him a glance from under her lashes, then picked up her pace. "Sure."

"I did. She was wearing your baseball cap. She was wearing your clothes. She looks exactly like you, for Pete's sake."

She stopped walking and looked at him. "Her hair's different than mine."

"She had it tucked up under that ball cap. She looked exactly like you." He took a deep breath. "But she doesn't feel like you."

"What?"

He was really working on getting himself slapped today. "Not *that* way. Geez, who's the pervert here?"

"You are."

"When I kissed her, I didn't feel the way I felt when I'm around you."

He had her attention now.

"I didn't feel like the blood running through my veins had turned to fire, and I didn't feel as though my heart was going to crash right out of my chest."

Even the baby had stopped crying.

"I didn't feel like it was *true*. When I kissed you last night it felt like the truest thing I'd ever done."

"It did?"

"Abby, I didn't feel alive when I kissed your sister. That's what I feel when I'm with you. Alive. Like the life force is sizzling through my veins, like I want to be alive."

"Shane, what are you saying?"

"I'm in love with you."

A light came on in her face, then died just as quickly. "You are not. You want me to have that house don't you? You're carrying this big brother thing to a ridiculous extreme."

"Big brother thing?"

"You know. Giving me outings. Building Belle swing sets. Protecting me from spiders and unworthy tenants."

"I have sure as hell never felt like your big brother!"

"You haven't? You haven't just decided you'll help me get the house, just like you helped me with everything else?"

"I don't give a damn about that house."

"I don't, either."

He cocked his head at her.

"I mean obviously, I like the house. And obviously I'd like to have a house to raise my daughter in, but Shane, if you felt for one second that I only fell in love with you because of that house, I'd give it away, to the first person who wanted it. The girl with the purple hair and the iguana. I'd walk away from it in a second."

"What did you just say?"

"That I'd walk away from the house tomorrow."

"No, before that."

"That I'd give to the girl with the iguana."

"No, before that."

She suddenly was looking everywhere but at him. "I love you," she whispered. "I never meant to fall in love with you, or anybody. I wasn't going to get married to keep that house. I couldn't."

"But if love came along?"

"I don't think," she whispered, "it's a very good idea to say no, when love comes along."

"You know something, darlin', I don't think it is, either."

"Oh, Shane, I need you to kiss me."

"No."

"Please?"

"No."

"Why?"

"Because I know where that kiss will go. Right up the steps to my apartment. And, Abby, that's not what I want from you."

"It's not?"

He shook his head. "I want it to be true. And deep. And committed. I want it to be forever. I want to do the right thing always, and be the best man, always. And that doesn't mean sneaking you up the stairs to my room."

"What does it mean?"

"It means marching you down the aisle, with the whole world looking on. It means you wearing a beautiful dress, and carrying a bouquet of flowers."

She laughed through her tears. "Shane, you hate crowds."

"It won't matter to me if there are a million people in that room. I'll only be able to see one of them. You. I want to marry you. So I can wake up beside you always. So that I know those songs I hear you singing are because of the joy I've put in your heart. So that when I think of growing old I feel this wonderful anticipation. So that I can be a daddy to Belle, and a few more just like her.

"I want to be the very best husband in the whole world. And I don't think that will be very difficult with the very best wife."

She threw herself into his arms, and covered his face and his throat and his ears with kisses.

"I warned you," he growled, then groaned, and returned her kisses, and held her to him.

Belle was standing up in her stroller, crowing, trying desperately to get out. He went over and scooped her up and held her close, and then Abby was nestled into his arms, too.

And then Shane McCall smiled, and felt whole.

"Abby, will you ever forgive me because I asked you to marry me today?"

"I don't think forgiveness will ever be a part of my memories of you proposing to me, Shane."

"It's April Fool's day."

She laughed.

"But this is no joke."

"I know."

"I want you to marry me. I want you to marry me as soon as it can be arranged."

"Yes. And that's no joke, either."

They walked back to the house, shoulder to shoulder, he carrying the baby and she pushing the empty stroller.

Her sister was waiting anxiously on the porch.

Brittany looked back and forth between them, and then smiled. "Is it what I think it is?"

Abby smiled shyly. "Shane has asked me to marry him."

"Oh," Brit squealed. "I'm so excited. I want to help plan the wedding! This is so wonderful." And then she flew down the steps and hugged her sister, and Shane and the baby, and his arms went around them all.

His new family.

A brand-new circle of love.

EPILOGUE

ABBY stood in front of the mirror, her breath caught in her throat. The reflection told her dreams did come true, even if she could still hardly believe it. It was the first time she had ever tried on the completely finished dress.

"Mrs. Pondergrove, how can I ever thank you?" Mrs. Pondergrove had given her the dress. Given it to her, a virtual stranger. "Of course, I'll refund your money."

Mrs. Pondergrove looked insulted. "My dear, the look on your face is thanks enough. Besides, as the dress got closer to being done, it didn't feel quite right. Not for the woman I'm having it made for. In a week or two, maybe I can drop by with the new dress I've found. From a photograph in a magazine. It's truly lovely."

"I can't wait," Abby said sincerely.

But she knew she wasn't talking about the dress at all. She was talking about life, stretching in front of her, a glorious adventure to be shared with a glorious man.

Her life, suddenly, everything every woman always dreams her life will be.

"Abby," Brit said catapulting through the door, beautiful in her peach bridesmaid's dress, "do you have it on?"

She skidded to a halt, and her eyes filled with tears. "I

have never," she whispered, "seen anything as beautiful as you."

Abby smiled. "Take a look in the mirror, sister."

Corrine came in, quieter, her face glowing. Her peach dress would not have looked out of place at a fashion show. When she saw Abby, her eyes filled with tears, too.

"Stop it, both of you," Abby said sternly. "You'll get me going and nothing will ruin this dress quicker than a few tear stains."

"I have to get it out of my system," Brit insisted, dabbing at her eyes with a hanky, "Or I'll be crying at the wedding and spoil all your pictures. I can't believe Saturday is almost here. How did it come so quickly? I'm a nervous wreck. Abby, how can you look so serene?"

"Because you've looked after everything. I don't have a single thing left to worry about."

"Corrine, that reminds me," Brit said anxiously, "we still have to cover Belle's stroller in white and put the flowers on it. And how are we going to keep her dress clean until we get her into the church? And she won't let me put flowers in her hair!"

"You worry too much," Corrine said, with a tolerant smile.

"No, I don't! You need someone like me to worry. Then everything gets done."

Abby laughed, and she noticed, happily, that Corrine did, too. She thought maybe Corrine's life had not had enough laughter in it.

"Well, enough of the fashion show, ladies," Brit announced. "I have to get over to the church and see how I'm going to fasten the sprigs on the altar. Daisies and babies breath, with a single rose in the center of each arrangement."

For a strange moment, Abby felt transported to the church. It was as if she had walked through the doors. In her mind's eye, she saw herself, going up the aisle in her long white dress, the train floating behind her. The pews each had a bow, just as Brit had described. Spring flowers cascaded out of huge vases on the low stairs leading to the altar.

But the church was empty, save for herself.

And him.

Shane was standing at the altar. As she came down the aisle, it seemed as though he was talking to someone, but there was no one there.

And then he heard her.

And turned.

And the light in his face was what she had always known it could be. The pain of his past had been transformed into strength. She did not know what he had been before, but she knew he was more now than he had been then.

Wiser. More tender. Stronger.

One of those rare men who knew each moment was a miracle. She knew, as he took her hand, she was in the presence of the greatest of all miracles.

Love.

"I thought you said crying would ruin your dress," Brit said. Her sister came and gently wiped the tears from her cheeks. Abby gazed into her sister's eyes and recognized the beginning of a transformation here, too. She opened her arms.

And then all three sisters were holding each other, crying softly, laughing, and wiping tears away.

When they let go of each other Abby saw that Mrs. Pondergrove had quietly slipped away.

Abby looked at her sisters, and felt again the great and abiding presence of the miracles in her life. "Brit, you were right," she said softly. "Peach is your color. Our color. And you were right to make each of these dresses just a wee bit different, like your personalities. You two will be dancing until dawn."

"Oh, God," Brit said, "I don't believe this. In between planning the wedding and getting ready for my bakery's grand reopening, I completely forgot. I don't have a date for the dance. I can't believe this. Me without a date!"

Abby exchanged a look with Corrine over the top of Brittany's head. "What do you think sisters are for?" Abby asked her, softly, and then linking arms the three sisters walked toward the future.

* * * * *

REQUEST YOUR FREE BOOKS!
2 FREE NOVELS PLUS 2 FREE GIFTS!

Harlequin Romance

From the Heart, For the Heart

YES! Please send me 2 FREE Harlequin® Romance novels and my 2 FREE gifts (gifts are worth about $10). After receiving them, if I don't wish to receive any more books, I can return the shipping statement marked "cancel". If I don't cancel, I will receive 6 brand-new novels every month and be billed just $3.84 per book in the U.S. or $4.24 per book in Canada. That's a savings of at least 15% off the cover price! It's quite a bargain! Shipping and handling is just 50¢ per book in the U.S. and 75¢ per book in Canada.* I understand that accepting the 2 free books and gifts places me under no obligation to buy anything. I can always return a shipment and cancel at any time. Even if I never buy another book, the two free books and gifts are mine to keep forever.

116/316 HDN FC6H

Name _____ (PLEASE PRINT) _____

Address _____ Apt. # _____

City _____ State/Prov. _____ Zip/Postal Code _____

Signature (if under 18, a parent or guardian must sign) _____

Mail to the **Reader Service:**
IN U.S.A.: P.O. Box 1867, Buffalo, NY 14240-1867
IN CANADA: P.O. Box 609, Fort Erie, Ontario L2A 5X3

Not valid for current subscribers to Harlequin Romance books.

**Are you a subscriber to Harlequin Romance books
and want to receive the larger-print edition?
Call 1-800-873-8635 or visit www.ReaderService.com.**

* Terms and prices subject to change without notice. Prices do not include applicable taxes. Sales tax applicable in N.Y. Canadian residents will be charged applicable taxes. Offer not valid in Quebec. This offer is limited to one order per household. All orders subject to credit approval. Credit or debit balances in a customer's account(s) may be offset by any other outstanding balance owed by or to the customer. Please allow 4 to 6 weeks for delivery. Offer available while quantities last.

Your Privacy—The Reader Service is committed to protecting your privacy. Our Privacy Policy is available online at www.ReaderService.com or upon request from the Reader Service.

We make a portion of our mailing list available to reputable third parties that offer products we believe may interest you. If you prefer that we not exchange your name with third parties, or if you wish to clarify or modify your communication preferences, please visit us at www.ReaderService.com/consumerschoice or write to us at Reader Service Preference Service, P.O. Box 9062, Buffalo, NY 14269. Include your complete name and address.

HRI1

If you enjoyed this story from Margaret Way, here is an exclusive sneak peak from her irresistible new tale IN THE AUSTRALIAN BILLIONAIRE'S ARMS. Available April 2011 from Harlequin Romance®.

Sydney, Australia was supposed to be the perfect place for Sonya to lie low, until an innocent friendship catapulted her into the spotlight! David's a powerful enemy, but it's her own attraction to him that's more terrifying. Sonya's afraid that once she's in his arms she won't want to run again....

"WHO ARE *YOU* TO PULL ME INTO YOUR ARMS? What is your agenda? We both know you have one." Sonya had lost sight of her own.

"Agenda? Don't talk rubbish." David's response was curt. "You know I'm attracted to you." He could have laughed at the sheer inadequacy of the word. Magnetized? Mesmerized? Spellbound?

"Now this is very interesting." She was transformed into a state of the utmost hostility. "*You're* attracted to *me!*" The entrenched defence mechanisms were back in place.

"Neither of us sought it," he said. "Neither of us wanted it. It just happened."

"Just happened?" she cried. "Oh, you're very convincing."

"So were *you*, just then, beautiful Sonya. Okay, I admit my mistake. I was the aggressor. But it's too late now to make a fuss. I'm sorry if I hurt you."

She took a deep, shaky breath, feeling weak and ashamed. "You are mad, mad, *mad!*"

"You're so right," he agreed tonelessly, his handsome face taut.

"You are leaving."

HREXP0411

It was a statement, not a question.

Still, he turned back. "You'd prefer me to stay?" There was hard mockery in his brilliant eyes when the temptation to stay was overwhelming.

"You are *leaving*," she repeated. "This is not your finest hour, David Wainwright."

"I agree. I'm afraid I overestimated my powers of self-control. So how do I go about making reparation? I'm too much of a gentleman to ask you to account for *your* behavior. There's a lot of passion dammed up behind the Ice Princess facade, isn't there, Sonya? Floods of it!"

She felt like she was thrashing about in a cage. "I've had enough! I know what you're up to. You are *not* exonerated. You are wanting me to fall in love with you. That is your strategy. I should have been prepared."

Will Sonya risk everything and give in to the passion she feels for David?

Find out in
IN THE AUSTRALIAN BILLIONAIRE'S ARMS.

Available April 2011 from Harlequin Romance®!

CARA COLTER

Dancing with heartbreaker Prince Kiernan Chatam
is a dream come true for most girls, but for
streetwise dance teacher Meredith Whitmore,
it's simply a fabulous career break.

But as Meredith slowly uncovers the man behind
the royal mask, she's in for the surprise of her life…
and she might just get her happy ending after all.

*Find out if this modern-day Cinderella
meets her match in*

To Dance with a Prince

Available March 2011.

www.eHarlequin.com

HRI7716